The Artistic Ape

THREE MILLION YEARS OF ART

The Artistic Ape

THREE MILLION YEARS OF ART

Desmond Morris

RED LEMON PRESS

Take your journey through art beyond the printed page!
Whenever you see this symbol, use our free app to access exclusive videos and extra content. Simply download *The Artistic Ape* app from iTunes or Google Play, then point your device at the symbol to launch one of twelve videos. *The Artistic Ape* app requires an Internet connection, and can be used on iPhone, iPad or Android devices. For direct links to download the app, visit **www.redlemonpress.com/apps**

This app is compatible with iPhone 3GS, iPhone 4, iPhone 4S, iPhone 5, iPod touch (4th generation), iPod touch (5th generation), iPad 2 Wi-Fi, iPad 2 Wi-Fi + 3G, iPad (3rd generation), iPad Wi-Fi + 4G, iPad (4th generation), iPad Wi-Fi + Cellular (4th generation), iPad mini and iPad mini Wi-Fi + Cellular. Requires iOS 4.3 or later. This app is optimized for iPhone 5. Android users must be using a device with version 2.2 or later.

First published in Great Britain by
Red Lemon Press Limited,
Northburgh House
10 Northburgh Street
London EC1V 0AT, UK

© 2013 Red Lemon Press Limited

Text copyright © 2013 Desmond Morris
Desmond Morris archive material © 2013 Desmond Morris

The moral right of the author has been asserted.

ISBN 978-1-78342-002-5

A CIP catalogue record for this book is available from the British Library.

Printed and bound in China

1 3 5 7 9 8 6 4 2

www.redlemonpress.com

Red Lemon Press Limited is part of the
Bonnier Publishing Group
www.bonnierpublishing.com

CONTENTS

Acknowledgements

I would like to acknowledge the enormous amount of help I have had from my wife Ramona during the writing of this book. I am also extremely grateful to the brilliant team involved in the creation of the book, especially Silke Bruenink, Martina Challis, Jane Walker, Leah Germann, Jo Connor, Katie Knutton, Kate Manning, Sarah Benton, Alexander Goldberg and Jason Newman. My sincere thanks also go to the following for valuable discussions on specific points: David Attenborough, Paul Bahn, Robert Bednarik, James Bomford, Richard Dawkins, Ellen Dissanayake, Julian Huxley, Vassos Karageorghis, Damon de Laszlo, Julie Lawson, Silvano Levy, Rona Marsden, James Mayor, Lee Miller, Andrew Murray, Herbert Read, Michel Remy, Peter Robinson and David Sylvester.

Finally, I owe a special debt to the many artists I have known over the years and with whom I have had many enlightening discussions on the nature of art, especially Jankel Adler, Sven Berlin, Francis Bacon, John Bratby, Alexander Calder, Richard Hamilton, Barbara Hepworth, John Latham, Mervyn Levy, LS Lowry, Conroy Maddox, Oscar Mellor, Edouard Mesens, Joan Miró, Henry Moore, Sidney Nolan, Victor Pasmore, Roland Penrose, Walter Poole, William Scott, William Turnbull and Scottie Wilson.

Foreword

Desmond Morris began writing *The Artistic Ape* in his 85th year, having gathered the material for what has turned out to be his *magnum opus* over more than 60 years of working in the fields of science and art. He has travelled the globe extensively, visiting over 100 countries in his quest for first-hand knowledge of human art forms, and has seen much of what he describes here in situ. He was able to hold the Makapansgat Pebble in his hand in the cave where it was first treasured three million years ago. He has visited many of the cultures we hear of in the Tribal Art and Folk Art chapters, and through his own work as a widely respected surrealist painter he has met many of the artists he writes about in the chapter on Modern Art.

By combining his deep knowledge of human behaviour with a personal understanding of the artist's instinct, Desmond Morris is able to present us with an overview of the evolution of art and an intriguing analysis of human endeavour in art. We learn about thousands of artefacts; more than 300 are depicted in this book. We hear about cultures and societies stretching far and wide around the globe and across the expanse of history. Finally, the author arrives at the point where he can identify and analyse nine universally relevant roles of art. *The Artistic Ape* is a profoundly personal book. It is written by a scientist whose roots were in the academic world before he became a well-known television broadcaster and who, all the while, remained an active surrealist painter whose work is exhibited and collected around the world.

Martina Challis
London, 2013

1 Introduction

Scan page to view video

Introduction

THE DEFINITION OF ART

In my previous books I have focused on the ways in which human beings are similar to other animals. I have looked at our primeval behaviour patterns and the manner in which these have survived in the modern world – our sexual and parental activities, our feeding and drinking, our grooming and sleeping, and our playing and fighting. When doing this, I deliberately ignored those aspects of our lives in which we differ from other species, but now I want to turn the spotlight on one of the most exciting ways in which we have manifested ourselves as a unique animal – on the complex activity that we refer to as art.

The evolution of art has, for me, been the most fascinating of all human trends – more than any other activity it has set us apart from other species. In the past, this evolution has proved extremely difficult to define, especially for those specialists who write on the subject. In most cases, these experts are far too close to their subject to see it clearly as a general pattern of human behaviour. The result is that they offer narrow definitions that usually exclude huge segments of artistic activity. They then argue among themselves as to what is art and what is not.

The cause of this confusion stems from the fact that specialised students of aesthetics nearly always lack any knowledge of human biology and evolution. So they are incapable of seeing how the artistic impulse first arose in the tribal societies of our remote human ancestors, and how it then went on to flower into the amazing phenomenon that we see all around us today. Only if we first examine and understand these biological roots of art, can we then go on to fully appreciate all the subtleties and nuances of

> '...the artistic impulse first arose in the tribal societies of our remote human ancestors...'

the advanced forms of aesthetic expression. It is this examination that I will attempt in the present book.

First, what are the more general definitions of art that have been proposed in the past? There are literally hundreds, most of which are virtually meaningless. One describes art as 'the making of something to please the eye'. Another states that art is 'a creative operation of the intelligence'. Yet another that art is 'everything that is created by man and appeals to his aesthetic sense'. It is Shakespeare, in 1606, who gives us the first useful description of art, when he makes King Lear speak of art 'that can make vile things precious'. In other words, art is a transformative process. Shakespeare is telling us that art is an activity that allows us to take the unpleasantly mundane and make it remarkable and wonderful.

> 'Shakespeare is telling us that art is an activity that allows us to take the unpleasantly mundane and make it remarkable and wonderful.'

In the following century Goethe comments that in art 'the best is good enough'. In 1814 John Keats adds that 'the excellence of every art is its intensity', and Elizabeth Barrett Browning asks 'what is art, but life on a larger scale?'. All three are emphasising the fact that art improves the quality of something and makes it a more powerful experience. With these definitions we are beginning to see a consensus of opinion that art is something that takes the everyday experience and somehow magnifies it. The French artist Jean-François Millet makes this more explicit when he says that art is 'treating of the commonplace with the feeling of the sublime'. In 1864 Gustave Flaubert was even more dramatic, commenting that 'Human life is a sad show... ugly, heavy and complex. Art has no other end... than to conjure away the burden and bitterness.' A few decades later, Oscar Wilde offers his conclusion that 'art consists in the perfect use of an imperfect medium'.

Moving into the 20th century, the art critic Clive Bell tells us that art is the means 'by which men escape from circumstance to ecstasy'. And in her book *What is Art For?* Ellen Dissanayake expresses the same idea, but in more sober terms, when she says that 'art can be called an instance of making special'.

To sum up all these views, art can be seen as a human activity that rewards us by allowing us to experience an accentuated version of our otherwise humdrum existence. It makes the commonplace more impressive and the boring more entertaining. It also makes the mild more intense and the threadbare more elegant.

For thousands of years our ancestors employed this device as an accessory attached to other activities. Implements, weapons, clothing and buildings were all taken beyond the purely practical and made more complicated than was necessary for them to function efficiently. These elaborations made them seem more important because they stood out from the rest. Their visual intensity, the skill involved in making them and the time they consumed all gave them an aura of significance.

It was not until 1803 that Benjamin Constant famously coined the phrase *'L'art pour l'art'* – art for art's sake. The idea was that art could only truly be called art if it was completely freed of any other considerations. Taken to an extreme, this meant that a Christian icon, for example, was a worthless piece of art because it carried a religious message. Even if the icon was exquisitely produced, as a work of art it was inferior to a mediocre landscape that carried no religious or political message. This approach has infected much modern thinking about the arts.

A brilliantly styled Ferrari is considered less of a work of art than a modest piece of sculpture. This is an attitude that has to be avoided if one is to gain a true perspective of human art as a deep-seated and age-old preoccupation.

In light of the above, it is necessary for me to provide my own definitions of our uniquely human activities – those that we do not share with other animals. There are three main ways in which human behaviour differs from that of all other species – the pursuit of art, the pursuit of science and the pursuit of religion. All other so-called 'higher activities', such as politics and commerce, are in reality no more than ways of organising human society so that it can satisfy its basic animal needs and, in addition, pursue these three key goals.

My definitions of art, science and religion are as follows:

Art is making the extraordinary out of the ordinary
– to entertain the brain.

Science is making the simple out of the complicated
– to understand our existence.

Religion is making the believable out of the unbelievable
– to reduce the fear of dying.

In the text that follows I will attempt to show how our unusual evolutionary story has encouraged art to develop from a tiny, modest beginning to become one of the three great obsessions of human existence. I should explain that to make this huge subject easier to handle, I will be confining myself to the visual arts. However, the underlying principles of what I have to say often apply just as well to music, drama, dance, storytelling, poetry and the other more obscure art forms such as perfumery.

After what is intentionally going to be a brisk ride through three million years of the visual arts, from the prehistoric to the ultra-modern, I will have given enough examples to allow me to examine the eight basic rules by which I believe all human art operates. I apologise in advance for the inevitable omissions.

Such is the richness of this subject that it would take a thousand encyclopedias to cover the subject of human art comprehensively. What I have set out to do, by presenting a balanced selection of examples, is to organise the material in such a way that it makes sense in a condensed form, and wherever possible I have tried my best to avoid the specialised jargon of art historians and theorists.

2 The Roots of Art

Scan page to view video

The Roots of Art

THE ANTHROPOLOGY OF ART

Human beings are unique among the monkeys and apes because they are the only fully developed primate predators. We now know that wild chimpanzees will occasionally kill and devour a small mammal, but this is not their usual way of feeding. Like all other primate species except man, chimpanzees are predominantly herbivorous, concentrating their diet largely on fruits, berries, roots and nuts, with insects and birds' eggs as valuable supplements.

The problem with being a herbivore such as a monkey is that you have to spend almost all your waking hours searching for food and then, once you have found it, picking, preparing and eating it. What is more, the act of feeding is highly repetitive and without any great climactic moments.

The life of a large carnivore is very different. A great deal of effort is put into the hunt, but once it has proved successful there is a pause for a great feast. After this there can be a period of relaxation before the next hunt begins. This applies equally to big cats, such as lions and leopards, and to primeval human hunters. But there is an important difference between them too. When a lion has feasted on its kill, it sleeps. In fact, so efficient is its way of life that it sleeps for about 16 out of every 24 hours. But human hunters are different. If they have succeeded in the hunt it is not because they have evolved huge fangs, powerful jaws and sharp claws – it is because they have used their intelligence.

'If they [human hunters] have succeeded in the hunt it is not because they have evolved huge fangs, powerful jaws and sharp claws – it is because they have used their intelligence.'

This particular evolutionary advance, which would eventually give human beings global domination, was not in increased muscle power but in increased brain power. Human hunters were puny creatures compared to the 'professional' killers of the animal world, but they overcame the weakness of their primate bodies by employing teamwork and cunning. They supported this by the unique evolutionary device of developing 'interrupted breathing' into verbal speech.

'So the human animal evolved essentially as an intelligent, talking carnivore. This is what made it great.'

Many other species have modified their breathing to produce squeals and roars, hoots and grunts and other brief vocalisations that carry simple, single messages, such as 'I am angry', 'I am in pain', 'I am sexually aroused' or 'I am hungry'. But none has then gone on to combine these vocal sounds into a complex language of the type found in every human tribe on earth.

The early human hunters became genetically programmed to develop these complex forms of vocal communication. Every child, with or without specific teaching, quickly learned to talk while growing up, so that by the time the child became an adult he or she could engage freely in verbal communication with other members of the group. The child was not, however, sufficiently finely tuned by evolution to develop the same language in every case. The details were learned from other members of the tribe, with the result

Right Preparing the meat for the tribal feast.

that this new evolutionary mechanism, so vital for communication within a tribe, also tended to isolate one tribe from another. Even today, with modern global travel, literally hundreds of different languages still survive in the world and cause endless confusion wherever people from one culture encounter those from another.

So the human animal evolved essentially as an intelligent, talking carnivore. This is what made it great. It hedged its bets by not abandoning its old herbivorous diet, so that when meat was short it could regress to its ancestral fruit-and-root way of life. And even when meat was plentiful, it strengthened its nutritional intake by adopting an omnivorous, 'meat-and-veg' form of feeding. This evolution gave us the so-called primitive hunter-gatherer society, with a marked division of labour between the sexes – the males specialising as hunters, the females as gatherers.

'...even at the moment of satiation, the human feasters had to express themselves in some way rather than simply go to sleep like the well-fed lions.'

It was this way of life that was to create the social context in which human art could find a foothold and start to grow. It all began with the arrival of the human feast. As already mentioned, when a specialist hunter like a big cat makes a kill and gorges on the meat, it then goes to sleep. But the human hunters were not evolutionary specialists; they were, in origin, evolutionary opportunists. This meant that their nervous systems were geared up to high activity levels. To put it in simple terms, cats are lazy and monkeys are busy. But how do you busy yourself when you have made a major kill of a prey animal large enough to feed the whole tribe?

The answer is that you make the feast into an outstanding occasion. There are no dramatic feeding occasions for ordinary monkeys or other herbivores. Every day is a long, long sequence of tiny acts. But for our remote humanoid ancestors life was becoming punctuated by great moments of triumph, on the special occasions when the group of male hunters brought home the kill. The primate urge to be ever active meant that, even at the moment of satiation, the human feasters had to express themselves in some way rather than simply go to sleep like the well-fed lions. Sleep would have to wait while some sort of celebration was enacted.

To make these triumphant feasting moments seem more significant, something had to be added to them – and this something was the first form of what today we call art. Clothing and body decoration had to become more distinctive, giving us the first form of visual art. Stories had to be told about the adventures of the chase. The hunter's tale of 'the one that got away' is probably the oldest story ever told. This was the beginning of poetry and literature. Songs had to be sung and rhythms beaten out to announce to the world the tribe's great success. And this was the beginning of music and dance.

In this way a tradition of expressive elaboration of key moments began, and it was soon extended to other special occasions, such as birth, coming of age or marriage. In addition to celebrations there were also rituals associated with going to war, with death, with ancestors and with superstitious fears. Each of these gathered its own unique display of ritual decorations and events and, like verbal language, these differed from tribe to tribe. All the tribes performed vivid and dramatic celebrations – the members of the tribe all decorated themselves, sang, danced and told stories – but the details differed. And as the tribes grew, multiplied and spread out over the whole of the globe's land surface, the variety of the celebratory techniques became more and more impressive.

Today, much of the hard evidence of this has been lost to us forever, because the displays were only ever intended to last as long as the celebrations (like the floats in a modern-day carnival). Happily, early explorers often brought back examples of the artefacts involved and placed them carefully in museums, where we can still study them. And the tribal storytelling has often survived in the form of highly stylised myths that have been handed down orally from generation to generation.

We need to return for a moment to the definition of art – the making of the ordinary into the extraordinary. It could be argued that, since the primeval art forms I have been describing were limited to the extraordinary moments in the life of a tribe – the successful hunt, the coming of age, the funeral and so on – there

Right Elaborate body decoration that transforms a tribal celebration into an extraordinary event.

was nothing ordinary about them in the first place. But this misses the point. It would have been possible to enjoy the feast in silence and without any dancing or visual decoration. The arrival at the tribal camp of a large carcass could have been treated as just another quiet moment in tribal life. The death of a member of the tribe could have been dealt with in a simple manner, without any accompanying ritual or ceremony. There was nothing to force early tribesmen to perform elaborate displays on these occasions, but they nearly always chose to do so. It was this transformation of the everyday aspects of tribal life – from the ordinary to the extraordinary – as a way of highlighting these exceptional events that was at the heart of the evolution of human art.

The next question, inevitably, is how did human beings manage to bring about this transformation? What are the rules of the various forms of elaboration that make ordinary clothing into extraordinary costume, or ordinary speech into haunting story or mesmerising song? The difficulty in answering this question is caused by the complexity of even the simplest of human forms of expression. To find some easier answers we must look elsewhere.

We can learn a great deal about how to convert the ordinary into the extraordinary by looking at the displays of other animals. When a fish, a reptile, a bird or a mammal engages in aggressive or sexual behaviour it often begins by performing some kind of conspicuous threat or courtship display. This can involve colour changes, stylised movements, exaggerated postures, body transformations, loud calls and unusual cries. With these actions, the animal in question announces that it is changing from its ordinary, everyday mood into an unusually heightened condition in preparation for fighting or mating.

The key to all these actions is that they make the animal more conspicuous. This is a dangerous step to take because, in becoming more conspicuous to a rival or a mate, the displaying animal also becomes more exposed to a possible predator. It must therefore present two kinds of appearance: ordinary and quietly inconspicuous, or extraordinary and boldly conspicuous. The latter condition must be restricted to just those times when a rival has to be intimidated, or a potential mate has to be wooed. During those brief moments, a risk has to be taken as the displaying animal gives vivid display a priority over safety and security.

Although this has nothing directly to do with human art, the transformation of the displaying animal does involve a sudden change from an ordinary, humdrum condition to an extraordinary one. In this respect it parallels what happens in the case of human art. And this is, of course, the reason why we find so much beauty in nature. We admire the beautiful colours of the peacock's tail, the ritual dancing of courting fish or the elaborate songs of humpbacked whales precisely because, in their efforts to make themselves extraordinary, they follow many of the same basic rules that we do when we make art.

What are these rules? There are eight important ones and I will be examining these in detail at the end of the book.

First is the rule of exaggeration.
Supernormalisation and subnormalisation of display units occur.

Second is the rule of purification.
Colours and shapes become purified and therefore intensified.

Third is the rule of composition.
The display units are arranged in a special way to create a balanced presentation.

Fourth is the rule of heterogeneity.
A display is neither too simple nor too complex. It has an optimum level of heterogeneity.

Fifth is the rule of refinement.
The display units and the intervals between them become more precise.

Sixth is the rule of thematic variation.
Once a particular display pattern has been developed, it is varied in many ways.

Seventh is the rule of neophilia.
The playful need for novelty – the 'new toy' principle – demands that from time to time established traditions must be abandoned in favour of new trends.

Eighth is the rule of context.
The time and place in which the display is made are carefully selected and even elaborately prepared.

3 Non-Human Art

Scan page to view video

Non-Human Art

DRAWINGS AND PAINTINGS BY ANIMALS

In any examination of the roots of human art it is valid to ask whether any other species is capable of indulging in this kind of activity. In nature there is no evidence of this, but what happens when animals are offered the basic equipment with which to attempt some form of picture making? Are they capable of making marks that demonstrate visual control?

The first evidence that a non-human animal, with encouragement, might be capable of creating some sort of visual pattern emerges from a study made in Russia at the beginning of the 20th century. In 1913 Nadezhda Ladygina-Kohts began a three-year study of a young male chimpanzee called Joni. At one point she gave the animal a pencil and watched as he started to make lines on a piece of paper. They are the first known examples of non-human picture making.

Kohts later went on to make similar tests with her young son Roody. She commented on the differences between the drawings of the ape and those of the human child: 'even after extensive exercises in drawing [the ape] did not go beyond drawing straight, sometimes crossing, lines haphazardly scattered on the paper.' Her child started out in the same way but soon graduated to more complex shapes. 'Joni's drawings generally are monotonous, while Roody's reflect rapid progress and diversity.'

'...although the ape never reached the stage of making pictorial images, his pattern of abstract lines did show some progress.'

These drawings reveal that although the ape never reached the stage of making pictorial images, his pattern of abstract lines did show some progress. In the early

drawings there are only long, repeated lines made in a seemingly random fashion, while in the later drawings he is showing some degree of visual control because here short lines repeatedly cut across his longer ones.

Kohts goes on to say that throughout her study she never observed the ape indulging in 'the imitative activity of the human child' or attempting to make any identifiable shapes on the paper. She makes the interesting point: 'This is true in spite of the fact that Joni had been no less enthusiastic in drawing than Roody. Joni often cried for a pencil; it could be taken from him only by force. He drew with keen and lively interest and looked at the objects with great attention.' She adds that the ape, when without a pencil, 'drew with his finger, which he had previously dipped into ink'.

Kohts' careful study of ape drawing, which is unlike any study that had gone before it, makes three important points. It establishes that a young male chimpanzee will not only make scribbles on a piece of paper if given a pencil, but will also modify these as time goes on, thus confirming some degree of visual control. In addition, the ape finds this activity so exciting that he becomes upset if prevented from drawing, and he will even invent a substitute for a pencil if he is denied one.

Kohts fails to comment on how strange this is. Why on earth should an ape become distressed when prevented from performing an activity that appears to offer it no obvious natural reward? The drawings it makes are of no use to it and yet they, or at least their creation, seem to have some value to the animal. In our search for the roots of art, this aspect of the chimpanzee's drawing activity is more significant than the contents of the drawings themselves. The pattern of lines may be boring, but the intensity with which they are made is extraordinary. It is as though the brain of a higher primate is somehow programmed to become engrossed by the act of picture making, even if the pictures themselves are little more than simple, near-random scribblings.

The Alpha experiment

The next important step in the study of non-human picture making did not occur until 1951, with the publication of a scientific paper devoted entirely to the subject of ape drawings. Its author, Paul Schiller, was an American psychologist working at the famous Yerkes Primate Research Center in Florida, USA. His research centred around an elderly female chimpanzee called Alpha.

This study established beyond doubt that in the drawings of a chimpanzee it is possible to demonstrate not only a change of style, as Kohts had found, but also a distinct and undeniable sense of design and patterning. Experimental cards with various markings already made on them by Schiller were given to Alpha and she was allowed to draw on them. Repeatedly it was seen that the position and nature of the human markings on the cards influenced the way in which the ape then scribbled on them. This proved that the ape's drawings were definitely not random, but were visually organised and controlled. It also demonstrated that it was possible to manipulate the animal's drawing actions experimentally.

Summing up the information obtained from the Alpha experiment, it is possible to say that this adult female chimpanzee showed the following composition tendencies:

- to restrict her scribbling to the surface of the paper;
- to mark the corners of a blank sheet of paper before filling it in;
- to mark a central figure;
- to balance an offset figure;
- to complete an imperfect figure;
- to cross strong lines at right angles;
- to make symmetrical markings around a triangle.

The Congo experiment

Armed with this conclusive evidence that at least one chimpanzee was capable of making marks on paper that were under its visual control, I was determined to take this further. I was able to do this at the Zoological Society of London when I took charge of a young male chimpanzee called Congo in May 1956. His first drawing was made in November of that year, and he already demonstrated that he possessed Alpha's ability to exert visual control over the positioning of his lines. This was revealed by accident because there was a small mark on the piece of card on which he made this first drawing, and Congo focused his lines on this mark.

'He was so intrigued by what was coming out of the end of his pencil as his lines started to appear on the card...'

I also noticed that this chimpanzee worked with intense concentration when making his lines. At three years of age, Congo was a bundle of physical energy, endlessly inquisitive and boisterous in his actions. The striking feature of his behaviour when he was given a pencil and started making marks was that, for the moment, all his vigorous playfulness was inhibited. He was so intrigued by what was coming out of the end of his pencil as his lines started to appear on the card, that he sat quietly fascinated by this new kind of play. As soon as he had finished drawing he was up and hurling himself about in his usual, high-spirited fashion.

I was studying many aspects of Congo's behaviour but two weeks later, in December 1956, I gave him a more careful drawing test. It now emerged that he had a favourite pattern, a fan of spaced-out, radiating lines drawn from the top of

Above Typical fan pattern drawn by the chimpanzee Congo.

the page towards his body. This became a persistent motif, reappearing in over 90 of the 384 pictures that he made during my investigation, a study that lasted from November 1956 to November 1958.

My method of obtaining drawings from Congo differed from the one used with Alpha. She was an adult ape when tested, and all her drawings had to be made inside her cage with the experimenter outside. This made it difficult to standardise the tests. The disadvantage of this remote-control method of obtaining drawings is that it was impossible to ensure Alpha's position in relation to the drawing area was always the same. I was more fortunate working with Congo, because he was under the age of four during the two-year test period and could be handled like a small child. For a test session he could be put in an infant's high chair to which a large flat board (43 x 51 centimetres) had been attached. Sitting him in the chair helped to reduce irrelevant movement and to focus his attention on whatever happened to be placed in front of him. It also meant that the angle of his body was always the same in relation to the sheet of paper or card offered to him.

Great care was taken to avoid influencing the way Congo made his drawings. After a sheet of paper had been placed on the board in front of him, he was then handed a pencil or crayon and allowed to start work. Congo's eagerness to draw was such that he never hesitated; he always started making marks on the paper immediately and continued until he felt he had finished. The drawing would end in one of three ways. Either he handed the pencil back to the experimenter, or he simply put it down on the board or he started playing with it, rolling it about or holding it in his mouth. In cases where he failed to hand the pencil back, the experimenter would hold out his palm and wait for Congo to place the pencil in it. When this was done, the drawing was removed and another sheet of paper or piece of card was put in its place. After Congo had had a few seconds to scrutinise the new paper (and any pattern on it) he was once again handed the pencil and the whole process was repeated.

A typical drawing session lasted between 15 and 30 minutes and usually produced between five and ten drawings. Sometimes Congo was not in the mood for picture making and lost interest after the first few pictures. At other times he was insatiable, and on one memorable occasion he worked non-stop for practically an hour, producing the huge total of 33 works. But both these very short and very long periods happened rarely.

One of the surprising features of a picture-making session with Congo was the intensity with which he worked. He received no food reward for his efforts. Making the drawings was its own reward for him. He was not particularly interested in examining the finished work, but the act of creating it fascinated him. Furthermore he knew when he had finished. If encouraged to continue he would refuse, but if given another piece of paper he was immediately happy to start again on a new work. On one or two occasions, when for some urgent reason the experimenter had to stop the session, attempts to interfere with an unfinished work were met with a screaming fit and, on one occasion, a full-blown temper tantrum. It seemed extraordinary that a chimpanzee should be so upset when attempts were made to stop an activity as specialised as picture making. Why on earth should it have such a powerful appeal for an animal that shows no inclination to perform anything like it in the wild?

Congo's sessions were carried out in a quiet room with no distractions, but on one occasion he was filmed to provide a permanent record. He also demonstrated his picture-making abilities on live television. The fact that he was prepared to concentrate on this unusual activity in the presence of a film or television crew was remarkable. As he grew older and his 'family' ties became stronger, his reaction to the intrusion of strangers became more hostile. It reached the point where, if a visitor wanted to watch Congo at work, the artist was more likely to draw blood than pictures. Fortunately, by this time a large number of pictures had been produced and the Congo experiment had provided some important new information.

The pictures made by Congo belong to three main categories: drawings on blank sheets of paper, drawings on pieces of paper bearing pre-existing geometric shapes and paintings on coloured cards. The drawings on plain paper were done mostly at the start of the experiment to familiarise Congo with the procedure. The drawings done on pre-marked paper were introduced to test Schiller's claims with Alpha. Five months after the investigation had begun, the paintings were introduced to examine Congo's reactions to colours. From the first moment that he handled a paintbrush it was clear that Congo found painting much more exciting than pencil drawing. The reason seemed to be that for the same amount of physical effort he was able to create a wide, bold stroke instead of a thin line. It was a case of 'magnified reward', where an action produces a greater reaction than expected.

'From the first moment that he handled a paintbrush it was clear that Congo found painting much more exciting than pencil drawing.'

The earlier studies of primate picture making had all been done with drawings. Congo was the first non-human to create paintings. His very first one was produced on 17 May 1957 and he went on to paint many more, the last one being made on 9 November 1958. The early ones were a little hesitant, as he became familiar with this new medium, and the late ones, although bold, were beginning to show signs of boredom with the whole procedure. But in between these two extremes was a period when Congo reached a peak of visual control where every brushstroke was expertly placed exactly where he wanted it, with little or no accidental elements intruding. Congo's middle-period paintings represent the most extraordinary examples of non-human art ever produced.

The method employed with Congo's painting was very similar to that used with his drawing. He sat in the same chair and at first he was given all his paints together in a tray of small containers. He found the colours so fascinating that he spent most of his time mixing one colour with another, rather than applying them to the card.

Right Congo is seen painting with a primitive grip of the brush (top) and with a sophisticated grip (bottom).

Because of this a new arrangement was introduced. Six opened pots of colour were placed on a table, just out of Congo's reach, and a brush was placed in each pot. The colours used were red, green, blue, yellow, black and white.

At the start of a painting Congo was handed the first brush and allowed to paint until the brush was dry. He was then handed the next loaded brush after having given back the first one. The first brush was then placed in its pot ready for use again later. Each colour in turn, in a random order, was presented to Congo in this way until he showed signs of losing interest completely, despite the 'boosting effect' of the frequent colour changes. At that point the painting was considered to be finished. It was removed, a new card was presented and the whole process repeated. In a typical painting session, not more than two or three paintings were usually produced due to the great intensity involved in creating them.

Congo was, of course, able to use each colour as much or as little as he liked before handing back the brush. To that extent he could influence the colour balance of his paintings. On rare occasions he would refuse one particular colour altogether and wait for another one to be offered before continuing. His favourite colour was red and his least favourite was blue.

His overriding preference, however, was for any 'new' colour – one that he had not just been using. Each time he was given a different colour this boosted his excitement and kept the work going for longer.

After looking at the way Congo made his drawings and paintings, the question remains as to what we learnt from them beyond what we already knew from the earlier studies.

> 'On rare occasions he would refuse one particular colour altogether and wait for another one to be offered before continuing.'

The plain drawings

As already mentioned, Congo soon began to exhibit a fondness for a fan pattern and repeated this many times. In all but one case he created this fan by drawing the lines from the top of the page down towards the bottom, therefore making each line towards his body. In one exceptional case he did something quite extraordinary and totally unexpected. In a session that took place on 14 August 1958, Congo had already drawn a normal fan pattern but he then began a new one using a different technique. A strange intensity seemed to overtake him and, instead of beginning at the top of the page with each stroke, he started at the bottom. This meant that he had to make each of his radiating lines with a completely different arm movement. He found this extremely difficult and was emitting soft, almost inaudible grunts of concentrated effort as he did so.

To the observer it appeared that this drawing of a 'reverse fan' was costing Congo more mental energy than any of his 383 other pictures. Once it was complete, it was impossible to tell this fan pattern from all his others, but witnessing its creation it

Right Fan pattern
made by Congo, with
lines drawn from the
bottom to the top of
the page.

Below Congo drew
this circle and then
placed marks inside it —
creating a 'proto-face'.

was clear that it was special. It proved that Congo had by this
time developed a 'fan image' and that he could make it in
more than one way.

One other plain-paper drawing of Congo's was equally
surprising. His early work was largely linear, but in his later
work he sometimes drew a circular motif. On one occasion
he made a carefully drawn circle in the centre of a large sheet
and placed several small marks inside it. Again, it was created
with intense concentration and one felt certain that, had he
been able to talk, he would have identified it as a face. It is
very similar to the images made by a human child, just before
the child draws the first recognisable face. It was frustrating
that Congo never went further, stopping right on the threshold
of the moment when, had he been a child, he would have gone
on to produce his first truly pictorial image.

Congo was at a late stage in his two-year picture-making
phase when he made his 'face', and he was becoming
extremely 'physical'. Despite this fact, he was so fascinated
by the creation of this marked circle that he became almost
human in his self-control. As soon as the picture was complete
he relaxed and became his usual extrovert self again.

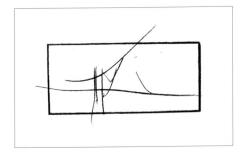

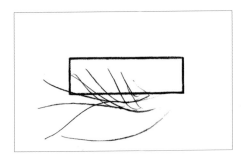

Top Congo made marks that keep within a large rectangle.

Middle The marks nearly keep within a smaller rectangle.

Bottom The marks cross a much smaller rectangle.

The experimental drawings

In addition to drawings on blank sheets of paper, Congo made a number of experimental drawings similar to those done by Alpha. The results were much the same, confirming Schiller's work.

Reaction to rectangles

It was clear from his drawings on blank sheets of paper that Congo was restricting his lines to the drawing surface and was trying to avoid going over the edges. But what happened if a hollow rectangle was placed on the paper that was offered to him? Would he now work inside this slightly smaller area? The first rectangle given to him measured 15 x 28 centimetres, leaving a 2.5-centimetre margin around it. Congo modified his drawing so that all his lines fell within the rectangle.

Next, a smaller rectangle measuring only 10 x 23 centimetres was offered. Again Congo tried to confine all his lines inside it, but a few strayed outside. When a third rectangle, this one only 5 x 18 centimetres, was presented to him he gave up trying to mark inside it and made most of his lines cross over it.

It was clear that the small rectangle possessed different properties from the larger ones, apart from its difference in size. The controlling factor appears to be one of ratio of sheet size to rectangle size, for it is only in the case of the small rectangle that the shape is narrower than the margin surrounding it. As far as Congo was concerned, this difference apparently changed the rectangle from a space to be filled up to an object to be marked over.

'...he marked the squares with gentle tick marks. It was almost as if Congo was autographing them.'

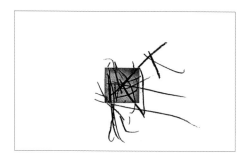

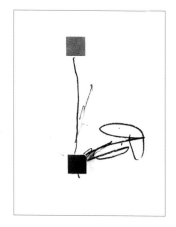

Marking of a central figure

When a small, centrally placed feature was present on the paper offered to Congo, on 34 of the 37 occasions he repeatedly marked the central shape and largely ignored the rest of the sheet. This was true whether the central shape was a square, a circle, a bar or a cross. When the central figure was made very small he marked it, but he also drew lines on other parts of the paper. It was as if the visual impact of these small central shapes was not powerful enough to attract all Congo's lines towards them.

Response to multiple figures

Eight tests were done to see how Congo would react to the presence of several figures on the sheet before him. In six of the eight tests he marked each of the small squares on the paper individually, in turn and quite deliberately. The presence of more than one square seemed to fascinate him, and instead of his usual bold scribbling he marked the squares with gentle tick marks. It was almost as if Congo was autographing them.

When three thin bars were placed, one above the other, down the middle of the page, Congo proceeded with great care to join them up with several vertical lines down their length. This surprising response was repeated when two squares were placed in the centre of the page, one at the top and one at the bottom. His immediate – and quite unexpected – reaction was to draw a bold vertical line down the middle of the page.

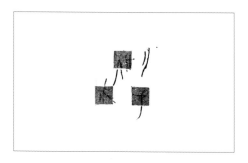

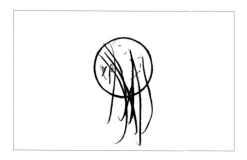

Top Congo marked a small, centrally placed square.

Middle He marked a small central figure.

Bottom Congo made marks on each of three small squares.

Right Congo joined up three vertical bars.

Far right He joined two small squares.

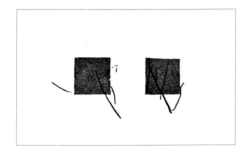

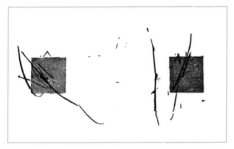

Above Congo's reaction to two squares being shown further and further apart.

A three-part test was then done to see what would happen if two squares were placed side by side near the centre of the page, and then were moved further and further apart on the next two sheets. In all three cases both squares were individually marked by Congo but then on the third sheet, where there was a large open space between them, he treated this as if it were a blank area to be drawn on and placed a bold scribble right in the centre of the page. Here Congo obeyed two separate urges – to mark and to fill – on the same page.

Response to an offset figure

A total of 33 tests were carried out to investigate Congo's sense of balance. In each test he was offered a sheet of paper on which a 5-centimetre square was placed to one side or the other. Would he mark the square, balance it or do both? The answer was that in 16 tests he did both, in 11 he balanced but did not mark and in 3 he marked but did not balance. Three others were impossible to classify.

When Congo's efforts at left–right balance were studied more closely, it was clear that when a square was strongly offset he was achieving an overall balance by placing marks in the centre of the 'large open space' available to him. Although this had a crude balancing effect, what he was really doing in these cases was simply 'filling a space'. To ascertain whether he was capable of achieving true left–right balance, we studied cases where the square was only slightly offset and there it became clear that true balance was being achieved. Here Congo made marks that were not in the centre of the large open space he had available to him, but to one side of it. If the square was displaced

Right Congo balanced an offset square.

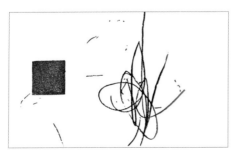

Above Congo balanced an offset square with equal displacement.

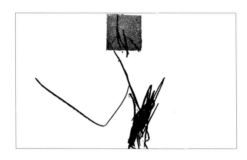

Above Congo demonstrated vertical balance.

Right Congo's reaction to a single vertical line.

slightly to the right, say, Congo would make marks that were equally displaced to the left.

This remarkable spatial awareness of the chimpanzee was further illustrated when, in a test where the square had been placed at the top of the page, Congo balanced it with marks at the bottom.

These tests made it very clear how, when Congo was drawing or painting on a plain background, the position of his own marks would influence the position of the marks he had yet to make. This explained why he was repeatedly demonstrating an attractively balanced composition when drawing on plain sheets.

Response to intersecting lines

When Congo was given sheets with a single vertical line, his reaction depended on the position of that line. If it was dead centre, he criss-crossed it with more or less horizontal lines. If, however, the vertical line was slightly offset, then Congo treated it as if it were the edge of a page and confined his marks to the larger blank space.

Although a number of other tests were made, the ones described here are sufficient to demonstrate that Congo was capable of a surprisingly advanced sense of composition when placing his lines on paper. When he graduated from drawing to painting, the addition of the colours and the broader strokes, combined with the rules that he had established for himself in terms of arranging his lines on the space available to him, meant that he would go on to create some abstract compositions. These were not only satisfying to him, but were also appealing to human eyes.

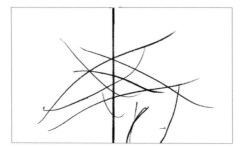

The paintings

As already mentioned, Congo's paintings went through three phases. In the first phase he was getting to know this new medium and some of his marks were accidental. However, by the second painting session he had already begun to take control of the brushes and was able to make a simple kind of bold fan pattern. His third session took place on live television and, despite the distractions of a TV studio, he was sufficiently excited by the act of painting to produce two pictures.

It was not until his 14th painting session, on 22 July 1957, that Congo showed he had fully conquered this new medium and was painting with complete confidence. Now, as one watched him at work, it was clear that every mark, every line and every spot were boldly placed exactly where he wanted them. His original, simple fan pattern had now become a complex one. Every line was carefully positioned in relation to every other line, and the whole composition was designed to fit into the space available for it, and also to fill that space.

On the following day, when he was again painting live on television, he was so sure of himself that he produced a large, complex fan pattern. It even had a new feature in the form of bunches of stippled marks across its base. And there seemed to be a single centrally placed black spot, although this could have been

Right Congo's painting shows a complex fan pattern, 1957.

an accident. In August he started varying his main fan pattern. In one instance he grabbed his grooming brush and dragged it through the wet paint, creating a central area of fine lines. He also added heavy horizontal lines across the base of his fan pattern and a cluster of five small white spots at its very centre.

By his 22nd session, on 2 September 1957, Congo had reached a peak of bold control. Now there was not a single accidental mark on the paper. Every line was exactly where he wanted it, and he used the space available to him with the confidence of a professional human artist. He was playing with his fan pattern, tilting it to one side as it progressed, creating a stippled fan bundle or splitting it in two. (Of the ten paintings he created that day, all are now in private collections in Europe and North America, including one that was obtained by Pablo Picasso and another by Joan Miró.)

In the weeks that followed, Congo continued to produce abstract paintings of a quality not seen, before or since, in any non-human animal. Each time he would explore some new variation. He created a lop-sided fan, a subsidiary fan, a fan with a curved base, a split fan with a central yellow spot, a split fan with a central black spot and a split fan with a central blue mark. He was enjoying that most human of aesthetic games – thematic variation. Those who watched him work during this phase simply sat in wonder, hardly able to accept what their eyes were witnessing.

Below Congo's painting shows a lop-sided fan pattern, 1957.

Right A subsidiary fan pattern, 1957.

Right A split fan pattern with a central yellow spot, 1957.

Right A split fan pattern with a central black spot, 1957.

This peak period in Congo's painting continued throughout the rest of 1957, during which time he made about 30 more high-quality works. Then in 1958 he entered his third phase in which, although the boldness and confidence remained, his level of interest began to wane. Many of the works were dashed off quickly, with great intensity but with less attention to detail. The elaborate fan patterns slowly vanished to be replaced by vigorous horizontal shapes and wild circlings.

Congo's picture-making abilities

To sum up all aspects of the Congo investigation, it can be said that a chimpanzee is capable of the following behaviours.

Self-rewarding activation

A typical drawing or painting session with Congo involved no reward or encouragement of any kind. Congo was given no food, and the experimenter was careful not to show approval or give praise for any particular kind of drawing or painting action. Making a drawing or painting was its own reward.

To test this, on one occasion a food reward was deliberately given when Congo had made a drawing. The effect was revealing. As soon as he had made some more lines he held out his hand for a second reward. Each time this was repeated he did less and less drawing before holding out his hand. Eventually any old scribble would do and he did not even bother to look at what he was doing, just so long as he was given a food reward for it. The careful attention the animal had paid previously to design, rhythm, balance and composition was gone – and the worst kind of commercial art had been born. This experiment was never repeated.

'…its [the ape's] compositions are superior in rhythm and balance to those of the human infant.'

Compositional control

Congo clearly showed that he could restrict his work to a given space, fill that space and balance his compositions. In this respect he outperformed a very young human child. There was a special reason for this. When ape and child are extremely young they both make simple scribbles, with poor muscle control. When they are a little older and the muscle control has improved, the child has already started to make pictorial images. He or she is now so intent on drawing 'mummy', 'daddy', 'cat' or 'house', that these pictorial units become more important than any overall composition. It is only later that these units become combined into a composed 'scene'. Because the chimpanzee never reaches the pictorial stage, its focus remains fixed on the overall arrangement of lines and on variations of those arrangements. This means that its compositions are superior in rhythm and balance to those of the human infant.

Right Congo painting showing a split fan pattern with a central blue mark, 1957.

Calligraphic differentiation

The term 'calligraphic' is used here in the broadest possible sense to refer to the nature of the component elements of a picture, as opposed to the interrelations between those units. In this respect the human child is far superior to the chimpanzee. At a very young age the child will start to combine simple lines and shapes into more complex units, in a slow progress towards pictorial images. Although Congo did not reach the pictorial stage, this did not mean that he lacked any kind of calligraphic growth. There is a film of him making a perfect circle with a single movement of his wrist, something he would never have done in the early stages. He also learnt to make loops, criss-crossed lines and such details as small, subsidiary fan patterns. So he was capable of demonstrating limited calligraphic differentiation of a primitive kind.

Thematic variation

The key principle in human art of thematic variation was strongly present in Congo's work. The most dramatic example of this is in the way he varied his favourite fan pattern, creating a reversed fan, a split fan, a stippled fan and so on. Once he had the fan motif fixed in his mind he enjoyed the visual game of varying it in as many ways as he could. This also applied in his physical play, where he would invent a new game, such as jumping onto a branch and then leaping off it. He would do this time and again, making the leaps bigger and more daring until eventually he would abandon it and move on to something else.

Optimum heterogeneity

When a picture is about to begin the paper or card is blank – therefore homogenous. Each line or mark placed on it makes it more heterogeneous. If an ape or a human went on adding mark after mark after mark, eventually the page would reach its heterogeneous maximum – completely covered in a dense mass of lines and shapes. This is confusing to the eyes and lacks visual appeal. Somewhere between the two extremes there is the happy medium of optimum heterogeneity. There is enough detail to make the picture interesting but not so much that it becomes a bewildering mess. To put it another way, the artist knows when to stop. This applies to Congo just as much as to any human artist.

Picture making by other primates

This study of Congo's picture-making abilities confirmed the findings made by Schiller with Alpha, and added some new elements. Following the two-year Congo experiment six other young chimpanzees were also given a few of the drawing tests, with squares placed on the papers. Although only a few such tests were done, these apes clearly showed the ability to mark a central square and to balance an offset square. In other words, they too were making lines that were under visual control, and not just random muscular movements that happened to leave marks on the paper.

Also in the 1950s, a female gorilla called Sophie began making drawings and paintings at Rotterdam Zoo. When given a set of Congo's experimental sheets,

Right The female gorilla Sophie seen painting at Rotterdam Zoo in the late 1950s.

she too demonstrated visual control of her lines. She filled a blank page, marked a central square and balanced an offset square. Sophie's paintings had a distinctive style. She worked with a remarkable delicacy for such a large animal, with the same concentration as Congo and with no reward other than the making of the pictures themselves.

The most surprising parallel with Congo came with Bernard Rensch's discovery in Germany of a capuchin monkey called Pablo. The monkey was capable of creating a well-formed fan pattern. Rensch photographed the animal in the act of doing this, using a stick of white chalk on its cage wall. He compared the symmetry of the fan patterns of Congo and Pablo and cited these as examples of rhythm or 'regularity preferences' of an aesthetic nature that are clearly demonstrated in non-humans.

The fact that a capuchin would also make a fan pattern was important in a special way. I had often wondered whether Congo's arm movements, when making his fans, had been influenced by the chimpanzee's tendency to drag bedding towards him when making a bed before settling down to sleep at night. This series of actions, pulling the bedding towards himself from different directions, is something observed in wild chimpanzees. It occurred to me that Congo's fan patterns may originally have been favoured by him because they were the result of a similar sequence of arm movements. However, because capuchins do not make beds in the wild, this explanation does not seem so likely. Rensch's idea of animals favouring rhythmic repetition seems more appropriate.

Right The capuchin monkey Pablo making a fan pattern.

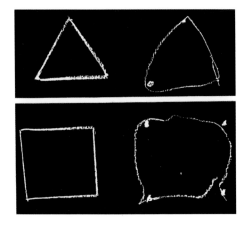

Above The drawings on the right by the chimpanzee Julia show copying ability.

One of the most unusual experiments with chimpanzee drawing was published in 1965, also by Bernard Rensch. It showed that a chimpanzee called Julia could be persuaded to copy simple shapes. Rensch says 'never before has an ape succeeded in copying a previously drawn figure near it… We drew on a small blackboard with chalk a triangle or a square and made next to it three or four points which were the endpoints of the figure. Then we demonstrated to the animal the shape of the figure by tracing the lines with our finger. Julia learned gradually to connect the three or four points in one stroke with chalk lines.'

Rensch's copying test was successfully repeated once more. In 1976 a two-and-a-half-year-old male chimpanzee called Nim, who was being taught sign language at Columbia University by Herbert Terrace, made reasonable copies of a circle, a square and a triangle.

Much later, in 1997, Gregory Westergaard reported on a group of ten captive capuchins from an animal research centre in Maryland, USA. When provided with lumps of clay, stones, tempera paint and leaves, the monkeys would spend up to 30 minutes 'reshaping the clay with their hands and decorating it with the paint and the leaves'. The Maryland experimenters make the point that 'captivity may have liberated in the monkeys a talent for art. Because they do not have to forage for food and defend themselves against predators, they seek out other activities… such expressions are the inevitable consequences of an intelligent but restless mind.'

Right The drawings in the bottom row by the chimpanzee Nim also show copying ability.

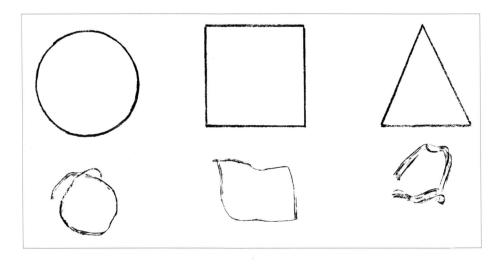

Above Painting by
an elephant called
Hong, Thailand.

'...elephants in Thailand were painting pictures of recognisable subjects, such as flowers and trees.'

Recent paintings by non-primates

In recent years there has been a dramatic widening of the interest in picture making by non-human species. Any animal that could be persuaded to hold a brush was enlisted to create paintings that could be sold to a gullible public. This development has done considerable harm to the serious study of non-human picture making. These splish-splash works involve no visual control and the shapes made are largely accidental. They are simply muscular actions that happen to leave behind marks.

There is one important exception to this rule and that concerns the remarkable hoax of elephant painting. It was drawn to my attention by Richard Dawkins that elephants in Thailand were painting pictures of recognisable subjects, such as flowers and trees. He suspected they were fakes and I agreed to investigate. I discovered that there were painting elephants at work at their easels all over Thailand. The explanation was simple. When logging using animal labour was banned in 1990, 3,000 domesticated elephants were suddenly unemployed. Many of them died, while others earned a meagre living doing tricks for tourists.

The elephants' future looked bleak. Luckily for them, two Russian artists living in New York, Vitaly Komar and Alexander Melamid, had learned of the plight of the Thai elephants. The pair decided that they would do their best to open an art school for the elephants to give them a new occupation. This took time, but by 1997 they had established the Asian Elephant and Conservation Project and were soon organising special camps in Thailand where elephants could paint and their pictures could be sold to visitors.

The project was a great success despite the fact that the paintings themselves were rather disappointing, consisting of little more than a collection of random strokes. However, the fact that they were genuinely made by elephants wielding brushes in their trunks was enough to see them being sold to admirers in large numbers. The sales raised funds to help the elephants survive the crisis caused by their sudden redundancy.

That was the situation at the start of the 21st century, but then something strange began to happen. As the years passed the nature of the paintings changed. Suddenly the random daubs were no more, and in their place came startling pictorial images. The elephants were now painting pictures of flowers, trees and even animals. One particular elephant called Hong was able to create a picture of a walking elephant holding a flower in its raised trunk. No other non-human animal had ever produced a pictorial image of any kind, and the original efforts of elephants had all been below the level of those made by apes. How had Hong and a number of other Thai elephants graduated to this advanced form of picture making in a period of only a few years?

To find the answer to this question, in 2009 I visited one of the Thai elephant camps at Nong Nooch, near Pattaya, where I was able to watch three female elephants painting pictures of botanical subjects. Each of these animals has its own personal keeper, or mahout.

A painting session begins with three heavy easels being wheeled into position. On each easel a large piece of white card (76 x 50 centimetres) has been fixed underneath a strong wooden frame. Each elephant is positioned in front of her easel and is given a brush loaded with paint by her mahout. He pushes the brush gently into the end of her trunk. The man then stands to one side of his animal's neck and watches intently as the brush starts to make lines on the card. Then the empty brush is replaced by another loaded one, and the painting continues until the picture is complete.

Right An elephant called Mook painting a vase of flowers, Nong Nooch, Thailand.

To most of the audience, what they have seen appears to be almost miraculous. Elephants must surely be almost human in intelligence if they can paint pictures of flowers and trees in this way. What the audience overlooks are the actions of the mahouts as their animals are at work. This oversight is understandable because it is difficult to drag your eyes away from the brushes that are making the lines and spots. However, if you do so, you will notice that with each mark the mahout tugs at his elephant's ear. He nudges it up and down to get the animal to make a vertical line, or pulls it sideways to get a horizontal one. To encourage spots and blobs he tugs the ear forward towards the canvas. So, very sadly, the design the elephant is making is not hers but the mahout's. There is no elephantine invention, no creativity, just slavish copying.

Investigating further, after the show is over it emerges that each of the so-called artistic animals always produces exactly the same image, time after time, day after day and week after week. Mook always paints flowers, Christmas always does a tree and Pimtong a climbing plant. Each elephant works to a set routine, guided by her master. The inevitable conclusion, therefore, is that elephants are not artists. Unlike the chimpanzees, they do not explore new patterns or vary the design of their work themselves. Superficially, they do appear to be more advanced but it is all a trick. Having said this, it has to be admitted that it is an amazingly clever trick. No human hand touches the animal's trunk. The brain of the elephant has to translate the tiny nudges she feels on her ear into attractive lines and blobs. And she has to place these marks on the white surface with great precision. This requires considerable intelligence and a muscular sensitivity that is truly extraordinary.

'...it is clear that the chimpanzee brain is capable of obeying a number of basic aesthetic rules.'

Animal art

Looking at all the non-human picture-making activities, particularly the detailed studies of the chimpanzees Alpha and Congo and some smaller studies of other apes, it can be said that it was possible to prove visual control of the marks being made. All the other animal examples lack this proof and provide us with no more than abstract patterns that may be visually organised or may be no more than random scribbles or daubs. Without experimental tests of the kind done with Alpha and Congo, it is impossible to tell what is happening in those cases.

Where visual control is operating, it is clear that the chimpanzee brain is capable of obeying a number of basic aesthetic rules. This tells us more about the precursors of human art than anything done by children or primitive cultures. It is as though the ape stands at the very threshold of art – the birth of art – and for that reason these primate drawings and paintings are of special importance for any study of the evolution of human art. In his book *Monkey Painting*,

Thierry Lenain states baldly that 'A monkey painting is not a work of art.' His reason for this statement is that the animal is only interested in making the painting, not in studying it afterwards.

I find this a strange and unacceptably narrow definition of the word 'art'. Keeping a finished work for later enjoyment only applies to a certain type of art. Lenain's definition excludes all forms of performance art, for example, which exist only in the moment when they are being made. And it excludes all forms of ritual art or folk art that are discarded and destroyed when the rituals or the festivities are over. His definition also excludes all forms of child art, for children, like apes, show little interest in their drawings or paintings after completing them. As Ben-Ami Scharfstein says in his essay on inter-species aesthetics: 'Even mature artists sometimes enjoy the process of creation much more than its results....'

Of course, nobody who has made a serious study of ape painting has ever claimed that it is a great form of abstract art. It is not. But with its simple visual rules it does contain the germ of aesthetics and, like child art, is therefore a valuable tool in the search for a deeper understanding of the nature of human art.

Also, for what it is worth, Congo did on one occasion show a passing interest in his finished works. On the day that his paintings had been framed for an exhibition, he went up close and stared at them intently, even reaching out to touch one of them.

Right Congo staring intently at one of his newly framed paintings.

4 Child Art

Scan page to view video

Child Art

THE PERSONAL UNFOLDING OF THE ARTISTIC IMPULSE

Give any two-year-old child a pencil and paper and he or she will enjoy scribbling. At first the scribblings are random, but as time passes they start to become organised. Favoured shapes begin to appear out of the tangle of random lines. Gradually these shapes become more distinctive and, as the child approaches a third birthday, pictorial images are created. At this point, the human child enters a world that the chimpanzee never reaches. The best that an ape could manage was to draw a circular shape and make a few marks inside it. If this is the apex of ape art, it is the very first step of child art.

The early stages of development
The young child stares at what he or she has drawn and declares 'mummy' or 'daddy', and thus identifies what has been created. Once this connection has been made, the child embarks on a long series of developmental stages, during which the first crude circle with two blobs for the eyes and a line for the mouth will eventually become a well-drawn human face. The seven drawings shown here over the next three pages, which were all made by the same child between the ages of 2 and 13 years, illustrate this process.

   Drawing 1 was made on the first day that this child started scribbling. She was 2 years and 11 months old and her markings are already bold and exploratory. At this stage, like a young chimpanzee she is enjoying the fun of watching her lines emerge from the end of the crayons. Drawing 2, made during a second session on the following day, now reveals a central feature in the form of a crude circle. Although still clumsy, this represents a refinement from the wild scribbling of the previous day, with a self-imposed control that creates a geometric unit, or 'diagram'.

Right The scribble stage, age 2 years 11 months.

Far right The appearance of a central circle, age 2 years 11 months.

Below right The first pictorial image, age 2 years 11 months.

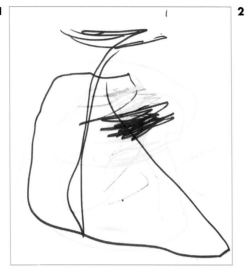

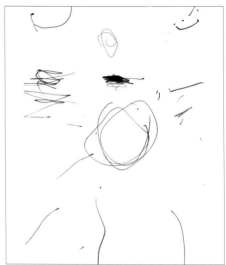

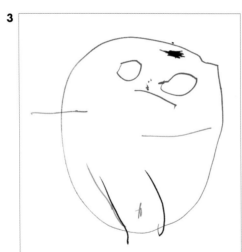

'...before the child has reached her third birthday, her brain has developed to a point where she can produce a representation of the human form...'

The young chimpanzee Congo also reached this stage, although far less quickly, and was eventually able to draw good circles.

Drawing 3, made on the third day of these drawing sessions, shows one of the first pictorial images made by this child. The circle has now become a body, and inside it are a small patch of black hair, a pair of round eyes, a few dots for a nose, a line for a mouth, two lines for arms and two more for legs. The abstract circle of the previous day has become an entire human being. Technically it could not be simpler but here, even before the child has reached her third birthday, her brain has developed to a point where she can produce a representation of the human form in which she has summarised the most important details of human anatomy. This is the stage that a chimpanzee never reaches – it is the point at which human art begins its long journey.

4

Above A bolder
pictorial image, age
4 years 1 month.

5

Above A separate
head and torso, age
4 years 10 months.

Drawing 4, made 14 months later at the age of 4 years and 1 month, shows a dramatic increase in the artist's confidence and power. However, the drawing still clings to the earlier image of a figure, with (green) arms and legs coming out of the central circle. There is as yet no separation between the head and the body of the figure. This is known as the 'cephalopod' stage in child art and, remarkably, is common to all children. In the mind of the young artist the whole of the person being portrayed is contained within the central circle. It is as though the primeval face that the child creates starts to sprout arms and legs before it has grown a torso from which these limbs can emerge. In the child's mind, the face is the most important feature of the human being, the limbs are second and the torso third. The neck, hands and feet are usually also a little late to arrive. This is a case of a pictorial image revealing to us the way in which a small child sees her companions.

Drawing 5 was made nine months later, at the age of 4 years and 10 months. It shows the next stage in visual development, where the arms and legs have now moved down from the head and are attached to a separate torso. The head and trunk are now two distinct units, but they still lack a neck between them. Fingers are present at this stage, but bizarrely there are no hands. Each finger protrudes separately from the surface of the arms.

Drawing 6 was done at the age of 10, after a long gap. The child's attempt to depict a whole scene, with the human figure performing some action within that scene, is typical of this stage. The body proportions are well worked out, and the artist has carefully added small details such as the goggles worn by the swimmer.

The final picture (Drawing 7) was made at the age of 13 years and 2 months. Although the figures are still flat and the illusion of depth is missing, the lines are now placed with much greater precision and refinement. There is also much more attention to detail, with the pupil and iris of each eye clearly shown as well as the eyelashes, eyebrows, eyelids, individual hairstyles, a necklace and even the small detail of the philtrum depression between the nose and the upper lip.

The first five of these seven drawings are typical of the kind of development that takes place in the early stages of child art.

Right A figure is drawn as part of an action scene, age 10 years.

Below right Images now have refined detail, age 13 years 2 months.

The similarity between the drawings of one child and another is remarkable, as if all children must go through these phases – not because of their education but because of the way in which all human eyes see things at these young ages. The final two pictures, made at the ages of 10 and 13, have become more personal and individual. By this time many external factors are at work on the child artist, influencing the style and content of the paintings. About the only common features that are present in art made at this age are a certain stiffness and an inability to deal with depth. With special tuition, however, even these shortcomings can be eliminated by this later stage of childhood.

From scribbles to pictorials

What tuition cannot do is to influence the very early stages of child art. Young children are in an exciting new world of their own, discovering their own abilities to make recognisable images on paper. In the 1950s, Rhoda Kellogg made a detailed study of over one million drawings by young children from 30 different countries; she was staggered by the degree of similarity between them. Differences in the external environment hardly seemed to matter, and the same images cropped up time and time again.

Kellogg eventually drew up a chart of five basic stages, starting from the very first scribbles. She named these five stages as follows: scribbles, diagrams, combines, aggregates and pictorials. Kellogg recognised 20 different scribble units and studied the way in which they were purified into six basic diagrams, such as circles, squares and triangles. She then noted the way in which once they had been established, these simple diagrams could be combined in many different ways to make slightly more complex visual units. Each of these combines contained two elements; for example, a square with a triangle on top made a shape that would

Below left Rhoda Kellogg's chart sums up the five stages of children's drawings, evolving from scribbles through to pictorials. The chart reads from the bottom to the top.

Below right Kellogg's second chart shows houses drawn by children from 13 different countries.

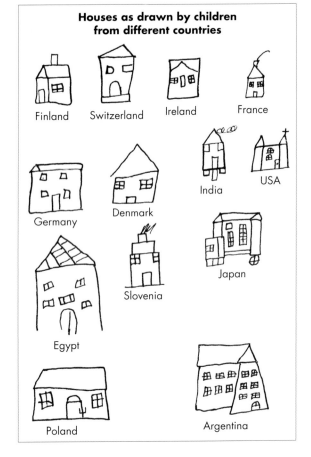

later become the basis for the drawing of a house. These combines then went a step further to create aggregates of several basic elements. And the aggregates in turn became the foundation for the earliest pictures of subjects such as people, houses, boats and flowers.

According to Kellogg, this visual development in young children was so internal and so independent of external environmental details that it was as though some kind of 'universal imagery' was operating at this level. No matter which country the children came from, they all produced the same kind of human figures, with the arms and legs coming out of the head. And no matter what kind of home they lived in, they almost all drew a little box-shaped house with a sloping roof.

Apart from the human figure and the house, there are several other basic pictorials that all young children seem to discover for themselves, and which contradict what they see in the outside world. Perhaps their strangest invention is the 'sunburst'. When children between the ages of four and six draw a sun in a simple landscape picture, they almost always show a circle with lines radiating from it. Yet when they see the real sun in the sky, they see a round object without radiating lines. A child might on rare occasions observe a sun, half hidden by clouds, emanating a ray of light – a sunbeam – but when this happens there are never beams of light emanating in all directions from around the sun's rim. Yet this is what we see on the paper, time after time; it is another example of an internal process of visual discovery that takes place as the child grapples with his or her first pictorial images.

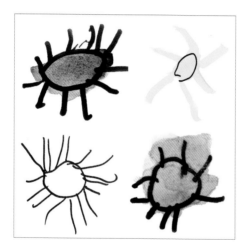

Right Some examples of a child's-eye view of the sun, taken from different sources. The sunburst motif seems to be common to all young children.

The mystery is why do children all over the world draw the sun with these radiating lines? Do they see radiating sunbeams when they look at the sun? Rhoda Kellogg thinks not. She states categorically: 'I do not think the Sun is a reality object.' What she means by this is that when small children draw a sun they are not consciously trying to copy a precise visual memory of the real sun. Instead they are engaged in an internal journey from very simple shapes to more complex ones, and the sunburst image is simply a stage on this journey.

In this way the first drawing of a human figure grows gradually out of circles and crosses, with the sunburst arriving as a halfway stage in this developmental process. In other words, when it first appears the sunburst motif is not a sun at all but just another of the simple patterns that the young child makes while exploring

Right This drawing by a seven-year-old girl shows the sunburst in the sky.

the possibilities of lines on a page. Kellogg makes the point that the sunburst is not drawn until after the child has made crossed circles, suggesting that it is a modification of the crossed-circle motif. Much later, at age seven when whole scenes are depicted, the sunburst motif will go up into the sky and take on its new role as a sun radiating sunbeams.

Child art is, therefore, like an unfolding visual language. Children play with simple shapes without reference to the outside world. They then combine these shapes in various ways until suddenly one of these combinations starts to remind the child of something in the real world. Once a rectangle has become a motor car, a triangle has become a sail or a spiral has become an animal's curly tail, then the child moves on to another phase altogether – the pictorial phase. During this phase, little by little the details of the face or the body or the vehicle or the house will start to undergo improvements that match them closer to external reality.

This process of refining images can sometimes be difficult because the images have been invented, rather than copied. The child realises that the arms on the human body are sticking out from the sides of the head, and this does not feel right. But it takes some time before the next refinement can take place, where the arms are shifted down to a separate body unit below the head. Once this has been achieved, however, the child will never revert to the head–arms image. The child may find improvements difficult, with the favourite, familiar old motifs stubbornly refusing to change, but once these changes have taken place there is no looking back.

The rules of the young artist

Adults sometimes try to influence children as they draw but soon discover that young artists have their own rules. When an adult started asking questions about a two-year-old's drawing during her first-ever drawing session, the answers were not always as expected. When asked to identify each part of her drawing, the child gave the answers indicated by the printed labels shown below. She made a clear distinction between the (brown) hat and the (green) hair. The eyes were given great importance and had huge black pupils. The nose was a minute dot between the eyes. The fingers were spread out along both arms. A row of small dots running from just below the mouth to the bottom of the figure was identified as buttons.

Two large, circular features in the centre of the body appeared to be breasts, each with a nipple indicated, but were surprisingly identified as buckles. Presumably this meant that they were two halves of a buckle that could be joined together to hold a belt in place – a rather sophisticated concept for a two-year-old. The child's mother was breastfeeding a new baby at the time this drawing was made, and it seems likely that this was influencing the circular features of the drawing. It would be interesting to know whether the child had intended the circular shapes to be breasts, but did not wish to verbalise this and so invented the buckle interpretation, or whether they really were intended to be buckles but their shape was perhaps unconsciously influenced by the mother's breastfeeding. When an adult pointed out that there were no feet at the ends of the legs, the two-year-old first-time artist replied, with the tone of a veteran who has been asked this question many times before: 'I don't do feet.'

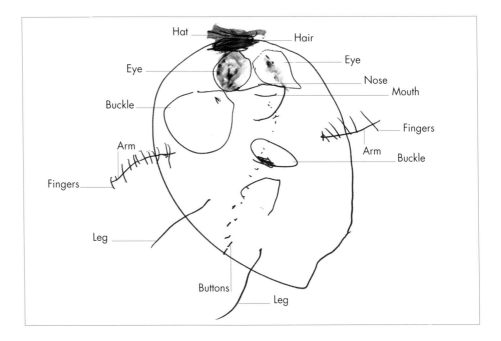

Right Drawing of a human figure by a two-year-old girl.

If you examine cave art and the elegance of its images, the contrast with child art is striking. The cave paintings at Lascaux in southern France have been called the 'birth of art', but this seems a ridiculous claim. Whenever a young child starts scribbling, *that* is the birth of art.

It would be wrong to suggest that all children develop at the same rate as one another and go through identical stages in developing their motifs. There are considerable similarities, it is true, but there are also some striking individual variations. Some children prove to be slow starters while others are prodigies. Take one example, when six children of different ages were asked to draw a giraffe.

The drawing of the youngest in this group, the five-year-old, is more advanced than those of the six-year-olds. It is the only one that shows the giraffe's special survival mechanism of feeding from tall trees. The others will eventually catch up with him, but at this stage he is slightly ahead of them. The drawing by the 15-year-old is significant because it demonstrates the end of childhood as far as art is concerned. By law, this boy still has three years to go before he is technically an adult in the eyes of society, but as an artist he has already matured. Like the prehistoric cave artists, he has reached a stage where he can portray animal forms with accuracy. Unlike them he has, with a Magritte-like perversity, decided to combine these forms in an original way to create a strange chimera – a giraffe with an elephant-headed body. This brings an entirely new kind of imaginative process to the act of drawing, with a calculating intellect replacing a childlike intuition. It involves careful copying from the outside world, or from photographs of it, and a pre-planned manipulation of those copied elements.

'Like the prehistoric cave artists, he [the 15-year-old boy] has reached a stage where he can portray animal forms with accuracy.'

This teenage drawing is so far removed from the work of the younger children that it helps to underline the nature of pre-teen art, and to identify its weaknesses and its strengths. Its weaknesses lie in its clumsiness, in the fact that the hand will not yet do precisely what the brain wants. Its strengths lie in the freshness and vividness of its created images – the younger child is on a long voyage of visual discovery, with the outside world as a servant rather than a master of this journey. Distortions in size and shape reveal young children's feelings about their world and what matters to them. The elimination of what is not important also tells us a great deal about the selectivity of children's minds, about what is relevant to them and what is irrelevant. Through their interest in playing with simplified shapes, these young artists also show how our ancient ancestors could have converted pictures into pictograms, and pictograms into the abstract geometric units that gave us our first written languages.

Right The results when six children were asked to draw a giraffe.

Martin, 5 years

Christopher, 6.5 years

Patricia, 6 years 11 months

Jennifer, 7 years

Clifford, 10 years

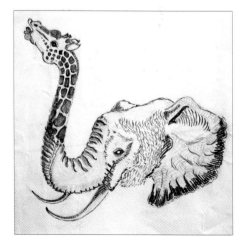

Richard, 15 years

5 Prehistoric Art

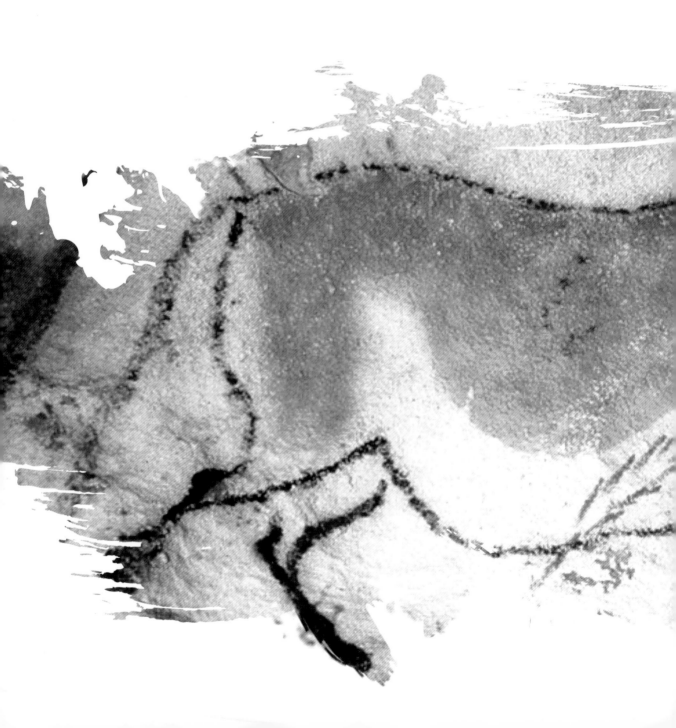

Scan page to view video

Prehistoric Art

FROM HUNTER-GATHERERS TO THE FIRST FARMERS

We know that the visual arts flourished long before the written word became established. In fact, the earliest written words were no more than a collection of stylised images. Our letter A, for example, is the head of a horned animal turned upside down. Our letter N started out as a snake. The spoken word came much earlier than the written word, of course, but even human speech was preceded by a form of visual art.

The earliest known forms of art

This is the story of the world's oldest known art object. Long ago, by the banks of a fast-running river in southern Africa, an inquisitive apeman caught sight of a strange face staring up at him from below the water's surface. There were many pebbles on the riverbed, each worn smooth by the current, but this one was different. It was shaped like a head, and its smooth surface bore the unmistakable features of a face: a pair of staring eyes, a wide nose, a mouth, a forehead and dark hair. The apeman picked up the pebble in his hand and gazed at it. The staring face he saw there fascinated him. He was so impressed by it that he carried it a long way back to the cave where he lived. And there he kept it. And there the pebble remained for the next three million years until anthropologists discovered it while digging for fossil remains in the cave.

This remarkable stone, known today as the Makapansgat Pebble, is the oldest known art object in the world. There is no evidence that it was fashioned by the apeman, but its presence in the cave confirms that he saw it as something important. It was the first knick-knack, the first collectible, the first *objet trouvé*, and its owner was not yet quite human. He or she was an Australopithecine, belonging to a group of animals that were halfway between apes and humans.

Right The three
million-year-old
Makapansgat
Pebble is the
world's oldest
known art object.

Right The three million-year-old Makapansgat Pebble is the world's oldest known art object.

How can we be sure of all this, when the event took place three million years ago? The answer is that the geological evidence forces us to accept that this is what happened. The smooth roundness of the pebble, which is made of red jasperite, indicates it must have come from a place where the movement of water had worn down its rough edges – this could only mean a beach or riverbed. There was no beach nearby, but not far from the cave flowed an ancient river. Raymond Dart, who first described the pebble in 1974, estimated that the nearest riverbed was 32 kilometres from the apeman's cave. Later studies suggested a more modest four kilometres, but even this was a remarkably long distance to carry any object.

The actual rocks of the apeman's cave, where the pebble was found alongside fossilised bones, contain nothing like it. The only possible explanation for its presence in the cave is that an apeman went to the trouble of carrying something that he could neither eat nor use in any practical way – and whose only possible interest must have been the accidental facial features on its smoothed surface – a considerable distance, until he could place in it his cave home. This is an amazing event to have happened three million years ago, and it is the earliest glimpse we have had, so far, of a symbolic act by our ancient ancestors.

If the Makapansgat Pebble proves that an early apeman was capable of appreciating what we might be forgiven for calling a ready-made art object, it says nothing about the actual making of an art object. For evidence of this we have to wait many thousands of years.

One of the earliest signs that our ancestors were engaging in the visual arts is the presence of coloured pigments and paint-grinding equipment in a cave at Twin Rivers near Lusaka, Zambia. It is not clear whether these pigments were used to

Above The *Venus of Tan Tan*, the oldest known art object made by a human being, is between 300,000 and 500,000 years old.

Above The tiny *Venus of Berekhat Ram* was found in 1986 in the Golan Heights. The figure is between 250,000 and 280,000 years old.

create body decorations or to paint surfaces or objects that are now lost, but there can be no doubt that some kind of primitive visual art was already being practised a very long time ago – between 350,000 and 400,000 years ago.

In 1999 archaeologist Lawrence Barham unearthed over 300 pieces of pigment of many colours: brown, red, yellow, purple, blue and pink. Some of these pieces showed signs of having been rubbed or ground to produce a powder. This means that our remote ancestors were busily collecting and processing a whole variety of pigments at an astonishingly early date. The wide range of colours is impressive, indicating that these early artists were capable of putting on quite a show and were probably already engaged in special rituals and tribal performances.

As regards the art objects themselves, new discoveries are being made almost every year, as refined dating techniques are applied to the ancient artefacts that our remote ancestors appear to have made. At present the oldest known art object made by a human is a small figurine called the *Venus of Tan Tan*, which was found in 1999 in Morocco by German archaeologist Lutz Fiedler. It was located deep in the ground next to some stone hand-axes, in a layer that dated from between 300,000 and 500,000 years ago. It is a piece of stone, six centimetres tall, that appears to have been roughly shaped into a human figure with a head, neck, torso, legs and arms. There are no hands, feet, face or signs of gender, but the stocky little figure has a bull-neck and short, stumpy arms. Traces of pigment suggest that it was once painted red.

Even those critics who believe that most of the object's 'human' features were accidentally made my natural processes, accept that the grooves were improvements made by human hands. 'Impact scars' have been identified in five of these grooves, confirming that they were made by a human wielding some form of implement. A similar figure, called the *Venus of Berekhat Ram*, was discovered in 1986 on the Golan Heights in the Middle East. Slightly later in date, it is between 250,000 and 280,000 years old and is very crudely shaped, like the *Venus of Tan Tan*. This tiny figure, which measures only about three centimetres tall, has three grooves incised by a sharp-edged stone, giving it a neck and arms.

These two very early figures go one step further than the Makapansgat Pebble. That was almost certainly an entirely natural object, but these figures were sufficiently humanoid in shape to attract attention and to encourage a little improvement by the addition of grooves. But they are still very primitive and far from deserving the name of human sculpture.

Evidence of human visual creativity from around 200,000 years ago, or even earlier, has been discovered in the Daraki-Chattan Cave in central India. It takes the form of quartzite petroglyphs, or rock carvings, consisting of both cupules (small circular concavities in the rock face) and engraved lines. The hammer stones used to produce the cupules were also found in the cave. Cupules of this

Right These 200,000-year-old cupules were found in the Daraki-Chattan Cave in India.

kind are something of a mystery, and even today no one understands their significance. Stretching over a very long time period, they appear all over the world and are one of the most common early art forms wherever their location. Sometimes there are just a few cupules, sometimes there are hundreds and occasionally thousands. They are made on horizontal slabs of rock, vertical walls and even overhangs. They clearly had some kind of symbolic or ritual significance, but what exactly that was eludes even the most expert cupule-hunters.

Turning from cupules to ornaments, the earliest known human adornments date from between 98,000 and 132,000 years ago. They consist of a collection of perforated *Nassarius* shell beads found at Es Skhūl in Israel. *Nassarius* is a species of marine snail not found in the area where these perforated shells were discovered, so they must have been specially obtained with some difficulty. It is easy to imagine these shells being threaded to make one of the world's first necklaces or bracelets. Strangely, similar perforated shells have been found at several other locations, including eastern Morocco (110,000 years old), Algeria and South Africa. The idea of a necklace fashion spreading so far afield at such an early date is difficult to grasp, but it appears to have occurred – unless the wearing of shell necklaces took place independently in four very different locations.

The earliest record of painting activity comes from an interesting discovery made recently in the Blombos Cave near the southernmost tip of South Africa. Ancient painting kits have been discovered there, although frustratingly the

paintings they were employed to make have so far not been found. The painting kits consisted of a pair of abalone shells containing paint made from red ochre.

Near these paint palettes were found stone tools that had been fashioned to prepare the ochre mixture, as well as shaped pieces of bone that may have been used to apply the pigment. Dating from around 100,000 years ago, this find is truly remarkable and means that carefully planned painting activities were taking place at this very early date.

Although the paintings at Blombos are missing, another early kind of human art has managed to survive there. Dating from between 70,000 and 77,000 years ago, it takes the form of geometric shapes scratched on the flat surface of two pieces of ochre rock. These are the earliest patterned engravings known at present anywhere in Africa.

Another controversial discovery made recently has led to the claim that the oldest known paintings in the world were made by Neanderthals between 42,300 and 43,500 years ago. The paintings were found on a

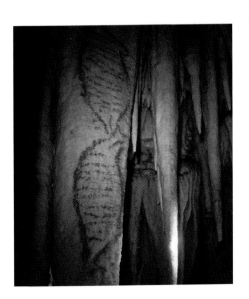

stalactite in caves at Nerja, 56 kilometres east of Malaga in southern Spain. The Neanderthals were able to survive in this part of Europe until around 37,000 years ago, and these images are the only known examples of Neanderthal art, apart from some decorated stones and shells. The images, painted in red ochre, look remarkably like dolphins, but they are thought to represent seals – we know that the Neanderthals ate seal meat. The early dates quoted were obtained by testing some charcoal deposits that lay only ten centimetres from the paintings and which were thought to have come from the lamps used by the artists when working. Critics want more accurate dating to be done, using a little of the pigment from the actual paintings.

Moving forward in time, the *Venus of Hohle Fels* is the oldest of a number of small, prehistoric female figurines that have been found at various sites across Europe. Her date is given as between 35,000 and 40,000 years old. A bone flute of the same date was discovered close to her, making it the oldest known musical instrument in the world. This Venus figurine is currently the earliest known example of true human sculpture. She is not a modified natural object – she is a fully carved figure and, as such, takes us into an entirely new phase of human artistic endeavour.

Discovered in 2008 by archaeologist Nicholas Conard beneath one metre of sediment on the floor of a cave in southwest Germany, the *Venus of Hohle Fels* is only about six and a half centimetres tall. This figurine, carved from mammoth ivory, displays four anatomical exaggerations: a pair of enormous breasts, big buttocks, greatly enlarged genitals and an excess of body fat. She also has three anatomical reductions, having no feet, hands or head. Her head has not been lost accidentally, but has been replaced by a ring for suspension. Coming from what must have been a 'feast or famine' culture, this Venus is clearly a celebration of feasting and sexuality. The deliberate lack of a head means that she is not meant to represent a particular individual. Instead, she is a generalised symbol of fecundity and may well have been worn as a good-luck charm to ensure pregnancy.

These then are the earliest discoveries in the prehistory of human art. From the Makapansgat Pebble three million years ago to the oldest piece of sculpture 35,000 years ago, we have been lucky enough to discover tantalising remnants of what seems to have been a major new preoccupation for our remote ancestors. It is important to remember that what we have found so far is only the tiniest tip of a huge iceberg. Confirming this thought is what happened next in the story of art.

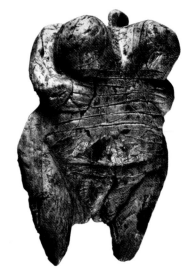

Below The *Venus of Hohle Fels*, found in southwest Germany, dates from between 35,000 and 40,000 years ago.

From the time of our earliest known prehistoric Venus, about 35,000 years ago, until the beginnings of the first human civilisations about 5,000 years ago, there was a long period of prehistoric art lasting 30,000 years. The number of discoveries made recently relating to the art of this period has multiplied dramatically. Hundreds of painted caves, decorated rock shelters, ancient burial sites and primitive settlements have been examined and their works of art described in detail.

Scholars have argued about the meaning of these art works – and there have been many fanciful interpretations. The truth is that we know so little about these distant cultures and have such small corners of their worlds to study, that it is possible to construct almost any outlandish explanation. Morris's law of academic debate that states 'the less light that has been thrown on a topic, the more heat it generates' has been much in evidence. In an attempt to keep interpretations as close as possible to the few known facts, I will separate the art of this period into its three main categories: portable figurines, cave art and rock art.

Above The portable figurine of the *Venus of Willendorf* was carved between 22,000 and 24,000 years ago.

'These figures were probably designed by women for women as symbols of maternity, not sexuality. They are visual hymns to childbirth, not courtship.'

Portable figurines

The *Venus of Hohle Fels* has already been mentioned as the oldest example of a piece of human sculpture. Several hundred more of these small prehistoric Venuses from the millennia that followed have been unearthed in careful excavations at sites ranging from Western Europe across to Siberia.

The most famous of these Venus figurines is the *Venus of Willendorf*, which was found in 1908 in Austria by the archaeologist Josef Szombathy. Larger than the one from Hohle Fels and more expertly carved, this figurine was created between 22,000 and 24,000 years ago. A little over 11 centimetres tall, she is made not from ivory but from limestone, and displays much more surface detail. Interestingly, the type of limestone used was not local, which indicates that the figurine was carried to the site where she was found. Originally the *Venus of Willendorf* must have been painted red because traces of red ochre still cling to her surface.

In common with the earlier figurine of the *Venus of Hohle Fels*, she has the same huge breasts and buttocks, conspicuous genitals, excessive fat deposits and a lack of feet. But she differs from the earlier Venus because she has hands and a head. Her hands and bizarrely spindly forearms rest on top of her breasts. Her head has no face and is covered with an elaborate hairstyle or some kind of headgear. As with the Hohle Fels figure, the complete lack of a face suggests that the Willendorf Venus was a generalised symbol rather than a representation of a particular individual. It is likely that she and all the other, slightly later Stone Age female figurines were either worn or carried as fertility charms.

Although the known examples of these figures were found hundreds of kilometres from each other and were made thousands of years apart, they do have a remarkably similar style. They are rounded, fleshy, simplified figures with a strong emphasis on prominent breasts, big bellies, wide buttocks and thick thighs. Hands, feet, faces and heads are frequently reduced or even omitted. Because the female's genitals are sometimes indicated these figurines have been viewed as sexual objects, but this does not fit the visual

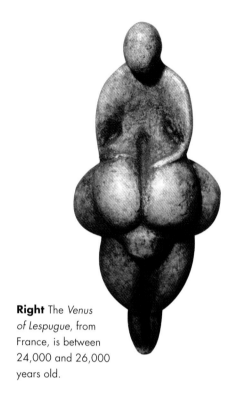

Right The *Venus of Lespugue*, from France, is between 24,000 and 26,000 years old.

Right The *Venus of Savignano*, discovered in northern Italy, is around 25,000 years old.

impact they make. These are not erotic breasts, they are lactating breasts; these are not the slender thighs of nubile young girls, they are broad, childbearing thighs. These figures were probably designed by women for women as symbols of maternity, not sexuality. They are visual hymns to childbirth, not courtship.

One of the most remarkable of these early figurines is the *Venus of Lespugue*, found in France in the foothills of the Pyrenees. Carved from tusk ivory and estimated to be between 24,000 and 26,000 years old, she was badly damaged during excavation. The image shown here is of a remodelled copy that presents her as she would originally have appeared. The prehistoric artist has dramatically exaggerated her body shape, giving her enormous, pendulous breasts ready to breastfeed the hungriest infant.

Despite the fact that these figurines come from widely scattered locations ranging from southwest France to eastern Siberia, they all appear to be from one genre. They are all small enough to carry or to wear as pendants, the largest being less than 15 centimetres tall. Several of them are pierced with suspension holes. They are nearly all faceless, and quite a few seem to have the same hair stylist, or is it hat-maker? It is hard to determine the exact nature of the strangely patterned head covering, and even more difficult to explain why, in most cases, it comes down to cover the upper part of the non-existent facial features.

In a few instances the stylisation of the female form reaches a whole new level. In the Savignano Venus from northern Italy, the usually rounded head is reduced to a tapering vertical spike. Her generous breasts, belly, buttocks and thighs, however, are all true to the great proto-Venus tradition. In certain other figurines a further level of stylisation reduces the female body to little more than a metaphor. Here, all that is left is a hint of a female form. There may be a pair of breasts, a pair of parted legs, a swollen belly or a protruding pair of buttocks. The message is still the same, but now the artist has reduced her pregnancy charm to the bare essentials. This is not laziness; this is sophisticated symbolic abstraction. It is the kind of shape refinement that a modern sculptor would be proud of – and the dates of these figurines are still very early.

Right These highly stylised female figurines, carved from mammoth bone, were found at Dolní Věstonice in the Czech Republic. They are 22,400 years old.

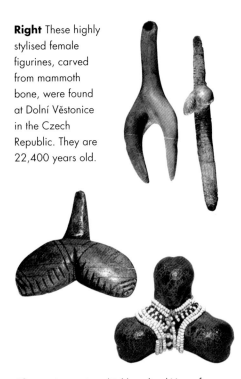

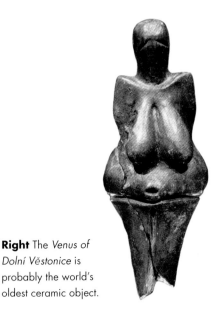

Above An ancient, highly stylised Venus from Dolní Věstonice in the Czech Republic and a modern version used by a Turkana girl in Kenya. The one on the left is 22,400 years old, the other less than 30 years old. The desire for children has a long history.

Right The *Venus of Dolní Věstonice* is probably the world's oldest ceramic object.

Some scholars may well feel uncomfortable with the description of these wonderful artefacts as 'lucky charms'. The great age of these little figures and their extraordinary rarity create an atmosphere of reverence in which many feel they should be given some loftier significance. They have been referred to as mother goddesses, as symbols of a creation myth, as emblems of security, as universal mothers, and so on. There is no evidence whatever to support such weighty descriptions. The simplest explanation is that the figurines were worn or carried in the clothing of women who were eager to have a baby. The fact that modern versions of the figurines are still in use today helps to confirm this. The young women of the Turkana tribe in northwest Kenya, for example, still wear similar 'Venus figure' pendants when they want to become pregnant. Once this has happened they pass these Venus figures on to their younger sisters. Like the ancient figurines, these lucky charms are reduced to having little more than breasts and buttocks.

Before leaving the subject of prehistoric sculptures, it is important to point out that stone and bone were not the only materials used. One of the Venus figures was made of baked clay and is generally recognised as the oldest example of ceramic art. She pre-dates the first pottery by over 10,000 years. Known as the *Venus of Dolní Věstonice*, she was found in a region that is now part of the Czech Republic. Only 11.5 centimetres tall, this Venus is between 25,000 and 29,000 years old and was discovered in 1925. She has several unusual features: a facial detail in the form of two slanting eye slits, squared shoulders and a conspicuous, well-formed navel. This navel is well observed because thin women have vertically shaped navels and plump women have horizontally shaped ones, and this navel is appropriately horizontal. The four holes in the top of her head are possibly the remnant of some kind of suspension device. Otherwise, this Venus is very much in the style of the carved figurines.

Looking at these remarkable female figurines of the Old Stone Age, it is clear that in this very early phase of human art there was already considerable sophistication in the way

Above The lion-headed man of Hohlenstein-Stadel was carved from mammoth ivory. He dates from around 32,000 years ago.

relevant details were exaggerated and irrelevant ones were reduced or omitted. Because the figurines were concerned with pregnancy and fertility, those related features of the female form were dramatically magnified. Other features were ignored, but this was not due to laziness or clumsiness. We know from the paintings that were being made at about the same time on the walls of caves that the artists of the Old Stone Age were capable of elegant precision when portraying their prey species. It seems likely, therefore, that these artists would have been able to make much more accurate sculptural figurines had they wished to do so. The presence of some realistic animal sculptures in a few ancient caves shows just how accurate the artists could be if they tried. Even at this early stage we are seeing images being manipulated and modified to make a greater visual impact. We will find the same process at work when we come to examine tribal art and modern art.

Although the so-called Venuses are the most interesting examples of prehistoric sculpting and modelling, they were not the only figures to appear during these very early days. There were also animal figurines and a few remarkable zoomorphic figures. The best of these figurines is the lion-headed man of Hohlenstein-Stadel. Significantly he is about 29 centimetres tall – much bigger than any of the Venuses – and therefore not in their special category of body adornments. At 32,000 years old, this imposing figure must be the oldest known zoomorphic chimera in the world. Its existence is a remarkable testimony to the early artist's imagination, where two species were combined to make a fanciful monster.

The impact of the lion-headed man relies not on exaggeration or reduction, as the female figurines do, but instead on disrupted context. The lion's head appears where there should be a human head. The figure is made extraordinary because the head is deliberately placed out of context. This disturbed natural arrangement of the elements of a figure or scene is a visual device that will become extremely popular in later ages, when artists juggle contexts to create monsters of many kinds ranging from minotaurs and centaurs to demons and dragons.

Cave art

Around the time that the female figurines such as the *Venus of Lespugue* were being carved, a new chapter in the prehistory of human art was about to be written. Cave walls in southern France were soon to be decorated in a remarkably accomplished manner. Although we know that pigments had been in use much earlier, this is the oldest known example of the results of their careful and imaginative use. The discovery of the Chauvet Cave in 1994, with cave paintings that were made as far back as 25,000 years ago, came as something of a shock – because here on the walls was evidence that an art style common 10,000 years later had already begun. The idea that a particular style of art could last for that long is hard to understand today, when almost every year brings its own new art fashion.

Over 300 painted caves from this prehistoric period have now been found in France and Spain. Some contain only fragments, while others are so richly decorated with images that they have given rise to many arguments as to why our remote ancestors executed these early works of art with such skill and passion. The most impressive cave paintings are at Lascaux in southwest France. When Picasso first saw them he snorted, 'We have invented nothing' – the 'we' in question being himself and his contemporaries. For those of us who were lucky enough to enter that cave when it had just been opened to the public, it was indeed a humbling experience. It was hard to accept the idea that Stone Age humans could create works of art of such quality.

One of the first books published about the Lascaux paintings was *Lascaux, or the Birth of Art*, written by the Frenchman Georges Bataille. His title is dramatic but wide of the mark. These paintings were not the first fumblings of a new human endeavour. This was not the birth of art; instead, at the very least it was its adolescence. What this cave had done was to neatly preserve for us a tiny corner of the art of those early days. Who knows what was happening outside that cave? Art must have been thriving, but all that external work has been lost to us. By its very nature it would not survive, except where freak conditions managed to protect it from the ravages of time.

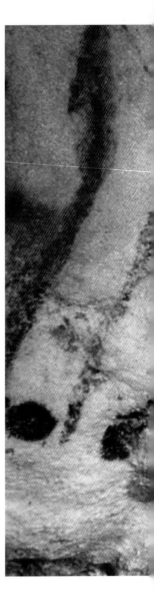

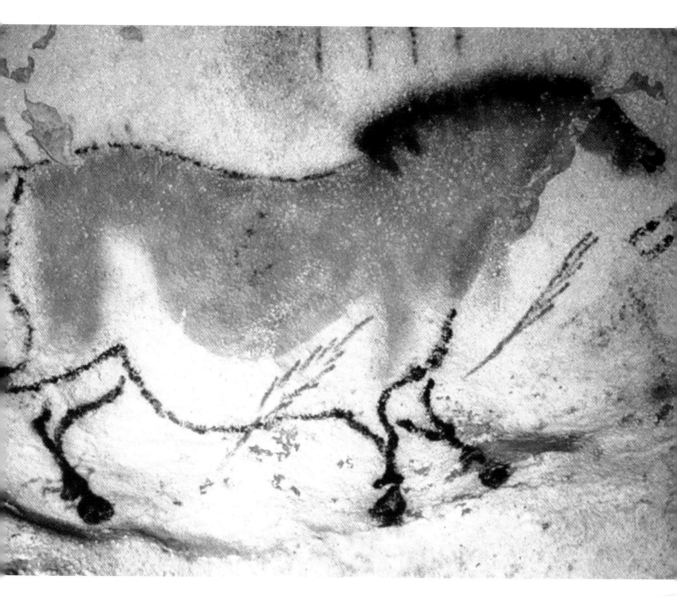

Above A painted horse on the wall of the cave at Lascaux in southwest France.

So how and why did these Stone Age hunters become such expert creative artists? Several imaginative explanations have been put forward in the past, but they make little sense. One theory sees the paintings as the work of ancient shamans, who would enter the cave in a trance-like state to perform magic rituals and then paint their visions. But these are not the works of artists who have been in a trance. They are the paintings of artists who are striving hard to create an accurate portrayal of the animals in question. To do that you need to be consciously in control of your actions – and completely free from any trance-like state. These prehistoric artists were careful, painstaking technicians, not spiritual chanting diviners.

A close examination of the images on the cave walls reveals two kinds of image: small abstract signs and large animal portraits. The animal portraits are often close to one another, but there are no deliberately grouped scenes – no compositions, only juxtapositions. Each animal is to be seen on its own, and if another one is close by that is simply because of lack of useful space on the cave walls. Indeed, sometimes one animal is half obliterating another one that was painted earlier.

These animal images are extremely unusual because, of all ancient and tribal art, they alone strive to be naturalistic. There is no exaggeration, no playing with shapes and no distortion of proportions. The usual modifications seen in other early art forms are missing. These artists are setting out, for some reason, to copy nature as closely as they can. And given the primeval conditions in which they are working, with flickering lamps to light their work, rough cave walls as their canvases and the simplest of painting equipment, their achievements are nothing short of amazing.

'There is no exaggeration, no playing with shapes and no distortion of proportions. The usual modifications seen in other early art forms are missing.'

Back in the 1930s, one man who was impressed by the precision of these early painters was the Australian artist Percy Leason. In his own work he was meticulous to a fault, and when he set eyes on the animals portrayed in the Spanish cave of Altamira he was shocked by what he saw. Others were talking about how lifelike the portrayals were, but Leason saw them differently. With his keen artist's eye he noticed that the belly of each animal seemed to be pushed forwards towards the viewer. Also, the legs were stiff and the feet were in a tiptoe posture, indicating that they were not weight bearing. It dawned on him that these animals were not 'lively', but were in fact all dead. They were being portrayed lying on the ground after they had been killed – presumably by the artist's fellow-tribesmen during the hunt. Although Leason was not aware of it at the time, the same strange tiptoe feet were also in evidence on animal paintings in other caves, such as those at Lascaux in France.

The portrayal of the animals was so accurate that these postural details had been carefully introduced into the paintings, but their significance had been missed by the archaeologists studying them. To prove that he was right Leason undertook the somewhat gruesome task of visiting an abattoir and painstakingly photographing the animals in it before and after they were killed. The ones that had just been killed were photographed from above as they lay on the ground, and they matched the postures of the cave paintings perfectly.

Leason published his photographs and his views about cave art in an archaeological journal in London in 1939, but with the outbreak of World War II his paper went largely unnoticed. There was one response, however, from another artist, William Riddell, who specialised in painting scenes of mammoth hunts and other prehistoric activities. He could not accept that the cave artist drew from a

Right A bison cave painting at Altamira, in Spain.

Below A cow painting at Lascaux, in southwest France. Both these cave paintings show the tiptoe position of the animals' feet.

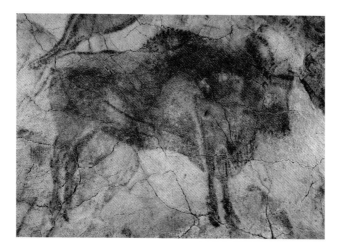

dead model stretched out on the ground before him, as Leason had implied. This simply could not be done in the recesses of a dimly lit cave. Instead, Riddell argued, the cave artists depended on visual memories of the dead animals lying in front of them following a hunt.

Riddell was right about one thing. There was no way that a dead bison could have been dragged into a cave as a model for an artist to copy. His idea that the artists had incredible visual memories is, however, equally implausible. Although Leason and Riddell agreed that the cave paintings depict dead animals, they both seem to have overlooked the obvious explanation of how this was done so accurately. The reason for their oversight is that we tend to look upon prehistoric painting solely as a cave activity. This is because all we have left today are the images protected deep inside caves. We focus so much on these that we seem to think that nothing but hunting was going on in the outside world. A human society that can create great cave art must also have had a lot going on outside, including no doubt sketching, drawing, body painting and who knows what else.

We know that these early tribes had stone implements and would not have survived the cold without making warm clothing out of animal skins. We also know that they had a variety of pigments at their disposal. Indeed, they probably had more colours than those that have survived on the cave paintings we see today. Only the most enduring ochres have stood the test of time. When a great kill was made, it would be a simple matter for an artist to take a stick of charcoal and record its outlines on a 'canvas' of stretched skin. Armed with this he or she could then make a more detailed painting on a rock face or withdraw to a cave. The outside paintings would not survive, but a few of the inside ones would.

'By portraying their greatest triumphs on their cave walls these early tribespeople were able to celebrate their victories...'

Riddell thought that copying an image was too modern an idea, but how else could the cave artists be so accurate? This is the common-sense solution that explains how these artists made such precise portrayals.

If that is how they executed their work, the question remains as to why they should want to go to so much trouble. One clue comes from the range of species shown on the cave walls, which does not correspond to the mixture of animal bones found nearby. In other words, a lot of the animals these people ate, especially the smaller creatures, were not considered important enough to have their portraits painted. Only those animals whose capture would be so dramatic that it would be the cause for a great celebration, were considered suitable for an act of commemoration on the cave walls. The artists' favourites were the mighty bison, the wild ox (aurochs), the fleet-footed horse, the antlered deer and the armoured rhinoceros – all animals to command respect and, apparently, to deserve it. By portraying their greatest triumphs on their cave walls these early tribespeople were able to celebrate their victories and perhaps, at the same time, appease the gods of the animals they had killed.

The strangest feature of this ancient cave art is that it lasted almost unchanged for so long. Two images of bison from the Chauvet and Altamira caves confirm this, one having been painted as early as 25,000 years ago and the other only 15,000 years ago. If they had been painted by two modern artists we would be convinced that they went to the same art school. Here is another explanation why the more recent cave painters of Lascaux and Altamira are so skilled – they had 10,000 years of practice behind them.

At this early stage, the cave artists were still learning their skills, although even then the majority knew what they were doing and produced good work. If only we could see what was happening in their daily lives outside the cave – what a revelation that would be. There is nothing more tantalising than attempts to study our ancient past.

Two cave paintings of the mighty bison.

Above This painting in the Chauvet Cave in France may be as much as 25,000 years old.

Right This painting in Spain's Altamira Cave is only 15,000 years old.

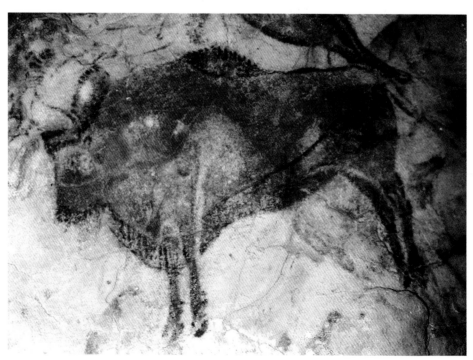

Right This cave painting at Lascaux portrays a dead bison with its entrails hanging out.

Finally, if there are any lingering doubts about the fact that all the animals in the cave paintings are dead, it is worth pointing out that some of them are shown very dead indeed. A bison at Lascaux has its entrails hanging out, and one at Altamira is curled up in an awkward posture that would never be seen in life, even during sleep. At the Chauvet Cave there is an extraordinary portrayal of a rhinoceros with blood spurting from its mouth. It also has several other red marks on its body, suggesting that it has suffered considerable injury.

I mentioned earlier that there are two kinds of image on the cave walls: small abstract signs and large animal portraits. Now that I have discussed the latter, the former may be easier to understand. If all the animal images are portraits of freshly killed prey, then the small signs can be read as indicators of the events that saw the animals fall. In some cases this portrayal is explicit, as when a horse at Lascaux is depicted with arrows or spears across its body. In other cases, spears or other weapons are shown on or next to the body. Some of the more mysterious signs may well be symbols of traps set for the prey. Of course these are only guesses, but they are easier to accept than some of the more arcane suggestions that have been put forward in the past.

One particular animal portrayed in the Lascaux Cave has puzzled observers so much that they have been reduced to calling it a mythical creature, 'a kind of unicorn'. Cave artists simply do not paint mythological animals. They are down-to-earth naturalists. The 'creature' is seen as having two unnaturally lengthy horns protruding from its head. However, if one interprets all the painted lines near the animals' bodies as spears, then it is clear that this is simply a horse that has been killed by two spears to its head.

One of the most remarkable qualities of prehistoric cave art is that the proportions of the animals are so accurately presented. Almost all other prehistoric and ancient art involves exaggeration, simplification and stylisation. Those early artists emphasised aspects that were important to them and ignored other elements. They did not seem to care if their objects or images did not look exactly like the natural shapes on which they were based. But the cave artists did care about this, and the reason seems to have been that each of the animals they portrayed on their cave walls was not a generic symbol, but a personal portrait of an individual animal killed in the hunt. Where portraits of any kind are concerned it is always important to make the image look like the 'sitter', and so it was with the cave art. The remarkable way in which the cave artists managed to make their images extraordinary can be attributed to the skill with which they created the natural shapes of the animals' bodies using just a few deft strokes. With great dexterity they could depict a well-proportioned bison, bull or horse, and with the minimum of detail.

Rock art

A third major category of prehistoric art is less protected than cave art – it is the rock art that is exposed to the outside air, and to all the buffeting and abrasion that this brings. Fully exposed rock paintings, or pictographs, are rare for obvious reasons, but there are many locations where a helpful rock overhang has given partial protection and enabled some painted rock art images to survive for thousands of years. Incised images called petroglyphs are more common on fully exposed sites. These have been hacked out of the hard rock surface and they too have managed to survive for many thousands of years. Their shortcoming is that they are notoriously difficult to date accurately.

'Humans first arrived in northern Australia about 60,000 years ago and were doubtless already creating some kind of art even then.'

The most extraordinary rock paintings that have survived to the present day are those from northwest Australia. Humans first arrived in northern Australia about 60,000 years ago and were doubtless already creating some kind of art even then. Much of their earliest activity was probably centred on body painting and has been lost, and the earliest dates we have so far for their rock art are still hotly debated.

These first Australians set up their camps in convenient rock shelters, the floors of which have given up some datable remains and also, in many cases, pieces of ochre that could only have been used for making colours. Examination of these ochre pieces has so far given dates varying between 10,000 and 40,000 years old. The oldest dates found by direct examination of the rock paintings themselves are between 25,000 and 30,000 years old. One interesting case from the Kimberley region was a buried fragment of painted rock that appeared to have fallen from a rock ceiling above. This was accurately dated to between 38,700 and 40,700 years old.

In western Australia incised rock art has been dated to 26,000 years old using a new micro-erosion technique developed by rock art specialist Robert Bednarik. Rock engravings found in southern Australia have been dated using a different method based on analysis of the 'desert varnish' that gets clogged up in the incisions over thousands of years. These results give very early dates, of about 40,000 years old, but this figure has been contested.

The unusual feature of the rock art of Australia is that, in some regions, it is still being practised by Aboriginal tribes today. When westerners first encountered this, they were fascinated to discover that the artists involved were recording an elaborate tribal mythology and reworking it regularly to keep it bright and fresh. It would seem that in this part of the world there is a continuous rock art tradition that goes back thousands of years to the work of the first settlers.

Above These highly stylised Bradshaw figures are painted under a rock overhang in northwest Australia.

When examining the style of this work it becomes immediately apparent that it differs strikingly from the cave art of Western Europe. From the earliest examples right up to the present day, the paintings and incisions on the Australian rocks are highly stylised and show little attempt to create naturalistic images. From the start, Aboriginal art on this continent is wildly imaginative and inventive, exaggerating and distorting natural shapes and paying little heed to realistic representation.

Surprisingly, it is the earlier examples of rock art that are the most elegant and refined. By comparison the later ones, although displaying images that are bold, lively and dramatic, lack the subtlety of the more ancient works. The best examples of these early images are found in the rock shelters of the Kimberley region in

Right These drawings of groups of Bradshaw rock art figures in northwest Australia show elaborate body adornments on the arms and hips.

northwest Australia. Called the 'Bradshaws' after their Victorian discoverer, and also known by their Aboriginal name *Gwion Gwion*, these painted figures are breathtaking due to the inventiveness of their design.

Considering the great age of these rock paintings, their survival in the open air without the repainting so common in the later Aboriginal work is something of a miracle. A special study by Jack Pettigrew had revealed the secret of their survival: they have in effect been fossilised. The actual paint has been replaced by biofilms of pigmented micro-organisms. A mulberry colour has been preserved by a black fungus; a cherry colour by red bacteria. In other countries, a biofilm covering has sometimes destroyed early artworks but here, miraculously, it has preserved them.

Despite this biofilm protection, after 40,000 years the images are usually rather worn and sometimes indistinct. So the examples shown below are careful drawings, rather than the originals, in order to show the detailed design of the figures. Almost all the Bradshaw figures are tall and spindly, with elaborate hairstyles and headdresses, and highly characteristic tasselled body ornaments and costumes. In appearance and dress they are quite unlike the typical Aboriginals we know from later times. The differences are so great that Grahame Walsh, who studied the rock paintings in the field for 30 years, was forced to conclude that the people who made them were of a different race entirely. They belonged to a pre-Aboriginal race that has long since disappeared. Politically, however, this is highly controversial because it interferes with the territorial claims of modern Aboriginals, and Walsh's conclusions have caused much angry discussion.

Whatever the outcome of this debate, the most important feature of these very early rock paintings is that they reveal an amazingly elegant and skilfully stylised portrayal of human figures. The aesthetic sensitivities involved here are advanced, once again emphasising the fact that human beings have been able to

'...the most important feature of these very early rock paintings is that they reveal an amazingly elegant and skilfully stylised portrayal of human figures.'

Right Dreamtime ancestor figure and lightning man, Kakadu National Park, Australia.

produce high-quality art for tens of thousands of years. Later Aboriginal rock art lacks this refinement but makes up for it with its complex symbolism. Each image is part of tribal mythology, and once a figure has been painted onto a rock face the tribespeople started to think of it as having a life of its own inside the rock.

Once an image has a symbolic role it is vulnerable to simplification. There is no longer a burning need to portray the image either elegantly or meticulously. Instead it can be reduced to an emblem, a simple sign that carries a much bigger message, just as a crude wooden cross can stand for the crucifixion of Christ. Ultimately this can lead to symbols that are so reductive that they become little more than abstract signs or patterns, a kind of visual shorthand. This has happened all over the world, often rendering the interpretation of very early rock art either difficult or impossible.

When local tribesmen make symbolic rock art today, it is of course possible to relate their myths and beliefs to the shapes and patterns they make on the rocks. Even then, however, there is some uncertainty because the tribesmen do not always tell the truth about the meaning of their signs.

Whatever the specific meanings of particular signs or images may be, their general significance is clear. They are markers identifying a particular place as belonging to a particular tribe or culture. They are the 'I was here' statement. It is important to say who the 'I' is, and so this is done through the visual telling of tribal myths or legends, or in some other way that relates the marks to their creators.

The same process occurs today in city ganglands where decorative graffiti includes specific gang signs – small emblems of territorial ownership. Rival gangs will send 'taggers' to spray over these signs, and the insulted gangs will send out 'tag bangers' to kill them if they can catch them in the act. Leaving your mark is an age-old preoccupation and has led to the creation of a great deal of art, both ancient and modern. Ancient rock paintings, which are often hard to date accurately, appear all over the world.

One special way in which prehistoric artists have 'made their mark' is by leaving handprints. The artist placed his or her hand on a rock surface and then either spat or blew coloured pigment at it. When the hand was removed, its outline was left on the surface. This activity has occurred at ancient sites as far apart as France, Australia and Argentina. The oldest stencilled hands date from about 30,000 years ago. The handprints in the Patagonian region of Argentina were made between 9,000 and 13,000 years ago. In their case we know that a hollowed-out bone was used as a pipe to blow the pigment onto the hand.

Right Prehistoric handprint stencils on a cave wall in Patagonia, Argentina.

The white, yellow, orange or red pigment must have been taken up in the mouth, mixed with saliva and then blown down the bone tube. Interestingly, in most instances it is the left hand that is painted, revealing that the right hand was used to hold the pipe. So, even at this very early date human beings were predominantly right-handed.

Furthermore, in some cases it is been claimed that careful measurement of the hands has shown that the artists were female. So it is possible that much of the prehistoric painting was done by women rather than men, as has been assumed in the past. In the North American state of Utah, the indigenous Paleo-Indians have left their mark on their traditional territories in an impressive way. Huge panels of rock-art figures can still be seen there, dwarfing the visitors who travel to study them. The Great Gallery in Horseshoe Canyon is a rock face 61 metres wide and 4.5 metres high. The schematic figures on its surface were made between 1,500 and 4,000 years ago.

In Africa, the famous Tassili frescoes on the edge of the Sahara Desert have survived thanks to the dry climate and their remote location. A staggering 15,000 works have been located there to date, covering a period of production ranging from 2,000 to 15,000 years ago. Many of the animals depicted, such as the hippopotamus and the giraffe, have long since vanished from the region.

Below Large-scale prehistoric figures at the Great Gallery in Horseshoe Canyon, Utah, USA. Paleo-Indian art such as this shows a high degree of stylisation and purification of body shape.

Right Symbolic motifs at the male circumcision rock shelter of the Dogon tribe, Mali. Each circumcised boy adds his own painted symbol.

Further north, the Dogon tribe in Mali circumcise their young males in a special ceremony every three years. It takes place in a rock shelter whose walls are covered in paintings of masks, lizards and mythical beings, creating a dramatic atmosphere for the boys' ordeal. No African woman is allowed to set eyes on this rock art, which has been embellished and added to over hundreds of years. As with some of the Aboriginal work in Australia, this is a case of a prehistoric art tradition being continued right through to modern times.

Compared with rock paintings, rock carvings are much more time consuming, but are also much longer lasting. Incised rocks appear all over the world, but because of the labour involved in making the marks they are even more stylistically simplified than rock paintings. Many incised images are no more than unintelligible linear signs and symbols. The simplification process that has developed in the making of these petroglyphs often goes so far that, in the absence of tribal explanations, one can only guess at the subjects being portrayed.

Summing up, the richness and worldwide distribution of prehistoric art – whether it was carefully carved and carried as a lucky charm, was painted on a cave wall by the light of a flickering lamp or by reaching high on a rock wall in the open, or was painstakingly formed by pecking away at hard rock surfaces to produce lasting engravings – are testimony to the powerful creative impulse of those pre-urban artists. Their creature comforts may have been primitive and their technologies primeval, but their art shines through despite these shortcomings. Art is placed firmly in the forefront of those aspects of daily life that were of great importance to these early peoples.

Why did art play such a major role? The archaeologist Paul Bahn has summed up the answer in a single sentence. For rock art, he says, 'individual artistic inspiration was related to some more widespread system of thought and had messages to convey: signatures, ownership, warnings, exhortations, demarcations, commemorations, narratives, myths and metaphors.' These communication functions may indeed have been a driving force, but it is the manner in which they were carried out that is so remarkable. Time and again these ancient messages are recorded in a way that, even today, we find visually appealing and aesthetically attractive. We do not have to know the mythological details or the tribal histories to enjoy their art. No matter how mysterious some of the signs and symbols may be, they still appeal to our eyes. It is almost as if the human species is incapable of being artless, regardless of any material circumstances.

'It is almost as if the human species is incapable of being artless, regardless of any material circumstances.'

The art of the New Stone Age

About 12,000 years ago the age-old hunting way of life that had forged our species and had, in the process, given rise to human art came to an end. Hunting made way for farming. This transition began with improvements in the gathering of plant foods. These plants were now domesticated and crops were grown for the first time. When animals were attracted to these crops they were penned in and kept, to be killed for food as needed. Eventually the animals too became domesticated, being tamed, controlled and specially bred.

To operate this new feeding system, the nomadic hunters had to settle down. As farmers they had to stay in one place, become owners of specific territories and build settlements. At first these were made up of simple round huts, but by about 10,000 years ago the first rectangular houses had been built, rooms had been invented and burial rituals were taking place. Then, about 8,000 years ago, pottery was invented and the cooking of food could now become more efficient.

This New Stone Age, known as the Neolithic, came to an end about 6,000 years ago with the discovery of metal – heralding the arrival of first the Copper Age, then the Bronze Age and finally the Iron Age. With these new developments the small settlements began to increase in size and complexity. The villages became towns and urban life was beginning, leading to the great, ancient civilisations where specialists could flourish and all kinds of new art forms could blossom. But before that momentous stage was reached there was a period of primitive farming, between 6,000 and 12,000 years ago, when the human arts underwent some important changes. Caves and rock faces were abandoned in favour of the walls of the new buildings. Pottery provided new surfaces for painting and incising works of art. With textiles and weaving technology came the opportunity to impose art designs

Above left This example of incised rock art, which portrays a hunting scene, is located at Nine Mile Canyon, Utah, USA.

Left Some of the 3,000 Puako petroglyphs incised in lava rock on the Big Island, Hawaii.

on clothing. And with the gradual improvements in the construction of buildings, architectural art could begin to flourish.

As primeval superstitions became elaborated into the complex belief systems we call religion, the settled way of life was able to offer the newly invented supernatural forces purpose-built abodes of their own. The oldest known temple was built roughly 11,500 years ago at Göbekli Tepe in southeast Turkey. It went through several building phases, and between 8,000 and 9,500 years ago huge stone pillars were erected there. Amazingly for such an early date, the pillars are decorated with carved reliefs of a variety of animals, such as lions, cattle, wild boar, foxes, gazelles, donkeys, snakes, ants, scorpions and birds, including herons, ducks and vultures.

The existence of this stone building reveals how quickly the move from hunting to farming had an impact on human art. Some have argued that the 'temple' might in reality have been a communal dwelling-house, rather than a holy place, but as far as the art is concerned this makes no difference. What we are witnessing here is the birth of a new medium for artistic expression – architecture. It is rare to find a building from any date between 10,000 years ago and the present day that is purely functional. Even the simplest personal dwelling will boast a few features that go beyond practicality and become examples of aesthetic design or decoration. And where important occupants such as gods, kings or overlords are concerned, then the aesthetic factor becomes even more important as a display of high status.

Another location in Turkey, the extraordinary Neolithic settlement of Çatalhöyük, shows just how quickly dwellings became the backdrop for new art forms. Dating from 6,200 to 7,400 years ago, this cluster of rectangular houses

Below The world's oldest known temple is at Göbekli Tepe in Turkey.

Below right Carved relief figures on a pillar in the temple at Göbekli Tepe, Turkey.

was home to between 5,000 and 8,000 people but lacked a temple or any other major building. The ordinary dwellings, however, were sometimes decorated with both painted and relief murals.

On one wall at Çatalhöyük, a pair of leopards is modelled face to face in relief, each animal over one metre long. It was discovered that they had been replastered and repainted 40 times, showing that these relief images were highly valued over a long period of time. Although wild leopards in the Near East are now on the verge of extinction, these big cats were common in the region in the time of Çatalhöyük and must have been a serious threat to the domestic animals of the early farmers. Judging by the position of the legs and tails of the relief images, the leopards depicted were lying dead on the ground – probably the way that the inhabitants of the ancient city preferred to see them.

On another wall, a painted mural shows a huge red bull, also depicted in a death posture, with its tongue hanging out and its feet no longer weight bearing, like those painted by the ancient cave artists. It is surrounded by over 20 much smaller and very active human figures, some red and some black, and three small horses. The figurines found at Çatalhöyük were mostly of animals, but there were also a number of 'fat ladies' reminiscent of the much older Venuses of the Early Stone Age. The Çatalhöyük figurines were called 'mother goddesses' by the excavator, but significantly the most famous one was found inside a storage vessel, as if she had been placed there to guard the grain. To aid her in this important duty, the mother goddess figure was flanked by two large felines. These have been identified as leopards guarding the goddess, but in reality they are probably

Right A fertility figure found in excavations at Tell Halaf, in northeastern Syria.

Centre right This protective figurine found at Amlash, in northwest Iran, was made about 3,000 years ago.

Far right A contemporary corn maiden from England.

oversized domestic cats – the traditional enemies of the rodents that were the great pests of early settlements. Recent excavations have discovered a cat burial dating from 9,500 years ago on the nearby island of Cyprus, so it is highly likely that cats had already been enlisted as pest controllers to protect precious food stores at Çatalhöyük. Far from being goddesses, these female figurines were more likely to have been descendants of the Paleolithic 'lucky charm' pendants worn to ensure pregnancy. The new figures, associated with crops, were doubtless lucky charms to ensure another form of plenty – a good harvest. Their generous layers of fat suggested that they had been successful in this task in the past.

Small portable figurines of this type have been discovered in a number of countries in Eastern Europe and the Middle East. For example, at the Syrian site of Tell Halaf, near the border with Turkey, a number of ceramic figurines of seated females have been found. These women date from between 7,500 and 8,500 years ago and are depicted clasping their large breasts. Their heads have been reduced in size and lack detail. Using these distortions, the artists have moulded the figures into depersonalised symbols of fertility. As such, they could have been used as lucky charms to encourage either childbirth or a good harvest.

This tradition of small 'fat lady' protective figurines would last for thousands of years. Similar figures found at Amlash in northwest Iran have been dated to around 3,000 years ago. As with earlier figurines, they emphasise the thighs and buttocks of the female form at the expense of other features. Although fat, these figurines seem to be far less pregnant than the earlier Paleolithic ones;

this supports the idea that, when tribal hunting switched to farming, the figurines took on the new role of ensuring a rich harvest rather than a pregnant belly.

This tradition has been handed down to modern times in the form of the corn dolly (the word 'dolly' is derived from 'idol'). Also known as the corn maiden, she is made out of straw taken from the last sheaf of standing corn at the end of the harvest. She is then carried into the farmer's house and kept there safely until the following spring. At this time she is taken back into the fields so her spirit can enter the newly sown seed and protect the next crop.

The corn dolly explanation probably accounts for the function of the Neolithic 'fat ladies'. The term 'cult of the goddess' sounds more impressive when describing them, but the fact is that only one impressively large 'fat lady' figure has ever been found from this early period. She is from the Temple of Tarxien on the island of Malta and, had she survived undamaged, would have stood an amazing 2.5 metres tall. Although this Maltese 'fat lady', dating from about 5,000 years ago, has donned a skirt, her heavy thighs are still in evidence. It would seem that here, at least, the

Right The surviving lower half of the only known example of an over-lifesize 'fat lady' figure from prehistoric times. She was discovered in the Temple of Tarxien on the island of Malta.

tiny, Venus-like lucky charms that date as far back as 40,000 years ago have finally managed to blossom into a full-scale Earth Mother tradition. This benign belief system, which focused on the rich produce of the newly farmed lands, lasted throughout the Neolithic period. But with the discovery of metals that made good weapons, God underwent an unfortunate sex change and the great protective Mother Goddess became transformed into a thunderous God the Father.

Thanks to the success of the early farming methods, populations increased and soon there were enough surplus males to start wars. Male pride began to demand bigger and better settlements, villages became towns and towns became cities. The bad news was that male slaughter became commonplace. The good news was that male competition led to the growth of the first civilisations. With this dramatic development the human arts suddenly leapt to a new level of expression. How did this happen? With the growth of cities came specialist craftworkers, and these specialists produced extravagantly skilful jewellery, costume, ornament, furniture, sculpture, painting, carving and architecture. The art patron was born and his ego would thrust the visual arts up to new heights, both metaphorically and literally.

Right The mysterious alignments of the megaliths at Carnac in Brittany, northwest France.

Megaliths

Before this new flowering of the human arts occurred, one strange development deserves a special mention. No one has yet explained it satisfactorily, but it is so odd that it cannot be overlooked. A human obsession with very big stones seems to have started in Portugal about 7,000 years ago. These megaliths appeared in France by 6,800 years ago; Malta by 6,400 years ago; Corsica, England and Wales by 6,000 years ago; Ireland by 5,700 years ago; Spain, Sardinia, Sicily, Belgium and Germany by 5,500 years ago; Holland, Denmark and Sweden by 5,400 years ago; Scotland by 5,000 years ago; and Italy by 4,500 years ago.

Although the most famous megalithic site is undoubtedly Stonehenge in Wiltshire, England, the greatest concentration of standing stones is found in France, around the village of Carnac in Brittany. There are more than 3,000 megaliths, many of them arranged in long parallel columns. At the site of Menec 1,100 of these stones are arranged in 11 rows, and it seems likely that these formed some kind of ceremonial walkway leading to a large circular megalithic temple at one end, which is now lost.

Megaliths are so indestructible that even today this art form survives as a testimony to the determination of early humans to do something extraordinary. Whatever the true function of these gigantic monuments – and we will probably never know what it was – it remains an inescapable fact that the early farming communities who made them had no practical need for them. Despite this, an almost unimaginable amount of effort was expended on their construction. Some of the giant stones at Stonehenge, one of the tallest monuments, weighed up to seven tonnes and were transported over a distance of 225 kilometres. Other, even larger stones weighed up to 40 tonnes and were brought from 40 kilometres away.

The most complex of the megalithic monuments are the ones on the small islands of Malta and Gozo in the Mediterranean. There, the temples had a ground plan similar to the shape of one of the ancient 'fat lady' figures. It is almost as if when entering the temple you were entering the womb of the Earth Mother herself. Most extraordinary of all is the underground megalithic Maltese structure called the Hypogeum, built about 5,000 years ago. Because its builders had gone below ground level, they had to carve megalith facades out of the living rock. In other words, the temple design had become so important to them that they had to imitate it below ground.

Below The Hypogeum, an underground megalithic temple on the Mediterranean island of Malta.

Right A unique reclining female figure was found in the prehistoric temple, the Hypogeum, on the island of Malta.

The only known example of an ancient female figurine in a sleeping posture was found in the Hypogeum temple. It is perhaps not too fanciful to suggest that she represented an early drug cult, because cavities containing only soil were located in the walls of this underground temple, pointing to the cultivation of hallucinogenic mushrooms. The bones of 7,000 people were discovered in the Hypogeum, and 200,000 human body parts were found at another underground temple, the Xagħra Stone Circle, on nearby Gozo. By contrast, the great temples above ground contained no human remains, only the bones of sacrificial animals. It would seem that the megalithic structures of Malta and Gozo were either surface temples where important ceremonies or rituals were carried out, or submerged mass burial grounds situated nearby. At megalithic sites in other countries this same dual function of ritual and burial also seems to apply. In some places certain structures were primarily concerned with burial and others with ritual, as in the Maltese temple, but in others the two functions were combined and burials took place inside the ceremonial space.

All the figurines found at the Maltese megalithic sites were of large women. Men were conspicuous by their absence. On the Maltese islands, at least, the megalithic world was clearly dominated by a female cult – and one with remarkably generous thighs.

Not all the temple surfaces in Malta were unadorned, as they are at Stonehenge for example. Some were skilfully decorated with spiral relief patterns and images of animals. Again we are witnessing a very early culture that demonstrates the human passion for making their world as extraordinary as possible. Moving the huge stones, burrowing beneath the ground, decorating the surfaces, modelling the figures – all these activities were totally at odds with the ordinary daily lives of these people. Once again we come face to face with a human species that behaves in a manner unheard of elsewhere in the whole evolutionary story. This exceptional animal drags giant stones over great distances in order to create something unimaginably impressive but with no practical use at all; this imaginative animal gains deep satisfaction from creating a spectacle, from transforming ordinary rocks into extraordinary monuments.

Relief carvings appear on megaliths elsewhere in the world, and there has been a great deal of debate as to whether these are merely decorative or symbolic. Design motifs such as the spiral, the lozenge, the wavy line and the multi-semicircle were so favoured that in many regions they seem to form a powerful abstract repertoire that eases out any kind of pictorial representation of humans or animals. This suggests that these designs do indeed carry symbolic messages, but we will never know what they were. Some people may feel that, despite the limited repertoire, there is no need to view these ancient patterns as anything more than attractive decorations. But if we take a closer look at the incised megalith from Ireland's New Grange monument, the strangely irregular composition does seem to suggest something more than simply a recurring visual pattern. Tantalisingly, the artists who made these particular incision markings 5,000 years ago seem to be trying to tell us a story.

Right Spiral relief patterns on the wall of a megalithic temple on the Mediterranean island of Malta.

The world of the megalith builders was a strange one, being technologically primitive and yet architecturally ambitious. Hampered by simple tools but determined to create impressive structures, these Neolithic farmers demonstrated yet again the human determination to express oneself in a way that goes far beyond the limited means available. Like their cave-painting predecessors, these builders left an artistic legacy that outstrips all other aspects of their existence and has somehow managed to survive to the present day.

Finally, we can find an important clue about the meaning of the seemingly abstract patterns seen in much prehistoric art if we examine the bark paintings made by modern Australian Aboriginals. These artists are working in an age-old tradition that has managed to survive to the present day, and so in this special case we can talk to the artists and ask about the meaning of the patterns they produce. When we do this, something surprising emerges. It turns out that the designs that seem most abstract to us are, in reality, the most symbolically significant to them – it is the animal and human images that are considered to be the more decorative additions. A design may appear totally abstract to our eyes, but to the artist it depicts local features such as mud, grass, wooden stakes, tree saplings, a riverbed, flowing water, tree logs or a fish trap. If the artist had died 5,000 years ago we could never have guessed this, and we must therefore keep an open mind about the seemingly abstract patterns on ancient megaliths and other rock surfaces.

Right The incised patterns on a megalith at New Grange in Ireland are around 5,000 years old.

6 Tribal Art

Scan page to view video

Tribal Art

THE IMAGES OF TRIBAL SOCIETIES

Above The entire body has been reduced to a pair of breasts in this Bambara wood carving.

Although tribal societies are now disappearing rapidly, enough have survived into recent times to allow us to study their art in some detail. Early photographers took their cumbersome cameras into many remote corners of the world to record the displays and rituals they found there. Early explorers brought back examples of figurines and decorated artefacts that were associated with these rituals. Most of the cultures they visited have now been corrupted by contact with more advanced societies, but a few are still holding out. Yet even those tribes are on the verge of modernisation.

This decline in tribal traditions has been widespread, with tribal art forms weakening as their function changes. Tribespeople have little respect for foreign collectors of their art and often do only as much as is required to make a quick sale. The enormous effort that was put into creating their art for ritual purposes is no longer in evidence. This means that in order to understand the true nature of tribal art, we need to examine the older pieces that were acquired before commercialisation set in. Certain general features stand out when looking at this earlier work, which was mostly collected by anthropologists during the 19th and early 20th centuries.

Head and body distortion

No matter which tribe is involved, nearly all their art demonstrates a deliberate modification of natural shapes. For example, the parts of the human body that are of special interest to the tribe are emphasised at the expense of other body parts, with no regard for natural proportions. If heads are important to the tribe's artists, then three appear. If breasts are important, the rest of a figure's body is ignored.

The Bambara wood carving from Mali, West Africa demonstrates an extreme form of body distortion. More commonly, the exaggerations are less extreme – all the body parts are present but the proportions are modified. The Baule wood carving shows a woman's arms, legs, hands, feet, breasts and navel, but her head is far too big for her body. In real life a human head is one eighth of the height of the body. In the Baule carving it is one third. In other words, the head is more than twice the size it should be.

'The enlarged head is typical of most forms of tribal art, no matter which part of the world is involved.'

This type of distortion, which is based on the artist's interest in different parts of the anatomy, is found across many tribes. Because we identify people by looking at their face, the head is always going to be a favoured part of the body. An accurate portrait artist will exercise control and will keep the head of a figure to its correct size in relation to its body, but a tribal artist is free from any academic discipline and so allows himself considerable licence. The enlarged head is typical of most forms of tribal art, no matter which part of the world is involved. When randomly selected examples of human statuettes from six very different regions are measured (see table below), it soon becomes clear that head enlargement is a global tribal phenomenon. In each case the height of the head is given as a percentage of the total height of the figure. If the statuettes were true to nature they would all produce figures of 12.5 per cent, but not one of them comes even close.

If the 18 figures in the table are combined, it gives us an average head height of 30 per cent of the body height. This means that, taken as a worldwide genre, tribal figurines display heads that are about two and a half times too big for their bodies. It is remarkable that this happens in six totally distinct parts of the world, where there can have been no artistic influence by one group on another.

Just as the head is seen as the most important part of the body, so the eyes are sometimes seen as the most important part of the head – and are disproportionately

Above This Baule female figure from the Ivory Coast shows an enlarged head.

Head height as a % of total figure height by region and tribe					
AFRICA		**INDONESIA**		**NEW ZEALAND**	
Senufo	34%	Timor	28%	Maori	37%
Mumuye	35%	Sumba	25%	Maori	38%
Baka	37%	Sumba	28%	Maori	40%
MADAGASCAR		**NEW GUINEA**		**NORTH AMERICA**	
Sakalava	23%	Wosera	29%	Hopi	25%
Sakalava	26%	Sepik	30%	Hopi	31%
Sakalava	26%	Sepik	29%	Hopi	25%

enlarged in the same way. The Bemba tribe of central Africa, for example, create Janus helmet masks in which the eyes become so big that they almost obliterate the rest of the face.

This extreme form of distortion is not confined to just one tribe. It appears again on the other side of the world, in New Britain off the coast of New Guinea. The men of the Baining tribe wear huge masks with a pair of enormous, staring eyes to perform ritual dances on special occasions such as a birth, a coming of age or a commemoration of the dead. These masks are lovingly made from bark cloth, bamboo and leaves, but are used only once for their fire-dance ceremony and are then thrown away. The details of the masks' design are very different from those of the African Bemba masks, but they follow the same tribal aesthetic principle, namely ignore real proportions and exaggerate those elements that you feel are important. In a real human head, the width of

Above left Maori female figurine from New Zealand. The head height is 43 per cent of the body height.

Above right North American Hopi Indian Kachina doll. The head height is 40 per cent of the body height.

Right Oversized eyes on a Janus helmet mask from the Bemba tribe of central Africa.

Above Eye mask of the Baining tribe from New Britain, off New Guinea.

Below A headless and limbless fertility figure of the Makonde tribe from Tanzania, East Africa.

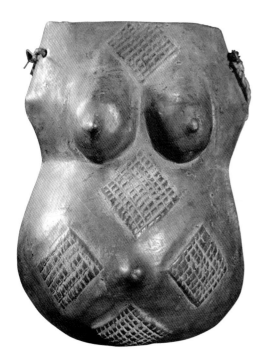

one eye is 20 per cent of the width of the head. In the Bemba and Baining masks, the width of the eye is roughly 50 per cent of the head, an exaggeration that sees the mask's eyes magnified two and a half times. This exaggeration gives these masks a dramatic impact with their magnified, unblinking stare.

For the Makonde tribe of Tanzania, certain rituals require a human fertility figure that has been dramatically reduced to the maternal essentials: milk-full breasts and a large pregnant belly. All other parts of the anatomy have been eliminated, even the head.

These examples are sufficient to demonstrate a basic principle of tribal art: that supernormalisation of some body parts and subnormalisation of others are accepted ways of intensifying an image. The negative side of this process – the subnormalisation of unimportant elements – has two degrees: size reduction and total elimination. The positive side – the supernormalisation of important elements – is usually restricted to less than three times the natural size. It could go much higher, of course, but that would distort the figure to such a degree that it would become unrecognisable. A human form with a head twenty times its natural size would look like a mask with a tiny appendage rather than a complete human figure.

In addition to the distortions of particular features, the overall shape of tribal artefacts also has a characteristic angularity and the elimination of detail. The line of a leg, the curve of a torso, the slope of a neck, the outline of a finger – they are all smoothed out by the tribal artist. Also, the general shape of human figures is usually more slender than average, which is the exact opposite of the prehistoric Venus figurines.

This overall smoothing and slimming of outlines give tribal artefacts a characteristic appearance. It sets them apart from other art forms and makes them immediately recognisable, even if they come from a tribe that is unfamiliar to us. The bumps and lumps of muscle and fat are ironed out into a more geometric vision of human anatomy. It is this simplification of form that made such an impact on the avant-garde artists of the early 20th century and set them heading in the direction of cubism and abstraction.

Body decoration

In addition to creating portable artefacts, many of today's tribes also continue the age-old tradition of body decoration when performing tribal ceremonies and rituals. Here it is more difficult (though as we shall see, not impossible) to distort the shape of the human body. As a result, a different kind of modification is favoured and a new rule comes into operation – instead of distortion we see intensification, instead of exaggeration we see purification. Bright, pure colours and strong patterns are added to real heads, making them more vivid and conspicuous. The most dramatic examples of this process can be seen in the tribes of New Guinea.

> 'Bright, pure colours and strong patterns are added to real heads, making them more vivid and conspicuous.'

In Australia, the body-painting displays of the Aboriginals still occur in certain regions, although they are less common today. The Aboriginals' body painting is far less colourful than that of their northern neighbours, the Papuans. Instead, Aboriginal body painting concentrates largely on powerful contrasts of black and white, with additions of yellow ochre. The same is true of most African face painting. The Nuba people of Sudan have strict rules as to which colour or pattern you may use in each age group. Boys are permitted to use red and white, but they must wait until they have been initiated into an older group before they can use black. Therefore black markings are a sign of status. Each man favours a

Right Dramatic variations can be seen in the facial decoration of these tribespeople from New Guinea.

particular arrangement of black lines, giving rise to some unusual and even asymmetrical designs.

To the east of Sudan, in the more remote parts of southwest Ethiopia, the Mursi people also favour facial decoration that is basically black and white. The women of the tribe add something extra to this: a dramatic enlargement of the lower lip. Just as tribal woodcarvers obey the rule of visual exaggeration, making some parts of their figurines larger than they should be, so the Mursi women do the same – except they use their own flesh instead. So they not only employ intensification of visual patterns and colours as a display technique, but they also manage, painfully, to obey the rule of visual exaggeration.

This enlargement of the lip is not an easy goal to achieve. When a girl reaches the age of 15 or 16, an older woman cuts a hole in her lower lip and inserts a wooden peg to prevent the wound from closing. Over time this peg is increased in size until finally a large rounded plate is inserted, stretching the lower lip to an abnormal degree. When they are big enough, these plates can also be painted to create an additional form of body decoration that amplifies the visual impact of the tribe's adult females. In Mursi society the larger a woman's lip plate, the higher her social status.

In addition to their woodcarvings, masks and body painting, tribal societies often express themselves by creating body ornaments such as necklaces, pendants, bracelets, earrings and finger rings. These ornaments may become the dominant form of artistic expression in some tribes.

Right Traditional body decoration of the Australian Aboriginals.

Far right The facial display of a woman from the Mursi tribe of Ethiopia, amplified by a large, decorated lip plate.

Among the Padaung branch of the Kayan people of upland Burma, the women wear brass neck rings from an early age. Initially five rings are fixed around the neck, but this number is increased gradually year by year. The total number worn by an adult is usually between 20 and 30 rings, but the ultimate goal is to reach 32 – a feat seldom realised. The Padaung also wear brass rings on their arms and legs, so an adult female might carry around a weight of brass totalling between 23 and 27 kilograms. Despite this encumbrance the women of the tribe are expected to walk long distances and work in the fields. In a strange way, these women have almost turned themselves into walking works of art. Despite the difficulties imposed on them by their ornaments, the women have become compelled to make the best visual display that their bodies can manage.

The neck rings of the Padaung women not only add a dramatic visual display element but, uniquely among neck ornaments, they also obey the aesthetic rule of exaggeration. They make the ordinary female neck extraordinary by stretching it far beyond its normal length. It is a basic gender feature of our species that an adult

Right Neck and leg ornaments worn by the women of the Padaung tribe, Burma (Myanmar).

Right The Samburu women of Kenya are proudly burdened by their heavy necklaces.

Below Earring decorations worn by a woman of the Fulani tribe from the Gambia, West Africa.

female's neck is longer and more slender than that of the adult male. The Padaung neck rings exaggerate this difference, making these women superfeminine in the process.

In East Africa, the women of the Maasai, Samburu, Rendille and Turkana tribes of Kenya also burden themselves with heavy body ornaments. They wear as many huge necklaces as they can acquire, or as their body can carry. It is said that a Samburu woman does not have enough beads until her chin is supported by her necklaces. As with the Padaung women, this urge to display their necklaces must cause these women considerable discomfort. But as the saying goes, 'Art is the only justification for pain.'

Many forms of body art must cause pain, and the fact that this pain is borne willingly is testimony to the importance of these visual displays. Each tribe seems to have its own speciality. The women of the Fulani tribe from the Gambia, West Africa seem to compete to see who can display the biggest gold earrings. The size and weight of these earrings are such that they cannot be pleasant to wear, but again these women seem to enjoy suffering for their art. They illustrate the principle that if art is to be taken seriously, it cannot be easy to create. To be serious, art must be difficult, challenging and sometimes even painful. Anything less makes it a trivial pursuit and little more than a childish game.

The most conspicuous display of pain through art is demonstrated by tribes who use the body's skin as a 'canvas' for a work of art. This art consists of two forms: scarification and tattooing. Both these methods allow the individuals who

Right Tribal scarification on a member of the Surma tribe, Ethiopia.

Far right Traditional Maori facial tattoo design, New Zealand.

Above Decorated loincloth with zip fasteners from the Turkana tribe in Kenya.

transform their own bodies into works of art to demonstrate permanently that they were prepared to suffer prolonged pain in the service of art. The designs must be as intricate and elaborate as possible to make them truly impressive. Art, in these instances, becomes a badge of bravery.

A remarkable feature of tribal art is that even when simple functional objects are being made, there is a deep-seated impulse to make them more visually attractive than is necessary for purely practical purposes. This applies even when living conditions are appallingly primitive. In remote areas of Kenya, for instance, the Turkana tribe wear little or no clothing in the extreme heat of central Africa. However, the women wear a small leather loincloth to cover their genitals. As a concealment device it requires no decoration, and yet even on this small scrap of 'modesty skirt' the artistic impulse is at work – in the form of carefully executed decorative additions. Small remnants of rarely seen western clothing are particularly precious and are incorporated wherever possible. The result, in one charming instance, is a loincloth with zip fasteners.

The three basics

When taken as a whole, tribal art demonstrates three basic features of human artistic activity. First, it shows that if an art object represents something, such as a human figure or face, it does not have to do so accurately, in a naturalistic way. Instead it can be selective, deliberately simplifying shapes by exaggerating some elements and reducing others.

Second, tribal art shows us that if a form of body decoration becomes linked to a social message in some way, it can then quickly become excessive and driven to painful extremes. When art becomes the servant of a competitive status display, for example, it can actually start to harm the body it adorns. This takes us back to what Paul Bahn had to say about rock art: 'individual artistic inspiration was related to some more widespread system of thought and had messages to convey…'.

Third, some tribal art, such as the decorated loincloth, shows that the human being feels compelled to add some kind of decoration to the most mundane belongings – even when existing in a social context of extreme poverty where it is barely possible to scratch a living. There is no special system of thought here, no cultural message to convey, no status display with which to impress one's companions. This is art for art's sake, pure and simple; it is a reflection of the basic human need to make some things more appealing and more attractive than functional necessity demands.

Most extraordinary of all is the way in which some small aesthetic gesture manages to surface in the bleakest environment. A close look at the scene in the photograph below reveals that this Turkana family is living in dire circumstances in a barren landscape in a remote part of Kenya. Their home is little more than a few animal skins thrown over a small hut made of rough sticks. Despite this, the two men standing in the only articles of clothing they possess have taken the trouble to decorate themselves by carefully placing white feathers in their hair. Even at this level of extreme poverty, each individual makes some sort of aesthetic gesture, underlining yet again the deep-seated nature of the human artistic impulse.

Right These Turkana tribespeople live in conditions of desolate poverty but still take the trouble to wear some body decorations.

7 Ancient Art

Scan page to view video

Ancient Art

THE BIRTH OF CIVILISED ART

When hunting gave way to farming as a way of life for the human species, dramatic changes followed. With surpluses of food and a more settled population, tribal settlements grew into large villages, villages into thriving towns and towns into huge cities. With the birth of the earliest civilisations, art took a dramatic new turn. Where the tribal leaders had been content to enjoy fleeting outbursts of artistic activity during feasts and rituals, the new rulers wanted to display their greater power on a more permanent basis.

The new art form

In almost all the ancient civilisations this more permanent display of power was achieved by attaching artistic expression to buildings. For hundreds of thousands of years human tribes had been nesting rather like birds, living in small round huts. When their dwelling-place developed into the rectangular, box-shaped hut it became possible to attach one box to another – and so the concept of a room was born. For people in the lower orders, that was how their homes remained: simple, functional, boxlike units clustered together. For the higher orders, these living units had to become much grander to enable their occupants to show off their new power.

'For the god-kings and the pharaohs, the overlords and the emperors, buildings had to become works of art.'

For the god-kings and the pharaohs, the overlords and the emperors, buildings had to become works of art. In addition to providing somewhere to live, these edifices also had to display the exalted status of these new leaders as they tried to control their ever-growing, urban supertribes.

Above Early houses with square walls in Çatalhöyük, southern Turkey.

To achieve this, a new art form was developed – architecture. It was the architect's task to elevate a simple dwelling into an abode fit for a king. This was done in three ways: the building was made bigger than necessary, it was more carefully designed and more lavishly decorated. The ruler's palace, the warlord's fortress, the god's temple and the great one's tomb were the new forms of art that started to spring up and dominate each of the ancient civilisations. Architects took the ordinary building and made it extraordinary by adding pillars, arches, reliefs, painted walls and sculptures.

In ancient Egypt, for example, it is important to make no attempt to separate the various elements of a great building. It was not a shell that contained works of art, like a modern art museum; it was itself a work of art. The building's design, reliefs, painted surfaces and statues all combined to create a supernormal space. Whether the building was a palace, a temple or a tomb, it did not *contain* works of art – it *was* a work of art.

The formidable tasks involved in the creation of these gigantic new art forms meant that the artist was not a single person but rather a whole hierarchy of individuals. At the very top was the patron – an emperor, a king or a pharaoh. He would exert a certain general influence on what form the art object would take. His ideas would be given to the architect, who would create specific designs for the structure of the building. The architect's designs would then be used by engineers, painters and sculptors, who would work under the direction of overseers. Once the plain walls had been erected, painters would add the pictorial and hieroglyphic images. Stonemasons would use the painted images as the basis for their time-consuming relief work. Once they had finished carving their reliefs, painters might then be brought back to colour the reliefs with pigments.

A great temple would only truly be completed as a work of art when it was in use as an enclosure for ritual performance. The performance would then bring in other art forms, such as music, song, dance and perfumery. Today we tend to approach the arts as separate elements – we have art galleries for the visual arts and concert halls for musical performances – but for the ancient Egyptians these were all combined. For this reason we know very little about individual Egyptian artists. There are no Egyptian Rembrandts or da Vincis. Or rather, they did exist but their names have been swallowed up in the great teams of people involved in the production of every temple or tomb.

One exception to this rule is Senenmut, the brilliant man who designed the magnificent mortuary temple of the female pharaoh Hatshepsut. The temple is arguably one of the most elegant works of architectural art in the whole of

Above The elaborately decorated surfaces of the Temple of Hathor at Dendera, Egypt.

Above This wall fragment of the goddess Isis (left) and Queen Nefertari (right) is an example of twisted perspective. The feet, legs, abdomen and face are shown in profile. The chest, arms and headgear are shown frontally.

Egypt, and Senenmut's role in its design is known because he gained power through becoming the pharaoh's secret lover. He was even allowed to build his own tomb in the precincts of her great temple. When you enter the tomb you are instructed to look upwards and there on the ceiling is a map of the stars, the oldest astronomical chart in Egypt. In addition to being a good architect and a good lover, it seems that Senenmut was also a good astronomer.

A remarkable consistency of style

The artistic teamwork involved in creating such great works of art is to some extent responsible for the stylistic consistency of ancient Egyptian art. Flamboyant, individualistic artists could not thrive in a culture where the patrons – the powerful new overlords – were demanding works of art on a monumental scale, works that were going to be used either for sacred rituals to please the gods or as royal tombs. In fact, the only stylistic variation we see in the art of ancient Egypt seems to come from the very top – and it concerns a preference for different degrees of plainness. With some temples, such as the one at Dendera, every square centimetre of the building is covered in relief designs. Yet the surfaces of the Great Pyramids at Giza were (originally) of smoothly polished white limestone, plain and undecorated. Before they lost their blindingly white skin these pyramids would have stood on the plains of Egypt as the largest pieces of minimalist art ever created, contrasting strongly with Dendera's elaborately decorated surfaces.

Apart from this variation, Egyptian decorations show a remarkable consistency of style that lasted for many centuries. Any work of Egyptian art is immediately recognisable as such. This consistency was due to the introduction of a number of set rules that were laid down concerning the way in which certain subjects were to be represented, and also the symbolic colours to be used.

With human figures it was felt that it was important to show as much of the body as possible. Depicting a three-dimensional object on a flat surface was difficult, but this problem was solved by employing a twisted perspective. The artist showed the feet and face in profile, but the torso and arms frontally. This gave the figures a strange stiffness,

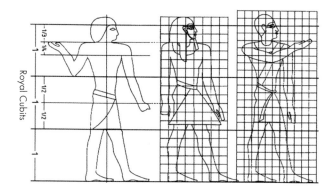

Royal Cubits

Above This diagram by John Legon shows the development of the Egyptian grid system for drawing the human image.

but it did succeed in showing both legs and both arms. The ultimate twist came when the artist wanted to show a frontal view of some kind of headgear, so the figure ended up with a face in profile under headgear that was shown from the front.

One of the aids employed by the Egyptian artists was a grid. It was based on the royal cubit (the length of the human forearm), a measurement used by builders and marked on their measuring sticks. By using such sticks it was possible for the artists to measure out the different parts of the human body and use these proportions time and again. In this way they were able to standardise and rigidify their human imagery.

Although body proportions in the art of ancient Egypt were reasonably normal, the size of a figure was related to its social importance and not to its natural bulk. For this reason, when the seated figure of the pharaoh Ramses II is shown with his favourite wife Queen Nefertari standing beside him, the height of her figure does not even come up to his knee. This is a special case of artistic exaggeration. It operates by enlarging the whole of the body in relation to other figures rather

Both these colossal statues show the pharaoh Ramses II and a much smaller figure of his wife, Queen Nefertari.

Right Ramses II is seen with Queen Nefertari standing beside him at Abu Simbel.

Far right Ramses is standing behind Nefertari in the statue from the Temple of Amon-Ra at Karnak.

'Wherever religion has become closely linked to art, the art has tended to become rigid and unchanging.'

than by enlarging certain body parts, such as the head, as happens in both child and tribal art.

There were many minor conventions that helped to restrict the artist's portrayal of figures in his work. The hieroglyphic symbol for a child showed a kneeling figure with a finger pointing at the mouth. If an artist was making a statue of an important figure who happened to be a child, he would depict the child making this gesture. He was not required to add any childlike features to the shape of the figure because the stereotyped gesture said all that was needed.

Painting and writing are in fact closely allied in Egyptian art – the Egyptian word is the same for both. Pictorial images became so symbolised that in a simplified form they began to stand for particular sounds, letters or words. Together these pictograms made up a written language consisting of highly stereotyped units, the units we call hieroglyphs. The existence of this pictorial language severely limited the amount of variability that any ancient Egyptian artist could impose on his work. It was still possible for him to fashion each hieroglyph in a more elegant or more careless way and thus impose some varying degree of quality on his work, but the overall visual style remained fixed.

The art of the ancient Egyptians retained its stylistic consistency for literally thousands of years. It did this by imposing strict constraints on what could be done and what was forbidden. As already mentioned, the art succeeded because it was not the work of flamboyant individuals but of teams of people working with almost military discipline. Just as the military loves uniforms, so this art loved uniformity. The rulers of Egypt were always craving stability, and their art reflected this. And as much of the work was aimed at the gods, rather than at a

Below Hieroglyphs on the wall of the Temple of Hatshepsut, Luxor, Egypt.

human audience, this too meant that innovation was kept to a minimum. Wherever religion has become closely linked to art, the art has tended to become rigid and unchanging. And that is what happened to the incredibly ambitious artistic projects of the ancient people who prospered along the banks of the Nile.

Although the intended audience of the major works of art, such as the temples and tombs, was not the Egyptian people but the gods and the dead, the living were not completely ignored. Both the elite and ordinary Egyptians eagerly pursued the minor arts of body adornment. In the higher levels of Egyptian society, elaborate costumes, jewellery and cosmetics were highly developed and used many new technologies. Both sexes were involved, and the excuse was given that the wearing of jewels would protect the person

Above An elaborate turquoise necklace from the Old Kingdom of Egypt.

Above A pectoral ornament from the treasure of Tutankhamun's tomb, showing the falcon-headed god with a sun disc.

from evil spirits. This was especially true of earrings, which would distract the evil ones and prevent them from entering the body through the ear canal.

Conveniently, the more beautiful the jewels, the better they were at distracting the evil spirits. In this way, as happened in so many other cases, art could flourish by acquiring a supernatural purpose. Gold, for example, was popular not simply because its purity made it visually appealing but also because it represented the flesh of the gods, the fire of the sun and eternal life (because it never faded). Every part of the body was adorned. In addition to earrings, finger rings, necklaces, brooches and bracelets, there were also anklets, diadems and fillets (headbands). These adornments were worn not only in life, but also in death, provoking thousands of years of tomb looting.

A new kind of visual art

About 2,000 years ago, when Egypt had fallen to the Romans, the early restraints on the portrayal of the human form in Egyptian art were relaxed. Under the influence of Rome, some amazing portraits began to appear. These have been found on

Right Three of the many true-to-life Fayum portraits, which were painted 2,000 years ago in ancient Egypt.

Below A stiffly formal statue of the Egyptian goddess Sekhmet, 1360BC.

Below right The lifelike Greek goddess Artemis.

the mummies of the individuals portrayed and have been described as the earliest form of 'modernism' in the history of art. They are modern in the sense that they are straightforward portraits created with painterly skill, which provide us with a remarkably lifelike image of the person in question. More than 1,000 such examples have been unearthed so far.

Each of the life-size portraits found at Fayum, about 80 kilometres south of Cairo, was painted on a thin wooden panel. The panel was then placed over the face of the mummy and fitted into its wrappings, so that when you looked at the mummy in its coffin it was as if you were staring straight at the person inside. What makes them so exceptional is that portraits like this would not be seen again for over 1,000 years.

Towards the end of the period of Egyptian greatness, the civilisations of Greece and Rome were starting to flourish on the other side of the Mediterranean. Their visual art was of a very different kind. For the Greeks at their classical peak, exquisitely naturalistic forms were the order of the day. The formal stiffness of Egyptian art was replaced by a flowing, organic style that celebrated the human body instead of regimenting it. One statue of a goddess was so lifelike that 'upon seeing her all men wished to kiss her'. Such was the skill of Greek sculptors in rendering human flesh.

There were three reasons for this approach to art in ancient Greece: one religious, one political and one technical. The significant religious change concerned the way in which the gods were seen. Unlike the Egyptians, the Greeks visualised their gods in human form, so the human body became more revered. Politically, individual merit was more admired in ancient Greece and artists were treated with greater respect. The great ones became famous and even today we know them by name – Praxiteles, Lysippus, Leochares... Technically these artists had the great advantage that they could now carve in marble or create their work in bronze, instead of working in stone. These new materials suited a more meticulous depiction of the subtle curves of human flesh.

These influences meant that the classical Greek artists were, above all else, taking the rule of refinement to a whole new level. The subtlety and sensitivity that they employed exceeded anything that had gone before – and, for that matter, a great deal of what would follow.

Sadly, many of the Greek originals are now lost and we know them only from Roman copies. Roman art itself was essentially an imitation of the Grecian images. The Romans were wonderful at making great art, but despite their impressive organisational and military skills they were surprisingly lacking in artistic innovation. Even their architectural designs leant heavily on Greek traditions. Architects had continued to flourish in Greece and Rome, as they had done in ancient Egypt. The biggest demand in ancient Greece was for the building of huge temples. So much skill went into the design of these buildings, with immense care taken to calculate the precise proportions of every detail, that they became major works of art. Their impact was so great that over 2,000 years later important formal buildings in Europe and the USA were still being based on ancient Greek designs.

Amusingly, modern copies of buildings ignore one important aspect of their ancient counterparts – their bright colour. The mellowed stone of the ruins of

Below The Parthenon (left) in Athens, Greece as it is today, and a full-scale replica (right) built in Nashville, USA.

Above A Roman amphitheatre at Arles in the south of France.

Above right The triumphal Arch of Titus in Rome.

Below The decoration on this Greek Red Figure vase portrays Odysseus and the sirens.

the ancient temples has become so strongly associated with them that naked stone has become the accepted finish. The idea of painting these buildings in red, white and blue – the original colours of the Parthenon – feels wrong.

The architects of ancient Rome had a much wider scope. In addition to building temples, there was a great demand for palaces, open-air theatres, amphitheatres, circuses for chariot racing, triumphal arches, public bathhouses and grand villas.

Inside their buildings both Greeks and Romans found additional ways to express their artistic urges. In Greece there was a flourishing tradition of vase painting that was so specialised and skilful that the very best vase painters became famous. Today more than 250 of them are known to us by name, and about 60,000 of their works still survive.

There were two main styles: the earlier Black Figure vases and the later Red Figure vases. The greatest of the Black Figure painters was Exekias. Both the Black Figure vases and the Red Figure ones frequently depict mythical scenes. One Red Figure vase portrays the famous scene in which Odysseus has himself tied to the mast of his ship to protect himself from the allure of the sirens.

There were also elaborate wall paintings in ancient Greece. Freed from religious constraint, these frescoes depicted scenes from ordinary life and tell us a great deal about the inhabitants of this ancient civilisation. Sadly few have survived the passage of time, although fortunately Greek frescoes in a tomb at Paestum, which date from the 5th century BC, have managed to last remarkably well. Discovered in 1968, the underside of the tomb's large flat lid reveals an elegantly restrained painting of a male diver jumping from a high diving board. The simplest explanation is that the tomb contained the body of an athletic diver. For those who prefer symbolism it is interpreted as the deceased making the great dive from life to death.

Around the walls of the tomb are scenes of a symposium, an all-male drinking session. The men recline on couches above the serving tables. There is an atmosphere of relaxed pleasure taking, with wine, music and song. As a tomb decoration, this subject matter is amusingly inappropriate and about as far from religious spirituality as it is possible to get. Dating from 470BC, this is a unique tomb where Greek frescoes have survived in their entirety.

Heavily restored frescoes from Akrotiri, on the island of Thera, show young boxers and antelopes, and those from Knossos, on Crete, show dolphins, fish and sea urchins. These frescoes date from the earlier Minoan civilisation of the second millennium BC. Again, the subject matter is friendly and decorative rather than solemn or mystical.

Above This decoration on a Black Figure vase by the Greek painter Exekias shows Achilles and Ajax playing a board game.

Below This painting of a diver on a Greek tomb at Paestum dates from the 5th century BC.

Below right This marine scene in the wall paintings at Knossos, Crete, dates from the second millennium BC.

The non-religious fresco tradition continues in the Roman era. The massive volcanic eruption in AD79 has neatly preserved the decorated walls of Pompeii and Herculaneum, two seaside resorts where the affluent holidayed in attractive villas. These were bustling towns, with bars and restaurants, theatres and a gymnasium, an amphitheatre and a forum.

The population's cheerful holidaying was rudely interrupted when Vesuvius exploded and they were suddenly suffocated by six metres of hot volcanic ash and pumice. The frescoes survived and tell us a great deal about what it was like to have been a wealthy citizen 2,000 years ago. Some of the images create the illusion of

Below This fresco in the Villa of Mysteries, Pompeii, shows a cult ritual in progress, AD79.

Above This Roman mural in a rich man's bedroom in the Synistor Villa at Boscoreale shows a colourful townscape.

Below Gladiatorial combat in a Roman mosaic from a villa at Nennig, Germany, from the 3rd century AD.

grand vistas while others depict bird-filled gardens. In the Villa of Mysteries at Pompeii, the walls of one room are covered in a series of ten scenes depicting some kind of arcane ritual, involving the ceremonial whipping of a naked girl who is being inducted into a mystery cult. In the scene opposite, a small figure is reading out some kind of incantation, while a cult member carries a large platter bearing ritual objects.

The painting of townscapes and landscapes was another unusual innovation at Pompeii. In the Synistor Villa at nearby Boscoreale, the bedroom walls of the wealthy Roman owner were painted in rich colours to create an atmosphere of luxurious urban architecture. Scenes like this are not so unusual as backgrounds to human figures, but employing an architectural scene or landscape as the central theme of a work of art is a remarkably modern concept. The frescoes of Pompeii included a number of townscapes, seascapes and landscapes as main subjects, something that would not be seen again for many centuries. The eventual collapse of Rome would prove to have a devastating effect on the progress of the visual arts in Europe.

Not content with covering their walls with art, the Romans also walked on it. The floors of Roman buildings were rich with astonishingly detailed mosaic scenes. There were the usual legendary and mythical figures, but the artists seem to have been more excited by the natural world around them. The mosaics come alive when they show scenes of the real world rather than the supernatural one. In one huge mosaic discovered at Lod in Israel, the central panel shows a collection of wild animals that were no doubt destined for the Colosseum in Rome. They include a lion and a lioness, a giraffe, an elephant, a rhinoceros, a tiger and an African buffalo. A mosaic from Pompeii depicts a fisherman's catch, which includes an octopus, a squid, a lobster, a prawn, an eel, a flatfish, a dogfish, a red mullet and various other fish species. Other mosaics show us scenes from daily life, including chariot racing, gladiatorial combat and gymnastics. Favourite subjects were gladiators and charioteers, the great sporting stars of the day. Unlike the Greeks, who banned women from their Olympics, the Romans seemed delighted to see their bikini-clad female athletes throwing the discus, weightlifting, running races and playing ball.

Artworks on a massive scale

Ancient civilisations were also thriving in the Far East. In those places where powerful rulers had taken control of the ever-increasing populations, massive projects were being undertaken. None was more impressive than the tomb of the Emperor Qin, built in the 3rd century BC and guarded by a vast underground army of life-size terracotta figures. This tomb was one of the greatest works of art ever attempted, with 700,000 workers involved in its making. Compared with an ordinary resting-place, it makes the word 'extraordinary' seem wholly inadequate.

The tomb's creator was the man who is credited with establishing Imperial China, having introduced a centralised government, a legal code, a written language, a formal currency and standardised weights and measures. He also

Below Emperor Qin's buried army of 8,000 terracotta warriors, Xi-an, China, 210BC.

rejected his predecessors' custom of entombing hundreds of living servants with him to care for him on his long journey to the afterlife. An earlier ruler would always insist on having his staff buried with him when he died. Although this ensured that they looked after him well when he was alive – to keep him going as long as possible – it was also a terrible waste of manpower. To avoid this, Emperor Qin supported the new idea of substituting life-size terracotta figures for living beings. However, the support of a few hundred servants was not enough for the emperor. Instead he commissioned artists to create an entire terracotta army, with over 8,000 warriors, 120 cavalry horses, 520 chariot horses and 130 chariots, all made to defend their entombed master. Identical figures were not permitted. Each warrior's face had to be sculpted as a recognisable individual. These warriors were, after all, representatives of a real army. To complete the emperor's entourage there were also terracotta officials, acrobats, strongmen and musicians.

> '...he commissioned artists to create an entire terracotta army, with over 8,000 warriors, 120 cavalry horses, 520 chariot horses and 130 chariots...'

There was a sting in the tail of this enlightened approach to entombment. Because the location of these valuable works of art had to be kept secret, the entire army had to be buried underground. The senior artists who had designed the tomb also had to be walled up with the emperor to ensure their silence. To give some idea of the scale of this gigantic work of art, the buried army was discovered one and a half kilometres from the emperor's pyramidal tomb mound. A whole necropolis surrounding the tomb chamber remains unexcavated. The chamber itself, booby-trapped to kill intruders, is thought to be a hermetically sealed space as big as a football pitch, with rivers simulated by flowing mercury, a ceiling decorated with heavenly bodies, surrounded by palaces and towers, and packed full of treasures.

As a work of art, Qin's tomb illustrates the rule of exaggeration in a special way. The individual figures may not show much exaggeration – their bodies are well proportioned without any deliberate distortions. The only concession to exaggeration among the individual figures is that higher ranks in the army are depicted by slightly larger figures, with generals being the tallest of all. But the real exploitation of exaggeration as a means of transforming the ordinary into the extraordinary lies not in the individual figures but in the vast scale of the operation. Qin displayed exaggeration by sheer numbers.

There is an interesting comparison to be made here with ancient Egypt. Like Qin's generals, the figures of the pharaoh Ramses II are taller than those around him. And the Great Pyramids at Giza, although simple in shape, are extraordinary

because of their massive scale. Even today this same strategy can be seen at work when some contemporary artists compensate for their lack of quality by creating works of art so huge that they become extraordinary simply by virtue of their size.

The use of an impressive scale as a way of exaggerating a work of art and turning it into an extraordinary

Above The great ziggurat at Ur in Iraq was built in the 21st century BC and has been partly restored.

experience was a feature of other ancient civilisations. The ziggurats of the ancient Middle East, the vast temple complexes of southern Asia and the awesome, blood-stained pyramids of the Aztecs and Mayas in Central America all made an impact through their sheer size.

During the time of the ancient civilisations, countless smaller portable artefacts were also made in addition to the monumental works of art. Some of these artefacts were decorative, some were made to display wealth and others were to satisfy superstitions, especially those concerning death and the afterlife. The rules of exaggeration and purification were much in evidence in many of these artefacts. When portraying humans or animals, artists enlarged important elements and reduced others. And the subtle outlines of biological forms were

Below The moated Hindu temple complex of Angkor Wat in Cambodia.

Above The huge Temple of the Sun at Teotihuacan, in Mexico, was begun in 100BC.

'With the collapse of the Egyptian, Greek and Roman empires ... their impressive artistic output disappeared with them.'

often purified by being simplified to smoother, more basic geometric shapes.

When the Egyptian, Greek and Roman empires, and the other civilisations of the ancient world, collapsed, their art disappeared with them. Much of the world entered a bleak, dismal phase when the visual arts were reduced to their lowest level. This state of affairs would last for centuries until, very gradually, new civilisations grew out of the dark ages. Only then would the next great phase of human creativity be able to flourish.

8 Traditional Art

Scan page to view video

Traditional Art

FROM THE SACRED TO THE SALON

Following the collapse of the ancient civilisations of Egypt, Greece and Rome, Europe entered a dark age in which the Christian faith came to dominate the arts. The only visual outlet for an educated man was to be found behind monastery walls, where beautiful illustrated manuscripts and highly stylised religious icons were laboriously fashioned for the greater glory of God. Sculpture was limited largely to Madonnas and crucified Christs. Serious painting virtually vanished.

It was not until the 14th century that a revival of the arts began to appear in Europe. A few sculptors and painters in Italy began to look back to ancient Greece and Rome for their inspiration. The sculptor Pisano in Pisa and the painter Giotto in Florence started to produce work that had a more lifelike, naturalistic appearance. This was the start of the rebirth of expressive art in Europe, and the following century saw it grow stronger and stronger. The subject matter was still deeply religious, but now the figures were presented as real, three-dimensional people, painted and carved with enormous skill. The anonymous artists of the medieval period were replaced by the great masters – Botticelli, Uccello, Michelangelo, da Vinci, Raphael, Titian, Tintoretto. Their genius would influence art for centuries to come, although it would rarely be matched.

From the 15th to the 19th century, European art remained predominantly concerned with representing its subject matter in a realistic, lifelike way. There were occasional variations, sometimes more sober, sometimes more flamboyant; sometimes more precisely lifelike, sometimes slightly more mannered and exaggerated. But essentially the respect for naturalistic, seemingly three-dimensional forms remained the basis for all fine art during this period.

There was, however, a gradual widening of subject matter as the centuries passed. In the early years religious and mythological scenes dominated, thanks to the remaining power, influence and patronage of the Church. Portraits also put in an early appearance and would remain a main source of income for artists for the next 500 years. Landscapes, interiors and still-life studies were also added later as acceptable subjects, as were animals and scenes of peasant life.

With this ever-increasing range of subjects the traditional, representational art of Europe seemed to be invincible. An art lover visiting a salon, a prince ordering a new portrait, a landowner commissioning another landscape featuring his mansion, a sportsman immortalising his favourite horse – all these patrons cannot have imagined, in their wildest dreams, what would happen to the world of the visual arts in the 20th century. But before moving on to that century of aesthetic upheaval, it is important to follow the unfolding story of traditional, representational art from the end of the 7th century to the close of the 19th century.

The control of the Church

During the 8th century the monasteries spread throughout Western Europe and became the main centres for intellectual and artistic activity. Monastic life was more than a spiritual withdrawal from the barbaric world outside the monastery walls; it was also the thinking man's solution to finding a way of life that provided material security. The greatest artworks of the period – illustrated books – were conceived and executed here. The most famous of these is the Book of Kells, which even today is considered to be the masterpiece of all Irish art.

Below The symbols of Matthew, Mark, Luke and John from the Book of Kells.

The book contains the gospels of Matthew, Mark, Luke and John, and the page shown here depicts their four symbols: Matthew shown as a man, Mark as a lion, John as an eagle and Luke as an ox. The extravagance and complexity of the pictorial illustrations and their surrounding geometric ornamentation have rarely been surpassed by any other illustrated volume from the Middle Ages. The traditional Christian figures and scenes are edged with ornate, interlacing patterns in bright colours.

It has been pointed out that the artists who created this book considered the illustrations to be more important than the text. In order to improve the overall appearance of a page the text sometimes suffered. Special efforts were made to avoid disrupting the design of a page, and the book's aesthetic quality was always given priority over its practical use. The Book of Kells was essentially a work of art first, and a work of scripture second. The monastery artists involved would never have admitted to this, but the truth is that their aesthetic sense had overpowered them – even to the point of obsessing them.

One of the great inventions at about this time was the page. Writing a text on the pages of a book is something we take for granted, but this form of presentation was a comparatively new departure. It gave the book's illustrator a sharply defined, rectangular, restricted space in which to work. It was as if his work was now framed by the edges of the page, allowing him to compose his illustration in a balanced, organised way. Illustrators echoed this by providing their images with inner frames within the outer frame. These inner frames became the subject of excessive decoration and ornamentation. It was a style that would last for centuries, as the monks laboured away in their isolated scriptoria behind their sheltered monastery walls.

Below The Garden of Eden, from the Grandval Bible, AD834–43.

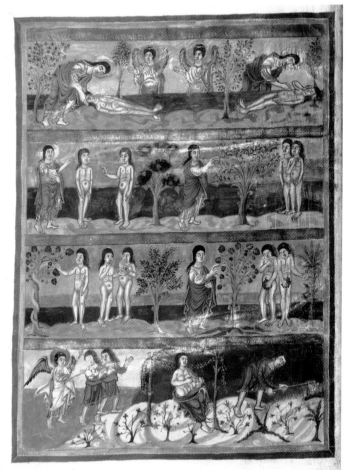

Another striking innovation from the 9th century is the use of the strip cartoon to tell a pictorial story. In the Grandval Bible, created in the French city of Tours between AD834 and 843, the story of Adam and Eve is depicted in a way that even the illiterate could understand. Eight scenes in four horizontal strips progress from the creation of Adam and Eve through to their expulsion from the Garden of Eden. The text is present above each of the strips, but it is relegated to an insultingly perfunctory role. Visual art has overpowered the written word.

During the 9th century all the arts continued to be dominated by the Church. Statues of the Virgin and Child as well as gold objects such as sacred cups, crucifixes and altarpieces were produced in large numbers.

The European art of the 10th century came under pressure from an unexpected source: Islam. This century saw a remarkable marriage of art styles in Spain. Under Muslim rule, one might have expected to see Spanish Christians being forced to adopt a Muslim style of abstract geometric painting, but this did not happen. The Muslim rulers were surprisingly tolerant in this respect, resulting in the development of an attractive hybrid form of art. The Christian communities in Spain had succeeded in retaining their Christian imagery while at the same time adopting Arab culture. In some regions Christians were allowed to keep their own churches and monks, and their paintings combined Christian subject matter with Islamic decoration. This combination proved to be a remarkably happy one, producing scenes that were clearly Christian in content but had a much more Islamic atmosphere than other art of the period. One of these Spanish monks, Beatus of Liébana, had written a commentary on the Book of Revelations. It became known as the Beatus Apocalypse and was made into a number of illuminated manuscripts.

Below Harvest scenes from the 11th-century Commentary on the Apocalypse by Beatus of Liébana.

'The Christian communities in Spain had succeeded in retaining their Christian imagery while at the same time adopting Arab culture.'

Left The Dragon and the Beast from the Beatus of Facundus, AD1047.

It would be wrong to suggest that these Islamic influences affected all the religious art produced in the monasteries of the 10th century. As with other periods, the monks churned out plenty of standard images to create more typical Christian scenes. But the exceptions are mentioned here because it is they that give a special character to the century, helping to show how the fiercely creative spirit of the human brain finds some kind of outlet even when hemmed in by strict sacred rules and regulations.

As the 11th century dawned, the laboriously crafted Beatus manuscripts continued to appear, reaching a peak of exotic colour and imaginative imagery in 1047 with the Beatus of Facundus. It was almost as if the Christian saints had found themselves transported into the Arabian Nights. The scenes depict nightmarish dramas and monsters, such as seven-headed dragons and beasts. Persecuted by the Muslims, the Christians in Spain secretly enjoyed converting the symbolism of the Apocalypse. Its monsters became the Muslim leaders, and their defeat in the Beatus became a symbol of deliverance from Muslim rule.

One of the most impressive artistic achievements of the 12th century can be found on the west wall of the Cathedral of Santa Maria Assunta on Torcello Island in the Venice lagoon. The vast mosaic created here depicted the biblical Last Judgement. The Byzantine artists brought in to produce this towering work clearly relished the section dealing with hell, which always seems to have more appeal to artists than depictions of heaven.

Above The depiction of hell in the mosaic of the 12th-century Cathedral of Santa Maria Assunta, Venice, Italy.

Right The mosaic of the Last Judgement in the Cathedral of Santa Maria Assunta.

Right The 12th-century mosaics in the apse of the Cathedral of Monreale near Palermo, Sicily.

By the 12th century, Byzantine artists were experiencing great popularity, and mosaics enjoyed a second golden age – but this time on walls rather than floors. The great monasteries and cathedrals of Europe were competing with one another to display the most impressive pictorial decorations, and the Byzantine craftsmen found themselves in great demand. Twelfth-century mosaics on a massive scale can also be seen at the Cathedral of Monreale near Palermo in Sicily. Its walls are completely covered in more than 6,315 square metres of biblical images, and it has been estimated that over 100 million pieces of mosaic and over 2,000 kilograms of pure gold were used in their creation. This was a clear case of making a work of art feel extraordinary by conceiving it as large, complex, minutely detailed, difficult to execute, incredibly expensive and immensely time-consuming. The decorated walls of this cathedral were as different from the walls of an ordinary dwelling as it was possible to make them, and therein lay their impact as a major work of art.

A continuing tradition

The tradition of illuminated manuscripts continued, and it is clear that the monks involved in this monotonous work were becoming increasingly imaginative in their renditions of biblical scenes. For example, they were fascinated by the idea of a plague of locusts as a visual subject. Knowing little about the anatomy of the locust, the artists were able to let their imaginations run freely. Even where they had better anatomical knowledge, as in the case of a human figure or a tree, they preferred to stylise their images – creating paintings of great character in the process.

One of the curious shortcomings of art up to this point was the lack of any emotions or facial expressions on human figures. Whether they were praying, fighting or being burnt alive, people all had the same deadpan expression. One 13th-century artist who began to add a spiritual intensity to his paintings was the Italian master Duccio. His work still had some of the earlier stiffness, but through the high technical quality of his painting he was able to add a depth of feeling. His Madonna may have been rigid, but she seems to be full of solemn grace as she holds the infant Jesus in her arms. This work represents a sudden leap forward in the history of art, with new technical skills surpassing most of what has gone before.

Centuries of highly stylised sacred art were about to give way to a more naturalistic approach. The portrayal of human figures was about to become more realistic. This did not mean that sacred art would suddenly disappear. Russian icons, for example, were still following the old traditions right up to the 19th century. But a new phase in the history of human art was about to begin, where the focus was on portraying the external world in a much more accurate manner.

Right Duccio, *Madonna and Child*, 13th century, Italy.

'His Madonna may have been rigid, but she seems to be full of solemn grace as she holds the infant Jesus in her arms.'

A new naturalism

A dramatic new development took place at the beginning of the 14th century as the move to create more natural scenes gathered pace. The central figure in this development was Giotto, whose images were described as creating 'the sense of living actuality'. His work has been hailed as the starting point of the Renaissance in European art, the rebirth of interest in the lifelike quality of classical figures from Greece and Rome. Figures began to have depth and shading; they started to adopt postures suited to the dramas in which they were involved. Their faces still sometimes showed little emotion, but in other cases dramatic facial expressions accompanied the mood of the event being depicted. The landscape became less flat and perspective was introduced. Giotto designed his pictures, it was said, 'according to nature'.

It has been claimed that Giotto's work showed a new peak of skilful painting and that his predecessors, with their flat, rigid, formalised figures, were simply not capable of doing any better. This is not true, however. We cannot tell whether the earlier artists would have been able to rival Giotto because they were all adhering to the religious preference for symbolic

> 'Figures began to have depth and shading; they started to adopt postures suited to the dramas in which they were involved.'

Right Giotto, *The Flight into Egypt,* 1304–6.

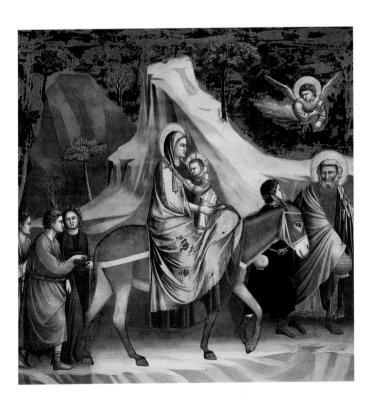

Christs and saints, rather than flesh-and-blood ones. It is wrong to see Giotto as technically superior to his predecessors, but rather as more daring than them.

Giotto did make one concession to the earlier rules: important sacred figures, although painted in a naturalistic way, still had golden halos around their heads. One suspects that he would rather have omitted them, but that would have been a step too far and would have landed him in trouble. His *Flight into Egypt* becomes a domestic scene of a travelling family if you can imagine the picture without the halos.

Giotto's introduction of naturalistic expressions, postures and gestures – accurately observed human body language – was an important innovation that would make a huge impact on art in the years to come. Following hard on his heels was another Italian painter, Simone Martini, whose figures showed even more naturalistic facial expressions. His work contains grimaces, shrugs and gestures of despair and horror. Martini's compositions were also planned with great care and restraint. His sense of rhythmic balance exceeds anything that had gone before it. In *The Miracle of the Child Falling from a Balcony*, Martini has frozen the action in mid-air, as though he has taken a snapshot of the scene with a camera. Saint Augustin is shown swooping down from heaven to save the child who is falling from a broken balcony but has not yet hit the ground.

Right Martini, *The Miracle of the Child Falling from a Balcony*, c.1328.

Right Masaccio, *Payment of the Tribute Money*, 1427, Florence.

In terms of sheer creativity, the 15th century offers the greatest riches in the history of traditional art. This was the height of the Renaissance. In Italy the young genius Masaccio, tragically poisoned at the age of 27, might have rivalled da Vinci had he lived; other major artists were Botticelli, Uccello and da Vinci himself. In Germany Dürer and Holbein were at work; in the Netherlands, van Eyck, Bosch, Memling and van der Weyden. And there were a hundred more artists almost as good.

The most innovative of all these great masters was the young Florentine, Masaccio. During his short life he introduced the idea of a scientifically calculated vanishing point into his art, creating true perspectives for the first time. He was also the first artist to give his figures proper shadows and to employ a single light source. When painting the murals for the Brancacci Chapel in Florence, Masaccio shaded all his figures as if the light falling on them was coming from the one high window in the building. This gave the figures a unity never seen before in any other mural work. He also introduced the idea of colours fading with

'In terms of sheer creativity, the 15th century offers the greatest riches in the history of traditional art. This was the height of the Renaissance.'

distance, his foreground figures being more intensely coloured than his distant ones. This use of colour increases the sense of perspective because, in real life, the invisible moisture or dust in the air makes objects appear gradually less colourful the further they are from you.

Masaccio also, incidentally, cunningly introduced the tilted halo, which made it less obtrusive and more like some kind of flat headgear. These innovations made Masaccio's paintings look more realistic than anything that had gone before, and it says something for the young Masaccio that da Vinci went to study his work in order to learn how to paint well. The *Mona Lisa* is said to be one of the first paintings to introduce atmospheric perspective, but this was a trick that da Vinci had learnt from his study of Masaccio's techniques – introduced nearly a century earlier.

Another Italian artist of this period who was obsessed with perspective was Paolo Uccello, who favoured scenes of pageantry. But although his subject matter took him away from the style of the more typical Renaissance painters, his mathematical analyses of problems of perspective were very much in keeping with the new mood.

Uccello's most famous works depicted the chaos of the battle of San Romano between the armies of Florence and Siena. He set himself the daunting challenge of showing the

Right Uccello, *The Battle of San Romano*, 1450–6.

confusion of the battlefield while at the same time presenting a composition that appealed to the eye of the viewer. Uccello's final work, *The Hunt in the Forest*, was painted in 1470 and was his most blatantly perspective-driven piece. Its arrangement is so carefully devised that it is impossible to ignore it when looking at this painting. The composition creates a sense of great depth and of seeing far into the forest where the hunt is taking place. Because of its remarkable use of colour and its imaginative originality, *The Hunt* remains a masterwork of the 15th century, even though it is slightly primitive in feeling for this period of European art.

Below Uccello, *The Hunt in the Forest*, 1470.

'*The Hunt* remains a masterwork of the 15th century, even though it is slightly primitive in feeling for this period of European art.'

Right Botticelli,
The Annunciation,
1480s.

In strong contrast to Uccello's rather personal vision of the world, a generation later the Italian master Sandro Botticelli took Masaccio's pioneering work several steps further. He created Renaissance paintings of such refinement that they leave all previous work trailing behind. They are technically so polished that they are almost painful to look at. Despite his outstanding technical skill, Botticelli's work did not remain popular and he was almost forgotten after his death. It was not until he was rediscovered by the Pre-Raphaelites in the 19th century that Botticelli's reputation once again rose to the level he had enjoyed during his earlier years. It says something for the richness of this period that an artist of Botticelli's undoubted skills could have seen his reputation slide into a steep decline so quickly.

Seven years younger than Botticelli, Leonardo da Vinci was a painter, sculptor, designer, draughtsman, architect, musician, scientist, theorist, mathematician, engineer, inventor, anatomist, geologist, cartographer, astronomer, botanist and writer. Despite producing the most famous painting of all time, his *Mona Lisa*, he only left us a grand total of fifteen completed paintings from his entire life's work.

Right Da Vinci,
Lady with an Ermine,
1488–90.

Some were destroyed because he kept experimenting with new techniques that failed to work. But the real reason for his small output was that he suffered from a chronic inability to finish things that he had started. Da Vinci was the world's greatest procrastinator and put things off so often and for so long that it is a miracle we have any of his work at all.

The *Lady with an Ermine* demonstrates several of da Vinci's innovations. First, he used oil paint instead of the traditional tempera. Oil paints had only just arrived in Italy from the Netherlands and, as always, da Vinci was ready to experiment with a new technique. (When he tried this with his great fresco, *The Last Supper*, it was a disaster and the painting started to disintegrate almost as soon as it was finished.)

Da Vinci also introduced a novel kind of posture for his sitter. In *Lady with an Ermine*, the sitter's body faces one way and her head the other. This twisting of the head to one side gives her a look of immediacy, as though she has just turned to look at something or someone. Her hand is caught in the act of stroking the neck of the ermine, rather that simply holding it – another element

Above Van Eyck,
The Arnolfini Portrait,
1434.

'...Bosch had the courage to ignore the usual restraints and the dictates of good taste in order to unleash his most outlandish visions.'

of frozen movement. The artist has added tiny highlights to her eyes, making them sparkle with life. His delicate shading of her flesh is another device he uses to increase the lifelike quality of his portrait.

Outside Italy, another great centre of important 15th-century art was the Netherlands, where oil paint had been in use for some time. One of the earliest Flemish masters was Jan van Eyck, whose fine detail rivalled that of da Vinci but whose figures were slightly more stilted and less lifelike. His most famous painting, *The Arnolfini Portrait*, is well known for the reflected figures of Arnolfini and his wife shown in the mirror on the far wall.

It was not until the following generation that a more adventurous master arrived to reinvigorate Flemish art. Born in 1450, his name was Hieronymus Bosch. We know nothing about his private life, but his huge triptychs reveal a dark imagination obsessed with monsters and bodily torments. Released from the duty of portraying the real world or the blandly acceptable sacred scenes, he set about inventing a nightmare fantasy of unspeakable tortures and humiliations. A naked man impaled on the strings of a harp, and a knight in armour being devoured by a ring of rat-tailed monsters – these are just two of the lovingly depicted horrors on display in the right-hand panel of Bosch's greatest triptych, ironically known as *The Garden of Earthly Delights*.

Bosch's monsters are made up of a combination of known animal details and inappropriate body parts. The result is to create a bestiary of relentlessly hostile creatures intent on inflicting as much pain and degradation as possible on wicked humanity. Nothing like this had been seen before in traditional art, and it vividly demonstrates the imaginative potential that is always lurking beneath the surface. For some reason Bosch had the courage to ignore the usual restraints and the dictates of good taste in order to unleash his most outlandish visions.

The Renaissance reached its peak at the start of the 16th century. Its crowning glory was the ceiling of the Sistine Chapel in Rome, covered in frescoes by Michelangelo between 1508 and 1512. Lying on top of a wooden scaffold, he completed 465 square metres of biblical scenes.

Right Bosch's vision of hell from *The Garden of Earthly Delights,* started in 1490.

His masterwork, measuring 13 by 40 metres, was originally intended to show only the 12 apostles, but he persuaded the Pope to give him a free hand and ended up painting no fewer than 343 figures.

The ceiling was followed by another huge work, *The Last Judgement*, which covered the chapel's altar wall. He began this second commission in 1535 and completed it in 1541. It was not well received; one cardinal declared the work to be obscene and demanded its removal because it showed naked figures 'shamefully exposing themselves' in a sacred place. It was condemned as disgraceful and fit only for a tavern.

Michelangelo's defence was that he intended to show human figures with equal status on Judgement Day, their nudity stripping them bare of any rank. In the end, the frescoes were not removed, but the genitals of the naked figures were covered up by a pupil of Michelangelo, who was brought in especially for this task.

Right Michelangelo, *The Last Judgement*, Sistine Chapel, 1535–41.

Right Brueghel the Elder, *The Peasant Wedding Feast*, 1566.

Peasants and portraits

Many other major artists continued the Renaissance tradition in Italy during the 16th century, among them Titian, Cellini, Tintoretto and Veronese. Further north, in the Netherlands, a family of painters called Brueghel began to turn their attention to more friendly scenes of peasant life. Previously peasants had been acceptable as spear-carriers or bystanders but not as the central figures of a composition, so this was a radical departure in subject matter.

'[Brueghel] heralded a new dawn for representational art as a visual record of daily life.'

Pieter Brueghel, the senior member of this family, had visited Italy to study Renaissance art but found the subject matter too lofty and detached from everyday life. Back in the Netherlands he began a series of paintings in which ordinary people went about their everyday tasks, and in so doing heralded a new dawn for representational art as a visual record of daily life. Previously only portraiture had given us such a record, while the rest of art had been devoted largely to sacred themes and sponsored by the Church. Not one of Brueghel's works was intended for a church. Indeed, some of his works were so anti-Catholic that on his deathbed he ordered his wife to burn them.

Brueghel was extraordinary for his period because he told no moral tales, made no moral judgements, saw no good and evil and presented neither hero nor villain. He was a dispassionate observer of the human condition; whether his subjects were hard at work or drunkenly sleeping, whether they were cripples or dancers, they were all treated with the same loving care in his intricately composed scenes.

Above Arcimboldo, *Vertumnus* (Emperor Rudolph II), 1591.

Right Panel from Grünewald's *Temptation of Saint Anthony, Isenheim Altarpiece*, 1516.

Another 16th-century artist who reacted against the lofty, sacred themes of the Italian Renaissance was the eccentric Italian Arcimboldo. His portraits are unique in the history of art. He appears to have been influenced by no one, and to have influenced no one himself. His bizarre portrait of the Holy Roman Emperor Rudolph II in the guise of Vertumnus, the Roman god of the seasons, sums up his oddity. Rudolph appears as a carefully arranged assembly of fruit and vegetables. Other portraits by Arcimboldo show heads made up of books, animals and plants. In each case they are ingeniously combined to create the impression, from a distance, that one is looking at a human portrait. Examined more closely their separate components become clearly visible.

No one knows why Arcimboldo indulged in these strange fantasies, but we do know that they were surprisingly popular with his patrons. It was not until the arrival of the Surrealists

in the 20th century that such perversely fantastic compositions would surface again. Arcimboldo's success in the 16th century reveals the extent to which, at any age, human playfulness is bubbling just beneath the surface of the fine arts.

In 16th-century Germany the religious artist Matthias Grünewald was also allowing his imagination full reign. In one corner of his great *Isenheim Altarpiece* he rivalled Bosch with the monsters he created to torment Saint Anthony. Another German artist of this century, Hans Holbein, was famous for his meticulous portraits but was also unable to resist a bizarre flight of fancy in one of his works. At the bottom of his portrait of two ambassadors is an inexplicable, distorted object in a position of prominence. Only when the painting is viewed closely at one side from an extreme angle does the significance of this strange shape become clear. It is a human skull mysteriously placed at the feet of the ambassadors by the artist, who skilfully employed a remarkable anamorphic distortion. This is yet another example of the undercurrent of imaginative creativity that is so often present just below the surface of traditional art, trapped in the straightjacket of representational duties.

Right Holbein the Younger, *The Ambassadors*, 1533.

Distorted vision or style?

Also in 16th-century Germany, Lucas Cranach the Elder was well known for painting unusually elongated figures, exaggerating their legs in particular. There has been much argument as to why he should want to distort the proportions of the human form. Another 16th-century artist, a Cretan-born painter known in Spain by his nickname of 'The Greek' – El Greco – was also controversial. His subject matter was relentlessly traditional, yet his strangely deformed figures were even more elongated than those of Cranach, abnormally so in fact. El Greco too has become the subject of academic disagreement.

There are two conflicting views. The first suggests that the vision of both artists was distorted by a serious eye defect called astigmatism. In other words, in their eyes the lanky figures looked normal. The rival view sees their distortions as merely stylistic. Most of the debate has focused on El Greco, the more extreme of the two artists. When his paintings are viewed through a special lens to correct for astigmatism they do indeed display normal proportions, which supports the view that he had poor eyesight. Secondly, his exaggerations become more extreme as he grows older, suggesting that his vision was deteriorating with age. Thirdly, it has been pointed out that when painting a figure from a sitter, there is no elongation, but when he is painting an imaginary figure it does appear. This makes sense because if El Greco had distorted vision, what he saw in his sitter and what he painted would match.

Right Cranach's elongated figure of Venus, 1530.

Far right El Greco's abnormally elongated figure of Saint Joseph, 1597–9.

The art of light and shade

The most notable artist working in 17th-century Italy was Caravaggio. An ill-mannered, violent, brawling young tearaway, his genius only surfaced when he put down his sword and picked up a paintbrush. Even then he was in trouble for hiring a prostitute to model as the Virgin Mary and for depicting the disciples as ordinary working-class men. He had to flee Rome after killing a man with his sword in a duel.

'What is truly extraordinary about Caravaggio is that he somehow managed to calm down long enough between brawls to paint great canvases.'

What is truly extraordinary about Caravaggio is that he somehow managed to calm down long enough between brawls to paint great canvases. Although his work centred on religious topics, he painted in a naturalistic style employing exaggerated light and shadow – especially the latter. Dead at the age of 38, Caravaggio's tempestuous spirit had robbed the world of someone with a remarkable talent.

Caravaggio was active at the very beginning of the 17th century. The greatest art during the years that followed was to be found further north, in the Netherlands, where the genius of Rembrandt, Rubens, Hals, van Dyck and Vermeer would flourish. Like Caravaggio, Rembrandt suffered from a serious character flaw. In his case it was not uncontrollable violence but uncontrollable extravagance that was his undoing.

Right Caravaggio, *The Supper at Emmaus*, 1601.

An epic spendthrift, Rembrandt went bankrupt despite being the most prolific and popular portrait painter in Amsterdam, with commissions pouring in. Rembrandt's house and all his treasured possessions were sold at a series of compulsory auctions. Later, after the death of his wife, he even sold her tombstone to raise some ready cash.

It seems astonishing that a man with such a weakness and such a chaotic private life should have been able to give us some of the greatest paintings of the 17th century. It is as though the creative spirit, with its essentially playful character, is all too easily linked with disruptive personality traits that are in one way or another strongly opposed to pious restraint or self-control.

Apart from his special commissions, Rembrandt was obsessed with the gradual ageing process he saw in his own face. He painted over 80 self-portraits between the 1620s and the 1660s. Like Caravaggio, he too was fascinated by the play of light on the human form, seen against a dark, shadowy background. For some, this makes him a relentlessly gloomy painter, but for others it allows the eye to concentrate on the subtleties of skin texture and the nuances of facial anatomy and expression.

While Rembrandt was working in Amsterdam, a little further south in Antwerp Peter Paul Rubens held sway. His visit to Italy as a young man had made a huge impact on him, leading him to marry the realism of northern Europe with the

Right One of over 80 self-portraits painted by Rembrandt, showing the ageing process.

'…the creative spirit, with its essentially playful character, is all too easily linked with disruptive personality traits…'

Above Vermeer,
The Milkmaid, 1660.

Above right

Velázquez, *Portrait
of Pope Innocent X*,
1650.

grandiose classical themes of the south. The result is a mountain of writhing human flesh in brilliantly composed scenes of mythological or biblical events.

In the following generation, Jan Vermeer turned his back completely on the grandeur of Rubens and also rejected the sombre tones of Rembrandt. His pictures focused on ordinary people and used brighter colours, especially blue and yellow. The biblical scenes were gone, the mythological dramas forgotten and the important sitters excluded. Vermeer bravely ignored the patronage of the rich and famous, and when he died all he left to his family was a pile of debts. Here was a man so totally dedicated to what he wished to portray that all worldly considerations were forgotten.

Vermeer's genius lies in the way he played with the light falling on his subjects from the high window in his studio. His modest subjects are caught in a moment of time in a way that suddenly makes the work of earlier artists look contrived and old fashioned.

In 17th-century Spain, a portraitist to rival those working in the Low Countries was Diego Velázquez. He was a favourite with King Philip IV, who made him the official court painter. Velázquez painted the king's portrait forty times – the monarch would sit for nobody else. He even had a key to the artist's studio and almost every day would visit him there to watch him paint. There are those who believe that Velázquez was the greatest portrait painter who ever lived, and in the 20th century Francis Bacon would produce a long series of paintings based on Velázquez's portrait of the Pope.

Still life and landscapes

In the early 17th century the realism inherent in Dutch painting found a special form of expression – the still life. A number of unusually skilled artists began competing to see who could produce the most impeccably naturalistic painting of everyday objects arranged on a table. To heighten the realism, the objects were usually shown in tastefully arranged 'disarray' following a meal. This was painting with a level of technical skill to rival a modern colour photograph.

Still life was essentially art for the upper-middle classes. By the 17th century the new, urban middle class was growing and prospering and wanted paintings to hang on the walls of their increasingly elegant houses. Flower paintings became immensely popular, but it was the tabletop compositions that represented the technical peak of this particular genre. Food, drink, cutlery, crockery, table linen and various ornaments were the central features of these works. Religious set pieces, mythological dramas, historical events and all human forms were banished. In their place came ripe cheeses, cracked nuts, bowls of fruit, meat pies, shellfish, bread and wine. Hedonists saw these paintings as a celebration of their good fortune at being able to eat well, and the pious could see them as a stern reminder that gluttony is a sin.

Although religious painting did not disappear altogether during the 17th century, this was a time when portraiture and still-life painting flourished.

Right Dutch still-life painting by Pieter Claesz, 1647.

Their execution reached a level of brilliance that has rarely been matched in other centuries. The increasingly important middle classes in the cities and towns were the major new source of patronage, and their influence on subject matter was inevitable.

Another secular form of art that began to be taken seriously in the 17th century was landscape (from the Dutch word *landschap*). Rustic scenes became popular in the spacious urban homes of the affluent Dutch, but these paintings were rarely pure landscapes. They were more usually settings in which small human figures were depicted skating on the ice or walking on the beaches.

A major figure in the development of landscape as a separate genre was the French artist Nicolas Poussin. He preferred to work in Rome, where he had come under the influence of classical subjects. Landscapes appeared in the backgrounds of those works, but it was Poussin who decided that they deserved to be brought into the foreground. To do this in a naturalistic way was a step too far for him, however, and his landscapes were heroic rather than rustic. Poussin seldom resisted the temptation to include small human figures somewhere in his compositions.

'The increasingly important middle classes in the cities and towns were the major new source of patronage, and their influence on subject matter was inevitable.'

Right Poussin, *Landscape with Saint James*, 1640.

New patrons

Taste in European art was strongly influenced by the great academies, the powerful organisations that tended to oppose innovation. The traditionally minded academicians considered religious, mythological, allegorical and historical subjects to be superior to portraits, scenes of everyday life, landscapes and still-life paintings. However, this view was bound to lose ground as dramatic changes were taking place in the structure of 18th-century European society. The newly rich landowners demanded images of their families, their estates, their mansions, their scenery and their domestic animals. Under this new patronage, artists shifted their focus of interest more and more towards these secular subjects and away from sacred and classical ones.

In England, Thomas Gainsborough and Joshua Reynolds supplied the images craved by this new breed of art patron. The clients of these artists sometimes enjoyed a double reward, with a family portrait set in the grounds of their impressive estate as in *Mr and Mrs Andrews* by Gainsborough. The newly wed Andrews couple pose in a relaxed manner on their property; these rich landowners were able to afford to commission this work even though they were only plain Mr and Mrs.

The Venetian artist Canaletto benefitted from the Grand Tour, which had become the fashion among the elite of northern Europe. In fact, Canaletto's

Below
Gainsborough, *Mr and Mrs Andrews*, 1750.

Above Canaletto, *Arrival of the French Ambassador in Venice*, c. 1740.

technically brilliant studies became more popular in England than in his Italian homeland. Unfortunately, the commercial success of his work saw its quality decline as he started to churn out canvas after canvas to meet the demand. A critic claimed that his new work was so mechanical that it must be the work of an imposter, with the result that Canaletto had to perform public painting displays to prove that this was false.

In France, before heads started to roll during the French Revolution, a trio of romantic artists were at work. Fragonard, Boucher and Watteau supplied the boudoirs of the elite with a series of charmingly decadent nudes and idealised theatrical costume pieces. These hedonistic confections were about as far from the sacred art of earlier centuries as it was possible to go. Indeed, they edged so close to the limits of propriety that they enraged some French art critics. These criticisms had little impact, however, since the paintings were commissioned by the royal court. Frivolous and blatantly erotic they may have been, but their patronage protected them.

Typical of this genre is François Boucher's *Louise O'Murphy*, a nude painting of one of Louis XV's mistresses, a charming Irish girl by the name of O'Murphy.

Above Boucher, *Louise O'Murphy*, 1752.

At the age of 13 she had been seduced by Casanova, who commissioned a nude painting of her. This painting so excited the king when he saw it that he took her as one of his younger mistresses and had his own portrait of her painted by Boucher.

If the wealthy art patrons of the 18th century tended to favour images of the grand country estates, the canals of Venice and the boudoirs of the French court, there was another, more squalid side to the century that those canvases ignored. It was a side that was to be captured in the art of William Hogarth. His paintings and engravings of the teeming city of London set about destroying any complacency that might exist about the state of British politics, city life and social morality. His savage visual satires brought home all the gross injustices and wanton degradation that existed in the urban society of his time.

Visual inventiveness

A revolutionary landscape artist of the early 19th century was the remarkable JMW Turner, who was obsessed with the extreme effects of light. It is said that he once had himself strapped to the mast of a ship in order to experience at first hand the visual impact of a storm at sea. His dying words were 'The sun is God.' Turner was fascinated by sunlight, fire, rain, wind, fog, storms and the violence of the sea. As he grew older his paintings became less and less detailed until eventually little was left except patches of light and dark.

The free, atmospheric quality of Turner's late work disturbed the art critics who had so admired his earlier, more conventional paintings. It was rumoured that he was going insane. His mother had ended her days in a mental hospital and Turner himself was becoming increasingly eccentric, spending his final years in Chelsea with his mistress Sophia Boot while pretending to be a retired admiral. When Queen Victoria was asked why she had not given him a knighthood, she replied that it was because she thought he was mad. Whatever the truth, the fact remains that the adventurous disregard for detail in his final works placed Turner almost a century ahead of his time in terms of visual abstraction, making him one of the most innovative artists in history.

'...the adventurous disregard for detail in his final works placed Turner almost a century ahead of his time in terms of visual abstraction...'

Left Hogarth, *The Tavern Scene* from *The Rake's Progress*, 1734.

Right Turner, *The Burning of the Houses of Parliament*, 1834.

Above Ingres, *Roger Delivering Angelica*, 1819.

Outside England, France became the focus of visual inventiveness in the 19th century. Major artists such as Ingres, Corot, Courbet, Daumier and Delacroix were about to take centre stage. The French Revolution had cleared the decks for an entirely new phase of art in which the artists would respond more directly to the visual impact of the world around them. An exception to this shift was the neoclassical artist Ingres, who stubbornly declared that he was a 'conservator of good doctrine, and not an innovator'. His critics accused him of plundering the past, to which Ingres replied angrily that they were scoundrels out to assassinate his reputation. His subject matter may have been allegorical and his technique may have been pseudo-classical, but his nudes were almost as erotic as their boudoir forebears from pre-revolutionary times.

Ingres had a great enemy – Eugène Delacroix – whose work was as full of natural movement as Ingres' work was with artificially set poses. The scenes depicted by Delacroix were so alive that you could almost smell and hear the action. His vigorous brushstrokes gave a rich, vivid feel to his images, with his figures nearly always caught in a frozen moment of violent movement.

Right Delacroix, *Liberty Leading the People*, 1830.

'The scenes depicted by Delacroix were so alive that you could almost smell and hear the action. His vigorous brushstrokes gave a rich, vivid feel to his images...'

Whether it was the slaughter of a king's concubines, the scene of a great rebellion or a wild fight between horses, Delacroix's swirling compositions were full of a dynamic force. He wanted his viewer to become caught up in the exciting event he was portraying. He was prepared to sacrifice any amount of fine detail to achieve this end, an attitude that went against everything that Ingres stood for.

The battle between the classicism of Ingres and the romanticism of Delacroix would soon fade into history with the arrival of a new revolution in art – that of the realists who wanted to portray ordinary people in a serious light. This was a revolution in subject matter rather than style. It was true that the Brueghels had depicted peasant activities much earlier, but their men and women were not meant to be taken too seriously. There was no 'dignity of labour' with them. The French artist Jean-François Millet, by contrast, saw peasants in a very different light, toiling away, tilling the fields and harvesting the crops. They were painfully earnest but carried the important new French message of *egalité*, although some critics attacked Millet for painting socialist propaganda.

Right Millet, *The Gleaners*, 1857.

A new approach to painting

A key figure in 19th-century art is the French painter Edouard Manet. His work is seen as the important bridge between the realism of the earlier part of the century and the impressionism of the later part. The Impressionists themselves recognised him as the father of their movement, but he always resisted exhibiting with them or becoming an official member of their group.

Manet saw himself as a realist, but there was a world of difference in the way he applied his paint. The careful, meticulous brushwork was gone, and in its place was a looseness that was disliked by the establishment critics who wondered why he did not finish his paintings. This freedom with brushstrokes, which allowed the viewer to see how the marks had been made, excited the younger artists. It was the starting point of a new technical revolution that would lead eventually to the even looser application of paint adopted by the Impressionists.

Manet's subject matter was Parisian daily life. In that respect he was a realist, showing people as they went about their business and enjoyed their leisure in the bars and cafés. He would often catch them in a moment of conversation or having a drink, and his compositions were more informal and spontaneous, with figures sometimes half-obscured by others or with faces cut off at the edge of the canvas. This was another aspect of his work that would have a profound influence on the Impressionists.

In 1874 a small group of Parisian painters, including Monet, Sisley, Pissarro, Degas and Renoir, came together to exhibit their new method of painting. One of Monet's works was entitled *Impression, Sunrise*, and a visiting critic remarked drily

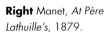

Right Manet, *At Père Lathuille's*, 1879.

Right Monet, *Impression, Sunrise,* 1872.

that it certainly made an impression on him, adding 'what freedom, what ease of workmanship! Wallpaper in its embryonic state is more finished than that seascape.' The critic dubbed the group the 'Impressionists' as an insult, but it was one that backfired. Their refreshingly different way of depicting the world gradually attracted supporters, and their movement went on to kick-start a whole new approach to painting that would herald the great upheavals of the 20th century.

The Impressionists employed several different techniques: paint was applied in short thick strokes that ignored fine detail; dabs of colour were applied separately without mixing, so that the eye of the observer had to do the merging; the painting was done quickly in order to capture a fleeting moment in time; the artists worked on location in the open air and not in the studio; blacks and greys were not used, dark tones being created from complementary colours; the artists did not wait for paint to dry before adding more strokes, thus creating deliberately blurred edges; great importance was attached to light conditions, such as the shadows of twilight, glancing sunlight, reflected light; shadows were shown as blue, from the reflection of the sky.

The results of this new technical approach were startling to those accustomed to the traditions of the great art salons. To many, the Impressionists' work was outrageous and appeared carelessly thrown together, but they persisted. There were about a dozen artists in the group, but a few stood out from the others. Claude Monet was perhaps the most extreme exponent of the new style, some of his works appearing to be little more than a collection of small dabs of coloured paint.

The Post-Impressionists

As an organised group the Impressionists held eight exhibitions in Paris, from the first in 1874 to the last in 1886. After that, a new group that became known as the Post-Impressionists emerged at the very end of the 19th century. The main figures in this movement were Paul Gauguin, Vincent van Gogh, Paul Cézanne and Georges Seurat. The most straightforward development was a technical refinement of Impressionist brushwork called Pointillism. It was a style created by Seurat and Paul Signac, in which the short dabs of paint of the Impressionists were reduced to mere dots of colour. Each dot was a separate colour, but when viewed from a distance the dots blended into larger shapes. Seurat had become interested in scientific theories about the nature of light and colour and was experimenting with complementary colours, colour halos and the effects of retinal persistence.

Below Seurat, *The Seine at La Grande Jatte*, 1888.

Van Gogh moved in the opposite direction; instead of reducing the short dabs of paint to delicate spottings, he made them even more visible and powerful.

Above Van Gogh, *Wheatfield with Crows*, 1890.

This process became stronger and stronger during his lifetime, ending up with an almost savage application of paint onto canvas. Van Gogh's work also differed from that of the Impressionists in that he often added dark outlines to make objects appear stronger and more conspicuous. There was a tortured air to many of his works, an atmosphere that reflected his own tormented personality. No matter how wonderful his art, he does not seem to have been a pleasant man. Jeanne Calment, the young girl who sold him his paints when he was at Arles, described him to me as 'filthy ugly, smelling of booze and with a vile temper'. And it is said that he could only gain pleasure from the most bizarre sexual rituals carried out in brothels. But he is another contradictory example of a melancholy life that gave rise to vibrant works of art.

'There was a tortured air to many of his [van Gogh's] works, an atmosphere that reflected his own tormented personality.'

Van Gogh's friend Paul Gauguin also suffered from depression and a failed suicide attempt. Gauguin ended his days in the South Pacific as a syphilitic drunk sleeping with very young local girls. After libelling the governor of the Marquesas Islands he was sentenced to prison but died of a morphine overdose before he could serve his time. Again, we see the paradox of a singularly unpleasant man creating important works of art.

Gauguin's paintings left Impressionism far behind. Seeing the Impressionists may have released him from traditional restraints, but he then went his own way into a primitive style with the illogical use of bright colours that had little do with the features they were depicting. A dog is bright orange, the earth is red, yellow, purple and green. Areas are left flat and details are only crudely painted.

Right *Gauguin, Joyeuseté (The Seed of Arearea),* 1892.

Gauguin's paintings of native life are laden with symbols and a strange, rather suffocating atmosphere. Despite the bright colours and vivid images, there was nothing pretty about his work. At the time it was created his art was revolutionary and it would make a huge impact on other artists arriving on the Paris art scene at the very end of the century.

Paul Cézanne, the other great Post-Impressionist, was a very different personality and far less troubled than either van Gogh or Gauguin. A wealthy religious man, Cézanne's biggest struggle was with the demands he put upon himself when painting. It is said that he might take several hours to make a single addition to a composition, and a still life might take over 100 painting sessions to complete. This was because he set himself a contradictory challenge: to present a direct observation of nature as it was before him, but at the same time to reveal its underlying abstract structure. Too little abstraction and he merely imitated nature; too much abstraction and he lost touch with nature. He wanted to depict the underlying geometric forms that lay just below the surface of natural shapes, famously saying that he wanted to 'treat nature by the cylinder, the sphere, the cone'. But in doing so Cézanne did not want to lose sight of a simple, direct observation of natural scenes.

'Too little abstraction and he [Cézanne] merely imitated nature; too much abstraction and he lost touch with nature.'

Right Cézanne, *The François Zola Dam*, 1878.

Cézanne could only achieve such a fine balance by prolonged concentration. His impact on the art of the following century would be enormous. His use of planes of colour and small brushstrokes would be taken as an analytical starting point for the first of the major movements of the 20th century – Cubism – that would see the art world plunge further into the abstraction of natural form, much further than Cézanne could ever have imagined.

A new art form

It is clear that two major influences were at work to alter the face of art in the 19th century. The first was a shift in patronage, away from the Church and the royal court and towards a thriving new middle class. The second was the invention of a scientific technique for making pictures, using chemicals instead of brushes and paints: photogenic art, or photography. From modest beginnings this completely new art form would eventually take over the role of recording events, places, people and objects.

Representational art had for centuries been entrusted with this social duty, and the dazzling skills developed by human hands holding paintbrushes had resulted in an astonishing archive of visual history from which so much has been learnt. What black-and-white photography lacked in inspired beauty was compensated for by scientific accuracy. The oldest surviving photograph dates from 1827. Taken by an inventive French country gentleman, Joseph Niépce,

Above The world's first photograph, by Joseph Niépce, taken in 1827.

it shows his outbuildings photographed from his study window. The exposure time was eight hours and the result little more than a blur, but it was a start.

A French painter called Jacques Daguerre took the next step, making his daguerreotype process public in 1839. His photographs were unique positives and extremely fragile. Exposure time was reduced to 30 minutes and gradually shortened in the next few years. However, by the mid-1850s he was overtaken by an English scientist, William Fox Talbot.

Fox Talbot had pioneered what he called 'photogenic drawing' in the 1830s. In 1839 he published a paper with the lengthy title 'The Art of Photogenic Drawing, or the process by which natural objects may be made to delineate themselves without the aid of the artist's pencil.' In 1841 he introduced a new development that he called the 'calotype', the world's first negative-positive process that made it possible to produce many positives from a single negative. Exposure time was now reduced to one to two minutes and this saw the beginning of photographic portraiture, even though clamps had to be used to keep the sitter's head completely still.

The 1870s saw the introduction of cheap and fast printing on bromide paper, and in 1888 in the USA the first Kodak camera appeared with a flexible roll of film that, at last, made taking photographs easy. The 20th century would see scientific picture making forge ahead, leaving handmade paintings robbed of their major duty of recording visual history. Black-and-white still photography would develop into sensitive colour photography, then cinematography, videotape and the rest. The world would no longer study paintings of kings and battles to learn what they looked like – they would see them on their cinema and television screens.

The impact of this development was already beginning to show itself in the painting of the final decades of the 19th century. The Impressionists were well aware of the growing role of photography, and it was a major influence on their decision to experiment with new ways of portraying the world. It would be only a matter of time before the artists working at the start of the new century would turn their attention away from representation and the restrictions of traditional art, to entirely new experiments in the creation of visual imagery.

From this brief survey of traditional painting, from the 8th to the 19th century, it is clear that certain of my eight rules of art are more in evidence than others. The pressure exerted on artists to fulfil the demands of patrons meant that strict limits had to be imposed on visual experimentation. The rules of exaggeration and purification suffered most. Whether portraying religious scenes or creating visual records of the external world, the traditional artist had to avoid any obvious exaggerations. The intensifying of colours and the purification of shapes also had to be kept to a minimum.

To take an extreme example, in Dutch still-life painting the suppression of these tendencies was almost total, so that the objects depicted were virtually identical with the real thing. What was extraordinary about these brilliant works is not their imaginative creativity but their demonstration of outstanding technical skill. Even here, however, most of my other rules were operating. Sensitive compositional control was active. The collection of objects shown in a Dutch still life was very carefully arranged. The balance and the visual rhythms of these works were carefully considered. Also, each still life was meticulous in the way it obeyed the rule of optimum heterogeneity. The compositions were always perfectly poised between the 'too simple' and the 'too complex'. The paintings were never too plain or too fussy. Part of the pleasure of viewing them is responding to the delicate balance between these two extremes.

'...the artists working at the start of the new century would turn their attention away from representation and the restrictions of traditional art, to entirely new experiments in the creation of visual imagery.'

Also, the breathtaking precision with which the individual objects were portrayed underlines the way in which the artists were obeying the rule of image refinement. And the fact that each work was a subtle variation on the general still-life theme follows the rule of thematic variation.

With other, more flexible examples of representational art, the suppression of exaggeration and purification is often less extreme. Portraits, for example, may slightly exaggerate the good features of a subject and reduce the bad features. Artists portraying mythical or sacred scenes may intensify their images to heighten the impact of their work. Many landscape artists will rearrange the scenery to suit their visual preferences. And towards the end of this phase in the history of art, experiments with intensified colours and shapes begin to appear on the scene.

So even where one of the main duties of the artist is to record the external world, my basic rules of art are still strongly in evidence. The burden of being the recorders of visual history does not turn artists into mere machines concerned solely with technical mastery and visual mimicry. They may suffer from constraints that are unknown to the child artist, the tribal artist or the modern artist but, even so, within the limits imposed upon them they still manage to obey their ancient creative urges.

9 Modern Art

Scan page to view video

Modern Art

POST-PHOTOGRAPHIC ART

Modern art – the art of the 20th century – can best be described as post-photographic art. Towards the end of the 19th century it became clear that the direct recording of the external world could now be done by scientific means, using chemicals instead of paintbrushes. A few artists ignored this takeover by the camera and traditional art did continue right through the 20th century, but from this point on it would always play a minor role. The major role would belong to the experimental artists who sought new ways of expressing themselves visually, now that the burden of recording had been taken off their shoulders.

'…when viewed as a whole the art of the 20th century is a bewildering mixture of styles and short-lived movements.'

The problem with this new freedom was that there were no rules telling an artist which way to go. Artists knew what they did not want to do, but that was all. Freedom is rather like a desert where you can take off in any direction you like but there are no signposts. As a result, when viewed as a whole the art of the 20th century is a bewildering mixture of styles and short-lived movements. A small group of artists would come together, try to do something different, give themselves a name and hope that collectors would respond. Art historians have been able to identify no fewer than 81 such groups or '-isms' between the years 1900 and 2000.

Looking back at these groups from today's viewpoint, it is clear that there were five main trends if we ignore minor theoretical differences. Each trend withdraws from the rules of traditional art in a different way. They can be summarised as:

geometric art – retreating from the natural world;

organic art – distorting the natural world;

irrational art – retreating from the logical world;

pop art – rebelling against traditional subjects;

event art – rebelling against traditional techniques.

In addition to these five trends, there were artists who refused to give up the earlier traditions:

super-realist art – competing with the camera.

These competing trends offered a greater variety of choices than had ever been seen before. In addition the 20th century witnessed a major shift in the patronage of art, from the Church and the royal court to the private collector and the public art gallery. The traditional art galleries were now joined by modern art galleries that were concerned exclusively with the new work, giving the public the chance to experience it at first hand. Failing that, lithographs, cheap colour prints, posters, postcards and illustrated art books made the images of modern art widely available to anyone who was interested.

'Modern artists were so deeply involved in experimentation that the general public often found their latest offerings difficult to accept.'

Although these developments meant that fine art was more accessible than ever before, in another way it became less accessible. Modern artists were so deeply involved in experimentation that the general public often found their latest offerings difficult to accept. Examples of modern art that we view as uncontroversial today in the 21st century were, on their first appearance, viewed as the work of lunatics and charlatans. It was rare for any new style of modern art to be accepted immediately, with the result that many of the most innovative artists found it hard to make a living. Pictures that sell for millions in today's auction houses were actually created by artists who were half-starving at the time they made them. This serves to underline the passion and the dedication of so many 20th-century artists, who lacked the usual support of the traditional patrons. They had a vision they were determined to explore, no matter how difficult this was in practical, day-to-day terms, and once again demonstrated the irrepressible creative urge of the human race.

Geometric art – retreating from the natural world

From 1900 up until the present day, there have always been artists who sought to explore the underlying structure of natural objects. Beneath all the tiny details and organic irregularities they detected an underlying geometry of simple shapes. Cézanne began this with his statement that he wanted to 'treat nature by the cylinder, the sphere, the cone'. At first sight, the move towards a cruder, coarser version of nature might seem ill-advised, but an unusual medical event explains why this is not so.

A middle-aged man who had been blind since childhood was given his sight by a new surgical procedure. When he opened his eyes his surgeon asked him what he saw, and he replied: 'There is light, there is movement, there is colour, all mixed up, all meaningless, a blur… a chaos of light and shadow.' The experience was quite painful until the man began to make out certain shapes. His eyes did this by starting to make out what we could call composition lines, places where a geometric contrast existed, something he could fixate on. He identified more and more shapes and lines until he could walk down a corridor without touching the walls. In other words, he learnt to see in an organised way by using the underlying geometry of the visual world. Cézanne's statement therefore has a special validity. When it sees any image, the human eye understands it by its underlying structure and avoids confusion by absorbing its basic geometry. A simplified shape therefore carries with it a pleasant sensation.

Below An African tribal mask of the kind that influenced Picasso.
Below right Picasso, *Les Demoiselles d'Avignon*, 1907.

So reducing the confusing detail of the visual world to simple geometry is something that we all do, without realising it, every time we set eyes on a scene.

The simplification of detailed shapes is also something that happens in a great deal of tribal art. In the early years of the 20th century one young Spanish artist, Pablo Picasso, was fascinated by the tribal masks he saw when he visited the ethnographical museum in Paris. It was said that he 'haunted the African collections' there, and Picasso remarked that the visits 'changed him'. In these tribal exhibits Picasso saw what Cézanne had been talking about – in this case the underlying geometry of the human face being exaggerated at the expense of personal portraiture.

'...the public response was that the painting was lewd, disgusting, outrageous, horrific and immoral.'

A third influence on Picasso at this time were some ancient Iberian stone sculptures with simplified facial features. These had recently been excavated in Spain. With these influences in mind, Picasso began work in 1907 on a painting that would stun his friends and herald an entirely new movement in the history of art. He called the painting *The Brothel at Avignon*. It showed five prostitutes posed as if parading themselves for a new client to choose between them. The three faces on the left were taken from the ancient Iberian sculptures; the two on the right were over-painted with two of the African masks he had studied at the ethnological museum. The planes of light and shade of the five figures revealed the influence of Cézanne.

The painting was considered too shocking to be exhibited and was only seen by Picasso's friends. It was hidden away for nine years before finally being put on show. Even then its title had to be censored and, against Picasso's wishes, the picture was primly renamed *Les Demoiselles d'Avignon*. Despite this, the public response was that the painting was lewd, disgusting, outrageous, horrific and immoral. Picasso kept it rolled up in his studio for the next 29 years, claiming that it was not finished. He would have been surprised to know that, in 1972, it would be described by a leading art critic as 'the most influential work of art of the last 100 years'.

The most surprising feature of Picasso's painting is the ugliness of the women who are supposed to be selling their bodies for sex. Picasso had been visiting brothels himself and, five years earlier, had caught a venereal disease from one of the girls, for which he had received medical treatment. (The doctor who cured him was rewarded with a Blue Period painting.) It has been suggested that it was this unpleasant memory that had caused him to give his female figures the 'ugly face of prostitution'.

Over the next couple of years Picasso continued to explore human figures of this general type, with their shapes becoming progressively more simplified and geometric. In 1909, out of these early experiments, he and his friend Georges Braque launched the first major movement of the 20th century – Cubism.

Above Braque, *Still Life with Violin*, 1911.

In the earliest examples it is still possible to detect the natural objects on which the geometric abstractions are based, but as time progresses it becomes increasingly difficult to do so.

Colour was gradually drained from these Cubist paintings until they ended up, at the peak of the movement's period, as a mixture of pale greys and browns. There is an atmosphere of severity and austerity about these works, as if the artists are encouraging us to take them seriously – something they needed to do, bearing in mind just how revolutionary these works were at the time.

This early 20th-century style of painting, known as 'analytical cubism', was based on the idea that the essence of a subject could best be transmitted by breaking it up into its parts. In the process the artist simplified the parts so they appeared to the observer as a mass of small interlocking slices of light and shade. The aim was to present a conceptual image in place of the usual perceptual one.

Once this idea had been carried through and subjects had been thoroughly fractured, dismantled and dismembered, a new phase gradually emerged – it was later given the convenient title of 'synthetic cubism'. Here, the dismembered elements were brought together again in a new synthesis, creating simpler, more rounded, more friendly paintings. This type of warmer, softer, more colourful cubism was to grow and mature, and for Picasso it became his basic style for many years to come.

Cubism was not alone in its move towards abstraction. Indeed, at about the same time other artists were making bold statements that rejected any sort of reference to recognisable subject matter, and were launching themselves into a totally geometric, fully abstract visual world. It comes as a surprise to discover just how early some of these works were made.

The Parisian artist Francis Picabia, for example, was strongly influenced by Cubism and created abstract compositions as early as 1912. Geometric abstraction was also appearing elsewhere. In Russia an avid supporter of modern art had assembled an impressive collection that included no fewer than 50 paintings by Picasso, including some of his most advanced Cubist works. On seeing these, young Russian artists immediately began pushing at the limits of this move towards abstraction, and the first totally abstract Russian painting was exhibited in Moscow as early as 1911. It was by Mikhail Larionov and was called simply *Glass*.

Larionov belonged to a small group who called themselves Rayonists because they were obsessed with rays of light. All their paintings were made up of these rays, which were a refinement of Picasso's Cubist planes. An important difference was that the Russians had taken the move towards total abstraction a step further. Their work contained no remnants of recognisable objects of the kind that could still be detected in the Cubist works. Their pictures were, to use their own phrase, 'independent of real forms'. With these works the Russians were running ahead of Picasso, taking his pioneering trend towards abstraction further down the path to its logical conclusion. Picasso himself would never do this, leaving the final stages of geometric abstraction to others. The Russians were not finished, however. They were about to push abstraction one final step further, to a point that was virtually impossible to exceed.

In 1913 the Rayonists were eclipsed by a new group who styled themselves Suprematists and were led by a remarkable man called Kazimir Malevich. He was about to make the most extreme geometric statements possible, creating abstract paintings so radical that it would be impossible to go beyond them without exhibiting a blank canvas. They may have been painted as early as 1913, but the precise date is not clear. We do know, however, that they were exhibited in 1915.

Below Picasso, *Mandolin and Guitar*, 1924.

The public reaction in Moscow to this new era of abstraction was described as 'howls of fury and derision'. Considering the early date, this is not surprising. But it did not deter Malevich, who continued to produce radical abstracts. In 1918 he went even further than the works he had shown in 1915 with a painting called *White on White*, in which a tilted white square sits on a white background. The white of the square and the white of the background are just different enough for the observer to be able to make out the position of the square.

A few years after the Russian Revolution and the introduction of communist rule, Malevich's work was banned. In 1926 the art institute of which he was the director was closed on the grounds that it was 'rife with counter-revolutionary sermonising and artistic debauchery'. Social realism was the only kind of art that Stalin permitted. Abstract work had to be hidden from the authorities to prevent its destruction.

Another member of the Russian avant-garde avoided these problems by living abroad for most of his life. Wassily Kandinsky left Russia for Germany in 1896 and produced his first fully abstract painting as early as 1910. His influence was not Cubism, but an encounter he had with a Monet painting of haystacks. This was Monet at his most extreme, with the haystacks no more than a blur of colour.

Right Malevich, *Suprematist Cross*, 1920.

This annoyed the precise-thinking Kandinsky. 'It really worried me, tantalised me,' he wrote, 'the painter had no right to paint in such a blurred fashion.' But then he was shocked to find that the painting, obscure as it was, excited him simply by its pattern of intense colour. 'It made an indelible impression on my memory,' Kandinsky recalled, and he realised that it was possible to make a visual impact without showing any recognisable features in a painting. It occurred to him that no one criticised music for being abstract and he described painting as visual music: 'Colour is the keyboard, the eyes are the harmonies... The artist is the hand that plays, touching one key or another....'

Kandinsky was taking a different route into abstraction and one that, because of its musical associations, looked very different from Cubism. His early 'improvisations', although completely abstract, were organic rather than geometric. His geometric works began in 1921 and are strangely stilted. In his effort to avoid any possible link to a recognisable object, he arranges his geometric units with exquisite care. Balance, rhythm and composition are oppressively obtrusive. In the end, Kandinsky's paintings become meticulous intellectual games rather than passionate visual statements. But for the period in which they were being painted, they were revolutionary statements.

Right Kandinsky,
On White II,
1923.

In Paris at about the same time, the French painter Robert Delaunay and his Russian wife Sonia, together with the Czech artist František Kupka, were experimenting with abstract patterns in very bright colours. They had taken abstraction from the Cubists and bright colours from the Fauvists and combined them to present something more appealing than the monotonously monotone Cubist works. Their movement, called Orphism, was short-lived because of the outbreak of war in 1914, but it did produce some significant examples of geometric abstraction and the Delaunays continued to paint in the same style after the war.

The Dutch artist Piet Mondrian moved to Paris in 1911 and stayed there until 1914. This was the height of the Cubist revolution, and Mondrian was strongly influenced by it. He began making his own abstract compositions while in Paris, removing all traces of recognisable objects. Later, in his mature work that he called Neo-plasticism, his austere compositions consisted of nothing but vertical and horizontal black lines with rectangular patches of the three primary colours red, yellow and blue. The only variation he allowed himself was in the precise positioning of the lines and colour patches. Once Mondrian had started working with this rigid formula he remained faithful to it for the rest of his life.

Below Robert Delaunay, *Circular Forms, Sun and Moon*, 1912.

Above Nicholson, Ben (1894–1982)·
1943 (Painting), 1943. New York, Museum of
Modern Art (MoMA). Gouache and pencil on
board mounted on painted wood frame, 9¾ x
10″ (24.6 x 25.3cm) including painted wood
frame. Nina and Gordon Bunshaft Bequest. Acc.
n.: 648.1994.

Another artist who followed a similar 'purified' path
towards what came to be called 'hard-edge abstraction' was
the Englishman Ben Nicholson. He too went further and
further towards the exclusion of everything except simple
geometric shapes, but in his case the favoured compositions
involved carefully arranged rectangles and circles. Some of
these were brightly coloured but in his later works he
sometimes even dispensed with colours, creating bleak
white-on-white reliefs.

Above Vasarely, *Oltar-BMB*, 1972.

Below Kelly, *Blue Curve Relief 2009.*

Extreme forms of geometric abstraction appealed to many other artists as the 20th century wore on. Later examples included the English artist Bridget Riley, the Hungarian-French artist Victor Vasarely, the German Josef Albers, the Frenchman Yves Klein and the Americans Stuart Davis, Barnett Newman and Ellsworth Kelly.

The work of one geometric abstractionist sets him apart from the rest. This is because although he limits his work to two simple geometric shapes – the square and the rectangle – he does so without using hard edges. His soft-edged shapes float in the centre of his huge canvases as if seen through a haze. Mark Rothko was a Russian-born American who spent several decades laboriously creating and re-creating his excessively simplified compositions, varying them only in the smallest degree. He appeared to be trapped inside one visual idea that had completely overtaken his imagination. The only change as the years passed was that his colours lost their warmth, his early reds, oranges and yellows giving way to dark blues, greens, greys and blacks. Rothko's final paintings became darker and darker and more and more depressing. A depressive himself, living on a diet of antidepressants, he was found one day lying dead on his studio floor having slit his arms with a razor.

One of the risks of simplification in art is that one starts to see more and more in less and less, until the experience has become almost trance-like. In the process it becomes haunting, but not necessarily in a good way, as Rothko discovered to his cost.

'He [Rothko] appeared to be trapped inside one visual idea that had completely overtaken his imagination.'

Right Rothko, *White Center (Yellow, Pink and Lavender on Rose)*, 1950.

Right Matisse, *Luxe, Calme et Volupté,* 1904.

Organic art – distorting the natural world

The 20th century differed from earlier periods in that now several completely different art trends occurred at the same time. The widespread rebellion against traditional art following the development of the camera meant that groups of artists, and lone individuals, were setting off in any direction except the purely representational.

While the long journey to geometric abstraction and simplification was taking place, alongside it was another major trend – towards the increasing distortion of the natural world. Here, the pictorial imagery was not being pared down to its underlying mathematical shapes, but was instead being deformed in some way – having its colour altered unnaturally perhaps, or its proportions changed or its details exaggerated or reduced beyond the normal. There could also be a degree of abstraction, but not towards more geometric units. Instead, the organic shapes would become less commonplace and more imaginary.

The earliest move in this direction took place in 1905 in Paris when a group of young artists shocked the establishment with an exhibition of paintings so brightly coloured and roughly painted that one of the major critics dubbed them '*les fauves*', meaning the wild beasts. Instead of being insulted, they adopted the name and called themselves the Fauvists.

They were a loose collection of painters who wanted their work to express their feelings and emotions rather than describe a particular scene in detail. The senior member of the group was Henri Matisse, and he was soon saddled with the title of 'king of the beasts'. His 1904 painting *Luxe, Calme et Volupté (Luxury, Calm and Pleasure)* became the icon of the first Fauvist exhibition. Even today it retains some of its wildness, with its extravagant colours and loose brushstrokes. Its impact on the more conservative critics in 1905 must have been tremendous.

Other artists exhibiting alongside Matisse were André Derain, Maurice de Vlaminck, Georges Rouault and Raoul Dufy. Their compositions owed a great debt to the Impressionists but were much more brutally painted. One critic referred to them as showing the nastiest smears of paint he had ever seen, but dealers and collectors, ignoring the comments of the bewildered and hostile public, loved them and started buying them up as fast as they could. This was unexpected where a new style was concerned. Usually it takes time for it to be appreciated, but perhaps the Impressionists had paved the way for this latest development.

Vlaminck's work looked as though he was trying to take up where van Gogh had left off. His landscapes have a similar intensity but with even more outlandish colour schemes than van Gogh's. A field of earth would, for example, become a sea of streaks of red, pink, blue and green on his Fauve canvas.

The Fauvists did not last long as a group. The members all went their separate ways. Only the king himself, Matisse, would remain faithful to the Fauvist tradition and adhere to it for most of his long life, placing colour above all else.

Right Vlaminck, *Landscape near Chatou*, 1906.

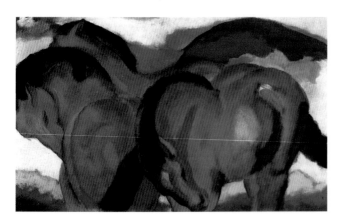

Above Marc,
The Little Blue Horses,
1911.

As the Fauvist movement came to an end, an even more adventurous group was about to make its mark in Germany. Called *Der Blaue Reiter,* or the Blue Rider, its members took the imaginative use of colour a step further. Franz Marc, who was passionate about animals, painted horses that were bright blue, red or orange and cows that were yellow. Colour no longer bore any relationship to nature, only to the mood of the painter.

Another member of the Blue Rider group was the Russian Wassily Kandinsky, whose compositions were already predominantly abstract. At this stage his watercolours were organic in concept and it would be some time before he abandoned these and moved on to his geometric compositions. His first organic abstract was painted in 1910, and it was not until 1921 that he switched to geometric shapes.

Kandinsky's organic abstracts were full of colour and movement, and to view them was like looking at landscapes exploding into fragments before your eyes. He said his key objective was 'emancipating form'. In other words, he wanted to disconnect the details of his compositions from recognisable features of the external world. The trick was to do this without making his non-figurative,

Right Kandinsky,
*Improvisation 28
(second version),*
1912.

abstracted details seem purely decorative. Somehow, they had to retain their organic validity without being in any way representational.

Much to Kandinsky's disappointment, the public and the critics were not impressed when the Blue Rider work was put on show. The main aim of the exhibition, he wrote, 'has hardly been attained at all'. Nor would it be attained, for the group's activities that had started in Munich in 1911 were about to be crushed by the outbreak of war in 1914. The foreigners among the main members of the group had to leave Germany, and the Germans Franz Marc and August Macke would soon be killed in combat.

In the meantime, during the interwar period the idea of distorting the organic world took another path, concentrating on the human form. Kandinsky had never tried to subject the human form to abstraction, but now several major artists began to do this without resorting to the geometric simplification begun by the Cubists. Picasso himself was one of these, shedding the geometry of his earlier works and turning instead to exaggerated human figures that retained their fleshy, organic qualities despite what was being done to them.

Right Picasso, *Nude in a Red Armchair*, 1932.

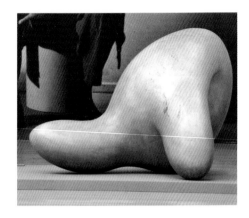

Above Arp, *Human Concretion*, 1932.

Sculptors were also experimenting with the human form as never before. Jean (Hans) Arp and Henry Moore were the two most adventurous, presenting nude figures in varying degrees of abstraction without ever losing sight of their organic nature. Their works were sometimes referred to as 'biomorphic abstraction' because their rounded outlines gave them a biological association, rather than a sharply angled, inorganic structure. It was still possible to identify some natural features, such as a head, a breast or a shoulder, but beyond that the anatomy was abstracted to a point where specific parts of the body could not be separated from the general shaping of the piece.

While the human figure was being subjected to varying degrees of abstraction, landscape was also receiving a

'Sculptors were... presenting nude figures in varying degrees of abstraction without ever losing sight of their organic nature.'

Right Arp, *Human Lunar Spectral*, 1950.

similar treatment. The English landscape artist Graham Sutherland responded to rocks, stones, tree stumps and thorn trees with the same metamorphic joy that Henry Moore approached the human body, transforming them into iconic images. In this respect Sutherland was unusual because landscape artists are usually overwhelmed by the visual impact of their subject matter and feel little need to subject it to any great degree of abstraction. Sutherland, however, saw the botanical and geological elements of the scenes before him as a starting point for the creation of dramatic new shapes.

In these works of the 1930s and 1940s, the process of organic abstraction is a partial one. It is still possible to recognise the objects that are being transformed. In this respect they do not go as far as Kandinsky's early watercolours where the sources are no longer discernible and the process of abstraction is complete. But Kandinsky's vision was about to take a new leap forward, thanks to the Armenian who called himself Arshile Gorky. After a harrowing escape from his home

Right Sutherland, *Thorn Head*, 1947.

country, Gorky managed to reach New York in 1920. As the years passed, he was able to establish himself as an artist there. Gorky was fascinated by Kandinsky's early abstractions and began to make his own versions in the 1940s, some of which were very large oils.

Gorky's paintings were greatly admired by a group of young American artists in New York. This admiration proved to be the trigger that set in motion a whole new school of painting – the American Abstract Expressionists. They achieved the unthinkable, in that they transported the creative centre of the modern art world from Paris to New York. Up until the 1940s the dominance of Paris had been unchallenged, but World War II ended that. Most of the avant-garde artists fled the violent chaos of Europe and settled as refugees in New York. There they were welcomed by Gorky and, although resented by some local American artists, their influence was inevitable. A new era in modern art was about to explode, with huge canvases being painted by a whole stable of newcomers including the Dutch-born artist Willem de Kooning. He had arrived in the United States as a 20-year-old

Right Gorky, *Untitled,* 1944.

Right De Kooning,
Montauk III, 1969.

stowaway and shared a studio with Gorky, rapidly coming under his influence.
Kooning's violently frenetic canvases were never finished. He went on working and
working them, the action of applying the paint for him being more important than
the finished result.

De Kooning took a step back from Gorky's total abstraction, using the female
form as the basis for his wildly aggressive brushwork. Attacked as a 'sexist pig
who… makes women look like crazed gargoyles', de Kooning is quoted as saying:
'Art never seems to make me peaceful or pure. Beauty makes me feel petulant.
I prefer the grotesque. It's more joyous.' De Kooning eventually abandoned the
human figure and turned to a frenzied form of total abstraction, bringing him more
into line with the other Abstract Expressionists working in New York.

Viewing the work of the American school of Abstract Expressionism objectively,
it has to be said that very little skill was involved in the making of their paintings.
Each artist had to find a signature device – some recognisable abstract motif –

that would identify him and distinguish him from the others in the group. Once he had achieved this he was free to enjoy endless thematic variation until he had completed enough huge canvases to provide one for each of the American art museums. It has been alleged that one artist even took the trouble to count the number of art galleries in the country so that he would know when to move on to another phase of his work.

Among the artists active in this movement, the main figures were Clyfford Still, Cy Twombly, Sam Francis, Robert Motherwell, Franz Kline, Hans Hofmann, Adolph Gottlieb, Mark Tobey and Jackson Pollock. Two of these Abstract Expressionists, Tobey and Pollock, took the trend towards organic abstraction to its ultimate extreme, with large canvases that were devoid of any focal points. Instead there was an overall pattern of extremely fine abstract detail that created the impression of a microscopic view of some kind of organic tissue. Pollock famously dripped and flicked his paint onto large canvases placed on the floor. He borrowed this idea from the German Surrealist Max Ernst, who was experimenting with dripping paint onto canvases in 1942 while a refugee in New York during World War II.

Far right Kline, *Untitled*, 1959.

Below Pollock, *Alchemy*, 1947.

For Ernst it was just one of many different painting techniques that his fertile brain invented, but when he showed it to the young American, Pollock took it up and adopted it as a lifelong preoccupation.

Pollock was an abrasive alcoholic who killed himself in a road accident at the age of 44, drunk at the wheel of his car. Although his drip paintings have been savagely attacked by many artists, critics and members of the public, it has to be said that his works have become iconic and are instantly recognisable.

The New York school's wild, large-scale experiments with colour, shape and pattern did expose their viewing public to an orgy of raw visual input, which must have made them think hard about the nature of the aesthetic experience. Many Americans, however, were deeply unhappy with the extreme degree to which their artists were taking this new trend.

A typical reaction from a gallery visitor was: 'To me most Abstract Expressionism is merely a form of juvenile doodling taken to absurd lengths.'

It has recently been claimed that the movement only succeeded because it was financially backed by the CIA, who wanted to create a contrast between the artistic cultural freedom of the USA and the suffocating straightjacket of social realism in the Soviet Union. Whatever the truth of the matter, the movement lost ground in the 1960s to be replaced by Pop Art and a return to pictorial imagery.

Irrational art – retreating from the logical world

A third way in which modern art reacted to post-photographic freedom was to retreat into the world of dreams and irrational fantasies. This move away from common sense and good taste began in 1916 at the height of World War I. A group of artists in Zurich were so horrified that the establishment could be sponsoring the disgusting slaughter of young men in the trenches and at the battlefront, that they decided to take up a philosophical position that was fundamentally anti-establishment, anti-authority and anti-war. They felt this could best be achieved by mocking, ridiculing and generally attacking anything associated with authority or orthodoxy.

The strength of this movement was that it had an important message – when society goes bad, those in charge must be told so and not allowed to make excuses for themselves. Its weakness was that it was essentially a negative movement. It was good at attacking the wrongs but not so good at putting something inspiring in their place. They called themselves the Dadaists. 'What we call Dada is a harlequinade made of nothingness…' is how one of them described the movement. 'What we are celebrating is at once a buffoonery and a requiem mass…

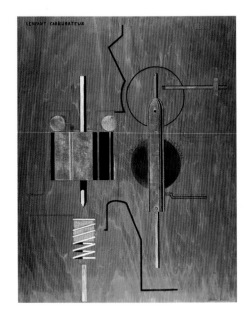

Above Picabia,
The Child Carburetor,
1919.

Above Baroness
Elsa, *God*, 1917.

The bankruptcy of ideas having destroyed the concept of humanity….' 'Dada wants to replace the logical nonsense of the men of today by the illogically senseless,' said another.

In addition to Zurich, Dadaist groups sprang up in several cities during the period 1915 to 1923. The Zurich group included the artist Jean Arp, who made some of his earliest works of art there. In Germany Max Ernst was creating his irrational collages and Kurt Schwitters his pictures made from street rubbish. In New York the Dadaists included Marcel Duchamp with his ready-mades, Francis Picabia and Man Ray.

One special feature of the Dadaist period was the introduction of an everyday object presented as if it were a work of art. The idea was to find something very ordinary and mundane, present it as if it were a valuable piece of sculpture, give it a pompous title and declare it to be great art. In this way, genuine works of art could be belittled and ridiculed in the typical Dadaist fashion. These commonplace objects were given the title of 'ready-made', or *objet trouvé*. The first person to present one as a work of art was an eccentric German performance artist called Baroness Elsa von Freytag-Loringhoven. In 1913 she took a large, rusted metal ring that she found in the street and claimed that it was a female symbol representing Venus. She gave it the title *Enduring Ornament* and said that if she commanded something to be art then it was art. Her most famous ready-made was a piece of plumbing in the shape of a sink trap, mounted on a carpenter's box and exhibited under the deliberately inflammatory title, *God*.

The baroness had a passionate attachment to Marcel Duchamp that appalled him. He had to issue an order that she was not allowed to touch his body. She would appear in public as a work of art: 'One side of her face was decorated with a cancelled postage stamp. Her lips were painted black, her face powder was yellow. She wore the top of a coal scuttle for a hat, strapped on under her chin like a helmet. Two mustard spoons at the side gave the effect of feathers….'

Baroness Elsa must have been a nightmare for Duchamp. Here was he, seriously pretending to be crazy in the service of the anti-establishment philosophy of Dada. And here was she, truly crazy and making him look like an effete poseur.

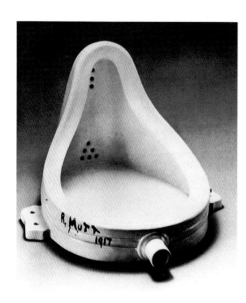

Above Duchamp, *Fountain*, 1917. (Although this work is always credited to Duchamp, he privately admitted that it was the creation of one of his female friends.)

'...anything can be made extraordinary if it is taken out of its ordinary setting.'

It is amusing to read the spluttering anger of Duchamp's biographers at the way she out-Dada-ed Dada.

The matter came to a head with the arrival of the most celebrated of all the ready-mades, a white ceramic urinal signed 'R MUTT 1917' and given the official exhibition title of *Fountain*. Presented as a serious work of art, this object caused a major scandal. The name of the fictitious artist R MUTT was a play on words in the baroness's native tongue (*Armut* in German means poverty). It appears that she gave the exhibit to Duchamp to place in an exhibition because he was a member of the show's organising committee. The rest of the committee rejected the exhibit in his absence, and Duchamp resigned in protest. The scandal was born and gathered momentum.

Today, a urinal exhibited as a work of art in a major gallery would not raise a single eyebrow, but in 1917 the public display of such an unmentionable object was considered utterly disgusting. Duchamp took the trouble to reassure his family that it was not his idea. In a private letter to his sister he made the telling admission: 'One of my women friends, using a masculine pseudonym, Richard Mutt, submitted a porcelain urinal as a sculpture; since there was nothing indecent about it, there was no reason to reject it.' Later, when *Fountain* had become famous, Duchamp pretended it was his idea and proceeded to make money out of limited editions of replicas. Baroness Elsa was unable to expose his lies. When the Dada period came to an end she returned to Europe and, in 1927, turned on the gas in her apartment, went to sleep and never woke up. Unavailable to defend herself, she was airbrushed out of the history of modern art, with Duchamp taking all the credit for her outrageous urinal *Fountain*, a work of art that has recently been referred to in reverential tones as 'the most influential item of modern art'.

Duchamp's own ready-mades were tame by comparison – a bicycle wheel, a spade and a wine rack. The earliest was a bicycle wheel mounted on a stool. Significantly, Duchamp did not call this a ready-made work of art and later commented that he simply 'enjoyed looking at it'. It was only called a ready-made some years later, after he had met Baroness Elsa.

Later, in 1919, Duchamp decided that a new way to make a strong Dadaist statement was to take the most revered work of art known to the western world and desecrate it. He took a postcard reproduction of the *Mona Lisa* and drew a beard and moustache on its face, exhibiting this artwork under the title *L.H.O.O.Q.* – a covert obscenity. He then made a second version entitled *L.H.O.O.Q. Shaved*, which showed a reproduction of the *Mona Lisa* without any modification, his only addition being the title beneath it. In this way, ridicule was heaped upon ridicule, in the Dadaist pursuit of joyfully destroying traditional art.

Regardless of who should take the main credit for the introduction of ready-mades as works of modern art, it has to be said that their influence has been enormous. Their essential message is that context is crucially important and that anything can be made extraordinary if it is taken out of its ordinary setting. Isolated in its new surroundings, placed on a plinth and beautifully lit, it is possible to view even the most mundane object in a new way. By stripping away its functional associations, the work can be examined visually in a virginal state.

Many artists have followed this trend in the years that came after the Dada revolution, and even in the 21st century new works are appearing that purport to be original aesthetic statements. In reality they are no more than latter-day re-runs of the eccentric Baroness Elsa's outrageous metaphors during the philosophical rebellion against the mass slaughter of World War I. If all those limbs could be blown off such healthy young bodies, she seemed to be saying, then it is fair game to portray God as a wastepipe.

The Dadaist movement covered the period from 1915 to 1923. After this time it developed into Surrealism, a more powerful and influential movement that would last for about 30 years and whose impact is still felt in many ways today. Like Dadaism, Surrealism was an essentially philosophical movement involving poets, pamphleteers and polemicists, but it also attracted highly talented visual artists. It is the work of these artists that has had the most lasting impact. Like the Dadaists, the Surrealists were motivated by their disgust for the establishment – an establishment that could permit the horrors of World War I. Some of the group's earliest members – Ernst, Arp and Man Ray – had been active as scattered Dadaists. They now came together in Paris under the leadership of the art dealer André Breton, who wanted to tame the chaos of Dada and organise a more systematic revolution.

Breton was inspired by Freud's studies of the human unconscious mind, and he set about defining the shape the new movement would take. Essentially, the Surrealists had to dedicate themselves to 'Pure psychic automatism… to

> '…the Surrealists were motivated by their disgust for the establishment – an establishment that could permit the horrors of World War I.'

express... the real functioning of the mind... in the absence of any control exercised by reason, and beyond any aesthetic or moral preoccupation....' Breton believed in 'the omnipotence of dreams, in the undirected play of thought'.

In other words, if rational control and conscious thought had given us a rotten society, why not try irrational freedom and unconscious imagining instead? Breton ran a tight ship and would settle for nothing less that total adherence to the rules that he laid down. There were ten of them; if you were to be a full member of the Surrealist group you:

1. **Must accept automatism and the unconscious as the mainsprings of creative activity.**
2. **Must be in favour of revolution against established traditions.**
3. **Must show contempt for all forms of religion.**
4. **Must support the communist party.**
5. **Must be an active member of a Surrealist group.**
6. **Must accept collective action and shun individuality.**
7. **Must exhibit work at Surrealist exhibitions and/or contribute to Surrealist publications.**
8. **Must limit paintings or writings to purely Surrealist exhibitions or publications.**
9. **Must not be expelled from any Surrealist group.**
10. **Must have been an active Surrealist throughout adult life.**

In the fervour of the birth of this new art movement, everyone eagerly agreed to these rules but they would soon be broken. The group was full of strong characters, and Breton's demand that they should shun individuality was asking for trouble. Like a stern headmaster, Breton began expelling unruly members while others abandoned him. Almost every Surrealist of any merit was either thrown out, walked out or disobeyed the group rules in a manner that should have seen them excluded. They all needed the education of being part of the Surrealist school, the indoctrination process giving them their lasting understanding of the key principles of Surrealist philosophy. But having been shown how to free their imaginations, members felt suffocated by their dictatorial headmaster and struck out into liberated creative worlds of their own.

Eventually Breton was left with an entourage of nonentities after all the major talents had scattered, but his importance should not be underestimated. The Surrealist movement changed the lives of all those involved, giving them the impetus to allow their art to risk new adventures of a kind never before attempted. These visual adventures were so rich that a classification of them helps to distinguish the different methods employed by the Surrealists.

Right Oppenheim, *Le déjeuner en fourrure (Breakfast in Fur)*, 1936.

Irrational juxtapositions

In this method, the separate elements of a work are familiar images taken from everyday life but combined in a provocatively unnatural way. René Magritte, Salvador Dali, Méret Oppenheim and Victor Brauner were the main proponents of this approach. All the parts of the compositions were recognisable, but they were then put together in an arrangement that made no rational sense and yet had a disturbingly powerful impact on those who saw them. By allowing their imagination free reign, the artists struck a chord with the unconscious thoughts of their audience, and surprised them with the perversity of their irrational associations. Oppenheim's haunting cup and saucer make hard ceramic into soft

Right Delvaux, *The Sleeping Venus*, 1944.

Above Fini, *The Ends of the Earth*, 1949.

Below De Chirico, *The Evil Genius of a King*, 1914–15.

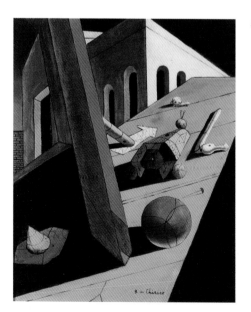

animal fur; fur into ceramic. The idea of drinking from this cup is strangely disturbing. These and many other illogical juxtapositions were popular devices for the early Surrealists.

Dreamlike scenes

Here, a precisely painted scene is infused with a dreamlike intensity. The technique is traditional and the images are recognisable, but the mood is one of mystery and ambiguity. The event being depicted is inexplicably strange and is laden with hidden meanings and unspoken dramas. In the best examples of this type of Surrealism it is possible to feel a powerful response to a painting without having any idea why. The artist somehow manages to hit an unconscious nerve and the viewer is forced to react. The chief exponents of this type of Surrealism were Paul Delvaux, Salvador Dali, Max Ernst, Leonor Fini and Dorothea Tanning.

A major influence on the Surrealist movement was the Italian Giorgio de Chirico, who was painting in this style even before the group had formed. His mysteriously haunting early work, made when he was in his twenties, was praised to the skies by the Surrealists. However, when his disappointing later work was rejected by them de Chirico rounded on his critics, calling them 'cretinous and hostile'. He angrily left the group but his impact had already been made.

'The event being depicted is inexplicably strange and is laden with hidden meanings and unspoken dramas.'

Optical illusions

With this technique, images are presented in such a contrived way that they can be given more than one interpretation. Dali employed this device repeatedly, and some critics saw it as mere cleverness. Others, however, believed that it made a significant impact by creating a visual confusion that made the onlooker re-evaluate the imagery being examined. One painting of this type shows a group of Africans sitting around their hut, but if the picture is turned on its side it becomes a portrait. Another shows a face that becomes a fruit dish or vice versa, and in the background a dog that becomes a landscape. Yet another shows three swans whose reflections become elephants.

Metamorphic distortions

Here, images are created by the irrational distortion of natural objects. Freed from any rational considerations, some Surrealists began to exaggerate recognisable elements in their compositions until they were completely out of proportion,

Below Dali, *Visage paranoïaque (Paranoiac Face)*, c.1935.

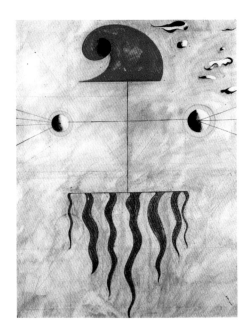

Above Miró, *Head of a Catalan Peasant*, 1925.

Below Tanguy, *Through Birds, Through Fire, but not Through Glass*, 1943.

or rearranged in an extreme way. But even at their most extreme, with these paintings it was always possible to detect the origins of the subject matter – usually human or animal forms. Joan Miró, Victor Brauner and Wifredo Lam all worked in this way.

Biomorphic inventions

This method invents ambiguous organic images that cannot be traced to a specific source but are influenced by biological principles. These Surrealists created an invented dream world where the elements were not taken directly from the external world, but nevertheless had an inexplicable validity. The main exponents of this type of Surrealism were Yves Tanguy and Roberto Matta, who created haunting private worlds that we were allowed to enter.

Automatism

With this method, the artist creates images by incorporating some automatic or accidental process. Many of the Surrealists experimented occasionally with automatic devices, but few of them made this their main form of expression. At least nineteen different automatic techniques were invented at one time or another by different Surrealists.

Surrealism was still active when World War II broke out in 1939. In a sense the movement had failed. It had been born out of a disgust for war, but the slaughter was about to start all over again. The Surrealists fled from Paris to New York to await the return of peace. When it came, there should have been a resurgence of passionate anti-establishment activity by the group, as there had been after World War I, but this did not occur. Surrealism as an active movement petered out in the early 1950s. However, although the group meetings and exhibitions ended, the influence of the major figures in the movement continued. Their imaginative imagery had a widespread impact on everything from advertising and literature to cinema and television. The word 'surreal' would eventually become common parlance.

Pop art – rebelling against traditional subjects

After World War II, advertisements became big business and the western world was soon being flooded with brightly coloured images of consumer goods, film stars and other famous personalities. In London and New York, groups of artists were looking for some way to break loose from the increasingly empty canvases of the abstract artists who had been holding centre stage for some years. They decided to hijack the commercial images and elevate them into the sphere of 'high art'. The idea was to do this in a solemn manner, as if these cheap commercial images were some new kind of sacred icon. The search was on for the most vulgar, lowbrow, hackneyed subject matter so that it could be treated as great art.

For some pop artists, their work was meant to be a sarcastic comment on consumerism. Visitors to art galleries would find themselves coming face to face with a portrait of a strip cartoon hero or an image on a food packet – they would be shocked to realise that this was what their daily world of artistic experiences had come to. Visitors were meant to see the irony of its treatment as great art. For other pop artists this mocking element was absent. For them, the elevation of popular art to the level of a museum exhibit was meant to alert the viewer to the fact that even the despised images of, say, the comic strip were worthy of serious consideration as art. Only when they were meticulously painted on a huge canvas as tall as a man and hung on a gallery wall would people realise that these lowbrow images were aesthetically significant. And there was also a feeling that by enshrining popular art in this way, the artists were creating a permanent record of the ephemera of the modern era.

Below Paolozzi, *I was a Rich Man's Plaything*, 1947.

In London, what is considered to be the forerunner of the pop art movement was a 1947 collage by Eduardo Paolozzi called *I was a Rich Man's Plaything*. It even contains the word 'POP' as though announcing the movement that was to come. As an organised trend, pop art was slow starting but by the early 1960s had made a big enough impact to reach a wide audience. 'Pop goes the easel' said a television art historian in 1962. Throughout the 1960s and into the 1970s it would attract several serious British artists, including Peter Blake, Richard Hamilton, Peter Phillips and Joe Tilson.

Despite its early beginnings, British pop art would eventually be overshadowed by its American counterpart, especially by the prolific output of Roy Lichtenstein and Andy Warhol. Lichtenstein's involvement had begun in an innocent way. His young son pointed to a Disney cartoon and said to his father, 'I bet you can't paint as good as that.' The result was a large 1961 canvas called *Look Mickey*, the first of many such works by Lichtenstein. His huge canvases

Above Lichtenstein, *As I Opened Fire*, 1966.

Below Warhol, *Big Campbell's Soup Can, 19¢ (Beef Noodle)*, 1962.

borrowed their imagery from such sources as *Secret Hearts* romances, or all-American war comics. Lichtenstein was attacked as a vulgar, empty copyist but defended himself by saying, 'My work is entirely transformed in that my purpose and perception are entirely different.'

Another American artist, Andy Warhol, worked along similar lines, borrowing examples of other people's commercial art – grocery labels, advertisements, posters – and enlarging them or colouring them up a little and selling them for large sums of money. Warhol made no apologies for what he did and is quoted as saying, 'Being good in business is the most fascinating kind of art. Making money is art and working is art and good business is the best art.' He was carrying off the clever trick of deflating the pomposity of the elitist world of fine art, while at the same time joining it himself.

At first the shock tactic of putting oversized copies of cheap commercial art into a major art museum and treating them like old masters was powerful enough to create a reaction. Could a serious artist really make a serious artwork based on a Mickey Mouse cartoon or a poster of a soft drink? Yes, they could, and the startled surprise at their humorous audacity made the initial contact with these works highly enjoyable. Pop art was much more fun than a few daubs of abstract art.

The problem for pop art was that once the shock had subsided, all that was left was the cheap commercial art that the serious artists had hijacked. As one art critic remarked, pop art was 'like a joke without humour told over and over again...'. The joke soon wore thin and by the mid-1970s the movement had started to fade away.

A related movement was junk art, in which any kind of rubbish was collected and turned into a work of art. The difference was that here the pieces of rubbish were transformed in the process, becoming elements in a composition. Although junk art was not named as a movement until 1961, it had surfaced much earlier in the work of the German artist Kurt Schwitters. He collected old bus tickets, sweet wrappers, cigarette cartons and any other bits of detritus that he could find in the street and then assembled them as works of rubbish collage that he called 'merzism'. He was the precursor of the junk art movement of the 1960s. Junk art had a better chance of creating lasting works of art than pop art because the commercial rubbish was being metamorphosed into something else. The bus ticket was no longer a bus ticket – it was now an integrated part of a composition. An oil painting or limited-edition screenprint of Mickey Mouse may have transformed the cartoon figure philosophically, but visually it was still, in both senses of the term, Mickey Mouse.

Right Schwitters,
*Merz Blauer Vogel
(Blue Bird)*, 1922.

Event art – rebelling against traditional techniques

With the disbanding of the Surrealists and the decline of the Abstractionists in the 1950s, and the demise of the pop artists and junk artists in the 1970s, young painters in the latter part of the 20th century were faced with something of a dilemma. Where could they turn? What visual rebellion was left for them?

The answer was to abandon painting and sculpture altogether, the traditional techniques that had lasted for thousands of years, and to revert instead to various kinds of event art. They gave this new departure a variety of different names – installation art, body art, performance art, conceptual art – but they all had one thing in common: the artist was no longer making a collectible object. The artefact was no more. These artists were, in effect, returning to the very roots of human art, to the celebratory moments of the primeval feast. It was all they could do, because the modern chemical and electronic technologies – photography, cinema, television – were absorbing so much of the new artistic talent. Visual creativity had moved on with the latest technological advances of computer-generated imagery and high definition, and the old world of the painted picture or the modelled sculpture was finally dying on its feet.

Once installations and events had gained momentum, it became an exciting challenge for an artist to find some novel way of involving people in a work of art. Some turned to strange lighting effects and haunting sounds, others to bizarre environments through which the visitor had to walk. The Japanese artist Yayoi Kusama, who was famously obsessed with dots, created dramatic spaces through

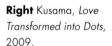

Right Kusama, *Love Transformed into Dots*, 2009.

which people could stroll, completely enveloped in a cocoon of bright colour and pattern. Large-scale outdoor events were executed by the artists Christo and Jeanne-Claude, who became famous for wrapping large buildings.

Some artists used their own bodies as works of art. The French artist Orlan creates what she calls 'carnal art'. 'Lying between disfiguration and figuration,' she said, 'it is an inscription in flesh.' Her studio was an operating theatre where she had herself filmed being disfigured in the cause of art. Cheekbone implants placed under the skin of her forehead turned her face into a unique visual image. An even more extreme example of carnal art is the Mexican Maria Jose Cristerna, who calls herself Vampire Woman. She has had multiple horns implanted into her head, implants embedded on her chest and arms and even implanted teeth to give herself vampiric fangs.

Other artists have used their body fluids to create revolutionary works. Andres Serrano exhibited a Christian cross made of blood, and he also placed a crucifix inside a perspex box full of his own urine. Called the *Piss Christ*, it caused outrage among devout Christians and his exhibit was vandalised in Sweden, France

Right Christo and Jeanne-Claude, *The Pont Neuf Wrapped*, 1985.

Above The human body as a work of art: the Vampire Woman of Mexico.

Below Serrano, *Madonna and Child II*, 1989. Figurine in luminous amber liquid.

and Australia. Serrano's work provokes controversy. It has been claimed that his later, less well-known work *Madonna and Child II* is also submerged in urine, but Serrano has never confirmed this to be true.

Some installations employ other liquids. British artist Richard Wilson filled a gallery room with hundreds of litres of sump oil, so that when you walked into a passageway that extended into the middle of the black oil-lake, all you saw at waist level was a shiny black, completely still surface. The knowledge that if the wall collapsed you would be drowned in a flood of thick, black oil gave the exhibit a sinister impact. Standing there was described as a 'disorientating and mesmerising experience… confounding physical logic'.

Certain installation artists go to great physical lengths to create their work. A Colombian artist, Doris Salcedo, went to the trouble of stacking 1,550 old chairs between two buildings. It was said that her work 'functions as political and mental archaeology, using domestic material charged with significance'.

Such high-minded phrases underline the weakness of much installation art. If we gaze at Goya's *Disasters of War* or stand in front of Picasso's *Guernica*, we are in no doubt that we are witnessing the victims of violence. We do not need to have this explained to us. If Salcedo's chairs were ones to which victims of violence had been tied and tortured then yes, the great pile of the now empty chairs would have a massive, sinister impact. But anyone coming across her installation and knowing nothing about her symbolic intentions would see only a pile of old chairs.

The truth is that the success of installation art depends on one thing: the originality of its oddity. No amount of accompanying philosophising will save it if it lacks outlandish originality. If Salcedo's 1,550 chairs look like builder's refuse they will fail as a work of art. If they look similar to builder's refuse but in some strange way different from it, they may succeed. We will remember the image and, if the installation has been a success, the oddity and novelty of that image will haunt us. Salcedo's most notorious installation, called *Shibboleth*, consisted of a crack in the floor 167 metres long, 1 metre deep and 25 centimetres wide, zigzagging the length of the Turbine Hall at Tate

Right Salcedo,
Shibboleth, 2007.

Modern in London. Some visitors fell into it, believing it was painted on the floor. Fifteen people were injured during the first month.

Some of the best installation art contains genuine visual surprises, some of which are brief and others more lasting. Creating new surprises is an increasingly difficult challenge, however, because each one must be unique or it will fail to be a surprise. Because of this, like other art movements before it installation art will soon fade into history to be replaced by something else. In the meantime, artists are being driven to ever more extreme measures.

In Sweden an installation called a 'genital mutilation cake' showed a life-sized human body, the head of which belonged to the artist, but the torso of which was a large black cake with a red filling. Visitors were invited to cut a slice of this cake and every time they did so the figure screamed in pain. Although it was intended to make a statement against female genital mutilation in Africa, the installation was mistakenly deemed to be racist and the art museum received bomb threats.

'Perhaps when the excesses of vast installations, decaying materials and dramatic light and sound have all been explored, we will see a return to a more modest scale...'

Perhaps when the excesses of vast installations, decaying materials and dramatic light and sound have all been explored, we will see a return to a more modest scale – to works of art that, while employing entirely new techniques, are once again suitable for adding to the collections of those who wish to enjoy the company of extraordinary objects in their ordinary environment.

Super-realist art – competing with the camera

It would be wrong to conclude this quick dash through the phases of modern art without a brief mention of those who have rebelled against the great rebellion. Some artists have continued to paint traditional, representational art as though nothing had changed. Many amateur artists still enjoy painting their landscapes and portraits, and a few professionals have also done so. There is still a small demand for official portraits, and although these are usually run-of-the-mill a small number of skilled portraitists have continued to face the challenge of recording the precise appearance of their sitters at the same time as capturing the nuances of their personalities. Both Salvador Dali and Graham Sutherland occasionally accepted a commission to do this and, momentarily, allowed themselves to forget their other, better known work.

Dali painted several straight portraits of people who were obviously important to him, either as patrons or in some other way. Although accomplished, his straight portraits are strangely stilted and lack his normal fluency. Unlike Dali and Sutherland, who only briefly interrupted their serious work to paint a few lucrative portraits, there were two 20th-century artists who remained doggedly stuck in the past as lifelong portraitists: the British artist Lucian Freud and the Italian Pietro Annigoni. The grandson of Sigmund, Freud became the highest-paid artist in the world in his later years, despite the fact that his portraits had become increasingly unflattering for the sitters. His roughly applied paint exaggerated every flaw. His early portraits, however, were as penetratingly precise as his late ones were heavily textured and ugly.

The Italian Annigoni was a throwback to earlier years – a formal court portraitist with great technical skills and little regard for the dramatic changes that were taking place around him in the fine arts. His portraits of the British royal family made all other 20th-century examples of this genre look rather ordinary by comparison.

Below Sutherland, *Somerset Maugham,* *1949.*

Apart from these occasional, commissioned portraits there was another strange genre of representational painting that was flourishing quietly in the corners of the art world during the 20th century. This genre has been given a number of titles: photorealism, super-realism, new realism, sharp-focus realism or, in the 21st century, hyper-realism.

The aim of photorealism is to make a painting with such meticulous skill that it is impossible to distinguish it from a photograph. All the merit is in the skill. It would be much easier to exhibit a colour photograph of the subject, but these artists are defiantly refusing to accept the camera's new dominance as the modern device that records the external world in all its precise detail. Hyper-realism goes a step further. While simulating precise photographic images hyper-realists also try to improve on them, but without interfering with the realism of their appearance.

Roberto Bernardi is a young Italian photorealist whose still-life studies were begun in earnest in the 1990s. Starting with photographic information, his finished works are made using the traditional technique of oil paints on canvas. Paul Cadden is a Scottish artist from Glasgow whose pencil drawings are so realistic that they appear to be black-and-white photographs and it is hard to believe they are drawn by hand. Each one takes up to six weeks to complete.

In purely technical terms these paintings and drawings are among the most astonishing ever created. But it has also been argued that there seems to be little point in them, creatively speaking, since they add little to what the camera can do. One sculptor who works in this genre, British-born Vancouver artist Jamie Salmon, is aware of this problem and has

Right Bernardi,
Cerchi Per Fetti,
2006.

Right Cadden,
After, 2013.
Pencil drawing.

devised a way to give his work a heightened reality. He does this by making his figures more than life-size. In this way, although their details are aimed at total reality, they have a presence at close quarters that gives them a powerful impact.

The London-based Australian sculptor Ron Mueck works in a similar way and has taken this process much further. Mueck creates huge figures that retain the precision of their details despite their size. His self-portrait *Mask II*, which shows his sleeping head, is three metres long.

To sum up the 20th century, when the camera advanced to a point where the burden of recording history was lifted from the shoulders of the artist, painting and sculpture began to change rapidly. One trend saw the simplification of complex organic shapes into their underlying geometric structure. The early experiments with Cubism led on to hard-edge abstraction and eventually to a completely blank canvas.

A second trend saw another form of abstraction in which organic complexities and irregularities were retained, but with less and less reference to specific subjects in the external world. This trend led eventually to intricate overall patterns lacking in any focal point.

A third trend saw a retreat from the rational world into the realm of dreams and the unconscious mind. This movement was concerned more with content than style and employed a wide variety of techniques – from the traditional to the outrageous – to achieve its goal.

Right Mueck, *Mask II*, 2002.

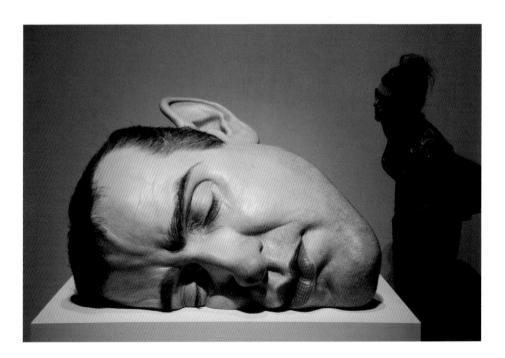

'...in most of these trends there was a tendency to become more and more extreme until eventually no further development was possible.'

A fourth trend saw a rejection of the typical subject matter of the visual arts and a pillaging of popular culture for its vibrant, if vulgar, imagery, which now became perversely elevated to the level of fine art. In its extreme forms, even society's refuse was used and transformed into works of art.

A fifth trend saw a rejection of painting and sculpture as the means of expression and a return to the primeval form of human art – the event. The art object was replaced by the art occasion, when the creative act became an event, a happening or an installation to be experienced on a special occasion. This ranged from extremely complicated environments to starkly simple ones, reaching its climax in 2012 with an exhibition of invisible art where visitors were offered a completely empty gallery. The only visible items in this last show were the labels explaining the nature of each type of invisibility. In one empty room, air conditioning units blew moist air into the gallery. The label explained that the water providing the moisture was originally used to wash the dead bodies of the victims of a drug war. In another room, a glowing white surface was said to have been created by allowing a horse to project its psychic energy onto the empty picture. This will be a hard act to follow for those seeking to be the most extreme exponents of event art.

Finally, there were those who rebelled against the rebellion and insisted on perpetuating the traditional role of the visual arts, that of recording the external world as precisely as possible with paintings and sculptures. Like the other modern art movements, even here there was a tendency to go further and further until at last, with dazzling skill, these artists ended up creating works that were so faithful to their subject matter that they looked exactly like colour photographs.

It is significant that in most of these trends there was a tendency to become more and more extreme until eventually no further development was possible. Geometric art ended with a completely blank canvas. Organic art ended with a mass of undifferentiated squiggles. Pop art ended with a heap of rubbish piled up in the middle of a gallery. Event art ended up with an empty gallery. And representational art ended up with such a precise copy of the external world that it could go no further.

Each trend had reached the end of its road, and the future lay elsewhere. So much has been tried in the past century that the future would now seem to be in the hands of the individual eccentric, the artist with a highly personal view of the world who can set aside the battle for visual freedom that was so comprehensively won in the 20th century.

10 Folk Art

Scan page to view video

Folk Art

UNEDUCATED ART IN AN EDUCATED WORLD

In modern times, the visual arts have split into three branches: the fine arts of painting and sculpture; the applied arts of architecture, interior decoration, industrial design, high fashion and landscape gardening; and folk art. Folk art can best be described as the traditional arts of down-to-earth working people in a world of trained art specialists and connoisseurs. Until the 19th century folk art was dismissed as peasant art and was completely ignored by educated society.

With the arrival of the Industrial Revolution folk art came under threat, and scholars suddenly realised that a valuable art form was facing possible extinction by the grim urban spread of factories and slums. Serious attempts to study folk art began, and today many museums collect and exhibit it. It may still be looked down upon by the professional worlds of fine and applied arts, but it is at least recognised as a valuable form of human creativity and, as such, has some special qualities of its own.

> 'The very existence of folk art is another demonstration of the deep-seated human urge to make our environment more visually exciting.'

The very existence of folk art is another demonstration of the deep-seated human urge to make our environment more visually exciting. The artists are largely anonymous and their work is not made for sale. It is true that we may find examples in antique galleries today, or being offered at auction, but that has nothing to do with the reason why they were made in the first place. They were created originally for the personal satisfaction of their owners.

The purest form of folk art is made by individuals for their own use or display, with no money changing hands. In some cases, however, particular folk artists excel in their work and others will go to them to acquire examples. This work is edging towards professional art, but it can still be classed as folk art if it is confined to the local community and follows local traditions. A village may have an expert woodcarver or metalworker, for example, whose work is acquired by other members of his or her community, but this is a far cry from the commerce of large-scale applied arts or the fine arts. The key difference is that these neighbourhood experts follow the local traditions unseen elsewhere, while ignoring the general trends and art fashions of the wider world.

> 'To the connoisseur's eye, folk art may seem fussy and overworked and lacking in elegant restraint.'

Folk art falls into six main categories. The first is textiles: costumes and soft furnishings. The second category concerns homes and their contents: external house decoration and internal decoration. The third concerns decorated vehicles, from ox-carts to art cars and from trucks to taxis. The fourth is wall art, from graffiti to street art. The fifth is festivals, from carnivals to flower pageants. Finally, there is the special category of folk painting, where untutored artists take up the paintbrush and paint for themselves in a manner that pleases them, ignoring the dictates of fine art connoisseurs. Their work is sometimes called naïve art, or outsider art, and in a few instances has become so famous that it has edged its way into the world of professional art.

In almost all these cases, two special qualities are almost always present: elaborate embellishment on the one hand, and painstaking craftsmanship on the other. Minimalist folk art is virtually a contradiction in terms. To the connoisseur's eye, folk art may seem fussy and overworked and lacking in elegant restraint. But to the folk artist its 'fussiness' and complexity are all part of demonstrating the need to make the daily environment as different as possible from the austerely drab and practical.

Textiles

A recent discovery of dyed flax fibres from 30,000 years ago has forced us to rethink the importance of textiles in prehistory. The wild flax fibres, found in a cave in the foothills of the Caucasus in Georgia, had been twisted, knotted and dyed black, grey and blue. There is other evidence that by 27,000 years ago, weaving was already quite complex and the human skill of textile making was already well advanced. We know this from the imprints left by textiles on clay. However, the earliest surviving actual fragment of cloth is only about 7,000 years old; it was found in Egypt where the dry, sandy conditions helped to preserve it.

As the centuries passed, the ancient practice of textile making became more and more skilful and the results, from elaborate costumes to huge tapestries, more and more impressive. With the Industrial Revolution, machinery took over the role of urban textile production and handmade textiles became a minor luxury. The age of jeans and T-shirts had arrived, and with it the loss of a major art form. Instead of spending hours making their own clothes and furnishings, people bought them ready-made. What would once have taken them weeks or even months to complete, was now reduced to a quick shopping trip.

This change did not entirely remove all aesthetic judgements, but it severely blunted them. The materials on display in the shops were not all identical – there were different colours and styles to choose from – but these were the styles imposed on people by the manufacturers. Local customs and personal preferences were overwhelmed by commerce. There were, however, pockets of stubborn resistance to the advance of this industrial juggernaut. All over the world, communities existed where ancient textile traditions were somehow kept alive. Pride in special skills refused to let them die. These cases of textile folk art are still with us today, and a few examples will show just how well they have managed to survive.

'Local customs and personal preferences were overwhelmed by commerce. There were, however, pockets of stubborn resistance to the advance of this industrial juggernaut.'

The three types of textile art that exist today are the mass-produced, machine-made textile; the handmade textile that is made for sale to others; and the handmade textile that we make for ourselves and is not available for sale. The fact that the third type exists at all in the modern world is remarkable and reflects, yet again, the basic human urge to make art. The second type – handmade art for sale – tells us that those who will not go so far as to make their own, will nevertheless pay extra for a handmade work of art. As artists, they may be passive rather than active, but they at least have not abandoned this particular area of artistic expression.

One of the sad features of handmade art for sale is that once a local community discovers that it has something of monetary value, it is usually tempted to start making quick examples for sale at the expense of quality. Fortunately, some communities make a distinction between textile art for personal use and art that is for sale. The tourist art may be degraded to increase earnings, but the personal art still maintains high standards. Eventually, however, even these high standards are lowered when the folk artists discover that discerning collectors only want the personal items and ignore the cheaper tourist ones. This raises the quality of the products, but there are still problems because the folk artists, although now working more carefully, will try to please the collectors by modifying their styles. They will add flowers and birds where once there were only geometric patterns, and they will make their colours more garish if they think the products will sell better. In other words, their aesthetic decisions are no longer strictly personal and one sees what has been described as the 'Disney-fication' of a sensitive folk art style.

One of the most remarkable survivals of a complex folk art form is found in Guatemala with an article of female clothing called a *huipil*. It is like a huge shawl or poncho with a hole in the middle, and the wearer throws it over her head. Its intricate geometric patterns carry a great deal of information about the wearer. Every village has a different style, so to a trained eye it is possible to tell exactly where the *huipil*-wearer comes from. But this is only the beginning. Her *huipil* will also identify her social and marital status, her religious background, how wealthy she is, whether she has any particular social authority and, finally, even her individual personality. It is as though she carries her whole CV on her body for everyone to see.

It is probably because the *huipil* carries this mass of information that it has managed to survive into the modern world. Its information and visual appeal have, quite literally, been interwoven in a masterful way. Comparing a group of these textiles from different villages, it is easy to see how inter-community competition can keep such an art form alive and maintain its high quality.

Moving south from Guatemala, a very different kind of folk art is to be found on the San Blas Islands off the north coast of Panama. Here the Kuna people, although officially Panamanians, have kept themselves as isolated as possible from the culture of the mainland. They have stubbornly refused to give up their traditional ways and have so far refused to accept attempts at modernisation. This resistance will probably not last, given the attractions of modern life, but for the moment the folk art of the San Blas Islands is still much as it was long ago. Its main feature is a pair of decorative panels that women wear on the front and the back of their blouses. These panels, called *molas*, are handstitched, employing a technique called reverse appliqué. They take several weeks of intensive work to complete. One expert has calculated that the best *molas* require 250 hours of sewing. Girls start making *molas* at about the age of seven and are usually proficient by the time they marry. From two to five layers of cloth are placed on top of one another and then holes, slits and shapes are cut in these layers to reveal the colours underneath. This negative process can be enhanced by the final addition of embroidery for fine details.

Below A traditional *huipil* from the Guatemalan village of San Juan Cotzal.

Unlike the Guatemalan *huipils*, where geometric patterns act as symbols, the *molas* avoid any kind of symbolism. It is true that early ones were often abstract patterns and that kind are still made occasionally today, but the abstract patterns are just that – they do not carry any secret messages. By far the most common subject for a *mola*, however, is some kind of pictorial depiction. A random survey of 2,000 *molas* revealed that almost half focused on natural history subjects – largely the animals and plants that the Kuna artists see around them. And they were not restricted to just a few favourites, but covered a wide range of species, a rich bestiary from insects to whales and a colourful flora from seeds to trees.

When designing a *mola*, a natural form is chosen as the main subject and then treated with a creative freedom that exploits and exaggerates the special features

Below A Kuna Indian *mola* with a crab motif.

Top A Kuna Indian *mola* showing embryos attached by their umbilical cords.

Middle A Kuna Indian *mola* depicts Christ in his tomb with an escape ladder and lamp.

Bottom A Kuna Indian *mola* of a jazz drummer.

of the particular animal or plant. There is no attempt at precise representation. A pleasing shape is more important than anatomical accuracy. There is no attempt to show perspective, a realistic scale or a landscape setting. The major motifs may be joined by minor ones that help to improve the composition, and any blank spaces left over are covered with a filler pattern of short lines, small coloured triangles or some other simple geometric unit.

The subject matter of Kuna *molas* is full of surprises. What other form of folk art would depict a pair of human embryos inside the womb, attached to their umbilical cords? The fact that the cords themselves, in isolation, are considered worthy of their own *mola* is also remarkable, but this is to some extent explained by the birthing customs of the Kuna people. When a Kuna woman is about to give birth she is moved to a special birthing hammock with a hole cut in it, through which the baby will fall. Beneath the hole is a wooden canoe full of water to break the baby's fall. Once the newborn baby has landed safely, the midwife steps forward and chews through the umbilical cord in two places – one near the baby and one near the placenta. The length of cord that is removed in this way is considered important and is buried beneath the woman's own hammock. It is therefore a valued object with which all the Kuna are familiar, and justifies its place, proudly displayed in a *mola*, worn on the chest of a Kuna woman.

One of the most remarkable features of Kuna folk art is that instead of being corrupted by the western images that have intruded onto the San Blas Islands, it has been strong enough as an art form to do the corrupting itself. Whether it is a Bible story or a photo seen in a magazine, the art has been adapted to the Kuna way of seeing the world and made into just another Kuna image.

The Kuna people have obviously enjoyed listening to the tales of missionaries, but appear to have seen them as appealing fairy tales to be freely interpreted. Where modern imports such as advertisements and magazines are concerned, the Kuna have been equally playful. They have transported everything into the colourful Kuna world and cheerfully distorted it to blend in with their special style of textile art.

Right An Uzbek *suzani* showing subtle variations in pattern detail.

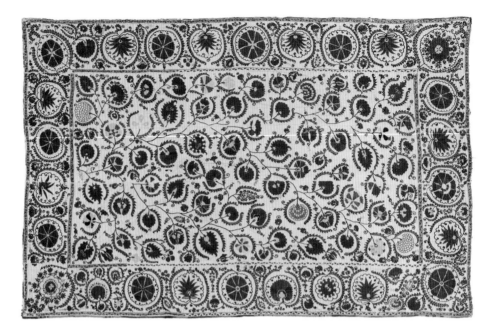

On the other side of the world, in Uzbekistan, the most admired form of local folk art is the *suzani*. The word means 'needle' in Persian and refers to a large, meticulously embroidered panel of cloth used as a decorative bedthrow, table covering or wall hanging to bring warmth and colour to a room. In recent years there has been a remarkable revival of this old traditional art form, which suffered badly during the 20th century under a ban by narrow-minded Soviet rulers. When the Soviet Union collapsed and Uzbekistan regained its independence in 1991, the old *suzani* tradition could come out of hiding. By the end of the 20th century, the western world had rediscovered the Uzbek *suzani* and the old patterns and techniques were once again being lovingly revived.

In earlier days, before the ban had been imposed, the creation of a *suzani* began with the birth of a daughter. It continued, with the help of family and friends, until the daughter was about to be married, when it constituted an important part of the bride's dowry. The elaborate design of the *suzani* was made by the village elder. She would make her drawing on a collection of four or six loosely attached strips. Once finished, the strips would then be separated and one of them given to each member of the family or to close friends. Because each embroiderer worked independently of the others, slight variations between the strips occurred. Some individuals could not resist introducing personal touches and embellishments, resulting in attractive irregularities in the overall design. Colour intensity could also vary from strip to strip as the dyes used were not always standardised, creating flaws that had their own strange appeal.

In one sense, this was art by accident. If the entire *suzani* had been made by one embroiderer, the various irregularities would probably have disappeared.

The patterns would have become more predictably repetitive, giving us what is known as 'pattern redundancy'. This occurs where, if you see one part of a pattern, you can guess the hidden parts. Precise repetition, over and over again, causes aesthetic boredom, and the unusual, co-operative way in which the *suzanis* are created manages to avoid this.

Suzanis were, for centuries, a strictly personal form of folk art and so were little studied by scholars. They were rarely mentioned in the writings of early merchants or travellers because they were not made for sale and were always kept inside the home as special family treasures. Only now are museums and collectors showing an interest in them.

The avoidance of pattern repetition that makes so much folk art visually exciting is sometimes less accidental that it was with the early *suzanis*. African-American quilting has a deliberately introduced system of pattern variation, giving these quilts an appealing irregularity of design that is sometimes reminiscent of the work of the 20th-century abstract artists. Although this tradition of asymmetrical patterning has become an essential ingredient of African-American quilting, it had its origins in stark necessity. When black female slaves on the early plantations were used by their American owners for spinning, weaving, sewing and quilting, the slaves would sometimes find a few moments to make quilts for themselves. To do this they had to make do with any piece of unwanted material they could find. They used scraps of cloth, bits of unwanted clothing and even feed sacks, giving their work an unavoidable irregularity of design. Later this irregularity became entrenched as a particular style of quilting and was done deliberately, even when material was plentiful.

Below African-American quilt from Gee's Bend, Alabama, USA.

In an isolated community in the small hamlet of Gee's Bend in rural Alabama, the quilt-making tradition has been continuous over many generations, right back to the days of slavery. One of the quilt-makers there commented: 'A lot of people make quilts just for your bed or for to keep you warm. But a quilt is more. It represents safekeeping, it represents beauty, and you could say it represents family history.' Such is the strength of a folk art tradition that has been kept alive in a small community.

What is remarkable about these particular examples of modern folk art is that they are now competing with the abstractions created by professional artists from the fine art world. Although the quilts are produced in a small hamlet by the direct descendants of freed slaves, they are exhibited at the very heart of modern art in museums such as the Whitney in New York. In this respect they are a testimony to the aesthetic power that lies dormant in all human beings, with or without professional training.

'Although the quilts are produced in a small hamlet by the direct descendants of freed slaves, they are exhibited at the very heart of modern art...'

Like the African-American quilt makers, the women of Tonga in the South Pacific have a deep-seated need to find some kind of creative expression. In their case it takes the form of making a decorated bark-cloth called a *tapa*. It is made by beating out the bark of the mulberry tree into thin, flat strips. Even today, the thud of the wooden *tapa* mallets is a common sound in Tongan villages, and where a group of women are working together they make a social event out of it, beating in a special rhythm. The strips they make are glued together to make large expanses of *tapa* cloth, which is then decorated with traditional designs using local dyes.

Some *tapas* are used as wall hangings or room dividers, but the most impressive ones are employed as ceremonial ground-coverings. Their size is remarkable,

Right A Tongan bark-cloth *tapa*.

Right This huge *tapa* is being prepared for the coronation of the king of Tonga.

the largest ones measuring as much as 3 metres by 60 metres. When the king of Tonga is about to celebrate his birthday, several hundred women will work together to provide him with a special *tapa* to walk on, so that his feet do not touch the ground beneath. When the king dies, a huge *tapa* is made along which his coffin is carried in procession to the royal tomb.

These five examples of a folk art involving some kind of decorated cloth – the *huipil*, the *mola*, the *suzani*, the quilt and the *tapa* – have been selected at random from the literally hundreds of different local traditions that still survive today. Each has its own special history and cultural significance. Together they show that, right outside the world of the professional arts, there exists a thriving interest in visual creativity, an interest that demonstrates itself in some form or another in every culture on earth.

In some instances, the local folk art remains an active part of the community. In others it may have been relegated to special events, such as weddings or festivals, but it still emerges when the event demands it. This is especially true of local costumes. Even the most industrialised nation can still see its pre-industrial costumes brought out on special occasions. They may lie neatly folded in a chest for most of the year, but they have not yet been completely discarded. We may have been seduced by the convenience of mass production and the comparative simplicity of modern clothing, but we cannot bear to see the end of our earlier forms of folk art. Almost every country in the world can still boast a traditional local costume that demonstrates the extraordinary attention to detail and the skilful craftsmanship that were invested when creating these impressive works of folk art.

Right Elaborate traditional costumes still worn in Vietnam by the Hmong people (right), in Greenland (far right) and in Mongolia (below).

Homes

The second major area of folk art activity concerns the home. It is true that in most towns and cities there is little evidence of folk art, but there are some striking exceptions. One of the most curious can be found in modern-day Egypt. On the front wall of some Egyptian houses a large painted scene depicts the owner's religious pilgrimage to Mecca to celebrate the Hajj. The Koran demands that 'before you die – go to the Hajj', and all devout Muslims are supposed to make this great trek at least once in their lifetime.

For many the Hajj is a daunting challenge and a major undertaking. Before leaving for Mecca Muslims are required to draw up a will, settle their financial affairs and make amends to anyone they have wronged – as if they are preparing to die. This is a wise precaution because every year several hundred pilgrims do die, usually trampled to death in stampedes that occur in the overcrowded conditions where emotions are at fever pitch.

For the rich, the journey to Mecca and back is not too difficult, but for the less wealthy it can pose a serious problem. When pilgrims do eventually manage it, they are so proud of their achievement that they want to advertise their successful pilgrimage, for all to see, on the facades of their houses. When they return home, they either paint the picture themselves or call in a local artist to help out if they feel unable to do the picture justice. Even then, this art has a rather primitive style, which gives it much of its visual appeal. The subject matter may concern an event in a foreign country, but stylistically this is local folk painting on a grand scale.

Right These modern Egyptian house paintings celebrate their owner's pilgrimage to Mecca.

The subject matter of these wall paintings usually includes the dramatically minimalist image of the Kaaba, or Cube. This is the starkly simple building at the heart of Islam, dramatically draped in black silk, around which the pilgrims must circle seven times. The paintings also often include the mode of travel employed to get to Mecca, including camels, ships and airliners. What is truly remarkable about these Hajj paintings is that they are the work of Muslim artists. Islam prohibits image making of any kind, and only geometric patterns are allowed. The painting of figures such as people or animals is strictly forbidden. Muhammad said that people who make such images will be punished on the Day of Resurrection. Yet despite this, here are huge folk art murals all over the walls of homes, in full view of the public, and the authorities have done nothing to stop them. The human urge to be creative has managed to flower even in the desert of religious suppression.

> 'The human urge to be creative has managed to flower even in the desert of religious suppression.'

Further south, it is possible to find places in tropical Africa where almost every building has been converted into a work of art. In northern Ghana, local communities have a long history of covering their houses with vivid geometric designs that are occasionally interspersed with pictorial images of humans and animals. To visitors these appear to be merely decorative, but to the women who make them they are deeply symbolic – a visual vocabulary. The artist's designs tell the world who she is. She is also making references to local folk tales and protecting herself by introducing images of pythons and crocodiles. The geometric elements include triangles, diamonds and lozenges, usually arranged in horizontal bands. Three earth colours are used – reddish-brown, black and white. They are

Right Painted mud house in Tangassogo, near the Ghanaian border, Burkina Faso, West Africa.

Above The painted houses of the Ndebele people in South Africa.

Below The decorated front doors of a Tunisian home.

covered in a water-resistant varnish obtained from the seeds of a local locust tree, giving them a life of about five years before repainting is required.

In South Africa, the Ndebele people also paint their houses using dramatic, geometric patterns. Superficially these patterns appear to be decoratively abstract, but there is in fact a secret code in operation. This house-painting tradition began in a strange way. After losing a war against the Boers, the Ndebele had expressed their grief through the symbols painted on their houses. These symbols were a secret language telling of their determination to resist the Boers. The Boer farmers did not understand the signs and allowed the painting to continue, assuming that it was merely decorative.

The painting continued as a private communication system, and any Ndebele could tell a great deal about the woman who had decorated a particular house just by looking at it. In effect, the patterns on the walls were the woman's personal prayers, values and emotions. A well-painted house demonstrates that the woman who lives there is a good wife and mother. The colours reflect the social status or the power of the home-owner. They can also be used to announce a marriage, offer a prayer or represent a current protest. In addition to all this they have to look attractive and make a strong visual impact. It is interesting that the facade of some houses is immaculate, while the door is neglected and covered in peeling paint. It is as though the frontal facade is seen as an isolated 'canvas' on which the owner can express herself. All the effort is put into creating that, and the door is ignored.

In Tunisia the exact opposite is the case. It is the front doors of Tunisian properties that are the focus of artistic expression. Each door is painted in a strong colour and most of them are covered with a mixture of protective symbols and decorative motifs. The symbols, which are intended to bring good fortune to the occupants of the house, are a mixture of personal emblems, Carthaginian signs and Muslim icons. They include signs of the Carthaginian goddess Tanit, such as fish or dolphins, and the Muslim hand of Fatima. In addition, the walls of the houses are painted white to protect them from the sun. Most of the doors are painted bright blue because, according to one scholar, the colour blue is supposed to repel mosquitoes. Others say that blue is a Tunisian symbol of happiness, prosperity and good luck, or that it reflects the colour of the sky and is therefore a symbol of heaven. Whichever is the case, it is true to say that with all their protective signs the Tunisian house-owners are taking no chances.

On the other side of the Mediterranean, in the Algarve region of southern Portugal, there are also local specialists whose services are required when local home-owners want to join in the display of their own region's version of exterior folk art. These specialists are not door-makers, however, but chimney-builders. Bizarrely, an Algarve house is judged not by the designs on its doors but by the complexity of its chimney pots. The chimney's design is described as 'the owner's signature'. As you travel around the world, it is as though each local community has chosen one particular aspect of its property to be the focus of its specialised folk art, and in the Algarve it just happens to be the chimneys.

If you are building a house in the Algarve, you will be asked 'how many days of chimney do you want?' The cost of a chimney is measured by how long it takes to construct – and the more you spend on your chimney, the greater your local status will be. Some houses have as many as four or five chimneys, even though only one is ever used – the others are decorative additions. Owners care for their chimneys assiduously, wrapping them up in plastic between April and May to prevent swifts and swallows from nesting there. The structure of these chimneys varies in shape from simple cones, cubes, prisms, cylinders and pyramids to designs incorporating intricate tracery, miniature clocktowers or houses and minarets. It is said that the idea sprang from the architectural influences of the Moors, who occupied this region centuries ago. The oldest surviving chimney in the region today, however, is said to date from 1817.

Right The chimney art of the Algarve, southern Portugal.

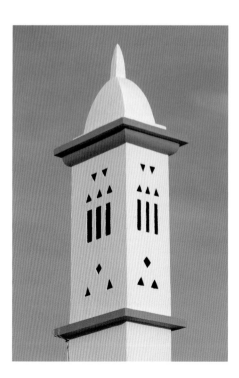
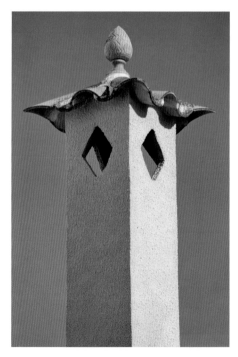

Leaving aside the external features of a home – the walls, doors and chimneys – there remains the question of the internal features, which tend to be dominated by the professional arts. DIY decorating may be popular and widespread but it rarely ascends to a level that could be called folk art. Perhaps because the interior of a house is more private, true internal folk art is seldom encountered. Where it does occur, usually some special environmental factor is at work to promote it. In countries in the extreme north, where temperatures are freezing for much of the year, the insides of houses will obviously play a much bigger role than their outsides. In Norway, for example, a particular kind of internal house-painting called 'rosemaling' can be found. It first appeared at the beginning of the 18th century when Norway was experiencing a boom period and people were looking for a way to express their new wealth in some visual form. Low-key and conservative on the outside, but warm and friendly on the inside, Norwegian houses were the obvious place to do this – and a new folk art tradition was quick to surface. The painted interiors of these houses are referred to as 'hidden gems that remain unknown to passers-by', and they became works of art of a highly characteristic kind. The painted rooms became so popular that only the poorest households displayed undecorated interiors.

The decorations were rococo in style, colourful and dynamic. Rosemaling translates as 'rose painting', and floral motifs were the dominant feature. The painting was everywhere, on bowls, boxes, chairs, cupboards, cabinets, walls

Right An example of Norwegian rosemaling.

and even whole ceilings. The designs used in rosemaling show varying degrees of abstraction, the stylised floral motifs developing into scrolls and flowing lines in blue, green, yellow, white and earth red. The work was done either by the home-owners themselves or by itinerant artists from the poorer, rural classes. These artists would travel from valley to valley, offering their services often for no more than room and board.

Rosemaling more or less died out in Norway in the late 19th century, but recently there has been a renewed interest and it has become accepted as an important rustic art form. When Norwegians started emigrating to the United States in the middle of the 19th century they were mostly from the rural districts where rosemaling was still flourishing. They kept their belongings in large, elaborately painted trunks. When their descendants inherited these examples of early rosemaling they became fascinated by the traditional designs and started a revival of this form of folk art in North America.

If it was the cold climate that forced folk art indoors in Norway, it was the complete lack of a house that had the same effect on another social group – the Romany. Living in caravans, the Romany people compensated for their cramped quarters by decorating their interiors as lavishly as possible.

Below The lavishly decorated interior of a Romany caravan.

The use of small wagons as homes by the nomadic Romany people was an idea borrowed from early travelling circuses in the mid-19th century. The Romany soon imposed their own decorative styles on the interiors, which became increasingly ornate until as a result of family competition they became iconic Romany symbols. A newly wed couple would have a specially built caravan called a vardo. It would take up to a year to complete and involve an elaborate combination of hand-carved woods, including oak, ash, elm, cedar and pine. Paintings were added to the woodcarvings, with horses, lions, griffins, floral designs and scrollwork all being featured. These added an almost overpowering richness to the decoration, aided by the liberal use of gold leaf.

'Romany decorative style was a folk art of amazing complexity and craftsmanship...'

This Romany decorative style was a folk art of amazing complexity and craftsmanship, and it is a sad fact that nearly all of it was destroyed – Romany funeral rites involved the burning of the deceased's caravan and its contents. After the motor car had replaced the horse as a mode of travel, many Romany people switched to modern trailers, and it is estimated that only about 1 per cent of them still travel in the traditional, horse-drawn, wooden caravans. Despite this modernisation, the interiors of the new trailers continue to display the Romany fascination with excessively lavish folk art decoration.

Vehicles

Another source of folk art is the vehicle – the mode of transport favoured by any particular community. It is true of course that the Romany caravan is a mode of transport but it is also a home and has been viewed as such here. When looking at non-residential vehicles it soon becomes clear that the majority, although well designed, are factory-bought and bereft of any personal touches. However, there is a fascinating minority where a huge amount of personal decoration is applied.

In Costa Rica there are the ox-carts, in Sicily the donkey-carts, in Pakistan the trucks, in Japan the *dekotora*, in Manila the jeepneys and in the United States the new phenomenon of 'art cars'. In each of these places there is local competitiveness to see who can display the most impressive embellishments, compelling some individuals to go on and on until their excesses are unmatched. The results are some of the most spectacular vehicles in modern history.

In Costa Rica the ox-cart was, for centuries, the main form of transport on the poor roads. With road improvements and the arrival of modern vehicles, ox-carts became obsolete. However, such was their visual appeal that they refused to die out altogether and have remained a cultural treasure ever since. The reason for this is the extraordinary lengths to which the cart-owners would go to compete with one another to display the most skilfully painted surfaces, especially the wheels.

The skill with which the wheels of an ox-cart were painted would reflect the

owner's personal prosperity. The local artists who did this work always painted freehand, without any mechanical aids, and their precision was legendary. This particular form of folk art started at the beginning of the 20th century, when ox-carts were essential for transporting coffee beans over the mountains and down to the coast for shipping. Each district had its own favoured designs and, even though each individual cart's decorations were unique, it was possible to tell which region it came from simply by examining its patterns.

Later, when modern transport methods were introduced, the ox-carts were kept for use in religious festivals and other kinds of public celebrations and parades. In 1988 the president of Costa Rica declared that the decorated ox-cart was to be recognised as a national symbol. Some of the best ones are now preserved as museum pieces, but a few can still be seen in use in rural districts. One of the most original and unexpected features of these carts is that each one has its own unique sound. Described as the song of the cart, this chime is produced by a metal ring hitting the hub-nut of the wheel as the cart moves along. In this way, an approaching cart can be identified even before it has been seen.

One of the most striking features of folk art is the way in which very similar traditions arise independently in completely different parts of the world. Once a functional working object such as a cart exists, it is as if the human urge to decorate its environment cannot resist embellishing the plain wooden surfaces that are in daily use. For example, the ox-carts of Costa Rica find a remarkable echo far away in the horse-carts of Sicily.

On the island of Sicily, the *carretti* used to be simple, plain, working carts drawn by horses in the cities and towns or by donkeys on the rough country roads. Before motor vehicles arrived in Sicily the carts were employed to carry not only workloads but also people for weddings and parades. As time passed these carts became more and more elaborately decorated, with every centimetre covered in carvings and painted scenes from Sicilian history and folklore. For the illiterate they even became a source of education.

'...the human urge to decorate its environment cannot resist embellishing the plain wooden surfaces that are in daily use.'

When every centimetre of space on the carts' wooden surfaces had been covered with decorative details, there was only one place left – the body of the horse. Before long, the animals were festooned with every conceivable kind of brightly coloured equine accessory. The most ancient and most important part of the *carretti* decoration is on the side panels of the cart. These display detailed historical scenes, some of them with medieval subject matter, for example depictions of crusaders attacking Arabs. Once panel painting had begun, neighbours competed with one another to see who could portray the most impressive scenes. Today the carts have become so valuable that they are no longer used for ordinary daily duties, but they are still brought out for special *carretti* parades. With modern forms of transport taking over ordinary travel duties, some Sicilians have felt deprived of their colourful vehicles and have gone to the lengths of applying the same designs to cars and small goods vehicles.

Although Sicily's horse-carts are unmatched elsewhere in the world, when it comes to decorated goods vehicles there is nothing to beat the amazing transportation trucks seen in present-day Pakistan. Here the word 'excessive'

Right A decorated donkey-cart from the Italian island of Sicily.

is insufficient to describe the lengths to which the owners of these trucks have been prepared to go to create a public spectacle, transforming the normally dull surface of a commercial vehicle into one of the most grandiose forms of all the folk arts. As one observer put it: 'They brighten up the roads like moving displays of indigenous art.'

'...the word "excessive" is insufficient to describe the lengths to which the owners of these trucks have been prepared to go...'

Today's trucks are the culmination of a long tradition of decorated transport in this part of the world. Even in the days of camel caravans the animals were adorned with tassels and garlands, good-luck charms and embroidered silks. When horse-drawn carriages appeared during the days of the British Raj, local folk artists were employed to embellish the woodwork. Later, this custom spread to include buses, lorries and trucks. Modern truck-painting began in earnest in the 1950s and is still thriving today.

Although there are some overall similarities in style, the decoration of every truck is unique. The folk artist's aim, it seems, is to cover every square centimetre of truck with designs, including the wheels, mudguards, bumpers and even the mirror frames. Special emphasis is given to the front and rear views, but the sides are also densely decorated. In addition to colourful abstract and floral motifs there are also large panels of pictorial images, often based on local celebrities and film stars. Some also carry written messages.

Right A decorated truck from Pakistan.

Nearly every city in Pakistan has its own unique decor, so that a local expert can tell at a glance where a particular truck has come from. For example, trucks from one region will be heavily trimmed with wood, those from another region with plastic, from another with beaten metal, from another with reflective tape and from yet another with camel bone. Individual truckers add their own words of wisdom to the designs of their vehicles. Amusingly, religious quotations are restricted to the front of the truck, while humorous statements such as 'Beware of lawyers' are placed on the rear bumper. So the trucks approach you reverently and leave you with a smile. Well-known celebrities are also a popular addition to the back panels of trucks. As with the Hajj paintings on Egyptian walls, this is a striking example of pictorial images being publicly displayed in a Muslim country.

In the Far East, Japan has its own version of decorated trucks but they are very different from those of Pakistan. They are an example of a truly modern folk art. Most forms of present-day folk art can be traced far back in history, but the *dekotora* trucks of Japan did not appear until the 1970s. At that time, some fishing transport truckers in the north-east of Japan started to personalise their vehicles. In 1975 a film appeared in which one of these truckers was the central character, and after this the *dekotora* trucks became a cult with a wide following. The aim of most *dekotora* truck-owners is to add as many embellishments to their vehicles as they can without making it impossible to drive them legally on the road. A few fanatics have ignored this rule and have gone so far with their modifications that their trucks can now only be admired at special exhibitions.

Right The dramatic *dekotora* trucks of modern Japan.

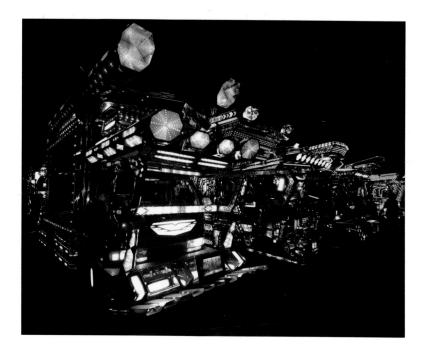

Right Jeepney decoration in Manila, the Philippines.

Stylistically, the Japanese 'art trucks' have more in common with robotics and science fiction than any other form of folk art. With their glaring, angular metalwork, they make the decorated Pakistani trucks look quaintly old-fashioned. Alternatively, it could be argued that the Pakistani trucks make the Japanese ones look armoured and defiantly aggressive. Whichever view one takes, it has to be admitted that the amount of time and energy put into these two remarkable types of folk art is truly astonishing. It yet again provides support for the idea that a deep-seated aesthetic urge lurks inside every human being, seeking some kind of outlet.

'Stylistically, the Japanese "art trucks" have more in common with robotics and science fiction than any other form of folk art.'

In the Philippines, the passion for decorating vehicles has taken a different route. Instead of employing huge trucks as giant canvases on which to impose a local form of folk art, the inhabitants of Manila have focused their creative attention on army jeeps. When the US Army departed the Philippines at the end of World War II, it left behind a number of surplus jeeps. These were converted into local taxis carrying about six passengers. As the years passed, more and more modifications were made until the jeepney, as it was now called, had been stretched backwards into a technicoloured minibus carrying as many as eighteen passengers.

The jeepney became festooned with eye-catching decorations as it grew in length, each minibus vying with its rivals to display the most outlandish adornments. It is perhaps as well that they were attractive in this way because in other respects the jeepneys were deeply unpleasant. One rider vividly describes his experience: 'It is a can of sardines. You travel shoulder-toarmpit, back-to-chest, shoulder-to-shoulder, elbow-to-hipbone, unavoidable thigh-on-thigh intimacy, buttocks accommodating forward to the seat's edge as another squashes back to mould into tight spaces.' In the case of the jeepneys, it seems, beauty is only skin deep.

Before leaving the subject of folk art vehicles, there is one unusual example that deserves mention, not so much for what it does as for what it fails to do. This is the 'art car' obsession that has emerged recently in the USA. There are now annual parades in Houston of as many as 250 personalised vehicles that are driven in procession through the streets. They come from 23 states and what they fail to do, unlike all other folk art forms, is to create a genre of unique-but-similar creations. The artists involved appear to have been working more or less in isolation from one another, each one producing his or her own individual display. The artists do not share any recognisable style, nor any of the thematic variation that is typically seen in folk art. The only feature they have in common is that they start out with ordinary road vehicles and then proceed to distort, deform and metamorphose them into something else.

It cannot be denied that art car creation is folk art because it is done by ordinary people, not by professional artists, and for their own satisfaction rather than any commercial gain. Indeed, indulging in this kind of 21st-century folk art must cost people dearly in both time and money. But perhaps because it is so new, it has yet to establish its own traditional style. Art cars reflect an American culture that is the moving force in most of the new cultural developments that are changing modern society. It is a culture that is more interested in progress than tradition, more devoted to novelty than to nostalgia, and that reveres individuality and originality.

Right Individualistic folk art in modern America – the art car.

Right Gangland district in east Los Angeles, USA.

Wall art

Public walls have provided a surface for folk artists for centuries. Occasionally these works have been made with official approval, but usually they are created without permission, illegally and on public property. When they are illicit they are referred to as 'graffiti'. They are universally hated by the authorities, who employ graffiti removal teams to obliterate them.

There are three types of graffiti. Some are pure vandalism, made as quickly and as crudely as possible and intended to deface the walls of valuable establishments. These are almost always made by disaffected young urban males, and are essentially an anti-capitalist insult written large. They are most common in poor city districts, especially where gangs have formed and taken charge of rival territories. In east Los Angeles, for example, the gangland walls are densely covered in scrawled graffiti of a primitive kind, with little attempt to create any sort of organised patterns. Similar disorganised scribblings can be seen on the walls of many cities around the world.

The second type of graffiti grew out of these early scribblings. Some of the rebel street artists began to take more care when spraying their paintings onto public walls. Instead of merely defacing property they began to decorate it. Their work was still unloved and unwanted, and frequently erased by the authorities, but the artists persisted and started to elaborate and dramatise their patterns. Little by little a distinct style began to emerge and a graffiti underworld developed.

Word spread from country to country, largely via the Internet, with the result that a recognisable 'graffiti school' was born. It was almost as though 'wall-ism' was a new art movement, created by anonymous guerrilla street artists working outside the law. When examples from different countries are compared, the stylistic similarity between them is remarkable.

The global selection of graffiti below shows examples that are based on abstracted writing. Each street artist has a code name that was originally no more than a scrawl from a black spraycan, but as the art form developed the ugly scrawls developed into increasingly dramatic and colourful designs. In most cases it is impossible to decipher the lettering because of the degree of abstraction involved. In some instances the abstraction is so extreme that the lettering is not merely distorted but completely lost. However, the fact that these graffiti all started out as lettering gives them a generic similarity. Many also include cartoon characters taken from magazines or films. When this happens the figures give the works a commercial, Disney-fied feel that nearly always degrades them.

The third type of graffiti is made by serious trained artists who have decided to use walls as a way of making public statements. Usually done with pre-prepared stencils that allow more sophisticated imagery to be placed on surfaces at high speed, this work may be street art but it is no longer folk art. This is fine art masquerading as folk art. The French artist Christian Guémy has been creating street graffiti for 20 years, specialising in portraits of the homeless as a way of reminding the establishment of their duty towards the poor.

Below A selection of graffiti examples from around the world: from Italy (top left), Japan (top right) and Hong Kong (bottom).

Top Stencilled street art by the Frenchman Xavier Prou, known as Blek le Rat.

Above Roadside graffiti on a wall in Barbados.

The reason that some artists have chosen to employ fake folk art as a means of expression seems to be that they wish to express their rebellion against the values of society. Instead of adopting outrageous imagery to make their anti-establishment statements, they have instead made their works deliberate acts of public vandalism. Their images may be traditional, but their locations are not. The main proponent of this type of street art is the Frenchman Xavier Prou, who works under the pseudonym Blek le Rat (R-A-T = A-R-T). He introduced the idea of using large stencils, and from 1981 to the present he has produced a stream of original images. His style has since been widely copied, notably by the Bristol artist Robert Banks, better known as Banksy.

With these sophisticated developments gaining ground, graffiti are in danger of losing their folk art credentials. To find modern examples that have escaped the sleek new styling and retain their primitive authenticity, it is necessary today to visit places where 'gangsta' art and stencil art have yet to penetrate. Two such locations are the Cape Verde Islands and the Caribbean island of Barbados, where it is still possible to see the kind of graffiti art that harks back to an earlier era.

Festival art

The fifth kind of folk art – festival art – takes us back to the primeval tribal feast where human art began. This is art that involves dressing up, wearing masks and transforming the home territory from its usual drab condition into a temporary wonderland of colour and pattern. Almost every culture has festivals of one kind or another, and they all involve a huge amount of artistic activity on the part of ordinary people for whom the only gain is the pleasure of participating in the special event.

One of the most common festivals is the annual carnival that takes place just before the beginning of Lent. As its name suggests, it permits one last moment of carnal pleasure before the self-denial period of Lent. Among the most famous carnivals are the ones held in Rio de Janeiro, Haiti, Nice and New Orleans. Throughout the Catholic world there are similar carnivals to these. The aim is always to achieve a greater height of vulgarity and costume excess than in the previous year. In the case of Rio, where a major carnival parade has been held for over 150 years, the excesses are outrageous. In one city, however, the carnival

Right The carnival in Nice, southern France.

Right Carnival scene in Rio de Janeiro, Brazil.

event has an entirely different look. The Italian city of Venice has a long traditional of masked balls where the revellers in this unique place opt for elegant extremes rather than vulgar ones. In fact, their feasts, parades, masked balls and costume parties all have a slightly sinister air.

A less sinister festival takes place each year in Belgium in the main square of Brussels, where a huge carpet of flowers is displayed. Flower festivals of this kind occur in many parts of the world. For their *Infiorata* held in June each year, the inhabitants of the town of Genzano di Roma, Italy cover an entire street with a floral carpet of elaborate patterns inspired by various examples of religious art. The flowers remain in place for two days, after which the whole display is demolished.

> '...the participants become engrossed in a sense of tribal belonging and group celebration.'

All over the world, the human species finds something to celebrate – almost anything will do just so long as people can re-enact the great primal feast of their remote ancestors. They usually have no idea why they are performing their particular ceremonies, but they feel a deep-seated need to express themselves dramatically in some way, abandoning their usual repetitive routines to indulge

Below The annual flower festival in Brussels, Belgium.

in a bizarre activity that is as far removed from ordinary daily life as possible.

Tradition will often give people some official reason for the festivities, and they may pay lip service to these explanations. Yet once the events are under way, these historical details are forgotten and the participants become engrossed in a sense of tribal belonging and group celebration. Briefly, here are a few examples of some of the stranger festivities.

The Spanish town of Buñol holds an annual tomato festival each August, called the *Tomatina*. Thousands of people crowd the streets, throwing tomatoes at one another until the entire town is drenched in a red mush. This began in 1945 as a brawl and occurred again the following year. It was repeatedly banned, but became more and more popular each year until finally, in 1980, it became fully established as a recognised festival.

In South Korea there is the annual Boryeong Mud Festival each summer, which lasts for two weeks and attracts over two million visitors. Mineral-rich mud, which is used to manufacture cosmetics, is transported from the nearby mud flats to create the 'mud experience'. The seafront offers a mud pool, mud slides and mud skiing, and coloured mud is provided for body painting.

In Ladakh, in northern India, the Ladakh Festival is held every year in September. Buddhist monks wearing dramatic masks dance to the rhythm of cymbals, flutes and trumpets, their actions depicting the many legends and fables of Ladakh.

In November each year, Mexicans celebrate the *Dia de los Muertos*, or Day

Below The carnival in Venice, Italy.

Below right The annual *Tomatina* festival in the Spanish town of Buñol.

Above The Ladakh Festival, India.

of the Dead, which is a festival of remembrance for the departed. The belief is that the dead are lurking in Mictlan, a spiritual limbo, and with the help of the festivities they can find their way home for a brief visit with their loved ones. It is a time of reflection about the meaning of death, which is seen as a continuation of life and therefore something to be embraced and celebrated.

The essence of all these festivals is that they provide a brief, dramatic alteration in the visual environment. A street becomes a magical parade or a carpet of flowers, a town is full of skeletons or ghosts, a whole district is turned red with tomato juice or brown with mineral mud. Suddenly everything is magnified – more colour, more patterns, more displays, brighter costumes. The ordinary is made extraordinary on a grand scale, a scale so large and so theatrical that it cannot last. It would be too much for everyday life, but once a year it can flourish and in the process release a huge amount of folk art energy.

Below Day of the Dead, Mexico.

Folk painting

The final category of folk art concerns individuals who feel an urge to express themselves on paper or canvas, despite being untutored in the fine arts. Referred to as naïve art, outsider art, Sunday painting or, in French, *l'art brut*, the work of these folk artists was always ignored in the past. Professional artists looked down on them and collectors showed no interest in them. They were not deterred, however, as their motivation was private and personal and they had no interest in selling their paintings. They were driven to create their pictures out of a compulsion to make works of art for their own sake.

Thousands of these amateur artists are working away quietly in the corners of every society. They fall neatly into two distinct groups. The first comprises those who imitate professional artists, producing modest versions of what they consider to be a valid subject, such as a landscape, a portrait, a still life or a flower painting. Their work fills the halls of local exhibitions and, although it may never make a major impact, it nevertheless provides the artists with yet another outlet for the human aesthetic urge.

The second group is made up of those artists with a strange and highly personal obsession with a particular kind of subject matter, who pursue it relentlessly and with such intensity that their technical shortcomings are no hindrance. Indeed, those shortcomings may well add to the quality of their work by making it so different from professional art that no attempt is made to compare the two. The naïve work is judged on its own terms, as a separate art form, rather than as a clumsy version of the professional work.

Right Rousseau,
The Dream, 1910.

A few of the artists in this second, idiosyncratic category have seen their eccentric work break through the barrier between the amateur and the professional art world, and have become fully accepted by major galleries, museums and collectors. The most famous of these was a French tax collector, Henri Rousseau, who began painting when middle-aged and was ridiculed by the Parisian art world during his lifetime. Born in 1844, he was a self-taught artist. He was obsessed with jungles and painted large canvases depicting them in great detail, even though he had never visited one. The nearest he came to a jungle was at the Jardin des Plantes in Paris, or in book illustrations. Today his paintings are looked upon as masterpieces and hung in museums.

In the USA, a New York clothing manufacturer called Morris Hirschfield began painting when he retired from his business. Born in Poland in 1872, he moved to the United States as a teenager and worked in a clothing factory. Eventually he was able to start his own company specialising in women's coats and slippers. Hirschfield retired in 1935 and spent the last ten years of his life painting. His pictures were strongly influenced by his lifetime's work of dealing with fabric design and pattern making. The results were stiff and full of tiny detail. In 1943, two years before he died, he was given an exhibition in New York but, as with Rousseau in Paris, his work was ridiculed and he was cruelly dubbed 'The Master of the Two Left Feet'. However, like Rousseau's paintings the intensity of Hirschfield's work was remarkable, and his paintings are now museum pieces.

Right Hirschfield, *Girl with Pigeons*, 1942.

In Britain there have been so many of these idiosyncratic naïve artists that for many years the Portal Gallery in London exhibited nothing else but their work. Known as the Portal Painters, some of these artists were so eccentric that even today there is little information about them. One was a reclusive Londoner called Fred Aris. His bizarre rendering of the story of Jonah and the whale shows Jonah stepping from the whale's mouth wearing a smart suit and carrying a briefcase. His paintings of cats reveal an intense understanding of what it is to be feline, despite the fact that the animals are given human eyes. Aris was a cafe-owner in south-east London, with no interest in the art world. He always refused to give interviews or have a solo exhibition, in case it attracted too much attention to him. Every few months he would arrive at the gallery with a new painting, check his account with them and then leave after a few moments. They had no phone number for him and could only contact him by post. Nothing is known about his private life. He wished to remain as anonymous as possible and let his meticulous paintings speak for him.

> 'All have a personal vision, and their deep-seated urge to be creative controls their lives.'

These are just a few examples of the countless hundreds of naïve artists who exist all over the world. Looking at their life histories it is clear that they all have one thing in common, namely that whether they are liked or disliked, whether their work is supported or ignored, they will not stop or modify what they are doing. All have a personal vision, and their deep-seated urge to be creative controls their lives. Practical considerations do not enter into their thinking. Like all the other folk artists mentioned earlier, they are a testimony to the human passion to make life less ordinary.

This rapid survey includes only a tiny fraction of the huge mass of human folk art that has been created – and is still being created – on a global scale. For every patterned textile, personalised house, decorated vehicle, dramatic wall-painting, multicoloured festival and obsessed Sunday painter that I have been able to include, there are a thousand other examples. All are made by folk artists who are just as passionate and just as devoted to giving their time to activities that bring them no more than personal satisfaction and childlike excitement. When Ellen Dissanayake described the human species as '*Homo aestheticus*', she had good reason for doing so.

Below Aris, *Black Tom Cat.*

11 The Roles of Art

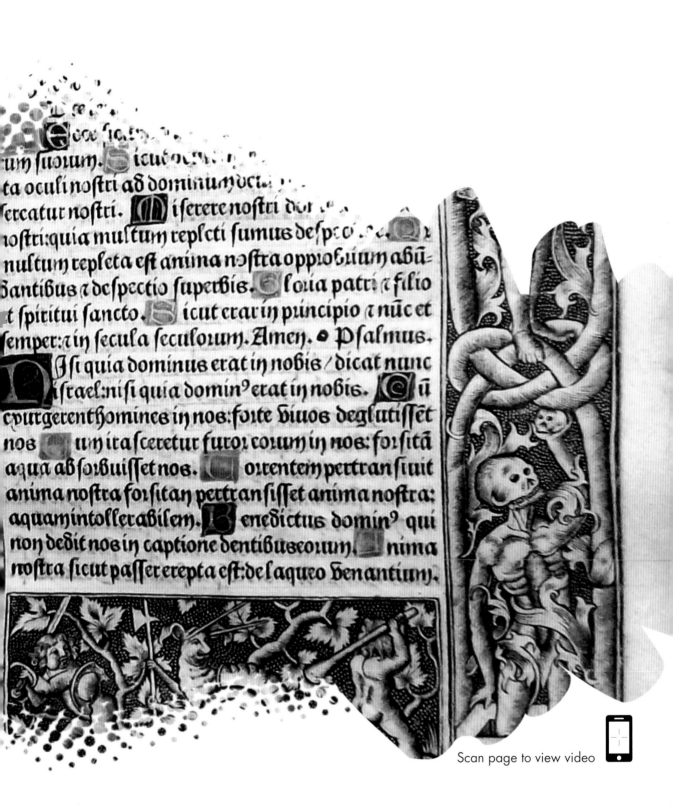

...ccc sia...
...um suorum. Sicut oc...
ta oculi nostri ad dominum dc...
...ercatur nostri. Miserere nostri do...
nostri:quia multum repleti sumus despc...
multum repleta est anima nostra opprobrium abū
dantibus ꝛ despectio superbis. Gloria patri ꝛ filio
et spiritui sancto. Sicut erat in principio ꝛ nūc et
semper:ꝛ in secula seculorum. Amen. ⚬ Psalmus.
Nisi quia dominus erat in nobis / dicat nunc
istrael:nisi quia domin⁹ erat in nobis. Cū
exurgerent homines in nos:forte vivos deglutissēt
nos cum ita sceretur furor eorum in nos:forsitā
aqua absorbuisset nos. Torrentem pertransivit
anima nostra forsitan pertransisset anima nostra:
aquam intollerabilem. Benedictus domin⁹ qui
non dedit nos in captione dentibus eorum. Anima
nostra sicut passer erepta est:de laqueo venantium.

The Roles of Art

THE NINE LIVES OF CREATIVITY

In the previous chapters I have examined art from prehistoric times to the present day. Inevitably, there have been many omissions in such a brief survey. The human species has been so productive, so creative, that to tell the whole story in a single volume is out of the question. Yet by racing through its various phases it has been possible to paint an overall picture of the nature of human artistic behaviour.

My original definition of art was 'making the extraordinary out of the ordinary', and it is clear that this deep-seated urge has been present in all cultures at all times – and has shown itself in many different ways. It has never been enough for human beings simply to satisfy their basic survival needs of eating, drinking, sleeping and breeding. They have always wanted to go further. Genetically programmed to be endlessly playful, in both childhood and adulthood, they have never stopped asking questions and trying out new ideas.

The human brain demands activity. This has been the secret of the success of our species. It is our intelligence and our inventiveness that have given us dominance, not our physical bodies. We lack the lion's jaws, the crocodile's thick hide, the cobra's venom and the eagle's swift flight. But we have this buzzing, seething brain that gave us our first spear and took us into space. When we enjoyed a moment of triumph we wanted to relish it and to make it celebratory. We danced, sang and painted our bodies in bright colours, making the occasion an extraordinary one. Out of this grew our urge to decorate, first ourselves, then our belongings and then our surroundings.

Our clothing went from comfort to display; our eating pots went from plain to fancy; our weapons went from functional to ornamental. The urge to make things look extraordinary spread and spread. This fundamental urge to make our environments more elaborate and more colourful, driven by our innate playfulness, made us into what Robert Joyce called 'the aesthetic animal'.

This primeval urge soon developed new roles. Artistic activity, which was already an end in itself, was expanded and refined in the service of other human activities. Art was used as an aid in hunting magic. It helped to make primitive rituals more impressive, and later it embellished religious ceremonies. For the rich and powerful it provided a way of displaying their social dominance. Art was stylised to become a communication system, as painted symbols became simplified into letters and numbers and writing began. Art assisted warriors in battle, making them appear stronger and more threatening.

As the centuries passed, these ancient roles began to change, and today we have even more distinct forms of artistic expression. Art is still used in the service of powerful social institutions. For centuries, religion has been a major patron of the arts, and so have the social rulers – the pharaohs, the overlords, the kings and queens and their courts, the emperors and the tsars. They have all eagerly used the visual arts to enhance their activities. Today, the patronage of the Church and these rulers has diminished, but it still exists in many parts of the world.

'There has never been such a rich supply of art forms in the history of our species, and there is no sign that the demand is in any way declining.'

New patrons of art have also emerged. The richest members of the middle and upper classes have enjoyed becoming the new benefactors. They have made great collections and built new museums and art galleries. Free of influences from the Church and from powerful rulers, they have been able to assemble works of art that are selected for their creative merit, not for their propaganda value.

These art galleries, which were originally reserved for the elite, were eventually opened to the general public. Today every major city around the world has its museums and art galleries where millions of works of art are available for visitors to view. Private art galleries, which sell works to collectors or to those people wishing simply to decorate their homes, have grown dramatically in number. New printing techniques have also made inexpensive copies of famous works of art available to everyone. In addition, folk art has continued to flourish, providing many more outlets for human creativity.

For the modern citizen, the visual arts have more roles than ever before. There has never been such a rich supply of art forms in the history of our species, and there is no sign that the demand is in any way declining. Nor would we expect this to happen, in view of our deep-seated, inborn, primeval urge to transform the ordinary into the extraordinary whenever the moment is right.

It is possible to identify nine major categories when summing up the roles of art as it impinges on the modern citizen.

Sacred art – art in the service of religion

The role of art in the service of the major religions has changed in recent times. The Christian Church, in particular, is no longer the major sponsor of great art as it was in the past. The great cathedrals, churches, chapels and other holy places almost all date from earlier centuries. Their frescoes, decorated tiles, stained-glass windows, painted ceilings and statues are hundreds of years old. However, although they are no longer being created, these works of art are still being enjoyed. Every year, thousands of visitors flock to see early examples of religious art. Most of the people who gaze in awe at the Sistine Chapel ceiling are not themselves religious, but they still respond to the skill and grandeur of earlier religious art.

When visitors enter the Gothic chapel of La Sainte-Chapelle on the Ile de la Cité in the heart of Paris and marvel at the 600 square metres of stained-glass windows installed there 600 years ago, they may no longer be capable of experiencing a state of religious ecstasy. However they are certainly, for a few moments at least, giving religious art a role in their modern lives.

Today, instead of commissioning great works of art, Christianity seems to have settled for mass producing cheap reproductions to sell to the faithful.

Below La Sainte-Chapelle in Paris, France.

These items have little aesthetic value but can be worn or placed in the home or in vehicles as a form of religious protection. In general, therefore, it must be said that Christian art is living on its past, but there are a few interesting exceptions to this rule.

One of the first of the modern artists to make a major religious statement was Graham Sutherland. His large tapestry *Christ in Majesty* was installed in 1962 at the newly completed cathedral at Coventry in England. At a height of almost 23 metres, the tapestry is one of the largest ever made. When the new cathedral opened, reaction to this modern place of worship was mixed. Traditionalists hated it, calling it a 'ring-a-ding God-box', but it also had many supporters.

In France in the mid-20th century, a number of modern artists decided

Right Sutherland's
Christ in Majesty altar
panel in Coventry
Cathedral, England.

'...a number of modern artists decided that, despite their rebellious origins, they ought to leave their mark on a sacred building.'

that, despite their rebellious origins, they ought to leave their mark on a sacred building. Whether they were religious or not, the idea appealed to their now justifiably enlarged egos. The first of the great French modern artists to undertake such a work was Henri Matisse. Between 1947 and 1951 the Matisse Chapel, as it is now known, was built to his design at Vence in the south of France. It was unusual in that this was the first time a painter had designed every detail of a religious monument, including its architecture, stained-glass windows, furniture, cult objects and even the priestly ornaments.

Not wanting to be outdone by Matisse, with whom there was always a friendly rivalry, Pablo Picasso had to have his own chapel. Although he was born a Catholic, in adulthood Picasso had become a member of the Communist Party and was therefore officially against the Church. His solution was to decorate a deconsecrated 12th-century chapel at Vallauris, which was only 13 kilometres away from the newly opened Matisse Chapel at Vence. Picasso was living and working at Vallauris at the time and decided to fill the old disused chapel with murals depicting the conflict between war and peace. In this way he could cunningly have a decorated chapel to rival that of Matisse without having to make a religious statement.

While this was happening, the French artist Le Corbusier was also hard at work making his own mark on the religious scene. He had the advantage that he was primarily an architect and so was able to bring those specialised skills to his undertaking. In 1954 his new Catholic chapel opened at Ronchamp in western France. It was a revolutionary construction in which the whole building had effectively become transformed into a huge piece of modern sculpture.

The Abstract Expressionist Mark Rothko was also involved in the creation of a controversial religious building. Known as the Rothko Chapel, in Houston, Texas, it is described as 'an intimate sanctuary available to people of every belief'. It opened in 1971 and has been officially described as 'one of the greatest artistic achievements of the second half of the twentieth century'. Viewing the chapel's bleak interior with Rothko's fourteen vast, plain black panels has not, however, been to everyone's taste. Some describe it as surprisingly peaceful, but others have called it an 'austere, dead monument'.

'While Christianity still relies largely on architectural art completed centuries ago, other major religions boast some striking new buildings...'

While Christianity still relies largely on architectural art completed centuries ago, other major religions boast some striking new buildings that demand to be viewed as sacred works of art on a grand scale. One of the most impressive examples of this trend is the Hindu Mandir Temple built in the 1990s in north-west London. In recent years Muslim artists have been busy designing spectacular new mosques in many parts of the world. In the United States alone, 897 mosques were built between 2000 and 2010. As a work of art, perhaps the most dramatic new Islamic building is the Grand Mosque in Abu Dhabi, with its 82 white domes and space for 41,000 worshippers.

Below Le Corbusier's chapel at Ronchamp, France.

Below right The Rothko Chapel in Houston, USA.

Right The Hindu Mandir Temple in north-west London.

Far right The Sheikh Zayed Grand Mosque, Abu Dhabi, United Arab Emirates.

In recent years a new form of religious art has appeared on the exteriors of religious buildings – *son et lumière*, or sound and light. It has been used to tell religious stories to large audiences. The first display of projected light of this kind was aimed at the walls of a French chateau in 1952, and the idea soon spread around the world. Religious monuments became a favourite subject for this treatment, usually with a recorded narrative to explain to the large audiences what they were seeing. Recently, in Durham, in northern England, an international light show saw the city's cathedral covered in the illustrated pages of the Lindisfarne Gospels – a modern way of displaying ancient religious images to a wide public.

Right Religious *son et lumière* display at Durham Cathedral, England.

Status art – art in the service of social standing

Below The celebration of high status in the Mughal Empire.

Bottom The Hall of Mirrors in the Palace of Versailles, home of King Louis XIV of France.

From the very earliest civilisations, the dominant members of society have displayed their high status by sponsoring great works of art. They have built palaces, royal tombs, castles, stately homes and great monuments. Then they have stuffed them full of ostentatious art treasures – sculptures, paintings, furnishings, murals, decorated ceilings, mosaics and the rest.

In India, between the 16th and 18th centuries, the courts of the Mughal Empire were full of teams of artists creating illustrated manuscripts and paintings that glorified the visual splendours of their world. Colours were intensified and perspectives ignored. Nothing could have emphasised the lavishly high status of the Mughal nobility better than these gems of miniature art.

One of the most remarkable examples of high-status art is the home of France's King Louis XIV – the grandiose Palace of Versailles. It contains over 6,000 paintings, more than 2,000 sculptures and over 5,000 *objets d'art* and pieces of furniture. In our modern, democratic era it is hard to comprehend the creation of that much art for the home of one man and his court.

Today, in the western world at least, displays of great wealth and power have shifted from bloodline royals to self-made billionaires, from monarchs to multinational corporations. To find today's high-status art displays our attention must turn away from palatial facades towards towering skyscrapers and opulent mansions. Some of the most impressive of these new buildings have become works of art in themselves, but they also frequently contain lavish displays of artwork that confirm the high status of their owners.

Usually these modern 'alpha people', or 'A-listers', are rather private in their displays. These are kept for their guests, their rival 'alphas', rather than offered to the general public.

Right The home
of the American
computer billionaire
Bill Gates.

The most expensive private house in the world cost around US $1 billion and was constructed recently in Mumbai for an Indian industrialist. The private home of Bill Gates, one of the world's richest men, is modest by comparison, costing a mere US $140 million in the 1990s. It does however have some exceptional facilities. When you enter the house, called Xanadu, you are provided with a microchip pin that has been programmed with your personal preferences. As you move from room to room, electronic versions of your favourite paintings appear on the walls, your preferred music is played, and the temperature and lighting are adjusted to the level at which you are most comfortable. If you receive a phone call, computers ensure that only the telephone nearest to you will ring. If you are watching television and you move from room to room, the programme you have selected will follow you as you go, appearing on the screen nearest to you. In the library, at a cost of US $30 million, there is a copy of Leonardo da Vinci's original notebook.

> 'As you move from room to room, electronic versions of your favourite paintings appear on the walls...'

Where buildings have been designed for less private use, some owners have felt the need to confirm that they are engaging in high-status displays. In a few cases, they have been sufficiently assertive to emblazon their names on the facades of their buildings. Donald Trump's Trump Tower in New York is an example of this, and in Las Vegas Steve Wynn has actually autographed his huge edifice.

Away from the western world, a few high-status rulers still indulge in the antique art of palace displays. The Sultan of Brunei's family home – the Palace of Light and Faith – has 1,788 rooms, 564 chandeliers, a banqueting hall for 5,000 guests, 5 swimming pools, a mosque, a garage for 110 cars and air-conditioned stables for 200 polo ponies. It is the largest single-family residence ever built.

The more common way of experiencing high-status art today is to spend a few days in a palatial hotel that mimics the grandeur of the old palaces. This is high-status art on a rental basis. The excesses of some of these new hotels are remarkable. The foyer of the Atlantis Hotel in Dubai, for example, boasts an artwork that is technically staggering but of a kind that is far too flamboyant to be found in any art museum.

One of the sad aspects of the recent development of high-status art displays is the reduced quality of the artworks inside these dramatic buildings. The royal palaces of old were rich in artworks, but today's equivalents are less so. The pseudo-palaces – the palatial hotels – cannot risk exposing serious artworks to their guests in the bedrooms and suites where there is no security. Instead all the aesthetic effort now goes into the actual buildings, which themselves virtually become the high-status art displays.

Only in the high-security private mansions of the rich and powerful are there serious status displays of important artworks. These social 'alphas' can impress their rivals with the purchase of another Picasso, thereby satisfying the demands of status art. But others wish to make a bigger impact. To do this they have to make their collections available to a wider audience, which leads us on to the next major role of art in modern times – public art.

Public art – art in the service of the general population

In earlier centuries, the only form of high art available to the general public was the religious art in cathedrals and other sacred buildings. Apart from public statues and monuments, the status art commissioned by kings and rulers would have been seen largely by their courtiers and close followers. In modern times this has changed dramatically, and both rich benefactors and governments have made large collections of art available to the public in major galleries and art museums.

'Public art is not only available to everyone, but is theoretically free of any religious or political bias.'

The English sugar merchant Henry Tate gave us the Tate Gallery in London. The American mining family of the Guggenheims gave us the Guggenheim Museum of Art in New York, Bilbao and Venice. The American oilman J Paul Getty, who was famous for saying 'The meek shall inherit the earth, but not its mineral rights,' gave us the Getty Museum in Los Angeles. In many countries, governments also contributed to the establishment of great national galleries and museums.

The opening of these art collections to the general public in recent centuries has added a major new role for art. Public art is not only available to everyone, but is theoretically free of any religious or political bias. The artworks are judged on their own merit and on nothing else. Of course, there have been exceptions to this rule, as when the Nazis or the Stalinists removed what they considered to be decadent art, but in general the lack of censorship in the realm of public art has been remarkable. In cities where there might have been a clash of opinion between those who support traditional art and those who favour modern art, the problem has been solved by having separate galleries. In Paris, for example,

Below The Guggenheim Museum of Art in Bilbao, Spain.

there are the Louvre and the Pompidou; in London the National Gallery and the Tate; and in New York the Metropolitan and the Museum of Modern Art. There are also specialist museums for tribal art and folk art.

Today we tend to take this enjoyment of public art for granted, but it would have been unthinkable only a few centuries ago. The earlier works of great art would only have been seen by a small number of privileged people. Today, thousands of masterpieces are being seen and appreciated by millions. One could not ask for a stronger confirmation of the deep-seated human need for art. The only drawback of these visits to view public art is that they are, of necessity, very brief. For longer enjoyment, another category of art is needed: collectible art.

Collectible art – art in the service of the private owner

A major role for a work of art today is as an 'owned object' – something that is an inheritance, a gift or a purchase and is kept at home as a personal possession. Collectible art is obtained almost entirely from private art galleries or auction houses. Almost every home in the western world contains at least a few such items, and serious collectors who become obsessed with a particular genre may end up with literally hundreds of works of art.

At the top end of the scale of collectors are the rare 'status art' owners who collect a group of masterpieces as a demonstration of wealth. But far more common are the ordinary collectors who buy more modest works that happen to take their fancy. At the lower end of this scale are those who buy inexpensive prints or posters to display on their walls. It is rare to find a home that has completely blank walls, which means that the sales of inexpensive artworks on a global scale must be vast.

Right *The Trivulzio Hours, 1470.*

Right *The De Brie Hours*, 1521.

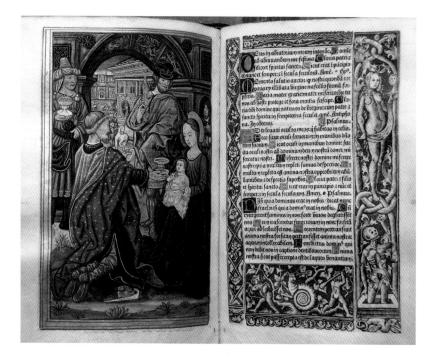

Finally, there is the 'owned art' that is collected in the form of illustrations in art books. Centuries ago, a noble family could enjoy owning a book of hours, a personal prayer book with its often unusual imagery. *The Trivulzio Hours*, for example, was made in Flanders in 1470 for the princes of Trivulzio in Milan. In addition to its traditional religious scenes it also depicts many strange secondary images, such as a monkey with blue genitals blowing on a horn and a bearded man holding a lance riding on a sheep. In other words, the artists who made these sacred illustrated books were, like the artist Hieronymus Bosch, allowing their dark imaginations to run free.

A handmade book of hours was such an exclusive product, available only to the loftiest members of society, that when printing arrived it was not long before less costly versions became available to a wider audience. An example of a printed book of hours is *The De Brie Hours* of 1521. Printed on vellum, this book follows the same pattern as the earlier manuscript volumes, with traditional biblical set pieces in colour combined with strange marginal scenes.

In the centuries that followed, the emphasis shifted from biblical subjects to the world of nature. Impressive volumes full of colour plates of animals and plants began to dominate the world of published art. This genre reached its peak with the publication of Audubon's *Birds of America* between 1827 and 1839. In the 20th century a new phase began with increasingly meticulous and technically perfected colour photographs of great works of art. By the end of the century many major publishing houses specialised solely in the production of high-quality art books.

Right Audubon's *Birds of America.*

Hundreds of these new books appeared every year, exposing a huge new audience to the visual arts. The colour plates would never be as good as the originals, of course, but they would nevertheless open the door to a vastly increased knowledge and appreciation of the visual arts. Compared with what was available to an ordinary citizen a few hundred years ago, the potential for exposure to the visual arts in modern times is staggering.

Technical art – art in the service of mass entertainment

With the introduction of scientific techniques to make visual images towards the end of the 19th century, a whole new trend in the arts was set in motion. It began with still photography, moved on to motion photography and then, with a jump from chemistry to electronics, developed from cinematography to television and from celluloid to advanced forms of computer imagery.

In today's home the oil painting on the wall, in its gilded frame, now starts to look antique, even if the picture on show is a modern abstract. In its place hangs a large, flat-screened television set, transmitting high-definition and 3D images. The computer screen provides

Below Computer-generated imagery and motion-capture animation technology were used in the film *Avatar* (2009).

another vast source of visual images through its search engines. Admittedly, many of the images displayed are what could be defined as 'aesthetically low grade', but the potential is there for any grade you care to choose.

Folk art – art in the service of local traditions

Despite the amazing advances in electronically transmitted images, and the dramatic rebellions of modern art movements, the older forms of folk art still survive in the 21st century. They stubbornly refuse to die away, and local communities continue to pursue old customs and traditions in the arts. The deep-seated desire to adorn the environment may have moved on from tribal face painting to modern tattooing, from tribal costumes to decorated vehicles, or from needlework to graffiti, but it remains a powerful form of aesthetic expression even in the 21st century.

> 'The deep-seated desire to adorn the environment... remains a powerful form of aesthetic expression even in the 21st century.'

All around the world, we can find examples of regional folk art that has changed little over the years, giving local communities a sense of identity and cultural history and setting them apart from other groups. It is true that many forms of folk art have succumbed to modern trends – when a western visitor asked a tribal warrior in a remote part of Africa to choose a gift that could be sent to him, he requested a T-shirt – but despite this many more stubbornly refuse to die out.

Right Folk art traditions survive in a Fijian village, despite a modern T-shirt.

Propaganda art – art in the service of a cause

At times of social change, unrest or upheaval, the visual arts are brought into play in a special way. They become political messages presented in the form of pictures and emblems. They are often so scurrilous that it is surprising the authorities have rarely attempted to ban them or punish the artists concerned. Outrageous political cartoons were especially popular in Britain during the late 18th and early 19th centuries, when artists such as George Cruikshank, James Gillray and Thomas Rowlandson pilloried establishment figures. The French were a favourite target – cartoons showed the downtrodden peasantry being exploited by the bloated, greedy clergy and nobility and then, after the Revolution, other cartoons showed the cruelty and vulgarity of the triumphant peasant class. In the golden age of British political satire – from 1790 to 1830 – no one was safe, not even the king.

To say that these caricatures were insulting is an understatement, but no official action ever seems to have been taken against the cartoonists concerned. Other artists with a political message were sometimes less fortunate. During World War II, when the Japanese had invaded China, Chinese banknote engravers solemnly added small anti-Japanese obscenities to their carefully crafted work. This cost one of the engravers his life. When the Japanese discovered what had been done, one engraver was tracked down and beheaded.

In the 21st century the tradition of savage political caricature lives on in the hands of artists such as Gerald Scarfe. His distortions of the rich and powerful are sometimes so exaggerated that it is surprising he has not come under attack from certain quarters. The explanation, he says, is that politicians would rather be caricatured 'as a smelly warthog than not caricatured at all'. He does find it odd, though, that some of them ask for prints of their grotesque portraits to hang on their walls.

Right Cruikshank's depiction of a royal birthday watched by the poor and homeless.

MERRY MAKING on the REGENTS BIRTH DAY. 1812.

Right Wartime Chinese banknote showing Confucius making an obscene gesture.

Although Scarfe and other modern political cartoonists seem to know no fear when it comes to making visual assaults on famous personalities, there is one figure that even they are scared of lampooning. They know that if they went to the extreme of caricaturing the Prophet Muhammad, their lives might be at risk. When a Danish newspaper carried cartoons of Muhammad in 2005, it caused an outcry that saw violent protests in which over 100 people were killed. Such is the power of political art.

Festive art – art in the service of celebrations

The birth of art, as a way of increasing the impact of tribal celebrations, has left its mark on the human species. So much so that even in industrialised urban societies, the urge to engage in colourful festivities remains a powerful form of expression. Many of the old religious festivals and ceremonies still survive and now, in addition to those, there are several major new categories, such as firework displays, sporting events, music festivals and pop concerts. Each of these has seen the birth of new visual art forms that help to transform such occasions into extraordinary experiences.

Pyrotechnic art has a long history but it was not until the 1830s, in southern Italy, that technical advances allowed the production of fireworks with bright colours – reds, greens, blues and yellows. Firework displays had always been noisy but now they could be visually appealing as well, and great public displays were devised for special celebrations. Pyrotechnic art reached its peak in 2000 with the millennium festivities and was prominent again in the United Kingdom in 2012 for Queen Elizabeth II's jubilee celebrations.

In addition to these great moments, there are also annual contests for pyrotechnic artists. Several countries are competing to be the leader in this field. In Italy there has been a *fiori di fuoco* each summer for many years, which is described as the

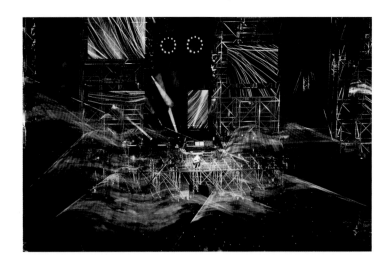

Annual World Championships for Fireworks. At Macau in the Far East the
International Fireworks Display Contest attracts competitors from Canada, Korea,
Japan, the United Kingdom, Austria, Taiwan, the Philippines, Portugal, France and
China. Great sporting events also provide a grand setting for the pyrotechnic arts, as
was obvious during the closing ceremony of the Olympic Games in London in 2012.

Spectacular musical presentations such as those of Jean Michel Jarre involve
visual displays on a massive scale, providing unforgettable images for those who
attend them. His Rendez-vous concert in Houston, Texas in 1986 had a live
audience of 1.3 million people – a world record at that time. In recent years,
performers of pop concerts take huge sets with them when they go on tour, and
music award shows also frequently bombard their audiences with imaginative
shapes and colours. Once a trend like this has started it soon escalates; audiences
come to expect a spectacular presentation, and each pop concert or award show
organiser must try to outdo the previous one.

Applied art – art in the service of commerce

One of the most ubiquitous forms of artistic expression today is commercial art –
art as an aid to selling a product. The modern world is full of designers, working
behind the scenes to make goods more visually appealing in order to outsell their
rivals. This applies especially to home decoration, furniture, household appliances,
food and drink, clothing, publications, means of transportation and buildings.

Everything in the home, from wallpaper and curtains to furnishings and kitchen
supplies, will have had a carefully designed 'visual impact' factor added to its
practical, functional qualities. A knife must not only cut well, it must have an
elegant shape; a chair must not only be comfortable to sit in, it must have an
attractive appearance; a food carton must not only protect its contents, it must
display an attractive exterior.

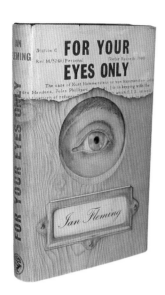

Above Book jacket design for an early James Bond novel by Ian Fleming.

Below The sports car as a piece of mobile sculpture – the Lamborghini Aventador.

The same is true of clothing, and an entire fashion industry depends upon this. James Laver has stated that clothing has three functions: modesty, comfort and display. The first two can easily be satisfied with very plain apparel – of the kind seen in some of the more extreme religious sects. But for the rest of the population, each article of clothing that is worn makes some sort of aesthetic statement, no matter how minor.

Every book or magazine will have a cunningly designed cover to encourage the prospective buyer to pick it up and examine it. Book jackets began as plain dust covers to protect the bindings beneath, and were discarded when the book was purchased. From the 1920s onwards publishers started adding attractive designs to their covers. By the 1960s the artwork for book jackets had developed to a point where their value was now being recognised and they were being carefully kept by serious book collectors.

When buying any kind of vehicle, several alternatives are nearly always available, each with the same practical features such as speed, economy and size, and differing only in the small details of its design. It is usually some quirk of sculptural design that finally decides which car will be bought, although the buyer may not even be consciously aware of this.

As we walk down a city street we are bombarded with displays in shop windows. Each is the work of a specialised window-dresser who treats the rectangle of the shop window as if it were the frame of a painting. Inside this frame the window-dresser arranges the goods for sale in an elegant composition that will attract potential shoppers.

Everywhere we look today we are flooded with designed images. They are not high art, so we rarely discuss them. Their impact is subliminal. The huge, global advertising industry that feeds the public with carefully crafted TV commercials, newspaper advertisements, magazine displays and roadside hoardings is hard at work, day after day, improving the visual impact of its work in order to sell the products of its employers.

In certain fields of commercial art, the creative spirits involved have in a few cases introduced examples of their particular genre that are so outrageous they are virtually useless. In these instances, applied art has almost become pure art. For example, modern female shoe design recently reached a level of exaggeration that makes the footwear startling to look at but dangerous for walking. The same kind of extreme exaggeration can also be seen in female hats, where dramatic visual impact has been given priority over practicality.

Above Shop-window dressing as an art form, at Macy's, New York.

Below Hats designed by Philip Treacy have reached new heights of design exaggeration.

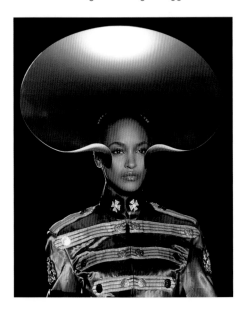

These are cases of commercial designers feeling the need to edge towards high art forms, despite the applied areas in which they work. They act as a reminder to us all that inside every commercial artist is a fine artist struggling to escape.

Finally there is the subject of photography. Although this began as a new, chemically induced art form, it quickly became the major technique for recording the visual world. This recording function became so important that eventually even a fuzzy snap of, say, an assassination or a celebrity in an embarrassing moment became a highly valued document. The aesthetic content of such pictures might be zero, but their archival value as a record of events was all that mattered.

This is true of much commercial photography today, but the more highly skilled photographers have fought against this trend. In extreme cases, they have turned this form of technical art into a fine art to rival that of the portrait painters and landscape artists. Indeed, their large-format, limited-edition photographs are often exhibited in art galleries and treated with as much respect as hand-painted works of art.

These then are the nine roles that art plays in our lives today. To summarise:

1. Sacred art has managed to survive even in an era dominated by science.
2. The dominant members of society continue to display their high status by their commissioned works of art.
3. An entirely new role for art has been the development of huge public galleries and museums.
4. Most domestic homes across the globe today contain at least a few works of art as private possessions.
5. The invention of photographic art led eventually to the rise of cinema and television as new forms of technical art.
6. Folk art persists in some form in almost every culture and keeps local traditions alive.
7. Wherever there is social or political unrest, some kind of political art surfaces to reinforce public opinion.

8. The most ancient role of all for artistic expression –
   the celebratory moment – survives in the form of great festivities.
9. Finally, wherever we look today, some form of applied art is employed
   to support commercial products.

Although we tend to take all this very much for granted, the existence of these nine roles represents a dramatic new spread of artistic expression that invades areas of human existence that were once drab but are now full of colour and design. This is particularly true of the applied arts. The commercial artist and the industrial artist are usually looked down upon by the exponents of the fine arts, but the truth is that the aesthetic impact of applied art on the ordinary citizen in the 21st century is much greater than is usually admitted. With the ever-increasing influence of mass education and modern communication systems, we can expect to see this trend continue to grow in the years ahead.

Below Bailey, *Untitled,* 2008. A recent study of skull and flowers by the British photographer David Bailey.

Untitled 40 (Human Skull & Blue Roses) 2008, David Bailey ©

12 The Rules of Art

Scan page to view video

The Rules of Art

ROADS TO THE EXTRAORDINARY

Before beginning this trip through three million years of art, I listed eight basic rules that govern artistic production. It is now possible to check these against the facts. Art was defined as 'making the extraordinary', and it follows that every work of art must, to some extent, differ from the ordinary.

The rules of art demonstrate how this has been done. Every work of art ever made differs in some way from reality. Even the photorealists, who do their best to contradict this and to make their paintings as close to the natural world as possible, accept one artificial convention: they present their images in rectangular units.

> 'There is always some degree of modification... that... heightens the intensity of what we are seeing.'

When we look at a particular scene our eyes focus sharply on the central area, but we can also see the surrounding region in a less focused way. We are aware of the peripheral features even though, at that moment, we cannot register the details. If we sense a sudden movement out of the corner of one eye, on one side of our field of vision, we will be aware of this and quickly switch our focus to concentrate on that new feature.

This double system of seeing the world enables us to give our main attention to what we are looking at, but without losing our awareness of events around us. Even when we are looking at a rectangular screen such as on a television set or a computer, we remain vaguely aware of the rest of the room around us.

The idea of these rectangular frames as a device to increase our focus on the central area of our field of vision is one that the modern media have inherited from the earlier world of art. Paintings have been framed in this way for centuries, and even before frames were used, as in the case of religious icons on panels of wood, the rectangular isolation of the work of art has been a favourite restriction.

When the photorealist presents a scene for us in a sharply defined rectangle, he or she is making at least one concession to artificiality. For all other art forms, however, the images themselves also show a degree of difference from reality, either intentional or accidental. There is always some degree of modification – a modification that personalises and heightens the intensity of what we are seeing. The question remains, therefore, as to under what general rules these modifications operate.

The rule of exaggeration

This rule involves the supernormalisation and subnormalisation of particular elements of the image being displayed. It is a common distortion in a great deal of prehistoric art, ancient art, tribal art and folk art. It is universal in the art of small children, and is also favoured by modern artists such as Paul Klee and Joan Miró.

The most consistent and important form of exaggeration concerns the human head. Anatomically this should be only one-eighth (roughly 12.5 per cent) of the height of a standing figure, but this is frequently exceeded. This enlargement is not limited to tribal art. It also occurs in ancient art, child art and modern art, as the illustrations below demonstrate (in each case the head height is given as a percentage of the total body height).

The exaggeration of the head is the most common form of body distortion, but there is often an exaggeration of the eyes when compared with the other features.

Below Exaggeration: in reality the human head is only 12.5 per cent of the height of a standing figure. It is 39 per cent in a pre-Columbian figurine of a warrior, Vera Cruz, Mexico, AD400–600 (left). It is 29 per cent in this child art figure. (centre). It is 33 per cent in Karel Appel's painting *Couple*, 1951 (right).

Right Dogu figurine with enlarged eyes, late Jomon period, Japan, 1st millennium BC.

Centre Ivory figure with huge lapis lazuli eyes, Egypt, 4000BC.

Far right Female figure with exaggerated navel, northern Syria, 2000BC.

Some early figurines emphasise the sexual features of the body. A number of Syrian figures from the second millennium BC exaggerate the navel in an unusual way, suggesting that perhaps their role was somehow connected with the act of giving birth.

It is rare to find an ancient figure with exaggerated feet. This part of the human anatomy is often omitted altogether, or appears simply as a small lump at the end of the legs. In more modern times, large feet have sometimes been portrayed where the artist wishes to emphasise the earthiness of a subject. In Miró's 1927 portrayal of a farmer's wife, he dramatically exaggerates the legs and feet to draw attention to the woman's deep agricultural bond with the earth of her farm.

It is surprising how flexible we are in our acceptance of human body proportions. We have in our mind the image of a basic body shape, and it requires vast degrees of distortion of a drawn or painted figure for it to cease to be 'human'. This flexibility has given artists such freedom in their depiction of the body, allowing them to make alterations in many different ways, to create images that carry powerful emotional messages.

Omitting parts of the body also fails to make it unrecognisable. Hands, feet, arms, legs, ears, hair – all these and other details can be omitted if it suits the artist's mood. These subnormalising acts have a double effect: they not only remove the importance of the omitted elements but they also enhance those that remain, exaggerating them by contrast. The shortening of the arms is a particularly common feature of many ancient figurines.

Right Miró, *The Farmer's Wife*, 1923, with exaggerated feet.

Below Figurines from ancient Greece, Mexico, Syria and Iran, all with arms reduced to stumps. Left to right: Boeotian 'papades' figurine, Greece, 6th century BC; Chupícuaro female figurine, Mexico, 300BC; female figurine, northern Syria, 2000BC; Amlash female figurine, northern Iran, 1000BC.

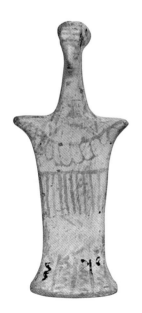

Above Giant statue of the pharaoh Ramses II at Memphis, Egypt.

Below An 18-storey-high fashion hoarding in Hong Kong, 2010.

In addition to creating disproportionate body parts, the rule of exaggeration also expresses itself in two other ways: by size and by number. Exaggeration by size is a way of making an object extraordinary simply by increasing its scale beyond the norm. In ancient Egypt, this strategy was exceptionally popular with the pharaoh Ramses II. In the world of commercial art, the same device is sometimes used today to increase dramatically the impact of a particular image. Advertising hoardings frequently present human images with dimensions that involve massive exaggeration.

The third form of exaggeration involves drastically increasing the number of creative units employed. The buried army of Emperor Qin from ancient China is a case in point. The emperor could have decided to protect his tomb with one gigantic figure towering into the sky, like the Colossus of Rhodes, but instead he opted for exaggeration by numbers. The impact, when coming face to face with his terracotta army, is just as impressive.

In modern times the most outlandish example of exaggeration through numbers must be the Tate installation *Sunflower Seeds* by the Chinese artist Ai Weiwei. In October 2010 he placed 100 million porcelain 'seeds', each individually handpainted by a team of 1,600 Chinese artisans, in the main hall of London's Tate Modern and allowed visitors to walk over them and lie on them.

'Advertising hoardings frequently present human images with dimensions that involve massive exaggeration.'

Right Weiwei, *Sunflower Seeds*, 2010, Tate Gallery exhibition, London.

Right Matisse, *The Red Room (Harmony in Red)*, 1909.

Below Marc, *Deer in the Forest II*, 1914.

The rule of purification

Pure, undiluted colours are rare in real life – they are nearly always contaminated with impurities and diluents. The artist can intensify his or her subjects by removing these contaminations. The art of children is full of primary colours boldly applied to the figures and backgrounds they paint. Even the most traditional of professional artists would sometimes allow themselves a few degrees of extra brightness. The Fauvists, some of the Surrealists and some of the Abstractionists allowed themselves great freedom with their colour choices. Freed from the duty of recording reality, there was no need to adhere to the muted colours of the natural environment.

The process of purification takes place with shapes as well as colours. An artist can purify a roughly spherical object, for example, by portraying it as a more perfect sphere. Rough edges with tiny irregularities can be purified by making them smoother. This simplifying of shapes can be employed to capture their essence, rather than to depict them in precise detail. This type of modification is present in almost all forms of art, especially in child art, tribal art and modern art.

Right The human head simplified to a rectangular shape. Left to right: 'Plank figure' of a mother and child, early Bronze Age, 2000BC, Cyprus; Cuchimilco female figure, AD1200, Chancay, Peru; 'Slab-head' figure, AD1000, Quimbaya, Colombia.

One curious form of purification found in ancient art sees the human head reduced not to a sphere, but to a rectangle. It is as if early artists were already slicing up the human form into geometric units many centuries before the Cubists. This happened, for instance, with the strange plank figures of Bronze Age Cyprus, the dramatic Cuchimilco figures of the Chancay culture in ancient Peru and the slab-headed figures of the Quimbaya culture in ancient Colombia.

A remarkable example of extreme purification in early art is to be found in the starkly simple figures from the Cyclades, a group of islands to the south-east of Greece in the Aegean Sea, and from nearby Anatolia. The art of this region, dating from the third millennium BC, often reduces the complex shape of the human figure to an elegantly smooth and simplified outline. All details and irregularities are omitted and each figure becomes a visual metaphor for humanity – the exact opposite of an individual personal portrait.

'...early artists were already slicing up the human form into geometric units many centuries before the Cubists.'

Right Anatolian female idols, third millennium BC, with increasing reduction from left to right.

The rule of composition

It is a general rule of visual art that the display units are arranged in a special way to create a balanced presentation. This rule is operating even at the level of the chimpanzee, who can place his lines in such a way that they establish a left–right balance. The same is true in the case of child art.

The ape and the child are aided by the fact that they are offered rectangular sheets on which to paint or draw. Prehistoric art lacks this restriction, with the result that composing a scene is more difficult. There is virtually no composition of figures in prehistoric cave art. What sometimes appears to be a compositional relationship between two figures is in reality no more than accidental juxtaposition. It seems likely that almost all cave art was 'portraiture' – in other words, that the artist was working on one particular figure and if it was placed near to another one this was a case of unplanned juxtaposition rather than deliberate composition.

The same is often true with rock art, although there are clearly some composed scenes, especially of dancing ceremonies and group hunting. In the rock art of the African Bushmen there are sometimes composed scenes where the narrative requires that the figures bear a particular relationship to one another. Because we can talk to surviving San Bushmen it is possible to interpret the meaning of these early rock art scenes. Puzzling figures can, with help, be identified as legendary dream-hunters or rain beasts. The irregular, open-ended space on which the artist is painting prevents him from refining his composition. As a result, at this stage in the development of art composition remains rudimentary.

In North American rock art a similar stage has been reached, and group hunting is once again the subject that creates a need for some degree of compositional organisation. At the Nine Mile Canyon in eastern Utah a large hunting scene is incised on the rock face. It is clear that its figures have been arranged to tell a story. On the right are several archers ready to fire their arrows at a herd of horned animals, many of which have young following behind them. Scenes of this kind are among the earliest examples of composed works of art, where individual figures are carefully placed in relation to the other figures in the scene.

Despite the existence of these 'composed' rock art scenes, it has to be said that the vast majority of rock art

Below Hunting scene from the Fremantle culture, Nine Mile Canyon, Utah, USA, AD500–1300.

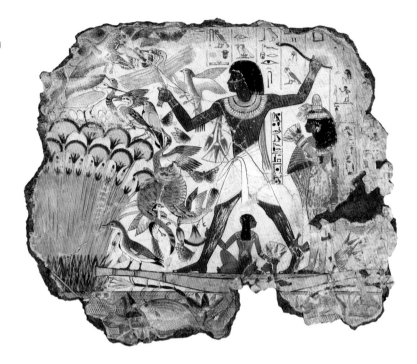

Right Ancient Egyptian wall painting of Nebamun hunting in the marshes, 1350BC.

images are not like this. Figures may be close to other figures but there is no sense of overall arrangement that could be called compositional. Even when we move on to the art of the great ancient civilisations, compositions of the kind we know from more recent works of art are still far from common.

In ancient Egypt, walls were often covered with images but these usually lacked any overall compositional treatment. There were frequently small 'composed' units surrounded by hieroglyphs, but these were usually minor statements within the general decoration of the wall. Occasionally a more complex scene was depicted, as in the famous case of a man hunting in the marshes, accompanied by his wife, daughter and cat. Because of his high status, the man is shown on a much larger scale than his wife. She stands on the boat behind him, and his daughter sits beneath him and clings onto one of his legs. The cat has flushed out some waterbirds, one of which it is holding in its jaws, while the man has grasped another bird and is about to despatch it with his killing-stick. The left side of the composition, although overcrowded with a variety of birds and butterflies, is full of movement – a rarity for ancient Egypt.

'In ancient Egypt, walls were often covered with images but these usually lacked any overall compositional treatment.'

The compositional quality of the work is spoiled, however, because of the ritualistic treatment of the human figures. They have to be shown flat and in profile, as was the custom, which makes their relationship with the naturalistically

Right Fresco at
Akrotiri, Santorini,
c.1600BC.

rendered wildlife rather awkward. Also, the figures are interrupted by lines of painted hieroglyphs (explaining that the man is enjoying himself) that disrupt the composition.

Even earlier than this Egyptian marsh-hunting scene, the plaster-covered walls of local houses on the ill-fated island of Akrotiri were decorated with frescoes. When a violent earthquake destroyed the island around 1600BC, these wall paintings were completely buried and were only recently rediscovered. They reveal that the owners of these houses had the entire wall surface painted with lively designs. The shape of each wall encouraged the artists to create a visually ordered work within these confines, giving us some of the earliest rectangular compositions known.

A later volcanic eruption had the same preservative effect on the wall paintings of Pompeii, but here there was a significant difference. Instead of always having the entire walls painted with a large design, the owners of the houses in this Roman city sometimes had the paintings restricted to smaller panels in the centre of the walls. This made the murals look remarkably like modern framed pictures hanging on the walls. They even had frames of a sort but these were painted on the walls, not made of wood.

In the luxury homes of Pompeii, some of the rooms were almost like picture galleries. Because the pictures are confined to sharply defined, rectangular spaces, their composition has been treated carefully. For the first time we see complex, balanced arrangements of the elements of the paintings. Modern composition has arrived.

From this point onwards, for 2,000 years artists have been attracted again and again to the sharply delineated rectangle as the most comfortable shape on which

Right A fresco in a rectangular panel, House of the Marine Venus, Pompeii, AD79.

Below The golden mean. When people were asked to choose which of these shapes they preferred, the most popular choice (35%) had the ratio of 21:34.

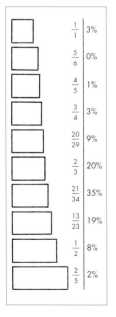

	$\frac{1}{1}$	3%
	$\frac{5}{6}$	0%
	$\frac{4}{5}$	1%
	$\frac{3}{4}$	3%
	$\frac{20}{29}$	9%
	$\frac{2}{3}$	20%
	$\frac{21}{34}$	35%
	$\frac{13}{23}$	19%
	$\frac{1}{2}$	8%
	$\frac{2}{5}$	2%

to place their works of art. Occasionally, for some special reason, they may have worked on a square shape or some fancy design such as an oval or a circle, but these are the rare exceptions.

Analysing the rectangular shape in more detail, it emerges that one particular height–width ratio is favoured above all others. A simple experiment was done to test this. A large number of people were offered a series of white rectangular cards on a dark surface, with the cards varying in proportion from a perfect square to a long, thin rectangle. When people were asked to select the card that they found most attractive, one stood out from the rest. The favourite rectangle had a ratio of 21:34. This preference was the subject of a mathematical treatise in 1509 by Fra Luca Pacioli. He believed that the 'divine proportion' had some deep significance for the human brain, giving rise to a sense of beauty when employed in visual compositions. Over the years this idea has influenced artists as different as Leonardo da Vinci and Salvador Dali.

What exactly is this seemingly magical ratio, today often called the 'golden proportion' or 'golden mean'? If the shorter side of the rectangle is one unit, then the longer side must be 1.618 units long. This figure of 1.618 is sometimes called the 'golden number'. Where it exists, if you divide the length of the rectangle's long side by the length of its short side, the answer will be the same as if you divide their combined lengths by the length of the long side.

This may sound complicated, and most artists probably never bother with it, but for some reason they cannot help obeying the golden proportion – even without knowing that they are doing so. It is the mathematical underpinning of visual compositions that makes them feel right when we set eyes on them.

There is a simple reason for this, and there is nothing mystical about it. It is concerned with the spacing of our eyes and the range and shape of our human visual field. As already mentioned, when we look at a fixed point in front of us it comes into sharp focus, and the rest of our field of vision is slightly out of focus. It is possible to test the range of your visual field by holding two forefingers in front of your face and then moving them away from one another to left and to right. If you keep your gaze firmly fixed at a point immediately in front of you, at a certain point your fingers will disappear from view. This means you have reached the edge of your field of vision. If you then do the same, but moving the fingers one up and one down, the same will occur but this time they will disappear sooner. In other words, because of the anatomy of your head, your field of vision is wider than it is tall, and the ratio is not far from the golden proportion.

So the reason we prefer rectangles with a particular ratio is that they make a good fit with our natural field of vision. This fact has not escaped the designers of electronic screens who report that: 'The Golden Rectangle shows up in the most

Right In Turner's seascape *The Fighting Temeraire* (1839), the main features lie on the golden mean.

Right The golden mean operates in Seurat's *Bathers at Asnières* (1884).

unexpected places. For example, it shows up in the 16:10 aspect ratio of the newest, most advanced LCD monitors, which provide more comfortable viewing than older, now obsolescent LCD monitors with 4:3 aspect ratios.'

The preference for this particular ratio is so deep-seated that it even operates within the rectangle. We do not enjoy seeing a picture divided down the middle by a major feature, because this splits the scene in two and reduces the chances of a flowing, rhythmic composition. If a main feature is offset to one side, however, the artist can then relate it elegantly with another feature that counterbalances it, and then one more to counterbalance that and so on – this produces a more complex and more attractive composition. An analysis of well-known paintings reveals that the artists have, probably intuitively, placed the most prominent features of their scenes right on the golden mean.

> 'So the reason we prefer rectangles with a particular ratio is that they make a good fit with our natural field of vision.'

In many cases we do not know whether the artists involved were making careful calculations before starting work, so that they could strictly obey the rules of the golden proportion, or whether their visual skills were such that they arrived at them automatically. One artist who made no secret of his calculations was Salvador Dali; when creating his major work *The Last Supper* in 1955 he announced that he was 'returning to the classical ideals' by 'researching the Divina Proportione' of Pacioli. From the exact measurements of the canvas, which precisely followed the golden proportion, to the height of the table, which followed a vertical golden mean, and to many other details, Dali's painting is a hymn to mathematical composition.

Right Dali's *The Last Supper* (1955) is a composition overburdened with mathematical principles.

The rule of heterogeneity

This rule says a work of art should be neither too simple nor too complicated. It should have an optimum level of heterogeneity. The rule is so basic that it was observed to be operating even at the level of the chimpanzee Congo. If interrupted before he had finished a painting he would scream in anger. If attempts were made to get him to continue after he had, in his own mind, completed a work, he refused to do so. This was not because he had tired of painting, because if then given a new blank sheet he would start again, proving that his refusal to add more to a picture was a genuine reaction.

This optimum heterogeneity response of the chimpanzee had not been expected. The idea that an ape brain could make a decision that a painting was finished seemed highly unlikely. It suggests that the animal had, in its mind, an idea of what constituted 'enough' marks on a page. Human children somehow know when one of their paintings is finished. This does not apply at the very early scribble stage, but as soon as pictorial images begin to appear and are organised into a composition, there comes a moment when the child will cry out 'Finished!' and put down the brushes or crayons.

This rule also applies to adult human artists, who nearly always prefer the middle ground between the underwhelmingly simple and the overwhelmingly complex. There are, however, two types of artist who break this rule. One is the sophisticated 'minimalist' and the other is the unsophisticated folk artist who suffers from what has been called 'horror vacui' (fear of the empty). The minimalist relies heavily on the famous statement by the architect Mies van der Rohe that 'less is more'. His idea was that if a work of art could be purged of unnecessary, fussy detail, its simplicity of form would give it a purity of concept. This philosophy was taken over by painters and sculptors, resulting in some of the most starkly empty exhibitions in the history of art.

On first entering such an exhibition there was a momentary pleasure to be gained from the shock of seeing such aggressively, perversely unimaginative works. It was as though, by breaking the rule of optimum heterogeneity so outrageously, the minimalist artists were celebrating a release from the tyranny of all forms of imagery.

The Scottish sculptor William Turnbull summed up the minimalist movement astutely when he said: 'Minimalism is just a diagram of an idea; and an idea is where art should start, not where it should end up.'

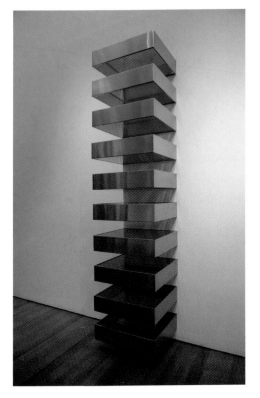

Below Donald Judd, *Untitled*, 1968.

Above Huichol beaded panel, Mexico, 20th century.

Once the initial shock impact of minimalism had worn off, the movement soon petered out. Much more lasting has been its extreme opposite – works of art that suffer from the horror vacui. Curiously, these works have never been given a name and have not spawned an art movement. This is because they are usually found not in the elite galleries of the fine art aficionados but in the more mundane world of folk art.

Few serious artists would indulge in the excessive procedure of packing every square centimetre of canvas with tiny details. For them, optimum heterogeneity is not maximum heterogeneity. It is what the Buddha called 'the middle way'. As he explained it, this is a path of moderation between the extremes of restraint and indulgence – it is the path of wisdom. Translated into aesthetic terms, the middle way is halfway between the depressing emptiness of minimalism and the overexcited ornamentation of the horror vacui works.

For many folk artists, however, there is a different consideration. Having no professional egos to protect, they set out to display as much expenditure of time and energy as possible. If one folk artist has painted 50 figures on his cart or taxi, for example, his rival will paint 100. And so the competition goes on until every available surface has been covered in the most minute detail, in a display of conspicuous craftsmanship.

The Huichol Indians of Mexico go even further with their horror vacui works of art. Their creations are so overcrowded that it is almost impossible to study the details or to relate them to one another. Any sense of composition or visual organisation has been lost. As a display of conspicuous effort they may be impressive but in every other way, by breaking the law of optimum heterogeneity so excessively, they have destroyed their value as coherent works of art. They do, however, provide good evidence in support of this law by showing what happens when it is so wildly abandoned. The essential feature of the horror vacui displayed by the Huichol is that it is not an isolated, personal idiosyncrasy, but rather a communal and competitive activity. If the artists of the tribe were not striving to outdo one another, it would not occur.

Right Extreme body tattooing.

Far right Multiple body piercings, London, 2007.

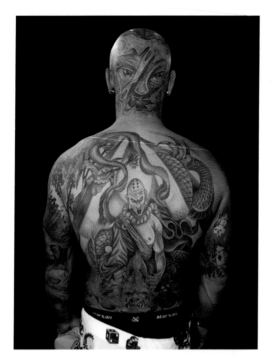

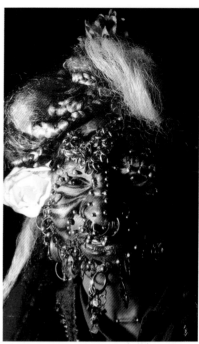

Horror vacui even operates in the sphere of body art, where some brave individuals have treated their entire skin surface as a canvas to be completely covered in the art of the tattooist. Another form of body art that has become popular recently is body piercing. A small number of rare individuals have taken this art form to extraordinary lengths. As before, this is a competitive activity and drives individuals on until there is no space left for an additional piercing.

'... some brave individuals have treated their entire skin surface as a canvas to be completely covered in the art of the tattooist.'

In earlier times there were periods when the fear of empty spaces took over an entire style of ancient art. Architecture has sometimes exhibited a severe case of horror vacui where the owners wish to show off and prove that their building is better than any of its rivals. The Blue Mosque in Istanbul is a case in point. Pictorial imagery was forbidden to its Islamic architects, but they made up for this with their intricate abstract designs and elaborate patterns. Hardly any surface in this huge building is left untouched.

It should not be forgotten that these examples of breaking the rule of optimum heterogeneity – from the bleak simplicity of the minimalists to the overwrought fussiness of the horror vacui artists – are extremely rare when considering the whole range of human art. The vast majority of artists choose the middle way, not because of any spiritual consideration but because it suits the manner in which their eyes examine the visual world.

Right Interior of the Blue Mosque, Istanbul, Turkey.

The rule of refinement

This rule states that as artists progress through their careers, from novices to experts, they strive to have greater control over their hand movements. As with sportsmen and sportswomen perfecting a golf swing or a tennis stroke, artists develop their manual skills to a point where their dexterity gives them the ability to place a stroke of the pencil, the pen or the brush exactly where they want it. In this way, the display units in their pictures and the intervals between them become more precise. Their art becomes more refined.

This process is at its most conspicuous in children's art. When children are very young they find it hard to get their lines to go exactly where they want. Their pictures are crude and imprecise. As they grow older, the lines come under greater control until, as young adults, they can apply them with a refined skill.

Some artists are naturally talented and can make their hands do anything they ask of them. Salvador Dali is a case in point. Others must struggle to achieve what they want, and some never do. Francis Bacon, for example, was always dissatisfied with his work and kept a sharp utility knife in his studio to slash canvases that disappointed him. When he died, nearly 100 destroyed works were found in his studio, mostly with the head region of portraits cut out.

Talking about Bacon's work, Damien Hirst poses an interesting question: How can it be that Lucian Freud is the better painter, but Francis Bacon is the greater artist? 'What's going on?' he asks. What indeed? The answer is one that contradicts the rule of refinement.

As already explained, refinement is the process by which an artist's hand becomes skilled. When small children start drawing, their muscle control improves and they become more and more accurate in placing their lines on paper. However, if they stop drawing when they become adult, the refinement process ceases. If asked to draw a figure some years later they will be unable to do so with any skill. Only if they keep drawing or painting will their skill develop. This can happen, if they are self-taught, simply through practice and observation, or they may be professionally trained to improve their technique. Ultimately they should be able to use their skill to make their hand create any visual image they want, including the precise copying of the external world.

Once artists can do this, they are then in a position to modify their images by the rules already mentioned, such as deliberate exaggeration, colour purification, compositional arrangement and degree of heterogeneity. They can do this to heighten the intensity of the visual message they are transmitting. The precise way in which this is done is what gives every artist his or her own personal style. Only the super-realists, who pursue the difficult goal of making their painted images look exactly like colour photographs of the external world, will lack a personal style.

To find an example of an artist who refined his skill and then, having developed the ability to portray the external world with precision, deliberately unrefined his work to a startling degree, one has only to look at the work of Picasso.

As a teenager, Picasso had already matured as a representational artist but then, to the dismay of the traditionalists, he spent the rest of his life deliberately unrefining this achievement. Because of the quality of his early teenage work, it was impossible to attack Picasso's later work as inept or incompetent. It was clear that he did not paint in this clumsy way because he was unable to create refined, traditional imagery. He had consciously chosen to discard his skills and to create these crude images instead. And it was not a passing fancy – he continued to paint like this for over 40 years, from the 1920s to the 1970s. Early critics had to find some explanation of this strange behaviour and they decided that there were only two possible answers: either he was mocking them or he had gone mad.

> 'He [Picasso] had consciously chosen to discard his skills and to create these crude images instead.'

It was not only the establishment that hated what Picasso was doing. Even the other avant-garde artists were horrified. The Swiss sculptor Alberto Giacometti left no doubt about how he felt: 'Picasso is altogether bad, completely beside the point from the beginning… Ugly. Old-fashioned, vulgar, without sensitivity, horrible in colour or non-colour. Very bad painter once and for all.'

The Russian Marc Chagall commented sarcastically: 'What a genius, that Picasso… It's a pity he doesn't paint.' The French artist André Derain said: 'One day we shall find Pablo has hanged himself behind his great canvas.' He was

Right Picasso,
The First Communion,
1896. Picasso
painted this at the
age of 15.

referring to *Les Demoiselles d'Avignon*, about which even Picasso's own art dealer, Ambrose Vollard, said: 'It's the work of a madman.' Picasso's great rival for the title of the father of modern art, Henri Matisse, considered *Les Demoiselles* to be a hoax. The formidable Swiss psychiatrist Carl Jung condemned the work as schizophrenic and 'practically satanic', adding that Picasso has a 'grotesque unconcern for the beholder'. Alfred Munnings, when president of the Royal Academy, made a speech in which he accused Picasso of corrupting art. Winston Churchill said that if he saw Picasso coming down the street he would want to kick him. And so the list goes on.

Today, in the 21st century, Picasso is looked upon as an old master and his paintings sell for huge sums, but in his own lifetime he was attacked for the way he had thrown away his refined skills. 'Any child could do that' was a common reaction. Picasso himself happened to agree with this particular criticism. When examining some children's paintings he remarked: 'When I was their age, I could draw like Raphael, but it took me a lifetime to learn to draw like them.' The difference, of course, is that the child is trying its hardest to progress beyond the crudity that Picasso is making his ultimate goal. He is doing this to rid himself of any association with the traditional art forms that see as their task the recording of what is visible in the external world. This is because his deeper concern is the dissection of the human body, and he needs a style that will focus the viewer on this process and not be distracted by the aspirations of traditional portraiture.

A survey of Picasso's massive output reveals that, although he enjoyed still-life subjects and the occasional landscape, the vast majority of his paintings are concerned with close-up views of the human form. Following the Cubist experiment, these human forms are crudely painted and usually deformed in some way. As mentioned above, the crudity is simply a shock tactic to make us focus on what really matters to him – the impact of rearranging human anatomy.

It has been claimed that the reason why Picasso repeatedly dissected the human head, chopping it up this way and that, was because as a child he had witnessed an autopsy of a female corpse with the head severed in two, a sight that made the small boy feel sick. This may have left a memory trace, and acted as a catalyst, but his lifelong fascination with rearranging human features has a more basic significance.

Right Picasso, *Seated Woman with a Hat*, 1939.

Somehow Picasso made the discovery that we look at a human figure in two ways. The first is a gestalt approach, meaning that we assess the complete figuration of all the details of the person. The term gestalt, meaning 'unified whole', is the basis of the way we view a traditional portrait. If, for example, we look at a photograph of a loved one, we do not examine separately the nose, then the eyes, then the mouth and then add them together to identify the person. We see the complete image and our brain tells us immediately who it is – we respond to the 'unified whole'.

Picasso realised, either consciously or intuitively, that if individual portraiture could be avoided by deliberately unrefining his technique, he could start to play with the human figure. Like a sculptor with a lump of soft clay, he could pull it this way and that to see how far he could go before it ceased to be human. He discovered that we identify an unknown face by the presence of eyes, a mouth and a nose. He wanted to know how far he could rearrange these details and still create something we saw as a human face.

Once Picasso started on this adventure of re-modelling the human body, he could not stop. The game went on and on. He was like a composer who had discovered a tune that could be varied in a thousand different ways. And once the public had overcome the shock of seeing such unfamiliar images hanging on the wall, they began to play the game with him. They forgave him for squandering the refinements of his juvenile work and accepted his adult discoveries as a new way of viewing the world.

'They forgave him [Picasso] for squandering the refinements of his juvenile work and accepted his adult discoveries as a new way of viewing the world.'

Although he was an extreme example, Picasso was not the only 20th-century artist to have started out academically and then thrown away his representational skills. Many of the important avant-garde artists of the period behaved in a similar way. Finding themselves free to explore new avenues, they abandoned their academic style and moved into areas where traditional refinement of technique was non-existent.

These were painters who had refined their skills but had then ceased to employ those refinements, but there were other artists who had no academic skills in the first place. Many of these so-called 'Sunday painters', the folk artists and even some of the avant-garde themselves were limited in their ability to portray the external world with accuracy and precision. Before the 20th century their work would have been dismissed as inept, but now, thanks largely to Picasso and the other major figures who were rebelling against naturalistic painting, they had a chance of being taken seriously. If their weaknesses gave their work a strangeness that had an unusual visual appeal, their shortcomings could become strengths.

Another way in which an artist may succeed without the benefit of a fully refined technique is where the person suffers from declining eyesight. If an artist's lenses have become discoloured with age this will interfere with his or her choice of colours. This was the case with Claude Monet in his old age. Between 1912 and 1922 his eyesight became so bad that he had to label his tubes of paint so that he knew which colour he was using. The colours in his later paintings lost their pastel subtleties and became much stronger. Also, his vision generally grew more blurred so that brushstrokes became less precise. These vaguer, more brightly coloured canvases have been viewed as Monet pushing his extreme Impressionist style further and further when, in reality, he was struggling to see any colours at all and was painting from memory, memorising where the different colours lay on his palette.

The two paintings by Monet shown here depict the same scene of the bridge over his lily pond; one was painted in 1899 when his vision was strong, and the other in the 1920s when it had deteriorated. The great irony was that people liked the more fuzzy paintings and imagined that they were a brave new innovation by the great artist. A crisis arose when, in 1923, Monet had a lens-removal operation to his right eye and could see true colours again. He was horrified by what he saw and started

Right Monet, *Bridge over a Pond of Water Lilies*, 1899 – good vision.

Right Monet,
The Japanese Bridge,
1923–5 – poor
vision.

destroying his paintings. His family and friends did their best to save some of them. He then started repainting canvases to correct the colours. His friends did their best to stop him 'improving' them. What Monet did not know was that the removal of a damaged lens has an unusual side-effect: the patient starts to see ultraviolet light.

The result of this was that when Monet painted with his right eye he was now 'over-blueing' his subjects. The left eye, which was getting even worse and was down to 10 per cent of normal vision, but which he would not allow his doctor to touch, made the world look redder. After the operation, he painted some pictures with his left eye and some with his right. The difference was startling.

Monet was not the only artist of his period to have bad eyesight. Mary Cassat also suffered severely from cataracts; van Gogh probably had glaucoma that made him see halos around objects and there are also claims that he was colour blind; Renoir, Cézanne and Toulouse-Lautrec were all short-sighted and unable to see details clearly in the distance; Pissarro had an infected right tear-duct that repeatedly developed abscesses and had to be treated and his eye bandaged; and Degas had a serious disease of the retina that eventually meant he could no longer see clearly what he was doing, giving his later work a dreamy vagueness.

One medical authority has even remarked that a good eye doctor might have had a dramatic effect on art at the end of the 19th century. Another doctor went so far as to say that 'maybe the whole Impressionist movement was a conspiracy of people

'...people liked the more fuzzy paintings and imagined that they were a brave new innovation by the great artist.'

who had bad eyesight'. Renoir's disability was even worse. He not only suffered from myopia that made long-distance objects appear fuzzy, but also from severe rheumatoid arthritis of his fingers. His arthritis was so bad that by the end of the 1880s his brushes had to be wedged between his fingers or strapped to his arm. He was confined to a wheelchair, and could only move his arm towards the canvas in short, sudden jabs, but he refused to give up and went on painting for years in this condition.

With Picasso's rejection of the refinement he achieved in childhood and Monet's loss of refinement due to physical disability, their success as artists begins to make the rule of refinement look questionable. With child art the principle is clear enough – the young artist becomes better and better at controlling the hand movements that make the lines and shapes go exactly where they are wanted. In earlier centuries, the improvement seen in the teenager was further refined by professional training and practice, leading to an adult ability to produce accurate representations of the external world.

The arrival of photography dramatically reduced the need for this adult phase of refinement. Artists could explore new ways of creating visual images. Traditional refinement became less important. But was it lost or was it changed? Was there a new kind of refinement in which an artist was aiming to perfect an image of his own invention, rather than one that matched the external world?

> 'If modern artists are making up the rules as they go along, how can they be judged?'

Many artists in the 20th century may not have possessed the traditional refinement skills of portraying the external world with great precision, but if that was not their aim, then they were not falling short. They were making new rules. If modern artists are making up the rules as they go along, how can they be judged? The old assessments of whether a portrait looked like the sitter, or a landscape looked like the piece of countryside that it represented, were easy. But what of an abstract artist or a performance artist, for instance; by what rules can they be judged?

The answer is that we can listen to what the artists have to say about how well they think they have succeeded; we can listen to the judgement of the experts; we can check their auction price records; we can listen to the opinions of our friends and acquaintances; or we can rely on our own personal reaction to their work. All five of these influences will be at work to some extent when we make a judgement about a non-representational work of art.

This is an entirely new situation for the visual arts. Never before has there been such uncertainty about the refinement – that is to say the quality – of particular works of art. Never before has there been such a variety of styles from which to choose. The law of refinement has arrived at a point in history where it finds itself at the centre of a minefield of conflicting opinions.

The rule of thematic variation

This rule states that once a particular motif, pattern or theme has been developed, it will be varied in many different ways. The most primitive version of this appeared in the work of the chimpanzee Congo. Once he had developed the concept of a radiating fan pattern, he started to vary it in a number of ways. The human child follows a similar path – once the child draws a human face, he or starts to alter and improve it, or change its expression, or its colour, or its size.

Today's adult artists produce new themes almost every year, but in ancient times, when social change was much slower, a particular theme could last for many years. In ancient China, for example, in the second millennium BC the intricate and highly characteristic relief patterns on the surfaces of the Shang dynasty bronzes lasted as a major theme for over 500 years. At the centre of these relief patterns is an animal mask called a Taotie. This is so highly abstracted, however, that it takes time to isolate it. A pair of eyes below a pair of heavy eyebrows is usually all that can be clearly identified. Despite the endless tiny variations in the Shang incision patterns, which make each work of Shang art unique, the overall theme employed is so characteristic that it is always easy, even at first glance, to see whether an ancient bronze belongs to this culture or not.

Right Thematic variation in Shang bronzes, second millennium BC, China.

Thematic variation is still commonplace among today's artists, but it operates at a more personal level. It is extremely rare for an artist to create a new motif and then abandon it after a single work and change to something very different. A new theme is almost always put through a whole range of variations before the artist becomes bored with it and switches to something new.

It is as if there are two opposing tendencies operating at once. One is the pleasure of familiarity and the other is the boredom of repetition. When an artist paints a particular scene, there is pleasure in doing it again because it is now an old friend and the visual problems inherent in it have been solved. But to copy it exactly would be too repetitious, so a compromise is reached – the theme is kept, but ways are found to vary it slightly.

This process becomes very clear when one examines a catalogue raisonné of a particular artist in which every work is illustrated in date order. It also becomes clear what frequently makes the artist jump from one theme to the next. To give just one example: with the Catalan artist Joan Miró, it soon emerges that it is the material on which he is painting that is likely to define a series of variations. In the 1930s, for instance, he painted nine variations of a particular theme working on a coarse canvas known as burlap. When he then switched to a finer Ingres paper, a new theme developed and he completed 31 variations of this.

Throughout Miró's long career he produced literally hundreds of short series of works, and it was usually (but not always) when he switched to a new type of material that he jumped to a new theme.

There will always be exceptions to this rule of thematic variation, with an artist occasionally making a sudden change – a single experiment – before returning to an ongoing series. The classification of an artist's output into distinct themes is never neat, but the fact that these themed series exist at all is of great importance to art historians in their efforts to understand the lifetime work of any major artist.

> '...there are two opposing tendencies operating at once. One is the pleasure of familiarity and the other is the boredom of repetition.'

The rule of neophilia

Neophilia is, literally, the love of the new. The playful need for novelty – the new toy principle – demands that from time to time established traditions must be abandoned in favour of new trends. This is something that has speeded up over the centuries until today it is moving bewilderingly quickly. The imagery and the style of cave art lasted for thousands of years with very little change. In stark contrast, scholars have recently been able to identify over 80 different major styles within the past 150 years.

The modern styles are defined as art movements, always with a title, which is usually an '-ism'. A few of these movements become so influential that they are known to the general public – Impressionism and Surrealism are two such cases. But there are many other modern art movements that are so short-lived or localised that their names mean nothing to non-specialists.

'...such is the power of the human imagination that something new is bound to emerge in the years ahead – to shock us, engage us and, with a little luck, inspire us.'

The neophilic urge has become much stronger in recent years because of the greatly increased speed of social communication. A young artist working in Tokyo today will be aware of what is happening in Paris, London and New York. Nearly all the recent art movements have burned themselves out in a few years or, at most, a few decades. However, once the best-known figures from these movements have become established as international figures, they can go on working in the style of their '-ism' long after it has ceased to be active. Surrealism, for example, started in the early 1920s and faded away as an active movement in the early 1950s, but its leading figures, such as Dali, Magritte, Ernst and Miró, all went on painting for many years.

So many experiments have now been done and so many techniques explored, that it is becoming increasingly difficult for today's young artists to create a new niche for themselves. Every novelty, every new act of rebellion seems to have been tried out. As at any stage in the history of art it is impossible to guess where it will go next, but such is the power of the human imagination that something new is bound to emerge in the years ahead – to shock us, engage us and, with a little luck, inspire us. The law of neophilia demands it.

The rule of context

This rule states that if an ordinary object is to be made extraordinary and turned into a work of art it needs to be displayed in a special context. The apeman who saw a face on a pebble in a stream and carried it several kilometres to keep in his home cave was the first known individual to have created a work of art.

Three million years later, a modern man in the shape of Pablo Picasso took home a discarded bicycle in the wartime Paris of 1942, rearranged the handlebars above the saddle and created a bull's head without adding any paint or other modifications. He and the apeman had acted in exactly the same way. Both had seen a strange image – a head – where it should not have been, and both carried the objects to their homes where they looked upon them in a new light as works of art. The new contexts alone transformed these lowly objects into art.

In the early part of the 20th century, this idea of making art simply by changing the context of an object was put into practice by the eccentric Dadaists. The Dada outrages have been followed by a large number of contextual 'dislodgements' in which mundane objects have been transformed into works of art simply by the way they are displayed. Kurt Schwitters, for example, began collecting discarded tickets

Right Emin,
My Bed, 1998.

and cartons, arranging them together, framing them and solemnly hanging them as pictures.

More recently, installation artists have reworked these early ideas and have started, once again, to display improbable commonplace objects as works of art. The most famous of these is Tracey Emin's unmade bed, exhibited exactly as it was in her bedroom. Lying around it are pill packets, cigarettes, condoms and other such items. Emin falls short of the Dadaist Baroness Elsa, however, because she fails to give it a shocking title. Emin says baldly, here is my bed, a work of art solely because I place it in a gallery.

Every time a painting is put in a frame or hung in a gallery, it is being given a special context. Every time a fancy costume is worn in a carnival procession, it is being exhibited in a special context. The rule of context states that every work of art can be enhanced by displaying it in a contrived setting. The influence of context is so powerful that even if the object has not been created by the actual artist, it can still be seen as art simply because it has been moved to a place, such as a gallery, where we expect to encounter art. A change of context alone can transform the ordinary into the extraordinary.

There is a second form of contextual manipulation that can convert the expected into the unexpected. Instead of the whole work of art being enhanced by placing it in a special context, one part of it is placed out of context in relation to the rest of the work. This is the stock-in-trade of modern artists such as Magritte and Dali, with Magritte placing an apple where a human head should be, and Dali giving an elephant the long legs of a spider. This contextual contradiction is not a new phenomenon, however; ancient art is full of centaurs, minotaurs and other such chimeras made extraordinary by contextual disturbances within the works of art. Perhaps the most extraordinary example of all is the 32,000-year-old lion-headed man of Hohlenstein-Stadel. This use of context as an aesthetic device has an amazingly long pedigree.

From the peaks of the most sophisticated urban civilisations to the troughs of the most poverty-stricken tribal remnants, the rules of art are operating – and have always operated – to drive human beings to embellish their environment. It may be a gesture as extravagant as decorating the Sistine Chapel, or as modest as putting three blue feathers in your hair. It may be as skilful as painting a masterpiece or building a pyramid, or it may be as simple as drawing a circle and putting lines inside it to make a face. None of these activities is essential for human survival. Food, drink and shelter are enough to avoid death. But human beings succeeded as a species by using their brains. As opportunists they exploited every situation and turned every challenge to their advantage. Eventually they reached a point where their level of success gave them the chance to celebrate their triumphs. Instead of sleeping, they danced and sang and painted their faces and wore strange costumes, making themselves extraordinary. This stimulated and rewarded the exuberant part of their brains and gave them a new pleasure, that of adult play.

Below By placing the head of an ibis on a human body, this ancient Egyptian artist has thrown both out of context, creating a supernatural being – the god Thoth.

With 80 per cent of their sensory input being visual, it is not surprising that human beings began to explore ways of making visual experiences more satisfying. They soon discovered that they could make colours more intense and the patterns more complicated; they could organise their visual field to suit themselves by making their own patterns and shapes, instead of relying on those found in nature. They could impose order, invent images and playfully create new visual experiences.

We succeeded so well as a busy, inquisitive, innovative species that our brains reached a point where they started to abhor inactivity. Prolonged solitary confinement in an empty cell is still considered a brutal punishment. Even when we had dealt with all our survival needs, we needed to keep mentally active; playing visual games or setting ourselves visual challenges was one of the ways in which we achieved this. By making the ordinary world into an extraordinary place, we entertained our brains and felt more fulfilled. By inventing what we call art, we found a way of enhancing our lives and of enriching the short time we are allowed to spend on this planet between the light of birth and the dark of dying.

Bibliography

Aarseth, Gudmund (2004) *Painted Rooms.* Nordic Arts, Fort Collins, Colorado.

Alland, Alexander (1977) *The Artistic Animal. An Enquiry into the Biological Roots of Art.* Anchor Books, New York.

Alschuler, Rose E. & Hattwick, La Berta Weiss (1947) *Paintings and Personality. A Study of Young Children.* University of Chicago Press, Illinois.

Anderson, Wayne (2011) *Marcel Duchamp; The Failed Messiah.* Editions Fabriart, Geneva.

Aujoulat, Nobert (2005) *The Splendour of Lascaux.* Thames & Hudson, London.

Bahn, Paul G. (1997) *Journey Through the Ice Age.* Weidenfeld & Nicolson, London.

Bahn, Paul G. (1998) *Cambridge Illustrated History of Prehistoric Art.* Cambridge University Press.

Bahn, Paul G. (2010) *Prehistoric Rock Art. Polemics and Progress.* Cambridge University Press.

Banksy (2011) *Wall and Piece.* Century, London.

Bataille, Georges (1955) *Lascaux, ou la Naissance de l'Art.* Skira, Geneva.

Bell, Deborah (2010) *Mask-makers and Their Craft.* McFarland, London.

Bellido, Ramon Tio (1988) *Kandinsky.* Studio Editions, London.

Berghaus, Gunter (Editor) (2004) *New Perspectives on Prehistoric Art.* Praeger, London.

Berndt, Roland M. (1964) *Australian Aboriginal Art.* Macmillan, New York.

Berndt, Roland M. & Phillips, E. S. (Editors) (1978) *The Australian Aboriginal Heritage.* Ure Smith, Sydney.

Boehm, Gottfried et al. (2007) *Schwitters – Arp.* Kunstmuseum, Basel.

Brothwell, Don R. (ed.) (1976) *Beyond Aesthetics. Investigations into the Nature of Visual Art.* Thames & Hudson, London.

Celebonovic, Stevan & Grigson, Geoffrey (1957) *Old Stone Age.* Phoenix House, London.

Chauvet, Jean-Marie et al. (1996) *Chauvet Cave. The Discovery of the World's Oldest Paintings.* Thames & Hudson, London.

Clottes, Jean (2003) *Return to Chauvet Cave. Excavating the Birthplace of Art.* Thames & Hudson, London.

Clottes, Jean & Courtin, Jean (1996) *The Cave Beneath the Sea.* Abrams, New York.

Dachy, Marc (1990) *The Dada Movement.* Skira, Geneva.

Daix, Pierre (1982) *Cubists and Cubism.* Skira, Geneva.

Davidson, Daniel Sutherland (1936) 'Aboriginal Australian and Tasmanian Rock Carvings and Paintings', *Memoirs of the American Philosophical Society*, vol. V. Philadelphia.

Dawkins, Richard (1986) *The Blind Watchmaker.* Longman, London.

Delporte, Henri (1993) *L'Image de la Femme dans l'Art Préhistorique.* Picard, Paris.

Demirjian, Torkom (1989) *Idols, the Beginning of Abstract Form.* Aridane Galleries, New York.

Dempsey, Amy (2002) *Styles, School and Movements.* Thames & Hudson, London.

Dissanayake, Ellen (1979) 'An Ethological View of Ritual and Art in Human Evolutionary History', *Leonardo,* vol. 12, p. 27–31.

Dissanayake, Ellen (1988) *What is Art For?* University of Washington Press, Seattle.

Dissanayake, Ellen (1992) *Homo Aestheticus. Where Art Comes From and Why.* The Free Press, New York.

Dupont, Jacques & Gnudi, Cesare (1954) *Gothic Painting.* Skira, Switzerland.

Dupont, Jacques & Mathey, François (1951) *The Seventeenth Century; Caravaggio to Vermeer.* Skira, Switzerland.

Ehrenzweig, Anton (1967) *The Hidden Order of Art.* Weidenfeld & Nicolson, London.

Eisler, Colin (1991) *Dürer's Animals.* Smithsonian Press, Washington.

Eng, Helga (1931) *The Psychology of Children's Drawings.* Routledge & Kegan Paul, London.

Fein, Sylvia (1993) *First Drawings: Genesis of Visual Thinking.* Exelrod Press, California.

Fosca, François (1952) *The Eighteenth Century; Watteau to Tiepolo.* Skira, Switzerland.

Foss, B. M. (1962) 'Biology and Art', *The British Journal of Aesthetics,* vol. 2, no. 3. p. 195–199.

Fraenger, Wilhelm (1999) *Hieronymus Bosch.* G+B Arts International, Amsterdam.

Gammel, Irene (2003) *Baroness Elsa.* The MIT Press, Cambridge, Massachusetts.

Gardner, Howard (1980) *Artful Scribbles. The Significance of Children's Drawings.* Jill Norman, London.

Getty, Adele (1990) *Goddess. Mother of Living Nature.* Thames & Hudson, London.

Gimbutas, Marija (1989) *The Language of the Goddess.* Thames & Hudson, London.

Goja, Hermann (1959) 'Zeichenversuche mit Menschenaffen', *Zeitschrift für Tierpsychologie,* 16, 3, p. 368–373.

Gombrich, E. H. (1989) *The Story of Art.* Phaidon, Oxford.

Grabar, Andre & Nordenfalk, Carl (1957) *Early Medieval Painting.* Skira, Switzerland.

Grabar, Andre & Nordenfalk, Carl (1958) *Romanesque Painting.* Skira, Switzerland.

Gray, Camilla (1962) *The Great Experiment: Russian Art, 1863–1922.* Thames & Hudson, London.

Graziosi, Paolo (1960) *Palaeolithic Art.* Faber & Faber, London.

Green, Christopher (1987) *Cubism and its Enemies.* Yale University Press, New Haven.

Groger-Wurm, Helen M. (1972) *Australian Aboriginal Bark Paintings and their Mythological Interpretation.* Australian Institute of Aboriginal Studies, Canberra.

Grozinger, Wolfgang (1955) *Scribbling, Drawing, Painting. The Early Forms of the Child's Pictorial Creativeness.* Faber & Faber, London.

Haddon, Alfred C. (1895) *Evolution in Art. As Illustrated by the Life-histories of Designs.* Walter Scott, London.

Hanson, H. J. (Editor) (1968) *European Folk Art in Europe and the Americas.* Thames & Hudson, London.

Hemenway, Priya (2008) *The Secret Code. The Mysterious Formula that Rules Art, Nature, and Science.* Springwood, Lugano, Switzerland.

Hess, Lilo (1954) *Christine the Baby Chimp.* Bell, London.

Joyce, Robert (1975) *The Esthetic Animal.* Exposition Press, New York.

Kelder, Diane (1980) *French Impressionism.* Artabras, New York.

Kellogg, Rhoda (1955) *What Children Scribble and Why.* Author's Edition, San Francisco.

Kellogg, Rhoda (1967) *The Psychology of Children's Art.* Random House, New York.

Kellogg, Rhoda (1969) *Analyzing Children's Art.* National Press Books, Palo Alto, California.

Kellogg, W. N. & Kellogg, L. A. (1933) *The Ape and The Child: A Comparative Study of the Environmental Influence Upon Early Behavior.* Hafner Publishing Co., New York.

Kluver, Heinrich (1933) *Behaviour Mechanisms in Monkeys.* University of Chicago Press, Chicago.

Komar, Vitaly & Melamid, Alexander (2000) *When Elephants Paint. The Quest of Two Russian Artists to Save the Elephants of Thailand*. HarperCollins, London.

Kriegeskorte, Werner (1987) *Giuseppe Arcimboldo*. Taco, Berlin.

Lader, Melvin P. (1985) *Arshile Gorky*. Abbeville Press, New York.

Ladygina-Kohts, Nadie (1935) *Infant Chimpanzee and Human Child*. Scientific Memoirs of the Museum Darwinianum, Moscow.

Ladygina-Kohts, Nadie (2002) *Infant Chimpanzee and Human Child*. Oxford University Press, Oxford.

Lassaigne, Jacques (1957) *Flemish Painting; the Century of Van Eyck*. Skira, Switzerland.

Lassaigne, Jacques & Argan, Giulio Carlo (1955) *The Fifteenth Century; from Van Eyck to Botticelli*. Skira, Switzerland.

Leason, P. A. (1939) 'A New View of the Western European Group of Quaternary Cave Art', *Proceedings of the Prehistoric Society*, vol. V, part 1, p.51–60.

Lenain, Thierry (1997) *Monkey Painting*. Reaktion Books, London.

Lewis-Williams, David (2002) *The Mind in the Cave. Consciousness and the Origins of Art*. Thames & Hudson, London.

Marshack, Alexander (1972) *The Roots of Civilization*. Weidenfeld & Nicolson, London.

Matheson, Neil (2006) *The Sources of Surrealism*. Lund Humphries, London.

Matthews, John (1999) *The Art of Childhood and Adolescence*. Falmer Press, London.

Matthews, John (2003) *Drawing and Painting. Children and Visual Perception*. Paul Chapman, London.

Matthews, John (2011) *Starting from Scratch. The Origin and Development of Expression, Representation and Symbolism in Human and Non-human Primates*. Psychology Press, London.

Mellaart, James (1967) *Catal Huyuk*. Thames & Hudson, London.

Mohen, Jean-Pierre (1990) *The World of Megaliths*. Facts on File, New York.

Moorhouse, Paul (1990) *Dali*. Magna Books, Leicester.

Morris, Desmond (1958) 'Pictures by Chimpanzees', *New Scientist*, 4, p. 609–611.

Morris, Desmond (1961) 'Primate's Aesthetics', *Natural History* (New York), 70, p. 22–29.

Morris, Desmond (1962) *The Biology of Art. A Study of the Picture-making Behaviour of the Great Apes and its Relationship to Human Art*. Methuen, London.

Morris, Desmond (1962) 'Apes and the Essence of Art', *Panorama*, Sept. 1962, p. 11.

Morris, Desmond (1962) 'The Biology of Art', *Portfolio*, 6, Autumn 1962, p. 52–64.

Morris, Desmond (1976) 'The Social Biology of Art', *Biology and Human Affairs*, vol. 41, no. 3, p.143–144.

Morris, Desmond (1985) *The Art of Ancient Cyprus*. Phaidon, Oxford.

Neal, Avon & Parker, Ann (1969) *Ephemeral Folk Figures*. Clarkson Potter, New York.

Oakley, K. P. (1981) 'Emergence of Higher Thought 3.0 – 0.2 Ma B. P.', *Phil. Trans. R. Soc. London*, B 292, p. 205–211.

O'Doherty, Brian (1973) *American Masters*. Random House, New York.

Otten, Charlotte M. (1971) *Anthropology and Art. Readings in Cross-Cultural Aesthetics*. The Natural History Press, New York.

Parker, Ann & Neal, Avon (2009) *Hajj Paintings. Folk Art of the Great Pilgrimage*. The American University in Cairo Press, Egypt.

Piery, Lucienne (2006) *Art Brut. The Origins of Outsider Art*. Flammarion, Paris.

Quinn, Edward (1984) *Max Ernst*. Ediciones Poligrafa, Barcelona.

Rainer, Arnulf (1991) *Primaten*. Jablonka Galeie im Karl Kerber Verlag, Köln/Bielefeld.

Rand, Harry (1981) *Arshile Gorky*. George Prior, London.

Ramachandran, V. S. & Hirstein, William (1999) 'The Science of Art', *Journal of Consciousness Studies*, 6, no. 6–7, p.15–51.

Raynal, Maurice (1951) *The Nineteenth Century; Goya to Gauguin*. Skira, Switzerland.

Rensch, Bernhard (1958) 'Die Wirksamkeit aesthetischer Faktoren bei Wirbeltieren', *Zeitschrift für Tierpsychologie*, 15, 4, p.447–461.

Rensch, Bernhard (1961) 'Malversuche mit Affen', *Zeitschrift für Tierpsychologie*, 18, 3, p.347–364.

Rensch, Bernhard (1965) 'Über aesthetische Faktoren im Elreben hoherer Tiere', *Naturwissenschaft und Medizin*, 2, 9, p.43–57.

Ricci, Corrado (1887) *L'Arte dei Bambini*. Nicola Zanichelli, Bologna.

Richardson, John (1991, 1996, 2007) *A Life of Picasso, Vols 1–3*. Jonathan Cape, London.

Riddell, W. H. (1940) 'Dead or Alive?', *Antiquity*, vol. 14, no. 54, p.154–162.

Ritchie, Carson I. A. (1979) *Rock Art of Africa*. Barnes, New Jersey.

Roethel, Hans K. (1979) *Kandinsky*. Phaidon, Oxford.

Rubin, William S. (1968) *Dada, Surrealism, and their Heritage*. Museum of Modern Art, New York.

Russell, John & Gablik, Suzi (1969) *Pop Art Redefined*. Thames & Hudson, London.

Sandler, Irving et al. (1987) *Mark Rothko 1903–1970*. Tate Gallery Publications, London.

Sawyer, R. Keith (2006) *Explaining Creativity. The Science of Human Innovation*. Oxford University Press, Oxford.

Scharfstein, Ben-Ami (2007) *Birds, Elephants, Apes and Children; an Essay in Interspecific Aesthetics*. Xargol Books, Tel Aviv.

Schiller, Paul (1951) 'Figural Preferences in the Drawings of a Chimpanzee', *Journal of Comparative Psychology*, XLIV, p.101–111.

Semen, Didier (1999) *Victor Brauner*. Filipacchi, Paris.

Shone, Richard (1980) *The Post-impressionists*. Octopus Books, London.

Sokolowski, Alexander (1928) *Erlebnisse mit Wilden Tieren*. Haberland, Leipzig.

Streep, Peg (1994) *Sanctuaries of the Goddesses*. Bulfinch Press, Boston.

Stuckey, Charles F. (1988) *Monet, A Retrospective*. Galley Press, Leicester.

Terrace, Herbert S. (1980) *Nim; A Chimpanzee who Learned Sign Language*. Eyre Methuen, London.

Tolnay, Charles de (1965) *Hieronymus Bosch*. Methuen, London.

Trevor-Roper, Patrick (1970) *The World Through Blunted Sight*. Thames & Hudson, London.

Twohig, Elizabeth Shee (1981) *The Megalithic Art of Western Europe*. Clarendon Press, Oxford.

Venturi, Lionello (1956) *The Sixteenth Century; from Leonardo to El Greco*. Skira, Switzerland.

Walsh, Grahame L. (1994) *Bradshaws; Ancient Rock Paintings of North-West Australia*. Edition Limitée, Geneva.

Whiten, Andrew (1976) 'Primate perception and aesthetics', in *Beyond Aesthetics; Investigations into the Nature of Visual Art*, ed. D. Brothwell. Thames & Hudson, London, p.18–40.

Willcox, A. R. (1963) *The Rock Art of South Africa*. Thomas Nelson, Johannesburg.

List of illustrations by origin

Picture credits

Front Cover: (montages left to Right) Getty Images; World History Archive; World History Archive; World History Archive; World History Archive; Corbis; Shutterstock; Back Cover: (montages left to right) Photo12; Wikimedia; The Desmond Morris Collection; World History Archive; Getty Images; Getty Images; Endpapers Front: Photo 12; Back: Shutterstock; Page headers (montages): Getty Images; World History Archives; Photo12; The Desmond Morris Collection; Chapter 1 opener (Montage): Page 10, left to right: Torsten Blackwood/AFP/Getty Images; The Desmond Morris Collection; Wikimedia; Photo12/Eye Ubiquitous/Nigel Sitwell/Hutchison; World History Archive; The Desmond Morris Collection; Chapter 2 opener: Torsten Blackwood/AFP/Getty Images. Chapter 3 opener: The Desmond Morris Collection. Chapter 4 opener: The Desmond Morris Collection; Chapter 5 opener: Wikimedia Commons; Chapter 6 opener: Photo12/Eye Ubiquitous/Nigel Sitwell/Hutchison; Chapter 7 opener: Getty Images/Wojtek Buss/AGE fotostock; Chapter 8 opener: World History Archive; Chapter 9 opener: World History Archive; Chapter 10 opener: The Desmond Morris Collection; Chapter 11 opener: The Desmond Morris Collection; Chapter 12 opener: World History Archive; Page 17: Torsten Blackwood/AFP/Getty Images; 19: John Scofield/National Geographic/Getty Images; 25: Courtesy of 'Child chimpanzee and human child' by Nadezhda Ladygina-Kohts's/www.kohts.ru/; 27: The Desmond Morris Collection; 29 bottom: The Desmond Morris Collection; 29 top: The Desmond Morris Collection; 31 top: The Desmond Morris Collection; 31 bottom: The Desmond Morris Collection; 32 top: The Desmond Morris Collection; 32 centre: The Desmond Morris Collection; 32 bottom : The Desmond Morris Collection; 33 top left: The Desmond Morris Collection; 33 centre: The Desmond Morris Collection; 33 left bottom: The Desmond Morris Collection; 33 bottom left: The Desmond Morris Collection; 33 bottom right: The Desmond Morris Collection; 34 top left: The Desmond Morris Collection; 34 left centre : The Desmond Morris Collection; 34 left bottom: The Desmond Morris Collection; 34 bottom left: The Desmond Morris Collection; 34 bottom right: The Desmond Morris Collection; 35 top left: The Desmond Morris Collection; 35 top centre: The Desmond Morris Collection; 35 centre: The Desmond Morris Collection; 35 bottom left: The Desmond Morris Collection; 35 bottom right: The Desmond Morris Collection; 36: The Desmond Morris Collection; 37: The Desmond Morris Collection; 38 top: The Desmond Morris Collection; 38 centre: The Desmond Morris Collection; 38 bottom: The Desmond Morris Collection; 40: The Desmond Morris Collection; 41: The Desmond Morris Collection; 42: The Desmond Morris Collection; 43 top: The Desmond Morris Collection; 43 bottom: The Desmond Morris Collection; 44: The Desmond Morris Collection; 45: The Desmond Morris Collection; 47: The Desmond Morris Collection; 51 top left: The Desmond Morris Collection; 51 top right: The Desmond Morris Collection; 51 centre: The Desmond Morris Collection; 52 top: The Desmond Morris Collection; 52 bottom: The Desmond Morris Collection; 53 top: The Desmond Morris Collection; 53 centre: The Desmond Morris Collection; 54 left: © 2013 Adapted from Rhoda Kellogg 'Analysing Children's Art' & The Desmond Morris Collection; 54 right: © 2013 Adapted from Rhoda Kellogg 'Analysing Children's Art' & The Desmond Morris Collection; 55: The Desmond Morris Collection; 56: The Desmond Morris Collection; 77: The Desmond Morris Collection; 59 top left: The Desmond Morris Collection; 59 top right: The Desmond Morris Collection; 59 centre left: The Desmond Morris Collection; 59 centre right: The Desmond Morris Collection; 59 bottom left: The Desmond Morris Collection; 59 bottom right: The Desmond Morris Collection; 64 Top: © Wikipedia; 64 Bottom: © D'Errico et al. (2009); 65: © Kota Kid; 66 top: Getty Images/Anna Zieminski/Stringer/AFP; 66 bottom: Getty Images/Jorge Guerrero/AFP/Stringer; 67: The Desmond Morris Collection; 68: Getty Images/Imagno/Hulton Archive/ Gerhard Trumler; 69 top: Getty Images/Danita Delimont/Gallo Images; 69 bottom: Getty Images/Werner Forman; 70 top: Getty Images/Werner Forman/Universal Images Group; 70 bottom: © Wikipedia; 70 centre left: © Wikimedia Commons; 70 centre right: The Desmond Morris Collection; 71: © loewenmensch@ulm.de; 73: © Wikimedia Commons; 75 top: Photo12/Oronoz; 75 bottom: Getty Images/Ralph Morse/Time Life Pictures; 77 top: http://venetianred.net/tag/chauvet-cave; 77 bottom: Photo12/JTB Photo; 78: Getty Images/ JEAN-PIERRE MULLER/AFP; 80 bottom left : Edition Limited/the Bradshaw Foundation; 80 bottom right: Edition Limited/the Bradshaw Foundation; 80 top: Getty Images/John Borthwick/ Lonely Plant Images; 81: Edition Limited/the Bradshaw Foundation; 82: © Photo12/JTB Photo; 83: Photo12/Eye Ubiquitous; 84: Getty Images/Andreas Rentsch/NonStock; 85: Photo12/ Eye Ubiquitous; 86 top: Getty Images/Cave Art Gallery/Flickr; 86 bottom: The Desmond Morris Collection; 88 top: © Wikimedia/Teomancimit; 88 bottom: © Wikimedia/Teomancimit; 89: Photo12/JTB Photo; 90 left: The Desmond Morris Collection; 90 centre: The Desmond Morris Collection; 91 top: The Desmond Morris Collection; 91 bottom: © muba; 92/93: Photo12/Damien Grenon; 94: Getty Images/De Agostini Picture Library; 95: Getty Images/Tony C French/Photo library; 96: Getty Images/DEA/A. DAGLI ORTI/Contributor; 97: The Desmond Morris Collection; 100: The Desmond Morris Collection; 101: The Desmond Morris Collection; 102 top left: Getty Images/Werner Forman/Universal Images Group; 102 top right: Getty Images/Michael Springer; 102 bottom: Getty Images/Werner Forman/Universal Images Group; 103 top: The Desmond Morris Collection; 103 bottom: Shutterstock.com/Sam Dcruz; 104 left: Photo12/Eye Ubiquitous/Nigel Sitwell/Hutchison; 104 right: Photo12/Eye Ubiquitous; 105 left: Photo12/Eye Ubiquitous/Mathew McKee/Hutchison; 105 right: Shutterstock.com/urosr ; 106: Photo12/JTB Photo; 107 top left: The Desmond Morris Collection; 107 top right: Shutterstock.com/Anna Omelchenko; 107 bottom: Getty Images/Sean Caffrey/Lonely Planet Images; 108 top left: Getty Images/Eric Lafforgue/Gamma-Rapho; 108 top right: Getty Images/Mike Powell/Stone; 108 bottom: The Desmond Morris Collection; 109: The Desmond Morris Collection; 113: © unknown; 114 top: The Desmond Morris Collection; 114 bottom: World History Archive; 115 top: The Desmond Morris Collection; 115 bottom right: Photo12/Institut Ramses; 115 bottom left: Photo12/Eye Ubiquitous/Julia Waterlow/Hutchison; 116: Getty Images/S.Vannini/De Agostini; 116 top: World History Archive; 116 bottom: World History Archive; 118 top left: World History Archive; 118 top centre: World History Archive; 118 top right: World History Archive; 118 bottom left: World History Archive; 118 bottom right: The Desmond Morris Collection; 119 bottom right: Getty Images/Walter Bibikow/The Image Bank; 119 bottom left: Shutterstock.com/Georgescu Gabriel; 120 top left: Photo12/JTB Photo; 120 top right: Getty Images/Ken Gillham/Robert Harding World Imagery; 120 bottom left: Photo 12/Oronoz; 121 top: Photo 12/Oronoz; 121 bottom left: Photo12/Anne Joudiou; 121 bottom right: Getty Images/Wojtek Buss/AGE fotostock; 122: World History Archive; 123 top: World History Archive; 123 bottom: Photo12/Ann Ronan Picture Library; 124: Photo12/Best View Stock; 126 top: Getty Images/Essam AL-Sudani/AFP; 126 bottom: Photo12/JTB Photo; 127: Shutterstock.com/Chameleons Eye; 131: World History Archive; 132: Getty Images/Werner Forman/Universal Images Group; 133: Getty Images/British Library/Robana/Hulton Fine Art Collection; 134: World History Archive; 135 right: Getty Images/Peter Barritt/Robert Harding World Imagery; 135 left: Photo12/Loeber-Bottero; 136: Photo12/Eye Ubiquitous/Mel Longhurst; 138: World History Archive; 139: ©2013 Getty Images/DeAgostini/G. DAGLI ORTI; 140: Photo12/Oronoz; 141: World History Archive; 142/143: World History Archive; 144: World History Archive; 145: Getty Images/DEA PICTURE LIBRARY; 146: World History Archive; 147: Getty Images/DEA PICTURE LIBRARY; 148: World History Archive; 149: World History Archive; 150 Top: World History Archive; 150 bottom: Getty Images/Coll-Peter Willi/Superstock Collection; 151: World History Archive; 152 left: Photo12/Oronoz; 152 right: Photo12/Oronoz; 153: World History Archive; 154: World History Archive; 155 left: World History Archive; 155 right: Photo12/Oronoz; 156: Getty Images/DEA/G. DAGLI ORTI; 157: World History Archive; 158: Getty Images/DEA PICTURE LIBRARY; 159: World History Archive; 160 top: Photo12/Oronoz; 160 bottom: World History Archive; 161: World History Archive; 162 top:

Photo Research Project Management Team: Tara Roberts, Jason Newman, Alexander Goldberg and Kieran Hepburn of Media Select International www.mediaselectinternational.com
Additional thanks to Valerie-Anne Giscard d'Estaing, Ann Asquith and Rick Mayston

Index